# Performing Worlds into Being:
## *Native American Women's Theater*

# Performing Worlds into Being:
## *Native American Women's Theater*

Edited by
Ann Elizabeth Armstrong, Kelli Lyon Johnson, and William A. Wortman

Miami University Press
Oxford, Ohio

Library of Congress Cataloging-in-Publication Data

Performing worlds into being: Native American women's theater / edited by

Ann Elizabeth Armstrong, Kelli Lyon Johnson, and William A. Wortman.

p. cm.

Includes bibliographical references.

ISBN 978-1-4243-3112-3

1. American drama–Indian authors. 2. American drama–Women authors.
3. Indians of North America–Drama. 4. Indigenous peoples–North America–Drama.
I. Armstrong, Ann Elizabeth, 1967- II. Johnson, Kelli Lyon, 1969- III. Wortman, William A., 1940-

PS628.I53P47 2008

812'.54099287'08997–dc22

2008040450

## Other titles from Miami University Press

***Poetry Series*** ❧ General Editor: James Reiss

*The Bridge of Sighs*, Steve Orlen
*People Live, They Have Lives*, Hugh Seidman
*This Perfect Life*, Kate Knapp Johnson
*The Dirt*, Nance Van Winckel
*Moon Go Away, I Don't Love You No More*, Jim Simmerman
*Selected Poems: 1965–1995*, Hugh Seidman
*Neither World*, Ralph Angel
*Now*, Judith Baumel
*Long Distance*, Aleda Shirley
*What Wind Will Do*, Debra Bruce
*Kisses*, Steve Orlen
*Brilliant Windows*, Larry Kramer
*After A Spell*, Nance Van Winckel
*Kingdom Come*, Jim Simmerman
*Dark Summer*, Molly Bendall
*The Disappearing Town*, John Drury
*Wind Somewhere, and Shade*, Kate Knapp Johnson
*The Printer's Error*, Aaron Fogel
*Gender Studies*, Jeffrey Skinner
*Ariadne's Island*, Molly Bendall
*Burning the Aspern Papers*, John Drury
*Beside Ourselves*, Nance Van Winckel
General Editor: Keith Tuma
*Rainbow Darkness: an anthology of African American poetry*, edited by Keith Tuma
*Talk Poetry*, Mairéad Byrne
*Between Cup and Lip*, Peter Manson

***Fiction Series*** ❧ Edited by the Creative Writing Faculty of Miami University

*Mayor of the Roses*, Marianne Villanueva; edited by Brian Roley
*The Waiting Room*, Albert Sgambati; edited by Eric Goodman
*Badlands*, by Cynthia Reeves; edited by Margaret Luongo
*A Fight in the Doctor's Office*, by Cary Holladay; edited by Brian Roley

# CONTENTS

# ACKNOWLEDGMENTS

The editors have entailed a number of obligations we are happy to acknowledge. The John W. Altman Humanities Scholar-in-Residence Fund provided foundational financing for the February 2007 conference and for some of the costs of this volume; Dianne Sadoff, Associate Dean, College of Arts and Science, was instrumental in assuring this funding. The many sponsors and hard-working volunteers for that conference are recognized on the conference website, staff.lib.muohio.edu/nawpa/sponsors.html. Judith Sessions, Dean and University Librarian, and Janet Stuckey, Head, Special Collections, Miami University Libraries, have continued to support NAWPA and its activities. Keith Tuma and Dana Leonard of Miami University Press and Sara Udstuen, Supervisor of Graphic Design, have made work on this book a pleasure and its final form a reality. Sue Wortman created the DVD, and in the process used photos and videos supplied by Spiderwoman Theater, Hugh Morgan, Michael Bendure and Randy Talley (Media and Community Relations office, the University of Arts and Science of Oklahoma), and Gion DeFrancesco, Amy Foster Munoz, and Daniella Briseno (Miami University Department of Theatre). Linda Sueyoshi of the E-Reference Service, Hawaii State Library, Hawaii & Pacific Section, provided a crucial newspaper citation.

Previous publication or presentation is acknowledged:
Vessela S. Warner's interview originally appeared in the *Baylor Journal of Theatre and Performance* and is reprinted here with the permission of *Journal's* editor, Carolyn D. Roark: "Dancing with Tradition: Two Generations of Quileute Dancers in Preservation of the Culture's 'Spirit Power': An Interview with Rochelle Warner and Bonita Cleveland, Members of the Quileute Tribe." *Baylor Journal of Theatre and Performance* 4.1 (2007): 121-34. The journal is now titled *Ecumenica.*

Monique Mojica's "Chocolate Woman Dreams the Milky Way" is a revised version of two oral presentations, the first offered at the Distinguished Lecture Series, University of Toronto, in January 2006, and the second at the Honoring Spiderwoman Theater/Celebrating Native American Theater conference, February 2007. It was revised and updated in January 2008 and has been published in *Collective Creation, Collaboration and Devising,* ed. Bruce Barton (Toronto: Playwrights Canada, 2008). An earlier version will appear in a forthcoming volume of essays on North American Native performance, edited by Steve Wilmer, and to be published by the University of Arizona Press.

Marcie R. Rendon's poem "What's an Indian Woman to Do" previously appeared in *Native Arts Circle News* [Minneapolis], summer 1994; *Sister Nations: Native American Women Writers on Community*, ed. Heid E. Erdrich and Laura Tohe (St. Paul: Minnesota Historical Soc., 2002), 138-39; and *Futures* [Minneapolis] 2.19 (Oct. 2000).



We gratefully dedicate this collection to: Robert, Kiefer, and Russell Bell; Reilly Ann Johnson, who has already demonstrated her own dramatic flair; and Susan H. Wortman.

# INTRODUCTION

*Ann Elizabeth Armstrong, Kelli Lyon Johnson, and William A. Wortman*

From its founding in 1997 the Native American Women Playwrights Archive (NAWPA) has defined itself as a *living* archive by sponsoring readings, performances, and conferences. Its most recent (and third) conference, in February 2007 at Miami University (Oxford, Ohio), was titled "Honoring Spiderwoman Theater/Celebrating Native American Theater." NAWPA welcomed some forty participants from four countries and a dozen or more Indian nations, presented three stage productions and a staged reading, and offered an array of public discussions, production histories, academic papers, interviews, and performance pieces, along with communal meals and conversation. We celebrated Native American theater not only by talking about it but also by doing it.

NAWPA was founded to collect, preserve, and make more widely known the work of living Native American women playwrights, with "American" including Canada, Mexico, Central and Caribbean America, and Pacific Islands. It now consists of manuscript plays, production documents (posters, publicity, programs, some video and audiotapes, reviews, and news stories), and related miscellaneous materials such as photographs, award citations, and other publications by the writers. This material is housed in the Miami University Libraries' Walter Havighurst Special Collections Library where it is stored in archival boxes and managed according to archival standards. The library in general tries to collect plays and other resources that complement this collection, including dramatic work by and about Native American men writers. The NAWPA website maintains a directory of the writers and lists their plays, their other work, and related materials and publications. This website also includes bibliographies of Native American drama, some digitized resources, related links, and information about submitting or inquiring: http://staff.lib.muohio.edu/nawpa. We hope in coming years to increase greatly the number of writers included and encourage new voices, record new productions, and stimulate continued—and vitally important—theatrical writing.

A conference event of this kind has to be collaborative. The many people involved directly in organizing and managing the events and the donors and active supporters outside the Libraries are cited on the conference website (http://staff.lib.muohio.edu/nawpa/conf.html). There were, however, more unusual collaborations: within the home institution, involving the library (NAWPA's home) and several academic departments and programs; in the field and at the conference, involving academics, playwrights, performers, directors, and producers (many wearing more than one hat, including being mothers and daughters and Indians and 21st-century North Americans with a variety of shared but also unique cultures). A lot of people wanted to make this event happen and worked together—across a variety of institutional, cultural, and geographic boundaries—to achieve success.

As an institution, Miami University has been notably supportive, as befits a university whose name honors the Indian Nation whose ancestors lived in this geographic area. The thirty-five-year active relationship between the Miami Tribe of Oklahoma and the University was formalized in a 2006 statement signed by leaders of the Miami Tribe and the university, and the university has designated the Vice President for Student Affairs as the official liaison to the Tribe and additionally a Coordinator of Miami Tribe Relations who manages the relationship and activities with the Tribe. Tribal students receive Heritage Scholarships; the Myaamia Project led by Daryl Baldwin (Miami) works to "preserve, promote, and research Miami Nation history, culture and language" through a range of scholarly and educational activities (www.myaamiaproject.org); in combination, the University Libraries, Archives, and Art Museum have committed to preserving important tribal artifacts and documents and mounting relevant exhibits. The cover of this book reproduces the painting "Young People's Dance" by Woodrow Wilson Palmer (Miami) held by the Museum. Frequent visits by the Tribe's chief, Cultural Affairs officer, librarian, and other leaders both maintain regular communication and publicly reaffirm the importance of the relationship, while the Tribe encourages curricular and extra-curricular enrichment activities by university students and faculty. Additionally, a dozen and a half or more units within the institution regularly support NAWPA's activities through financial contributions, staff time, facilities, and the generation of student interest and involvement. In partial answer, then, to the question Ric Knowles asks below, "How can the Western academy, in a collaborative relationship with Native artists, serve the healing, regenerative project?" this university's efforts suggest that the role—roles—of academic institutions can extend well beyond scholarly analysis (5).

That there was so much collaboration for the conference shows the appeal and the importance of Native American theater, theater that can transform experience publicly. The people involved talked and wrote articulately about their work—"works ripe with new ideas, rich with structural experimentation, and resonating with the sound of voices relating experiences from inside and outside the dominant cultural paradigm" (Howard 109). Yes, plays dealt with tragedy and crisis; writers, producers, and performers recounted the realities of production; academics analyzed and theorized. But throughout we saw and heard fresh perceptions of the human condition, rethought and reexamined American cultures, events, and people (the Cherokee Trail of Tears, Pocahontas, family dynamics, Hawaiian sovereignty), and relished good theater. Celebrating Native American theater was also, then, a celebration of strong women and men, significant cultural values, and the writers and performers who gave these voice, who performed worlds into being.

Although most of the contributions in this collection were originally presented at this conference, all have been updated or revised and then edited and arranged so that this book stands independent of the conference. The conference brought people together and occasioned the first drafts, but in revision, and with the addition of pieces not part of the conference, we have moved from the rather generic "Honoring…Celebrating" conference title to this more provocative theme, "Performing Worlds into Being." As readers will see shortly, the title is taken from the opening essay by Monique Mojica and Ric Knowles: the phrase is theirs but it also identifies an understanding that came out of the conference. The "explosion" of Native American theater occurring in the 1980s and 90s (and continuing) is now in the early years of the new century followed by an explosion of publication about it. New collections of plays and of essays (Geiogomah and Darby; Darby and

Fitzgerald; Huston-Findley and Howard; Mojica and Knowles; Nolan), articles in reference books and surveys (Haugo, Huhndorf, and Stanlake), Birgit Däwes' monograph, special issues of journals (Stanlake, Sullivan), and important author statements (several included here) all combine not only to celebrate but also to contextualize Native theater. We hope our book, too, has in its own way "performed worlds into being," in having taken an assortment of plays, statements, interviews, and essays and through the "performance" of revising and editing created a significant statement about the achievement(s) in and of theater by Native American women and the potential for continued creation of meaningful worlds.

**Section I: Looking Back, Looking Forward**

The title of this volume, *Performing Worlds into Being*, is taken from its first contribution, "Creation Story Begins Again: Performing Transformations, Building Cosmologies" by Monique Mojica (Kuna, Rappahannock) and Ric Knowles. In their collaboration, they celebrate the power of words, the potential of creating new and possible worlds, and the performativity of Native art. Gloria Anzaldúa has also insisted on the performative dimension of Native art, writing in *Borderlands/La Frontera* that because of the "tyranny of western aesthetics," Indigenous art has been both displaced and appropriated by European practices and institutions. When "[a]n Indian mask in an American museum is transposed into an alien aesthetic system," Anzaldúa asserts, "[i]t has become a conquered thing, a dead 'thing' separate from nature and, therefore, its power" (90). In contrast to these displacements and appropriations, "[t]ribal cultures keep art works in honored and sacred places in the home and elsewhere." More important, she writes, "[t]he works are treated not just as objects, but also as persons. The 'witness' is a participant in the enactment of the work in a ritual" (90).

Like the creation stories Mojica and Knowles elaborate, their words bring into being whole worlds, invoking many of the themes that appear throughout the rest of the volume: transformation, creation, community, participation, healing, and hope. They advocate for participation and collaboration in these processes, and they particularly emphasize relationship and responsibility, exploring the relationships between Native authors and academics, between artists and archives. In their contribution—both a dialogue and a performance—they argue that the wounds of colonization and genocide cannot be healed if academics continue to co-opt and appropriate Native art. Not only do academics need to take responsibility for their work with Native artists, Mojica concludes, but

> [t]he Native artist, too, needs to take responsibility for making work that matters, that provokes, subverts, takes risks, and refuses to be co-opted or commodified, work that touches, transforms, and has the power to heal. If theatre is a tool of transformation, which we know it to be, then we have a responsibility that the stories that we tell will be stories of our becoming, of our becoming whole. Which means that the stories that we tell must be creation stories. And like the academic who must take responsibility for the use of her research, the artist must live her art, must make creation story begin again in life as in art. It is not enough to make art out of atrocity and risk commodification of those stories. It is not enough to leave the stories on

> the stage without finding a way to make them transformative. To take, and provoke, response-ability. (6)

For Mojica, only through looking back at the atrocity and the resulting wounds can Native artists look forward to creation, to transformation, and to healing.

Jill Carter (Anishinaabe) similarly begins her analysis of Native performances with her own telling of a creation story. The story of Sky Woman, Carter writes, is a story of transformation and ritual, powerful components of the Native performance culture apparent in all of the contributions to this volume.[1] In "Blind Faith Remembers…This Ain't No Love Story, This Ain't No Masque: *Princess Pocahontas and The Blue Spots* as Transformative Ritual for the Grandmothers, the Ones Who Remain, and for the Ones Who Are Yet to Come," she analyzes the figure and the person of Pocahontas in order to contest gendered and racialized narratives about Native Americans through the legend of Pocahontas. Carter calls for Red Reading "on the literary artifacts of those who once read us, interpreting them through a Native lens and clarifying our understanding of the fears and fantasies that drove the colonizing body and that directed its documentation of our histories" (26). Mojica provides just such a reading in *Princess Pocahontas*, which resists such narratives and works toward the healing, transformation, and creativity that Mojica discusses in her work with Ric Knowles. Carter writes, "Our Elders tell us that we must remember, retain, and pass on our culture, languages, traditions, ceremonies, and stories if we are to retain nationhood and if our nations are to continue into the future." Mojica's *Princess Pocahontas and The Blue Spots* "in its reclamation of the mothers of the mixed-blooded peoples and in its re-appropriation of their stories, is her considerable contribution to this vital work around the survival, sovereignty, and continuance of the original nations of Turtle Island and to the spiritual restoration of their peoples" (8). Carter places Mojica's play within a Native literary tradition of performance that includes both storyweaving in the tradition of Spiderwoman Theater and what Carter calls the "aesthetic of the *mola*," a textile produced by Kuna women. Both of these traditions celebrate Native women's survival, autonomy, and creativity.[2] It is only through looking back—in this case, at Pocahontas—that Mojica, Carter, and many Native women may transform the future of their nations.

While the NAWPA conference primarily featured scholarship on dramatic theatrical presentations, it is important to recognize the wide spectrum of Native American performance traditions that frequently include dance, ritual, or other formats beyond the dramatization of scripted text. As part of the section "Looking Back, Looking Forward," Vessela Warner provides an important ethnographic interview with two family members, a mother and daughter of the Quileute tribe who keep alive their family's dance tradition. Warner presents their narrative in a unique format, allowing us to compare the two generational perspectives of Rochelle Warner and Bonita Cleveland. This is particularly relevant because it allows us to "look back" at the continuous

---

[1] Mojica uses the phrase "Native performance culture," which she attributes to Floyd Favel, in "Chocolate Woman Dreams the Milky Way" in Section III of this volume.

[2] Mojica discusses the *mola* in "Chocolate Woman Dreams the Milky Way" in Section III of this volume.

line of development of the dance tradition within the social context of the tribe and "look forward" to how a member of the current generation integrates these practices into her identity as she moves into the future. The interview subjects describe how the social dynamics of the tribe and family shape traditions such as the potlatch. They reinforce the importance of educating the general public about the tribe through their performances, and they share important historical moments and family traditions such as the naming ceremony, the Sacred Wolf dance, and other special traditions of myth, symbols, and ornamentation that make their art form unique. Bonita emphasizes that the challenge remains how to "understand the true meaning and values of the songs and myths. The riches of material matter as much as the riches of the spirit inside each dancer. Dancers can bring to life the robes they are wrapped with through the goodness and physical endurance they carry in their minds and bodies" (39). Throughout the interview, we see how mother and daughter carry these traditions forward.

**Section II: Honoring Spiderwoman Theater**

Spiderwoman Theater has maintained a close connection to Miami University, having performed *Sun, Moon, and Feather, Winnetou's Snake Oil Show from Wigwam City,* and now *Persistence of Memory* on our campus, having individually received Honorary Doctor of Fine Arts degrees, and having donated most of their papers to the Native American Women Playwrights Archive. Their history has been described in several places (see especially Haugo's and Stanlake's articles of 2005 and 2003), and in the interview included in this volume they comment extensively on the development of *Persistence of Memory,* a play itself that provides an important narrative of their careers and work. Their influence in American professional theater extends far beyond the Native American performance context. All three—Lisa Mayo, Gloria Miguel, and Muriel Miguel (Kuna, Rappahannock)—studied with major American studios and companies (such as Herbert Berghof Studio, Strasburg's Actor Studio, and Open Theater). All moved from independent careers into this very fruitful collaborative troupe that has significantly influenced and spawned other feminist and Native American theater companies. Along with their collaborative work as Spiderwoman Theater, they have also individually created solo shows and performed professionally in productions throughout the world. Their method of "storyweaving" pulls together the strands of personal stories with those of others (and history) to weave a rich tapestry that allows the everyday particularities of individual lives to resonate with profound significance.

*Persistence of Memory* is probably their final piece and is in a sense a retrospective of their career, yet it is much more than simply an anthology of memorable performance moments. Despite the improvisatory essence of Spiderwoman's work, the published texts of their plays read as powerful dramatizations of their engagement with their Indian heritage. (We hope the DVD accompanying this book helps overcome the limitations of print in presenting their multi-media work by including selected video clips used as an element of their performance, along with two clips from their latest performance.) In *Persistence,* especially because of its incorporation of their own performance history, the weaving together of their own work with that of their parents, children, and grandchildren, and the long view they have as performers and as women who have lived full lives, they transform their individual lives and histories into a profound affirmation of the human spirit. As our lives lengthen and become richer with memories, these persistent voices blend with the voices of those coming after us, and the stories are inter-woven, stories of violence and conflict, joy and love, loneliness and separation, or work and family. The persistence of memory...

> We go back eons. . . .We came from way, way ago to be here with you. (*Persistence of Memory* 54)

Three contributions specifically honor Spiderwoman Theater. Marie Annharte Baker (Saulteaux Ojibway) and Marcie Rendon (White Earth Anishinabe) offer uniquely personal poems that testify to the importance of Spiderwoman in their own artistic lives. Baker is a widely recognized Canadian poet (included, for example, in Moses and Goldie's *Anthology of Canadian Native Literature in English*) but has recently written plays (see her "Cannibal Woman Camp Out," included here). Rendon's poem, "What's an Indian Woman to Do," gets to the heart of an issue appearing in almost all Spiderwoman's work, "appropriation of native spirituality" (58). Later in the volume, we feature more of Rendon's dramatic writing and a description of her Minneapolis-based theater company. Murielle Borst (Kuna, Rappahannock) spoke intensely and entertainingly at the conference about Spiderwoman's technique and their influence on her own performance and written work. *Persistence of Memory* included a video clip from Borst's one-woman show *More than Feathers and Beads*, and she in turn demonstrated the Spiderwoman storyweaving technique in her own fiction, from which she read selections. Her talk was transcribed and then edited for this collection, in which form it has lost some of its performative verve, but it is clear that in her work, as in that of Monique Mojica, the Spiderwoman legacy lives on artistically into the next generation through both their biological daughters and other artists inspired by them.

**Section III: Voices**

Dianne Yeahquo Reyner (Kiowa) powerfully evokes family connections in her play *Weaving the Rain*. First presented in 2004 by the Thunderbird Theatre of Haskell Indian Nations University, *Weaving the Rain* was then performed at Miami University by the American Indian Repertory Theatre on February 19, 2007, during the conference. The play tells the story of the Two Crow family as they wait in a clinic for news of their father, who is suffering yet another health crisis as a result of cirrhosis of the liver. Because Reyner locates all of the play's action in a single set—this waiting room—the actors' words and actions must conjure not only the father's current health crisis but also the history of the family and, ultimately, of Native peoples in the United States. In order for the Two Crows to "understand that their survival is founded in the strength of the land and their culture," as Reyner writes in her author's statement, they must confront and understand the past, a confrontation that is played out on Reyner's set among the Two Crow family members—Margie Two Crow and her three children, Eve, John, and Michael (88). Two spirits help to guide the family through this confrontation—Roy Two Crow, a brother who died in his early twenties, and the Old Man, who in many ways embodies the past that Reyner seeks to evoke, engaging John in conversations about Indian lands and losses, about Fort Marion, and about the U.S. betrayal of Native Americans. The excerpts included in this volume also present both Margie and her daughter, Eve, as strong female characters, both of whom work inside and outside the gendered roles available to them as Native women. They struggle to connect, to understand their disparate experiences, and to hold the Two Crow family together, voicing diverse Native women's experiences in family and community contexts.

The next two plays are short comic pieces that portray completely different perspectives on Native American life and point to the stylistic diversity of Native women playwrights' work. Marcie Rendon's "Friends" is a ten-minute play with daughter, mother, and grandmother in the process of de-licing the daughter's hair. Throughout this black comedy, they explore humorous yet tragically ironic stories of their community, family, and romantic relationships. In Marie Annharte Baker's "Cannibal Woman Camp Out," Owl Woman has been charged by the Cannibal women, a council of mythical Native women elders, to go out there and "get us a man" (for what purpose isn't exactly clear). These original "bad girls" are being forgotten by their people and are no longer feared or reviled as they once were. Baker celebrates their unrestrained corporeality as she creates a comic and dystopian world ruled by Native women.

Monique Mojica performs her own world into being in *Chocolate Woman Dreams the Milky Way*, an autobiographical piece that both reflects on her life and work and analyzes the roles of memory, knowledge, history, and narratives in Native performance. As Chickasaw author Linda Hogan has written, "Self-telling is rare for a Native woman" (14), and Mojica's performance illustrates the multiple genres that self-tellings take for Native women artists as she "excavated some two-decade-old writing, dusted them off and had a look" (114). She finds scraps of dialogue, old scripts, fragments of stories, and old writing exercises, all of which, combined with her own memories and experiences, contribute to *saber sabiendo*, her ability to know knowingly. To know knowingly, Mojica reflects on and acknowledges the powerful influence of her ancestors. She honors these ancestors through an invocation with which Mojica performs yet another world into being: a possible world in which "I could place my feet upon those stars like stepping stones, [and] I would follow them to visit my ancestors. And we would drink cacao—*siagua* mixed with ground, roasted corn from gourds. We would smack our lips; wipe our mouths on the backs of our hands and talk. Wouldn't we talk! *Tegi!*" (125).

In her play "Pushing the Bear," Diane Glancy (Cherokee) relies solely on words to construct an entire world in performance. The actors in this play perform a world into being through narration only. Glancy includes no stage directions but focuses the action of the play only through the words of her characters. In this short work, Glancy dramatizes the story of the Trail of Tears through six characters, who also appeared in her novel *Pushing the Bear* (Harcourt Brace 1996). The piece comes to life through the juxtaposition of both dialogue and first-person narration describing their experiences and actions. Glancy began the process of telling her story of the Trail of Tears by driving the length of the Trail, listening, she explains, to the voices of the land. This movement across space is represented through the actors' words as they also voice the story of their progression along the Trail. This approach to "Pushing the Bear" exemplifies Glancy's vision of Native drama, which she has described in "Further (Farther): Creating Dialogue to Talk about Native American Plays." Native American plays demonstrate "[a] new oral tradition with breath, which is the condition of performance" (127). Through breath—through words—the past finds voice through performance, apparent in her contribution to this volume. The play offers "[a]ccess to unseen worlds(s). A cohabitation of this world and the other(s) (but without making unrealistic separations). Or *here are other worlds also which are here*" (129, italics in original). The land along and inside the Trail of Tears is another world that "also is here" and that Glancy calls into being through her characters' voices.

**Section IV: Collaboration and Community**

The final section of *Performing Worlds into Being* honors not only important Native American women writers for theater but also highlights the crucial role of the entire community that supports, encourages, and produces their work in a theatrical form. Unlike many other forms of art, theater requires an intense collaboration among a variety of artists: dramaturgs, directors, designers, actors, and technicians. Without that support, a writer's voice is frequently never heard. The essays in this section acknowledge the varied and specific ways in which many Native American women playwrights have positioned their work within their community of collaborators. Appropriately, then, almost all of the essays in this section are either written collaboratively or presented as interviews/conversations. This section begins with the local community-based and grassroots efforts of Marcie Rendon's "Theatre in the House" and the Thunder Road Theater of Tulsa. Then Victoria Kneubuhl's work extends the role of theater in articulating a community's history, taking inspiration from living history interpretation. Finally, the last essay on JudyLee Oliva's *Te Ata* looks at how a production can be both a community collaboration and a professionally produced mainstream theater event.

Native American theater companies take a variety of configurations, depending on their relationship to their audiences. Some create a grassroots approach that creates dramatic work about, by, with, and for the Native community. Others use a combination of community, educational, and professional theater approaches that combine community strengths with theatrical expertise. Or some even work outside of the theater, creating interdisciplinary collaborations in arenas like living history pageants, film, or digital media. Still others, as in JudyLee Oliva's ground-breaking production of *Te Ata*, aim to create mainstream commercial Native American theater. As Marcie Rendon and JudyLee Oliva and Christy Stanlake emphasize: Native American theater "belongs everywhere," without limitation (Rendon, "Theatre in the House" 138). Many have noted that there is a kind of ecology among artistic communities, and a sure sign of health among Native theater arts is the fact that there are community-based, educational, amateur (community), and professional theaters, all working simultaneously in various places, nourishing their audiences and providing training opportunities for emerging talents. While certainly there is room for growth, particularly in the area of professional support and funding for such theaters, it is important to note how each of these kinds of theaters play a role in making sure that Native stories are told and heard on the stage and that future generations of artists and audiences continue this important work.

Marcie Rendon breaks down the theater-making process she calls "Theatre in the House/ Raging Native Productions." In this short essay she articulates how theater has served as a profound "mirror" for her personally and for her community, one that locates and amplifies her voice.

Finding one's voice through the theater is a long journey, since once the play is written, then she faced the daunting challenges of finding people who want to participate in it as directors, actors, or producers ***and*** who want to attend it as audience members: "live theater is not something most of our community members are familiar with or have the money to attend" (139). However, building upon her training experiences with Playwright Center, Spiderwoman Theater, Ellen Maddow, and others, she adapted exercises to write and produce theater at people's houses, in parks, and in Native-owned coffee shops. Using a "fast and furious" process, Rendon taps into the creative potential of a community and builds upon the traditions and emerging talent in the group with whom she works. Because performers write their own lines from their own experiences, they have fewer hurdles in memorizing the work for performance. Publicizing the work within the Native community is also crucial since the audience is the key ingredient: "Without an attentive audience, the actor does not feel compelled to give a peak performance" (142). Rendon states that her goal is to "build the heart, soul, and enthusiasm" for this process so that Native communities maintain the tools to continue to create their own theater.

In "Thunder Road Theater and Community-Based Native American Theater," Vincent Scott, a Cultural Arts Specialist at the National Museum of the American Indian, interviews Julie Pearson-Little Thunder (Creek) and Jana Rhoads (Kiowa, Caddo) about their long-term collaboration in the building of their theater company. Since the mid-1990s, Rhoads and Pearson-Little Thunder have been bringing together different tribal communities through theater. They frequently use community-based theater methods to make intergenerational connections and foster stories of the elders in Native communities. While much of their work is situated within and between various tribal communities, their work also reaches a mainstream audience where they use theater to combat stereotypes and re-tell authentic histories. Pearson-Little Thunder and Rhoads note the importance of encouraging audience response with theater events planned in connection with tribal dinners and other communal activities. Their dramatic writing is adaptable to their community and exploits the strengths and talents of that community.

In "'Forceful yet transitory and fragile': An Interview with Victoria Nalani Kneubuhl" Ann Elizabeth Armstrong of Miami University interviews Native Hawaiian playwright Victoria Nalani Kneubuhl. Kneubuhl's dramatic work speaks to the many silences that exist in Native Hawaiian and women's histories, recovering those lost voices that are so transitory and fragile yet powerful. She discusses the importance of delving into the complex and contradictory histories to fully personalize her characters' lives for contemporary audiences. Kneubuhl describes *January 1893*, a historical pageant that was performed on the centennial anniversary of the United States's overthrow of Queen Lili'oukalani's Hawaiian government. Kneubuhl details the complexities of staging this three-day pageant with overwhelming community support and involvement, and she also explores the controversial audience reactions to the re-telling of this explosive and volatile history. Borrowing inspiration from living history interpretation, Kneubuhl has written other plays for the theater, such as *The Conversion of Ka'ahumanu*. This play, like much of Kneubuhl's other dramatic work, engages and explodes stereotypes of historical people and events by making the political intensely personal. Kneubuhl attributes much of her success to her close relationship to Hawai'i's Kumu Kahua Theatre Company, to family traditions that have provided her with support, and to a long tradition of women writers throughout history.

In "Native Drama in the Mainstream: A Case Study of the *Te Ata* World Premiere," JudyLee Oliva and Christy Stanlake provide a detailed analysis of a remarkable collaboration among the Chickasaw Nation, University of Science and Arts of Oklahoma (USAO), and professional theater artists in producing the play *Te Ata*. Oliva's play, *Te Ata,* follows the journey of a Chickasaw performer, Te Ata Thompson Fisher, through her youth in the 1920s into her more than forty-year career as a travelling performer across the U. S. and around the world. The play required a large multicultural cast and spectacular scenic effects, creating a stylistic complexity that made it a unique undertaking. Oliva and Stanlake argue for the importance of fully produced mainstream Native American theater that embraces spectacle and the full range of the expressive palette offered by professional theater production. They also analyze many of the misunderstandings and conflicts that occurred in the process of making this particular production, many of them that stem from the culturally biased and conventional practices of mainstream theater. Frequently, cultural misunderstandings rose to the surface, and the dramaturg (Stanlake) served to advocate for a Native American cultural perspective and reinforce the playwright's (Oliva's) vision of the work. The article praises many of the production's successes as well and asks readers to build upon and learn from their successes and failures in producing Native American theater for a mainstream audience in the future.

*Performing Worlds into Being* and the work of the Native American Women Playwrights Archive strive to bring various communities together. Our goal is to create a "living" archive that is enriched by the dialogue between scholars and artists, to honor the lineage of Native American theatrical performance through tributes to groups like Spiderwoman Theater, to nurture the voices of Native women authors so that they can continue to imagine and write worlds into being, and, finally, to engage members of the theater world and audiences in the collaborative act of performing and experiencing these worlds together. Each of the four sections of this collection speaks to one of these goals. As demonstrated by this volume, Native American women playwrights are clearly creative and productive, comprising a vital and dynamic force within their own communities. We hope to provide a bridge between these various worlds and to nourish the networks and resources of Native American theater artists.

Finally, a couple of words about our editorial efforts. Several contributions here come from Canadians: we have retained their spelling. The spelling of "theater" is itself somewhat controversial, but we have retained the preferences of the various authors while ourselves using "theater." Although we have had to reduce the length of a few contributions, we have also been able to include a DVD and, thus, are able to present the important illustrations accompanying Oliva and Stanlake's article about *Te Ata*, scenes from Kneubhul's *Conversion of Ka'ahumanu* and Reyner's *Weaving the Rain*, and several video clips that are important elements in *Persistence of Memory*. We remind readers that the plays reproduced here are copyrighted by their authors and all rights remain with the authors. Please contact the authors directly (or through the NAWPA website's "Contact Us" links: http://staff.lib.muohio.edu/) for permission to produce or use their work.

## Works Cited

Anzaldúa, Gloria. *Borderlands: La Frontera.* 2nd ed. San Francisco: Aunt Lute, 1999.

Däwes, Birgit. *Native North American Theater in the Global Age: Sites of Identity Construction and Transdifference.* Heidelberg: Universitätsverlag Winter, 2007.

Darby, Jaye T., and Stephanie Fitzgerald, eds. *Keepers of the Morning Star: An Anthology of Native Women's Theater.* Los Angeles: UCLA American Indian Studies Center, 2003.

Geiogamah, Hanay, and Jaye T. Darby, eds. *American Indian Theater in Performance: A Reader.* Los Angeles: UCLA American Indian Studies Center, 2000.

Glancy, Diane. "Further (Farther): Creating Dialogue to Talk about Native American Plays." *Journal of Dramatic Theory and Criticism* 14.1 (1999): 127-30.

Haugo, Ann. "Native American Drama." *A Companion to Twentieth-Century American Drama.* Ed. David Krasner. Oxford: Blackwell, 2005. 334-51.

Hogan, Linda. *The Woman Who Watches over the World: A Native Memoir.* New York: Norton, 2001.

Howard, Rebecca. "The Native American Women Playwrights Archive: Adding Voices." *Journal of Dramatic Theory and Criticism* 14.1 (1999): 109-16.

Huhndorf, Shari. "American Indian Drama and the Politics of Performance." *The Columbia Guide to American Indian Literatures of the Untied States Since 1945.* Ed. Eric Cheyfitz. New York: Columbia UP, 2006. 288-318.

Huston-Findley, Shirley A., and Rebecca Howard, eds. *Footpaths and Bridges: Voices from the Native American Women Playwrights Archive.* Ann Arbor: U of Michigan P, 2008.

Mojica, Monique, and Ric Knowles, eds. *Staging Coyote's Dream: An Anthology of First Nations Drama in English.* Toronto: Playwrights Canada, 2003.

Moses, Daniel David, and Terry Goldie, eds. *An Anthology of Canadian Native Literature in English.* 3rd ed. Toronto: Oxford UP, 2005.

Nolan, Yvette, ed. *Beyond the Pale: Dramatic Writing from First Nations Writers and Writers of Colour.* Rev. ed. Toronto: Playwrights Canada, 2004.

Stanlake, Christy, ed. *Nations Speaking: Indigenous Performances across the Americas.* Spec. issue of *Baylor Journal of Theatre and Performance* 4.1 (2007): 5-174.

---. "Native American Performance." *Oxford Encyclopedia of Theatre and Performance.* Oxford: Oxford UP, 2003. 924-25.

Sullivan, Sharon, ed. "NAWPA Supplement." *Journal of Dramatic Theory and Criticism* 14.1 (1999): 95-156.

# SECTION I: *Looking Back, Looking Forward*

## Creation Story Begins Again: Performing Transformation, Bridging Cosmologies

*Monique Mojica and Ric Knowles*[1]

MONIQUE

How *do we keep doing this Native theatre thing? How do we keep doing Native theatre that matters? That impacts. How do we keep doing this Native theatre thing, that* can *intervene: a suicide, an encroachment, a massacre? What would it mean to stop? How do we transform the stories that we tell? So that they can rejuvenate, regenerate? Who saves the lives of Native theatre artists? If what the non-Aboriginal public wants to hear and see is "the victim," and there is reward for that, if it lets them off the hook (no responsibility), and we believe (not without good reason) in the stories of our victimization (no accountability)? How do we transform the stories that we tell?*

RIC

In the midst of an explosion of Native theatre in Canada in the 1980s, Tomson Highway popularized a saying he attributed to Lyle Longclaws: "Before the healing can take place, the poison must first be exposed" (Highway 6). Twenty years later, we are still waiting for the healing to take place and too often reworking the victim narrative, in which everything that happens is traced back to the poison, to the original wound. The plays produced in the last twenty years have exposed much of that poison.

MONIQUE

*But we are not healed yet. The wounds are still fresh. And, paradoxically, we cannot wait to be healed. The vision must be put into practice for the vision contains the healing. We must be willing to ask ourselves and our audience to suspend our disbelief, to the extent of envisioning a world where* Indigenous *is not synonymous with* victim, *nor with the hoop of a nation that has been broken. There are links, bridges, medicine paths intact that can bridge what is known, or unconsciously known, and bring it into consciousness by performing possible worlds into being.*

RIC

Creation story begins again.

MONIQUE

Everything goes back to the original wound in a victim story. It's not that we need to stop telling those stories—stories of sexual abuse, of abandonment, of murder, of suicide, loss—they are part of us. But if we allow those wounds, that disenfranchisement, that disempowerment—that multigenerational trauma of colonization and genocide—to define our identities as Indigenous peoples, then that's all we've got. *We need to seize the courage to empower ourselves as the reflections of those things from our cosmologies that are whole and intact. By embodying that wholeness on the stage, we can transform the stories that we tell ourselves and project into the world that which is not broken, that which can be sustained, not only for Aboriginal people but for* all *the inhabitants of this small, green planet.*

RIC

This is a project of recovery, of reinvention, neither a nostalgic return, nor a naïve optimism. It is a bringing forward of what is not broken, of who we were and are prior to and outside of the disconnect that is colonization. It is not nostalgic because it moves forward; it is not

[1] This piece was originally given as a conference presentation with Mojica and Knowles speaking their parts as indicated here and with Mojica stepping away from the podium to perform "Sky Woman Falling." The authors also point out that "This contribution was written collaboratively, based on dialogue and conversations, but we have adopted the convention that what is written in italic type represents Monique's voice, while roman type represents our collaborative voice."

naïve optimism but a first step because it is a provision of something solid to stand on while building for a future. It's not a nostalgic return because it is outwardly directed, it is active, it's a revitalization of things that have always been there. It is not naïve optimism, but it *is* a suspension of disbelief, which is fundamental to the theatre: it takes courage, and suspension of disbelief, to perform into existence a future that we cannot yet see. It is an urgent, ongoing project of the present.

And the stakes are high.

MONIQUE
When we make a decision to create from a base of ancestral knowledge, we confront the rupture, the original wound. For me, using theatre the way that Spiderwoman taught me to approach theatre, from deep within the body's memory, has been a channel to bridge the disconnect.

We need, then, to have hope *with the wounds showing*. What makes it moving, and makes it matter, and makes it hit the body, is the *courage* to have that hope while showing those wounds. The courage to wear layers of costume in order to be naked, to put on a mask in order to be exposed. In order to be seen. This also means taking on the responsibility to one's self, to one's community, to the audience who is watching.

RIC
Creation story begins again.

Sky Woman Falling

(MONIQUE singing)

"Catch a falling star and put it in your pocket, never let it fly away..."

*(Gesture: catching stars)*

"Catch a falling star and put it in your pocket, save it for a rainy day..."

*(Gesture: catching stars too close to the roots of the Celestial Tree of Life)*

The Fall

*(Gestures: to hip; Pacal position; Starfish—skydiving)*

*(Singing: bass line from introduction to "White Rabbit")*

*(Gesture: back to Pacal position)*

Sky Woman Falling!

The roots of the Celestial Tree retreating farther and farther into Sky World

Star daughter hurtling in descent

> pieces of roots, crumbs of earth, seeds
> clutched in hand—the memories of home.

That is how it was, as I remember.

*(Singing)*

*(Gestures: to hip; Pacal position; Starfish—skydiving)*

"Go ask Alice

When she's ten feet tall

And if you go chasing rabbits

And you know you're going to fall"

Too close! Too close to the edge!

No! No! No!

Below—only water...

Mother, Father, all that I love left behind.

No good-byes, caresses, longing looks.

The twins hug each other inside me.

*(Singing)*

"Call Alice

When she was just small"

Sky Woman Falling!

A dying, falling star burns white-hot.

Free fall!

Terror chokes—terror-heart drumming panic inside the ears, inside the skull.

A throbbing between the shoulder blades

No! No! No! It didn't happen!

No! No! No! Let me quickly die!
Terror-heart cracks the breastbone and flutters free
My heart grows wings and is flying next to me
carried on soft air currents and
puffs of cotton ball clouds
Can't feel my hands or feet
Icy cold—not a sound.

*(Singing: bass line from introduction to "White Rabbit")*
"Go ask Alice
I think she'll know
When logic and proportion
Have fallen softly dead"

*(Gestures: to hip; Pacal position; Starfish—skydiving)*
Below, only water.
My spine will crack on impact—cheekbones shatter.
No! No! No! Make it stop NOW!
"The only way out of the pain is to lean into the pain..."
"Jam yesterday and jam tomorrow, but never jam today..."

*(Singing)*
"And the White Knight is talking backwards
And the Red Queen's 'Off with her head!'"
Suddenly buoyant
Under my arms, under my thighs
Great winged beings
break the fall—carry me slow floating
Below there is nothing—only water.
Not a sound.

*(Singing)*
"Catch a falling star and put it in your pocket..."

Touch me down on Turtle's back
Thirteen moons and great sorrowful eyes—
I am your new granddaughter
That is how it was, as I remember.

You know the rest of the story:
Muskrat gave his life so that from the tiny bit of earth
in his desperate little paw, the land grew and grew on Grandmother Turtle's back.
The twins were born—one in the natural way, one tearing through Sky Woman's armpit, leaving her dead.

From her body grows corn
From her body grows beans, squash, potatoes,
Tobacco.
That is how it was, as I—
"Remember what the doormouse said:"

I, too, am a granddaughter fallen from the stars
I call to Sky Woman: lend me your courage!
The courage of the valiant Morning Star when she rises each morning to greet her brother, the sun, at daybreak
And there, for some moments, we hang in the liquid pigment of a watercolour sky

*(Singing)*
"Feed your head
Feed your head
Feed your head"

[Or alternate ending:]
*(Singing)*
"I feel, I feel, I feel like a morning star,
I feel, I feel, I feel like a morning star.
I feel, I feel, I feel like a morning star,
I feel, I feel, I feel like a morning star."

MONIQUE
Doing Aboriginal theatre, and doing research for Aboriginal performance creation, means something different than it does for other communities. Doing Aboriginal theatre is about translation, building bridges, making reconnections. Each tiny fragment of research and creation contributes, accumulates, and adds up to something with which the disconnect brought on by "*la conquista*" can be healed. *To eat the food of a Nation—the chocolate, the corn, the salmon, the deer, the buffalo—is to ingest a whole cosmology; to lose them is to feed the disconnect.* Theatre research and creation also, and crucially, feed. They go straight into the body...

RIC
...and if they *don't* make it to the body they can't matter. Performance that matters—that *makes difference*—demands participation, transmutes this research and creation into the bodies of the audience as witnesses for whom, as Jill Carter has argued, dis-ease demands strong medicine, marrying traditional knowledge with contemporary methodology to make of performance a remedial re-membering.

MONIQUE
*What is found and created, then, is encoded on a cellular level, or between cells. It can be used to bridge the rupture, and impact on audiences, body to body, so that the transformation reverberates, amplifies, and goes on. It changes us on a cellular, molecular level.*

RIC
Creation story begins again.

MONIQUE
How does this happen? How is the connection made? What are the cords that connect us to what is not broken? One of the ways these connections are made is through the power of the word as invocation, through naming, and honouring, the living and the dead who came before us. Another way is by bringing our deities and cultural heroes to the stage, being *inhabited* by them, and becoming their reflections and manifestations. But this can't be done in isolation. Creation stories are about transformation, metamorphoses, beginnings. The transformative impulse does not come from individuals acting alone. It comes from building alliances, linking arms. It needs families, clans, Nations. It needs alliances across Nations. It needs healers, midwives, diplomats, defenders, and artists. It needs collaboration.

RIC
One of the most difficult and problematic forms of collaboration is one that we embody, collaboration across the traditional and traditionally disastrous divide between the (Native) artist and the (Western) academy. How can the Western academy, in a collaborative relationship with Native artists, serve the healing, regenerative project that we have been discussing, when Western scholarship has been one of the major technologies of colonization and disempowerment? It is a not insignificant fact that I make more money teaching and writing about Monique's work than Monique makes from writing and performing it. But it is also true that Monique's play *Princess Pocahontas and the Blue Spots* is better known within the academy than within the Native community or the theatre community. Widely disseminated and taught around the world in its public version as text, it has been seen by only a handful of people, and not by them for over fifteen years. This most performative and performatively regenerative of pieces, with its powerful invocation of women word warriors, has had its ongoing impact within the academy *as text.* And it is true that texts—books like the script of *Princess P*, or anthologies such as *Staging Coyote's Dream*—keep much that is important, and that would otherwise disappear, in circulation. But is this how the academy best serves Native theatre? Is one of Monique's most significant achievements to have, as editor of the Native Theatre issue of *Canadian Theatre Review*, forced Spiderwoman Theater to write down a script for *Winnetou's Snake Oil Show from Wigwam City*—their first publication? Is the academy's most useful role to kill orature into literature, box it into archives?

Western scholarship is traditionally best at defining, objectifying, preserving, and keeping the dead dead—dead and entombed in history and in books ("tombs")—

and keeping the victims of history victimized. How can scholarship reconfigure itself to help keep the ancestors alive? If the project now is to bring forward those things from the past that are not broken, to heal the dismemberment—to re-member—how can conferences, articles, books, anthologies—the traditional effluvia of scholarship and the structures of the academy—serve that project?

Perhaps one way is through collaboration that subverts the divisions (and the hierarchies that are implied in those divisions) between (Native) artists and (Western) scholars, and by subverting or perverting the objectifying taxonomies on which Western scholarship rests. Collaboration across difference does not involve ignoring difference; it means serving the work, and bringing one's own *position*—including whatever knowledges, skills, privileges, and power one has—to the service of the work. It means learning theoretical frames from the work itself. It means surrendering to knowledges one doesn't have. It means surrendering the safety of scholarly detachment and the protection of academic protocols and procedures—indeed, it may mean subverting those very protocols and procedures. It means taking responsibility for what our research performs in the world.

I don't want to idealize. There are dangers in this. When, for Aboriginal artists, does this collaboration consist of sleeping with the enemy? When does scholarly "support" become co-optation? When does the dissemination of Native work in print, in classrooms, in Western-style *theatrical performance*, become commodification? Who owns or benefits from the work, and whose interests does it serve?

MONIQUE

The Native artist, too, needs to take responsibility for making work that matters, that provokes, subverts, takes risks, and refuses to be co-opted or commodified, work that touches, transforms, and has the power to heal. If theatre is a tool of transformation, which we know it to be, then we have a responsibility that the stories that we tell will be stories of our becoming, of our becoming whole. Which means that the stories that we tell must be creation stories. And like the academic who must take responsibility for the use of her research, the artist must live her art, must make creation story begin again in life as in art. It is not enough to make art out of atrocity and risk commodification of those stories. It is not enough to leave the stories on the stage without finding a way to make them transformative. To take, and provoke, response-ability.

Creation story begins again.

## Works Cited

Carter, Jill. "Writing, Righting, Riting." *Alt.Theatre: Cultural Diversity and the Stage* 4.4 (2006): 13-17.

Highway, Tomson. *Dry Lips Oughta Move to Kapuskasing*. Saskatoon: Fifth House, 1989.

Mojica, Monique. *Princess Pocahontas and the Blue Spots. Staging Coyote's Dream: An Anthology of First Nations Drama in English*. Ed. Monique Mojica and Ric Knowles. Toronto: Playwrights Canada, 2003. 133-69.

Slick, Grace. "White Rabbit." 1966.

Vance, Paul, and Lee J. Pockriss. "Catch a Falling Star." New York: Marvin Music, 1957.

# Blind Faith Remembers...This Ain't No Love Story, This Ain't No Masque: *Princess Pocahontas and the Blue Spots* as Transformative Ritual for the Grandmothers, the Ones Who Remain, and for the Ones Who Are Yet to Come

*Jill Carter*

*This is what I have heard:*

*Long time now*

*She married he*

*Both of great power*

*She married he*

*Both Midewiwin*

*He became angry*

*Or afraid?*

*He became angry*

*Or afraid.*

*Long time now*

*She married he*

*He became angry—that's what them Mohawks say. But you know them—they're always angry—they're always causin' trouble...*

*He became afraid—that's what my mother tell me, an' her father tell she, an' his mother tell he—long time now: he became afraid because the medicine of she was more powerful than the medicine of he.*

*What to do? He asks. What to do?*

*There is a tree. Big tree. Some say pine; some say with many lights; some say tree: big tree.*

*Long time now*

*His councilors tell him to uproot this big tree*

*On that we all agree*

*Long time now*

*He uproots the tree*

*Brings she to the hole*

*And tempts her to look down—*

*Look down, he says. Look down!*

*She looks. He pushes.*

*End of story...*

*Fooled you!*

*Beginning of story...*

*Long time now*

*Sky Woman falls through the hole*

*Grabbing at what ever comes near her hands...tobacco, corn, strawberry...good medicines*

*Sky Woman falling holds on to the medicines.*

*Sky Woman falls through the hole*

*Falls a long time, long time now*

*Falls down to the waters...*

*And down in the waters they look up, see Sky Woman falling...long time, long time now*

*Birds call down*

*Muskrat looks up*

*Turtle looks up*

*Sky Woman flying*

*Human falling*

*Catch her, they say. Catch her.*

*Human falling. Birds meet her. Birds bear her up with their wings—some say they were gulls, ducks, swans—white feathered ones, white feathered wings.*

*White winged helpers meet human falling, catch her gently. Fly with her.*

*Below, Turtle waits.*

*Sky Woman flying with white-winged helpers; and Turtle waits on the waters below.*

*Sky Woman flying; white birds flying.*

*Gently they set her on Turtle's back.*

*Did she let the medicines fall? Earth clinging to the roots—sinking down into the waters.*

*Did she hold the medicines bare of earth? Each one says different.*

*Long time now…too hard to say.*

*But life on Turtle's back is hard without earth without trees without medicines.*

*Long time now.*

*Human falling.*

*Sky Woman flying.*

*And life begins on Turtle's back…*

*Long time now: this is the story of my coming—*
*Long time now—it is not the end.*

The story of Sky Woman is a story of transformation—a transformation from a time and space before to the times known by all the generations of life upon the Turtle's back. For the Anishinaabe peoples as well as for the Haudenosaunee, it is a story of our becoming through transformation; and this transformation is re-membered and celebrated through story and ceremony…long time now. For the Powhatan (the Anishinaabe alliance into which Pocahontas had been born), this time of transformation, that is Sky Woman's fall to earth, was recreated annually during the midwinter ceremonies (Allen, *Pocahontas* 19). The Powhatan (translated by Laguna Pueblo scholar Paula Gunn Allen as "people of the dream-vision" [*Pocahontas* 65]) shared with First Nations peoples across Turtle Island the understanding that life fulfills itself within certain sacred cycles and that during these cycles "times of transformation" are inevitable. Paula Gunn Allen defines this understanding of "transformation time" as "a particular point in that current that comes from the world of the supernatural that surrounds and infiltrates the human world, that decrees 'change chairs'" (*Pocahontas* 15). To receive, comprehend, and acknowledge this consciousness can serve the "blue spot" descendants of Pocahontas and others to properly read and interpret herstory, whether inscribed in English ink or in the breath and body of her relations in the communal circle or upon the greater stage.

Our Elders tell us that we must remember, retain, and pass on our culture, languages, traditions, ceremonies, and stories if we are to retain nationhood and if our nations are to continue into the future. And Kuna/Rappahannock playwright/performer Monique Mojica's *Princess Pocahontas and the Blue Spots*, in its reclamation of the mothers of the mixed-blooded peoples and in its re-appropriation of their stories, is her considerable contribution to this vital work around the survival, sovereignty, and continuance of the original nations of Turtle Island and to the spiritual restoration of their peoples. This project of healing requires a painstaking and precise descent through multiple layers if it is to be at all efficacious. And Mojica's contribution to this project provides not only a vehicle to facilitate this descent but also a map to document the path, as it works to lance the wounds of corrupted memory, to identify and extract the poison lurking in Euro-centered narratives and the distorted images that hold the Indigenous concept of self twisted in their thrall, to stimulate a depressed and enervated memory, and to inspire an organic knowing of the entitlement, obligation, and responsibility of Indigenous peoples to engage fully without fear or shame within Creation's web.

The legend of Pocahontas around which Mojica has constructed her project chronicles the story of a "savage" but "noble Indian Princess" who so loved a seafaring stranger that she defied her father and risked her life to save him only to be deserted by the object of her affections, "kidnapped" by his "countryman," tricked by a lesser suitor, and paraded in England as an object of conquest and a symbol of the "civilizing" and "transformative" power of colonization. As Paula Gunn Allen reminds us, this is an inheritance that comes down to us from the journals of said seafaring stranger (John Smith), the letters and journals of the tobacco baron and her chosen husband (John Rolfe), and the written testimonies of various old-world travelers remarking upon the languages, customs, and beliefs of the Algonquin peoples (*Pocahontas* 4-5). Our image of Pocahontas, then, has been formed for the most part by the worldview of a seventeenth-century British working class adventurer who (in his inscription of her person to the page) has severed her actions (and those of her people) from the cosmology that directed those actions. Furthermore, as Allen observes, Pocahontas's history has become a "love story" in Anglo-American tradition by virtue of its female protagonist, since narratives that feature women have been traditionally crafted as love stories (*Pocahontas* 59). Even the more recent renderings of her story (however loosely based on Smith's journals) cut her off from her "total biota or life system" and follow the tendency to locate her identity (female, "savage," "barbarian") as it is manifested in her relationship with an "actual human" bearing an actual human identity. Typically, this "actual human" with whom the female must engage to lay claim to any sort of personhood is, as Allen reminds us, always male (2). Hence, we, the "blue-spotted" descendants, the half-breeds, the mixed bloods, have come to see our "barbarian" grandmother through the colonizers' eyes—a besotted nubile who betrayed her people, a beguiled victim who was herself betrayed. And how then must we view ourselves (reflected as we are through the colonizing lens)—as misbegotten accidents of misbegotten passions, a hybrid harvest of besottment and betrayal? Have we seen this grandmother? We have seen her through the Other's eyes. Have we, then, known her? Do we recognize her? Can we, thereby, know ourselves?[1]

Monique Mojica re-grinds the lens through which we have come to view this grandmother, utilizing a process of "transformational dramaturgy" (Mojica, *Princess* 135) with which she and co-creatrix, musician/composer Alejandra Nuñez, enter into active engagement with the written testimony of Smith, Rolfe, and their compatriots, animating the "characters" on the page to test their credibility in action and weaving these with the words and actions of contemporary Native women. Out of this process has emerged an unanswerable challenge to the "historical canon" constructed upon the travel accounts originally designed to entertain, to titillate, to curry favor, and to attract financial support for further "adventures" by European explorers, entrepreneurs, pirates, and military personnel. *Princess Pocahontas and the Blue*

[1] This distorted mythology, however, carries even more profound ideological implications than the reduction of the political female sworn to serve her people to an adolescent individual driven solely by romantic yearnings. Eliana Crestani points to a marked shift in the representation of Pocahontas between the eighteenth and nineteenth centuries in American Pocahontas narratives. In the eighteenth-century mind Pocahontas was, as "wife of Rolfe," an ancestor of a noble family and an example of successful assimilation through interracial marriage. By the nineteenth century, interracial marriage was deemed neither acceptable nor proper as a vehicle towards assimilation, and "assimilation" became synonymous with "eradication" as policies were developed either to eradicate all traces of "Indianess" in the individual through re-education, indoctrination, and physical separation of the individual from family and community, or to actually exterminate. Pocahontas's image, then, as "savior of Smith," supports the concept of Manifest Destiny (the "noble savage" perforce recognizes and acknowledges the White captain's superior qualities) and the concept of the "doomed Indian." As "noble" as she may be, she is still a "savage"; she cannot be his wife. She, therefore, marries a lesser man and pines away her youth until she dies. These concepts "were to play a decisive role in the cultural acceptance of indigenes' removal or physical extermination" (Crestani 12).

*Spots* is a play that re-visions history, that re-educates, that opens a portal to the possibility of transformation in the here-and-now for its Indigenous spectators and that works efficaciously at multiple levels to facilitate active and actual transformation in the patent and metaphysical realms.

First produced in 1990 at Theatre Passe Muraille Backspace in Toronto under the direction of Muriel Miguel (director and co-founder of Spiderwoman Theater), *Princess Pocahontas and the Blue Spots* calls into account the manufactured stories of Pocahontas (Rappahannock), Malinche (Nahautl), and the Quechua Woman of the Puna. Effecting a seemingly effortless journey that traverses all directions—geographic and temporal—by means of thirteen seamless transformations, Mojica and Alejandra Nuñez (whom Mojica credits as "an intrinsic part of the tapestry, not an appendage" [personal communication]) weave the stories of these legendary grandmothers with those of three Cree and Métis "country wives,"[2] several contemporary Indigenous "Everywomen," Annie Mae Aquash and two female Tricksters, "Princess Buttered-On-Both-Sides," and the "Cigar Store Squaw."

In these latter characters, Mojica embodies two "faces" of Trickster (*Princess* 136-37) to play out and comment upon the contemporary squaw/princess iconography that continues to foster a dangerously distorted perception of Indigenous womanhood. While these corrupt perceptions may have taken root in the perverse fantasies of the newcomers to our territories, like foreign spores borne upon the wind, they have been disseminated as truth, sown within the soil to which they are not Indigenous, and taken root in the imaginations of our own peoples as well as of those with whom we share our lands. These distorted perceptions have displaced Native women physically, socially, and politically and continue to fuel the unconscionably high rates of battery, sexual assault, and murder that are perpetrated against Native females of all ages. This Trickster iconography (embodied in the "Princess" and the "Squaw") constitutes the imperceptible seam that connects each story explored by Mojica and Nuñez, weaving the legendary with the prosaic, the past with the present, the north with the south, and the descendant with the ancestor. Trickster is, after all, an irrepressible, creative force, arranging and re-arranging the universe in accordance with her whims. Her face winks mischievously within the flickering darkness of the chaos and the pain; but pushing against all expectations, she executes an impossible leap through time and space, reconfiguring the Story, righting old wrongs, and restoring the seemingly irreparable.

As Mojica herself notes, *Princess Pocahontas and the Blue Spots* begins in a space of "dislocation" (136) with the grotesque parody, Princess Buttered-On-Both-Sides, who transforms rapidly into "Contemporary

[2] Those European military personnel and fur traders who had been married in Europe had come to this land to establish themselves without their families. To facilitate their efforts in establishing themselves in North America, they required interpreters, guides, and strong alliances with the Indigenous peoples in their areas. To ease their loneliness and to ensure success and survival, they entered into "marriages" with Native women from the First Nations in their area. Where these women and their nations regarded such marriages as enduring covenants between willing, autonomous individuals and between the nations of whom they were citizens, the Europeans regarded such alliances as temporary measures of convenience. In too many cases to count, British and French soldiers and fur-traders "turned off" (discarded) their "country wives" (and the children born to them) as soon as they were sufficiently established and felt themselves ready either to send for their European families or to return to Europe to seek a wife. Abandoned and destitute without legal recourse, these women (with their children) had few options. Sometimes their estranged husbands gave them over as "country wives" to one of their colleagues. Sometimes these women were able to return to their communities. But in many cases, these women were left without resources, and they froze or starved to death outside the walls of the English and French forts.

Woman #1" possessing "no map, no trail, no footprint, no way home" (140). Anchoring all stories via the mock-tragic leap of her "Coyote in Drag,"[3] between Transformations One and Two, to the historical (and legendary) Pocahontas's leap onto the body of an English sea-captain, which is firmly anchored to Sky Woman's transformative leap, Mojica concludes the piece with an invitation—nay, an injunction—to reclaim our lives, to relocate ourselves, to leap blindly into the unknowable dark with only blind faith to light the way.

The displacement of the contemporary Native female is a direct result of the displacement of her grandmothers within the hoop of history. Maligned and misaligned, these ambassadors—upon whom lines of communication, harmonious relations, and business protocols between the Indigenous nations and the settlers had been built and upon whom the mobility and survival of the explorers and primary-resource-entrepreneurs depended—are those to whom contemporary Indigenous nations across Turtle Island owe our continuance (and/or, in the case of the Métis, Mestizo/Mestiza, and mixed-blood peoples, our inception). The relocation of contemporary Native women to their proper position in the nations' hoop depends upon the proper alignment of our understanding of these grandmothers as transformative female bodies bridging the liminal interstices in times of transformation between some and Others, us and them, ancestor and descendant, and upon our ability to learn from their example how we might do the same.

Like her mother, Gloria Miguel, and aunties, Muriel Miguel and Lisa Mayo, who comprise Spiderwoman Theater, Mojica utilizes a process of dramaturgical-and-performative-layering in the creation and execution of her works. This process—Spiderwoman's methodology of "Storyweaving"—has been authored by Muriel Miguel and developed over three decades by Spiderwoman Theater. While the outward manifestations of its praxis draw from and parallel certain exercises developed by Joseph Chaikin of the Open Theater of which Muriel Miguel was a core member (e.g., "Transformations" and "Inside/Outside"), its foundational philosophical underpinnings and aesthetic effects are uncannily reminiscent of traditional material-and-oratorical aesthetics belonging to the Kuna people of Panama of whom the Miguel sisters and Mojica are tribal members and of the Hopi tradition of finger-weaving for which Miguel named the process in honor of her best friend and co-founding member of Spiderwoman Theater, the late Josephine Mofsie Tarrant.

## Dramaturging the *Mola: Mola* Aesthetics

The *mola* is an important component of traditional female dress for the Kuna woman of Panama; and the art of *mola*-making belongs strictly in the female arena. In earlier times traditional adornments for the Kuna body included tattoos, piercings, and intricate designs painted on the body. In the late nineteenth century Kuna women began transferring the designs once used in body painting to hand-woven cloth. From there they began to experiment with appliqué,

[3] Mojica's conception of Princess Buttered-on-Both-Sides extends beyond her written description of the "Princess" as "one face" of Coyote. For her, this "Princess" is Trickster's self-creation. The "Princess" emerges from the Trickster within: she is, Mojica asserts, "Coyote in drag" (personal communication).

and eventually they developed a layering process that is an integral component of Kuna philosophy and aesthetics belonging not only to the *mola* but also to music composition, oratory, healing practices, origin stories, etc.[4] The process involves layering fabrics of variegated colors, one on top of the other. As upper layers are carefully cut away to expose the colors beneath, the story chronicled within each mola is revealed, emerging from the layers within (rather than being superimposed from the outside). And the arrangement of its layers and the integrity of the pattern are held in place with a network of delicate, invisible seams, with which the artist connects each layer to the others. Molas are assessed in accordance with specific aesthetic criteria; these are too numerous and complex to be adequately discussed here. But for now it may be worth remembering that in Kuna Yala the quality of a mola is judged by its thickness, its intricacy, and the imperceptibility of the stitches that connect its layers.[5]

Noteworthy also is that in the mid-1920s, the Panamanian police attempted to suppress the expression of Kuna identity by prohibiting puberty and curing ceremonies, the Gathering House, and the traditional style of female dress. In February of 1925, the people had been pushed past the point of endurance. Rising up in violent protest during the Carnival celebrations (which had been imposed upon the Indigenous population) and appealing to the United States for mediation, the people of Kuna Yala were finally able to negotiate a treaty that is foundational to the recognition of Kuna as a sovereign people within Panama today (Howe 146). In contemporary celebrations to commemorate Kuna sovereignty, that resistance is re-enacted by the people performatively on the streets every February. And amidst the dramatized recreations of oppression and civil disobedience, the "granddaughters of the revolution" proudly wear their finest *molas* for all to see. So the *mola*—a dense riot of texture, design, and color—whether it is being crafted, worn, or displayed is a celebratory marker of Kuna identity, of Kuna resistance, of Kuna survival. It is the "mark" of the Kuna woman. It is the test of her traditional knowledge, her memory, her artistry, and her ability to invent and adapt. It is the work of her hands. It is the raiment that reveals and magnifies her beauty.

**Layering as a Dramaturgical Tool**

Each story—each fragment of female experience—selected for inclusion in Mojica's play becomes a layer in the performative *mola*. As she and Nuñez sift through each of these layers, reducing it to its kernel or "essence," the collective *mola*-maker (in the persons of Mojica, Nuñez, and director Miguel) is cutting away inconsequential details, revealing the shape and color of truthful experience. The resultant multi-vocal perspective resists privileging the easy answers provided by a singular author or "authority"—the positivist course to an absolute truth. This is not, however, to suggest that the presentation of a multiplicity of perspectives constitutes an implication

[4] Oswaldo DeLeón Kantule (Achu), the son of a Kuna chief, Gathering House Orator, and history keeper, is a contemporary visual artist living in Canada, and his art expresses traditional Kuna understandings of the physical and metaphysical worlds that are realized in densely layered colors and textures, conforming to the aesthetic preferences and praxis of his people. When Mojica told Kantule that she regarded her dramaturgical and performative process as an extension of the mola-maker's aesthetic, he suggested that it would be "more accurate" to describe her work as "traditionally Kuna," because "everything is based on the Mola in Kuna Yala" (Mojica, personal communication).

[5] De Fernandez, Domitila DeLeón, and Oswaldo DeLeón Kantule. "Mola Make–Making Molas." Workshop. 16 June 2007. Textile Museum of Canada, Toronto.

that the truth is "relative" or that there is no truth. Rather, this process is a contemporary manifestation of a tribal process (common to many if not all Indigenous nations). This process mandates the preservation of tribal history as a communal responsibility, wherein each tribal member is expected to learn and retain fragments or "layers" of the communal story and is expected to participate in the transmission of that history, weaving into the grand design the details, shapes, colors, and fragments engendered by his/her memories, reception, and interpretations. As Laguna Pueblo writer Leslie Marmon Silko has noted, with regards to traditions of Pueblo orality, this process is engendered by an "inclusive" vision of the world that acknowledges that all levels of human experience are relevant and crucial, as it is somewhere within those levels/layers that physical and metaphysical truths may be preserved and recovered (31-32). And while Silko offers these observations as a direct address of Pueblo experience, her words speak to a foundational philosophy that directs the aesthetics of bead-workers, carvers, wampum-belt-artisans, and *mola*-makers throughout the Americas as much as it does that of Pueblo weavers and workers in clay.

### Cutting to the Core: The Pocahontas Layer and the Allen Connection

Since the myriad layers that comprise *Princess Pocahontas and the Blue Spots* are each anchored to the figure of a seventeenth-century Rappahannock girl, so maligned and misaligned that she has become unrecognizable to her own descendants, it seems only fitting to structure any theoretical negotiation of these layers in accordance with Mojica's process and to begin by cutting through to the base layer, which is the story of our "little Indian Princess." In so doing, the intent is to realign her image by situating her within an Algonquian (as opposed to a British) cultural context to thereby attain a more accurate reflection of her and of Mojica's ceremonial re-calling of this and the other grandmothers of mixed-blood peoples, to discover the thread-line that connects this base layer to the others, and to locate ourselves—the living generations standing with-out—as active agents existing within the living document that is Mojica's "performative *mola*."

Mojica's piece may begin in a place of dislocation and brokenness, but it begins with a clear vision to effect healing. Citing the late and revered Anishinaabe Elder Art Solomon, Mojica tells us "On the Precipice" of her second transformation, "It's time for the women to pick up their medicine in order for the people to continue....The women are the medicine, so we must heal the women" (quoted in Mojica, *Princess* 140). And the process of healing begins with Mojica's later invocation of not only the grandmothers who have passed but also the living "Word Warriors" (167-69) who continue to fight so valiantly to repair the breach in the hoop of our nations by restoring the Indigenous female to her rightful place in the circle. Prominent among these is Laguna Pueblo scholar Paula Gunn Allen who has coined the appellation "word warriors" to identify herself and other Native writers whose labors are devoted to the recovery and dissemination of historical truths and to the realignment of contemporary Indigenous societies in light of these truths.

In *Princess Pocahontas and the Blue Spots* Mojica draws inspiration from Allen's seminal work, *The Sacred Hoop* (1986), continuing its work and calling its author into her own project to preserve and heal the sacred feminine. So, too, it is only fitting that any critical negotiation of Mojica's project will answer Mojica's "cue" and call upon this eminent Word Warrior if it wishes to properly inform and serve the project of which it seeks to be a part. Thirteen years after Mojica's play, Allen has afforded us another layer to thicken the story, heighten the contrast, and deepen our understanding of the historic Pocahontas and the corruption of her image by the strangers who encountered her. So it is through Allen's eyes that we will look again at this grandmother and at Mojica's re-visioning of her, and perhaps, through the eyes of both, we will come to a new vision of ourselves—the "blue spot" descendants.

### Misnomers and Misinterpretation: When Is a "Masque" Not a Masque?

As we have seen, the First Nations peoples across Turtle Island have predicated the governance of communal life upon the acceptance and understanding of sacred cycles—those certain times when the world is transformed. And as Paula Gunn Allen has observed, for the Algonquian, the third coming of the English to Chesapeake Bay would mark a major transformational shift, which had been long prophesied for the people and their descendants:

> There be at this tyme certayne Prophesies afoote amongst the people enhabiting about us...which his [Powhatan's] priests continually put him in feare of....How that from the Cheasapeak Bay a Nation should arise, which should dissolve and give end to his Empier....That twice they should give overthrowe and dishearten the Attempters, and such Straungers as should envade their Territorye, or laboure to settell a plantation amongst them, but the third tyme they themselves should fall into their Subjection and under their Conquest. (Strachey quoted in Allen, *Pocahontas* 34-35)

In 1587 the Powhatan and their allies had wiped out Roanoke's "Lost Colony"; in 1595 (close to the time of Pocahontas's birth) in the waters just north of Chesapeake Bay a second colonial attempt at invasion was thwarted. Act three: 1607. Enter John Smith. His mission to establish settlement, locate the headwaters of the Chickahominy River, and to establish contact with "King" Powhatan (Allen 37). Captured by members of the Powhatan Alliance in 1608, he was taken to each one of the thirty-five member nations of the alliance, feted and feasted, until at last he was brought before Powhatan who was no "King," no "Chief," but High Priest of the visioning people.

The Powhatan midwinter ceremony in 1608 would mark not only the fall of Sky Woman that initiated a transformation from the life and ways of another Sky world to life on this earth but also the prophesied transformational time, which would be set in motion with the coming of the English Captain. Enter the "Princess." The meaning of her childhood name, Pocahontas, is unclear, but it relates to vivacity, mischief, and quick intelligence. As Paula Gunn Allen has noted, where the English translated the name and imaged the girl as "wanton," a Native interpreter would never relate her "mischief" to sexual precociousness; rather she would be characterized with certain four-leggeds who shared these aforementioned qualities—trickster figures (32). Allen notes also that "Pocahontas" was actually her childhood name. But in the European humanistic tradition, which fosters and celebrates "individualism," fluidity of identity is not acknowledged. And she goes on to remind us that in this culture, a person of European extraction is generally identified by one name from birth until death (17). Hence, in the English consciousness, through the English lens, Pocahontas remains a child and has been known as such...long time now.

By contrast, for countless Indigenous nations, names change as personhood changes. A naming ceremony announces the child to the community, but as the child grows, his/her works announce themselves and new names are bestowed. The child Pocahontas, so called for her vivacity and mischievous character, had also been endowed with her "first" name, the name she would grow into—Matoaks/Matoaka. She was so named for the "white (or snow) feathers" that were braided into her hair when she assumed her ceremonial obligations as a spiritual daughter of the High Priest of her people. These white feathers (Matoaks) adorned her hair during the midwinter ceremony and were, in Powhatan circles, a signifier of her position within the community. And as Allen reminds us, they connected her with Sky Woman, whose "plummet through the void was arrested by waterfowl—symbolized by white feathers or, on prepubescent women, by white down" (60); they marked her as a dreamer, a visionary, a priestess of the Midewiwin. Enter "Amonute": Pocahontas's third name means "Beloved Woman," and, as Allen points out, it clearly identifies her as a Midewiwin of high degree (18).

And then to mark yet another time of change she took a fourth name, the name she carried until the end of her short life: "And they blessed Rebekah and said unto her. 'Thou art our sister, be thou the mother of thousands of millions, and let thy seed possess the gate of those which hate them'" (Genesis 24:60). Enter Lady Rebecca, mother of the Blue Spots. Is this name marking the Beloved Woman's fourth and penultimate transformation a happy coincidence, or did she—after careful study—*choose* this name for her ceremony of baptism—the name by which she would announce herself as Christian convert, transformative body (Sky Woman) bridging two worlds, and mother to thousands of millions? But I get ahead of myself here...

(I will not speculate whether her conversion to the Christian faith was sincere or whether it was a politically expedient action. I certainly believe that Matoaks placed herself deliberately into the hands of the English after her adopted "brother" John Smith left Virginia, thus, in the minds of the Powhatan, severing the alliance between their Confederacy and the English. And I am inclined to share Beth Brant's speculation that Matoaks undertook conversion not only to re-establish ties with the newcomers but also in order that she might attain absolute proficiency in their language. [Brant 156])

Just as in her naming, the "little Indian Princess" has been relegated to a place of stasis, remaining in European consciousness immutably child-like and precocious, so too in the interpretation and dissemination of their actions, Pocahontas and her compatriots have been denied the rightful recognition owed to them as active, conscious agents of their own transformation by the confused misrepresentation of ceremony as spectacle and of strategic action as emotionally-driven reaction. Let us set the "scene": Captain John Smith, the bewildered and affrighted captive, is brought before the entire Powhatan alliance, headed by its High Priest who had been endowed with the title "Powhatan"—dream-visionary. After the prayers, offerings of tobacco, dancing, and song, our hero is laid out with his head resting between two flat rocks, which have been severally painted red and black to signify a liminal space "between two worlds"—a space of infinite possibility, a space in which lasting transformation may occur (Allen 49). Over the prone, confused, and terrified man loom two priests. Their bodies have been carefully painted half red and half black. Between two worlds, the body of each carries out its duties. Themselves transformative bodies, these priests negotiate the void between past and future, life and death, ancestor and descendant. One priest wields a club made of roots, the painted and carved detailing of which makes manifest the spirits that lie within. The second priest wields a straight club, topped by an ornate clamshell, which has been carved to resemble a blade. Whereas through European eyes, the clamshell "blade" may be seen to presage death, in Anishinaabe tradition the shell (miigis) is a signifier of life. More accurately, emerging as it does from water (the source of all life and the particular responsibility of Anishinaabekwe, 'Anishinaabe woman'), it is a signifier of the life-giving attribute of women and understood as such. Traditionally, a particular gesture effected with the clamshell "blade" will signify that the new soul has been formed, that transformation is complete. But how is our prone and helpless English adventurer to know all this? He has only his own experience and cultural perspective by which to assess the "Mascarado" in which he plays the principal role. He believes that he is about to be beheaded—and how could he not? He is no stranger to the practice. Certainly, he has witnessed this form of execution back in merry old England, where he has doubtlessly shuddered under the sightless gaze of countless gory sentries hoisted aloft on pikes outside the Tower of London and the palace of James I. At the very least, these solemn and colorful strangers will most likely use the tools they wield to beat out his brains.

And just when it seems that all is lost, Smith hears a high-pitched wail, which is, Allen observes, likely a sacred tremolo (50); and a young girl with swan's down in her hair separates herself from the crowd and throws herself on top of his prone body. John Smith, English working-class adventurer, is no more. In this ceremony of transformation, he has been adopted into the community of the dream-vision people. John Smith, alien threat, has ceased to exist for the Powhatan; rather he has become a "son" of their spiritual leader, just as Pocahontas/Matoaks/Amonute is a "daughter." And on the following day, this new son and the function he will fulfill as an integral member of this community will be announced in a naming ceremony wherein he will be ceremonially "born again" as a member of the Powhatan alliance.[6]

In the European tradition of the "well-crafted" love story, Pocahontas has not been characterized as an active participant in a communally "dramaturged" ceremony, nor has she been recognized as a precipitator of events before, during, and after Smith's captivity-drama. But then, by such a society wherein the European female was viewed as insensate chattel to be molded, trained-up, and controlled, how could she have been? Instead, what has been passed down to us is a portrait of a disaffected, bovine beauty, standing apart from her people and acting against the agenda of her community to satisfy her own ungovernable urges. It is a shameful portrait: and it bears no relation to the truth.

Indeed, among the peoples of this Algonquian alliance as well as among the Haudenosaunee and Pueblo peoples, women wielded considerable agency in the political, economic, infrastructural, judicial, and spiritual arenas. They held the property. They distributed the corn, goods, and other foodstuffs; women designed and built the dwellings as well as the ceremonial lodges; women had a deciding say in matters of policy and action (Allen 51); hence Allen's assertion that Powhatan women versed in the ways of mystery—the "Beloved Women"—wielded like agency in the spiritual and existential arenas is entirely plausible. If this is so, then there can be little doubt that Pocahontas, in consultation with her fellow-Midewininiwag, decided the fate of John Smith and *acted* in accordance with that decision. Where John Smith and the generations that follow him saw a precocious, rebellious, besotted prepubescent who, having conceived a passion for a bearded stranger, chose the colonizer over her own people, the Powhatan who had engaged in that ceremony of ritual death and rebirth read in the tableau of her body atop that of the prone adventurer the manifestation of their own active engagement in the prophesied time of transformation—a time that would herald the creation of a new people.

### Mojica Leaps: Urban Ceremony in the Secular Dream-Factory

The "masque" of performative ritual is open to misconstruction by one who understands the unfolding events as mimesis—an imitation of an action, either fictive or finished. From an Indigenous perspective, engagement in performative or mimetic acts for ceremonial purposes "literally" recreates those actions (Allen, *Pocahontas* 201), brings them into the

[6] Smith's "Generall Historie" is one of three accounts he authored about his experiences in Virginia, and it is the only account in which he recounts how Pocahontas saved his life. The absence of this incident in his other two accounts has fueled doubts regarding the veracity of his story and has certainly launched a scholarly debate, which "essentially rests now on the shared conviction that the rescue episode was in reality a ceremony of adoption" (Crestani 8, footnote).

here and now, and effectively transforms the "players" and the world they inhabit in that moment of their re-creation: Sky Woman falls to earth again and again and again, long time now...and in each new falling, new worlds find their genesis. In his admirable article, "The Hearts of Its Women: Rape, Residential Schools, and Re-membering," Canadian scholar Ric Knowles reads Mojica's performance as a "literal embodiment" and "re-membering" of the dismembered and distorted images of the ancestral mothers of mixed blood peoples on Turtle Island in an effort to "recuperate the reputations of the mothers of the mestizas" (255). Knowles's vision of Mojica's work, quite rightly, places it beyond the realm of mere mimesis, but that vision is still governed by an Aristotelian perception. For Knowles *Princess Pocahontas and the Blue Spots* is an instructional vehicle that seeks to deconstruct distorted mythologies, to realign fragmented and distorted histories, and in so doing to stimulate the transformation and repair of the dis-membered psyches of the Mixed bloods, Métis, and Mestizas across Turtle Island. In Knowles's model, I am a passive spectator in need of re-education, re-membering, and repair. His otherwise-excellent paradigm democratically equalizes the audience and homogenizes its reception of Mojica's work.

But in Mojica's play, I too play a "part." As a mixed-blood woman of Anishinaabe and Ashkenazi descent, I am after all a "blue spot," and the play is called *Princess Pocahontas and the Blue Spots*. It is my contention that Mojica's labors effect more than just spectacle through which a passive audience is re-educated and re-membered. Through these labors, rather, she has constructed an "urban ceremony," as it were, designed not merely to re-educate but to actively precipitate world renewal and transformation. Not only are my concept of history and perception of self transformed through this ceremony, I too, as a blue spot descendant, have a role to play in the birthing of a new nation. I too must leap blindly into the unknown. I too must be transformed into an embodiment of something larger than myself. I too will become Sky Woman for a moment, leap into the time of change, set up housekeeping there, and birth a nation. The "call to arms" here is not merely an exercise in intellectual stimulation, nor is it a call to the usual and recognizable conventions of political activism.

In her "Set Description" Mojica tells us, "The theme of the set, costumes and props is also transformation" (*Princess* 138). She then goes on to describe the ways in which one set-piece or prop can become "something else"; but this simply constitutes a detailed assertion of the multi-representational *nature* of these objects before us. With regards to the actual "theme" these embody, she remains coyly silent. Those of us who are intimately acquainted with Sky Woman will immediately recognize the indicators of her presence in Mojica's set. The tree with water, sand, and (pop) corn at its base immediately recalls the story of her coming. The pole, which is "pegged for climbing and decorated with the faces and clothing of the Métis women" (138), recalls for us the West Coast totem—genealogy, detailed history, and origin myth hewn in living wood.[7] The water, corn, and red paint are signifiers of ritual, which is after all, as Paula Gunn Allen reminds us, "a procedure whose purpose is to transform someone or something from one condition or state to another" (*Sacred Hoop* 79-80). The purpose of these ritual signifiers is not to stimulate our acceptance of or admiration for the multi-representational nature of the objects, which serve the storyteller's art, nor is it to fuel Mojica's considerable mimetic abilities as she embodies various ancestors and contemporaries; rather, these signifiers

[7] The word "myth" here in no way connotes "fiction" or "fantasy." I use "myth" in its purest sense to express the unimaginable scale and grandeur of these histories, their metaphysical origins, and the timeless truths they embody.

alert those of us who are comfortable in such mysteries that we are not mere spectators in a theatrical event but are perforce ***participants*** in a vehicle of our own transformation. We are participants in ceremony.

From nation to nation across the Americas, tribal prophecies state that the wheel of the Great Transformation, marked by the coming of the colonizer, would complete its revolution only in the time of the Seventh Generation—a time of necessary redress and reconciliation. That time is upon us. The wheel has turned. It is time to birth a new nation. Sky Woman is falling—long time now. In 1608, a young Beloved Woman with swans' down in her hair leapt "blindly" onto a strange body. She did not imitate the fall of Sky Woman birthing the generations of a new people; rather, *Sky Woman, birthing the generations of a new people, was born again in her.* In 1990, Monique Mojica leapt off the stage, concluding the first of a series of thirteen transformations. In her incarnation of Princess Buttered-on-Both-Sides—a slippery character and hard to grasp—she was not merely engaged in a soap-operatic parody of a young girl's self-effacing, self-destructive passion. As she leapt into the liminal void that separates the world of spectator from the world of performer, she closed the space between us and opened a door to new worlds, or at least the possibilities thereof.

As one of the generations of mixed-bloods living in story, prophecy, and ceremony, I receive her leap differently than my non-Native neighbors in the same audience, just as we receive Princess Buttered-on-Both-Sides differently. For the non-Native spectators, this "princess" is a pathetic signifier of an appropriated icon. Certainly, they recognize two beloved icons of White Americana, the Land o' Lakes butter spokes-model and the Mazola corn oil girl, peeking out from under her gaudy head-dress of illuminated corn-cobs;[8] and in the corn nuts she distributes, they surely recognize a plethora of ridiculous stereotypes or perhaps the corruption of something sacred. Hence, the descendants of the colonizing body can laugh ruefully at the spectacle and at its progenitors and so feel themselves to be comfortably allied with their Indigenous neighbors. But while Mojica's wry humor may inspire a momentary laugh in me, my reception does not stop here. Encoded within the parody, I am reminded of my responsibilities and power as an Anishinaabe woman. I am the cultivator, caretaker, and distributor of the corn. I must cling tightly to the medicines as I leap into the new realm that has been prophesied.

### Trickster: Two Faces, Two Worlds...<br>The Transformative Body Standing Between

At once masculine and feminine, bestial and godlike, creatrix and destroyer, Trickster offers two lessons for two different ways of seeing, two different ways of knowing, two different ways of being. To the passive spectator, she offers spectacle, diversion, humor. To her community, she sets forth the medicines, calls up the ancestors, solicits action, and invokes the forces that contain and define existence and that govern its transformation. That one, after all, is a principal actor in the "Mud Diver" story into which Sky Woman's fall ultimately sends her. And for all the chaos and confusion s/he has caused, our Trickster/Nanabush/Raven/Coyote is the agent of transformation facilitating the engenderment of sustainable life on the erstwhile hard, infertile surface of Turtle's back.

---

[8] Mojica's characterization of Princess Buttered-on-Both-Sides constitutes an intricate braid that inextricably binds the popular Maid of the Mist legend to these stunted "models" of American Indian femininity who have been created to carry on the "medicine show" tradition in the butter/margarine advertising "wars" that have been with us in North America since the early twentieth century. (Mojica, personal communication)

The interweaving of proud history and disfigured fantasy serve Mojica's ceremony well: our ceremonies have been misinterpreted, the image distorted, their content and import degraded—*long time now*. The bearded conquerors wrote our stories. And in so doing they shaped and controlled the images we held of ourselves. John Smith is the progenitor of this bastard child—"the little Indian Princess Pocahontas"; she has been conceived in his reception of ceremony; she has been stunted and disfigured by his misconception of the "masque." Now in this time of transformation, Mojica presents Smith's child according to *his* reception. But encoded in the distorted image, encoded in this bastard child, are an ancient story, an ancient knowledge, and an ancient ceremony of becoming. Princess Buttered-on-Both-Sides leaps into the space that separates spectator from performer; she bridges the gap between two worlds; she recreates Sky Woman's fall to earth; she transforms a post-modern, secular entertainment factory into a sacred ceremonial circle; she weaves past and present, ancestor and descendant, spectator and "actor," Anishinaabekwe, Aztec, Mayan, Woman of the Puna, Métis, and Mestiza into an intricate dance. Moreover, she invites the contemporary "dancer," who witnesses from the house, to accept this time of transformation, to accept that there is no way home, to pick up her medicine, to engage actively in the transformation, and to follow the example of Contemporary Woman #1 by giving birth to a nation. Sky Woman fell to earth. No way home. So Sky Woman planted the medicines she had brought with her from the time before and gave birth to the generations of life upon Turtle's back. To facilitate our organic and holistic understanding of our history and of what is required of us as liminal peoples caught in the interstices between nations, between cultures, between what we were, what we are, what we have been told we are, and what we can be, Mojica, through her embodiment of Coyote-in-Drag, inextricably weaves this metaphysical instance of originary "transformation time" to a more prosaic, albeit equally crucial, transformational moment of modern history. Just three centuries ago a Rappahannock Beloved Woman leapt forth into a time of transformation, built new alliances, successfully sustained the people's medicine, and gave birth to new generations of mixed-blood peoples:

> John, my husband, is a businessman, a merchant, and a tobacco planter. I know how to grow tobacco, it is our sacred tobacco plant...I provided John Rolfe with the seeds to create his hybrid tobacco plants and I provided him with a son, and created a hybrid people. (*Princess* 149)

The prophecies of the Dream-Visioning people had foretold the coming of a new nation that would subjugate the original peoples, a nation that would eradicate the old ways and impose new languages, new ways of knowing, and new spiritual practices. And as Allen convincingly argues, the Powhatan understood that such a force could conceivably eradicate the medicines and forever sever the connections between themelves and the Author of their creation (Allen, *Pocahontas* 232). Indeed, England's King James I had written his "Counterblaste to Tobacco" in 1604, explicitly linking the use of tobacco to devil worship, savagery, and the "beastly manners of the wilde, godlesse, and slavish Indians" (232).[9] Despite the potential for profit in the exploitation of our medicines, the colonizing body was threatened by and posed a threat to the continuance and

[9] I can't quite agree with Beth Brant's blithe dismissal of King James' tract: "but it doesn't appear that too many people paid attention to what he had to say" (Brant 159). James I, a devout Protestant, was still burning witches—and frequently. To link tobacco use with the practice of witchcraft would most emphatically discourage consumption of the "devil's weed" and cripple the industry. Back in the "New World," it would provide excuse for the utter eradication of the plant and for the execution of all those caught trafficking or using it.

survival (through cultivation) of the people's lifeblood—of their connection to mystery, of their knowledge of self and their place within Creation's web. It would require the wisdom of old stories, cunning manipulations, profound insight into the most cherished beliefs and deepest fears of the newcomers, political savvy, and diplomatic skill to transform the fearful objections of England into wholehearted support (built on greed) to save the medicine—to save the people. It would require strong magic; it would require a Trickster. Indeed, it still does...

Mojica's "Coyote in Drag" aims to please, delight, and entertain, even as she takes liberties, busts borders, and shows up without being invited. The third Transformation is introduced with the invocation the "matriarchs of metissaje"; and *that one* shows up to answer the call, bodily insinuating herself betwixt and between the layered incarnations of these grandmothers who struggle to re-right their stories. As she slyly animates various well-worn stereotypes, she presents the images of our grandmothers (at least on the surface) as they have been configured for and presented to us for centuries. As the "wrong virgin" of Transformation Four, who refuses to play in accordance with the "mode of the sacrificial virgin" into which the "Princesses" of the colonizing imagination have been stuck, she plays within the juxtapositions of the "real and the unreal" and provides a wordless but scathing commentary upon the dichotomy between the two. (Mojica, personal communication)

Historically, the real Malinche, betrayed by her own people, is said to have transformed herself into the volcano, known today as "Malinche Mountain" (Mojica, personal communication). Only such a topographical phenomenon could contain the power of her rage: "I spit, burn and char the earth. A net of veins binding me to you as I am bound to this piece of earth. So bound. A volcano, this woman..." (*Princess* 144). But such instances of mythical power have been so deconstructed and maligned by those who took it upon themselves to write our histories that the woman who turned herself into a volcano has been reduced to an eternally primitive virgin who ***gets thrown into*** a volcano...long time now. As the "wrong virgin" insinuates herself into the volcano that is Malinche, Princess Buttered-on-Both-Sides effectively unravels another one of history's lies. She tries on the "costume," peers into the "volcano," and walks away. Not only are the costume and the mask revealed to be ill fitting, set side-by-side with a powerful representation of the real, their inferior quality and patent artificiality are rendered hideously apparent. Textually, Princess Buttered-on-Both-Sides presents herself as an amusing (and therefore ***not*** dangerous) parody of what we have become; but her heart—her "bunny heart"—soars "like the noble rabbit" (***Princess*** 147). She is as clever, quick-witted, untouchable, and perhaps as unknowable as our grandmothers had to be. (Remember that Pocahontas—small, quick-witted, and mischievous—grew into Matoaks/Amonute/Rebecca.)

Historically, Malinche and Lady Rebecca have come to inhabit our imaginations as the kidnapped ones—the "fucked ones" and the Puna deities have been sterilized—robbed of their women's power—and transformed into cold icons to serve the story of the Other. But do these self-imaginings belong to the realm of the real or to the realm of the unreal? "Powhatan did seek to know the truth, because your countrymen will lie much" (John Smith quoted in Mojica, ***Princess*** 148). Was Matoaka kidnapped or did she allow the English to believe she was, wishing to live among them, to learn their doings, to telegraph those doings back to her people, and ultimately to forestall the complete eradication of her nation and its ways? Lady Rebecca states that she was a victim of "treachery"—"kidnapped" (Smith quoted in Mojica, ***Princess*** 149). But this is the story that we have been given. And Trickster surely loves to please her audience—at least, initially. In Transformation Twelve—the transfiguration of Contemporary Woman into Spirit-Sister, Spirit Animal—we are told:

> I walk resigned but not broken....I memorize every leaf, every hill, every bird, and every plot of mountain corn—knowing these things are the last things I will see....I promise to return....I promise to return to carry on the light...."If I survive this journey, it is only because my heart *has decided not to burst"*....Wordless, *I walk into the sea....* (*Princess* 165-67, italics added)

It is written that Pocahontas, in her fourth incarnation, wished to stay in England. Certainly Lady Rebecca as a woman with craft, wit, wisdom and diplomacy—certainly such a woman on a mission of such import—would have the good sense to exhibit utmost grace and tell her hosts what they wanted to hear. After all, she was not unaware that her English visit was an elaborate "masque," funded by her husband's business partners (but perhaps engineered by herself). As the main attraction, she was to embody the successful alchemy of civilization. She played the part of the "wanton savage" transformed into the noble Lady, who of course preferred this "brave new world" to her own.[10] Like Princess Buttered-on-Both-Sides, she sang the song that her audience most wanted to hear. And she served as an exotic spokes-model—an icon of civilized savagery—that would legitimize the fledgling tobacco enterprise and render its existence useful and attractive in the minds of the British financiers and political powers. Like Sky Woman before her, this Beloved Woman seized hold of the medicines, leapt blindly into a void, and carried them with her into the time of transformation, even as she promised to return.

As she does with Pocahontas (Matoaka/Amonute/Lady Rebecca), Mojica begins to re-right our vision of the Nahautl mother of the Mestiza by recalling all of her names: we have come to know her alternatively as Malinche ("Head Woman") or *La Chingada* ("The Fucked One"). And indeed Mojica initially invokes her as "Malinche," a title that has set her apart from her people in popular imagination and that has left us with the impression of a woman who was served by her people rather than a woman who served her people. This grandmother answers Mojica's call, but when she comes she flatly rejects the name by which she has been invoked insisting that "My name is Malinali" (143). Paula Gunn Allen has translated *Malinali* as "penance grass"—a sharp-edged grass that was used in the rituals of Meso-America to pierce the body and to offer up one's blood in sacrifice for the benefit of the whole community (*Pocahontas* 99). It is hard to conceive of this woman, named for the medicine of self-sacrifice, as "the fucked one," merely a conquest and/or a tool of conquest. Perhaps she is rather, as Mojica has her assert, a "smart woman," a "strategist," and "dangerous" (*Princess* 143). Her reference to her coiffure, "like two snakes" (*Princess* 143), weaves her tightly into the story of the Woman of the Puna and the Deity: "I wore a serpent skirt....I birthed a continent" (*Princess* 153). Likewise, we may imagine this deity as a passive, abducted victim, or we might take our cue from Mojica and imagine that "maybe it was the other way around" (153). The Woman of the Puna has been "virginized," sanitized, and robbed of her life-giving power, but her story has been corrupted by those who re-configured her image and re-wrote herstory. It belongs to the realm of the unreal.

In the realm of Indigenous self-actualization (the realm of *our* "real"), Serpent Skirt (Coatlique) and Serpent Woman (Cihuacoatl) held not only the power

[10] Indeed, our "Princess" was seen in attendance at performances of both *Twelfth Night* and *The Tempest* by William Shakespeare in 1616 (Allen, *Pocahontas* 283). I would give much to know what this "daughter" of Powhatan was thinking as Prospero's daughter began her entry into a marriage of political "statecraft" to firmly ally Milan and Naples? What must she have thought as Miranda spoke those lines? What hopes rose in her breast? What fears threatened to overwhelm her peace?

of life (to birth a continent) but also the power of death. Smoking Mirror (Huitzilopochtli) was the son of Coatlique; and the humans of this divine mother's choosing gave their lives in ceremony to her son. Their worshippers went about their daily business; and then one day, certain of these might find a small flint blade concealed within their clothing—a gift from Coatlique. The gift marked her choice. And the gifted responded by sacrificing themselves that the community might continue (Allen, *Pocahontas* 36-37). Within the cosmological portrait painted by Allen, there can be no mistaking: the conditions of life and death fall under the jurisdiction of the feminine here, and traditionally the practice of active and willing self-sacrifice is common among the people. Hence, it is highly plausible that a woman named for the implements of self-sacrifice might have, in full knowledge and having fully prepared herself to be possessed of skills that would be needed by the invader, been ***chosen*** by her nation and offered up as a dangerous gift—a "Trojan horse," as it were. And if things did not go according to design, did that constitute deliberate betrayal or self-serving harlotry? The story we have inherited—the literary artifact—has been crafted and preserved by the "victor." We, the "vanquished," have been taught to see these women as traitors and whores. As Mojica relocates them to their proper place in the circle, we are able to look at them from a new angle and, at the very least, begin to interrogate the literary artifacts we have inherited.

## Repairing the Web: Relocating the Heroine

Mojica weaves the stories of these vilified women, traitors, "fucked ones," from the distorted and corrupted images with which we have been left. Working within the Spiderwoman tradition of Storyweaving, which is her inheritance, Mojica invests her being with images (cigar store Indian princess/Indian beauty pageant contestant/the conquistador's slut/the betrayed, abandoned contemporary Native woman/the discarded, abandoned, prostituted, alcoholic mother of the Métis) and becomes ***the vessel*** through which these images right themselves, voice their truths, and present themselves to their descendants as they were and as they deserve to be presented. ("I come from the Spiderwoman tradition, they trained me, and that again is a very organic process of having it come from the body, from the image, from the story, from the gesture, out of the body, the word comes as a whole form..." [Mojica, "NAWPA" 3].) If the image is embodied truthfully in the storyteller, we trust that it will speak through her with equal truth. The "turned off" woman is no pathetic remnant; as the daughter of a Hudson's Bay Man, she is a member of Métis high-society (*Princess* 160). The moccasin maker, helpmeet to the French trader, is the ***best*** moccasin maker of the women of her nation. Given, as a precious gift to be appreciated and cherished, she has shod these men, made their canoes, made their snowshoes, and taught them to walk in the snow, hunted, fished, preserved food, translated, navigated, and built alliances and loyalties (*Princess* 158). Lest we forget, lest we continue to cover ourselves with shame and allow that to fester within, poisoning our minds and hearts, our grandmothers speak through Mojica to remind us that they were skilled specialists *chosen* by their peoples to preserve the newcomer, facilitate alliances and trade relationships, and birth new nations. The lives they led and the struggles they endured represent profound acts of sacrifice, enacted to preserve our peoples and our nations—and we, their descendants, must remember this with gratitude and pride.[11]

---

[11] For instance, after Pocahontas's adopted "brother," John Smith, returned to England, the alliance between the English and the Powhatan peoples was jeopardized, and the English established a policy of wholesale slaughter. This slaughter stopped when Pocahontas married John Rolfe and new alliances were established.

Mojica has transformed the well-worn "boards" of the public theatre into the liminal space wherein *ourstory* reveals itself through the eyes of foresight, faith, and anticipation as well as through the (paradoxically obfuscating) historical lens of 20/20 hindsight, despair, and cynicism. As we engage with the active embodiments of tribal memory, we begin to comprehend the treacherous, dimly illuminated spaces between what really directed the actions of our ancestors and what, we have been told, directed those actions. We are compelled to negotiate those spaces and to call up the remembrance of those things Mojica does not directly address in the play. For instance, we might recall that unlike Malinche, Pocahontas did not live to see her own son return to Virginia and take up arms against his own people (Brant 162). And this infuses us with an organic understanding that these grandmothers, who so trustingly gave, could not know how their trust would be abused, how their gifts would be despoiled and discarded. They could not know that this legacy of betrayal and despoilment would resonate through the generations causing the people to scorn their own ancestry and to turn on each other.

Appropriately, in Transformation Seven—appropriate because in this generation, the time for truth-telling is at hand—Mojica begins to expose the complex web of distortion and self-deception: many nations, many creation stories are embodied within the "virginized" Deity (*Princess* 152). She is Sky Woman, married to "the sun himself"; she is partnered with the "Lord of the Underworld" (evoking the Origin story of the Anasazi and Pueblo peoples—the point of emergence from the depths of the earth's belly); she is "Grandmother Spiderwoman," spinning the threads, revealing our place within the story. She is all women of all First Nations. And because "every step you took was to destroy [her] world" (153), she will not reveal her eyes. She will not tell the real story...she speaks in "parables" that only some will understand; the others will just have to guess: "You never knew if I was abducted or/ran of my own/free will/ to the/ Spanish miner/Portuguese sailor-man/ (or maybe it was the/other way around)" (153).

It begins with the Colonizer: he has, as Mojica tells us, "unsexed" her, "twisted and misaligned" (154) her image; but it does not end with him. And so the threads of Transformation Seven lead the storyteller inexorably to Amanda, contemporary descendant of Malinche, of the Virgin of Guadalupe, of Serpent Skirt, of the Women of the Puna:

> And when Amanda would go to visit her man, her *compañero*, in jail, she would be strip-searched. In order to smuggle liquor or alcohol for their wounds, anything that would bring some comfort into the prison, she would fill little bottles, and hide them in her vagina—the perfect hiding place. (*Princess* 154)

So begins a call to the living—here and now. We must stand up; and we must stand *with and for* each other. We, too, bear some responsibility for our condition. The men fall down and desert their women today (Transformation Eight), just as they did yesterday: "My husband didn't have a good hunt this season, so he brought me into the fort; and he left with flour, sugar, and brandy" (159). Indigenous people continue to victimize their own (Transformation Nine), just as we continue to vilify the distorted images of our own grandmothers, even as we buy into, live up to, and play out these distortions (e.g., the Cigar Store Squaw of Transformation Ten).

Weaving Annie Mae's story in subtle, nostalgic hues alongside a horrific testimony of the torture of a thirteen-year-old Chilean girl (Transformation Eleven), Mojica unites the descendant with the ancestor, the north with the south, and the colonizing oppressor with the Indigenous oppressor; we are all in the story; we weave the web; and we each bear responsibility for its design. American FBI agents are guilty of amputating Annie Mae's hands; but she was murdered by a fellow soldier in the struggle. Women in Chile continue to be tortured by their own "brothers." Our channels to the womb have ceased to be channels for the generations; they have, instead, become gateways to abominations and tortures, or hiding places for bottles of impotent, pitiful "comfort."

### The Storyweaver: Transformative Bodies in Action

To penetrate the layers of distortion and misconstruction imbedded within "history's" pages and so dis-cover the truthful essence of our nations' grandmothers, it is vital for the storyweaver in the Spiderwoman tradition to explore every available image of these grandmothers through breath and body. Breath marries itself to body; breath becomes sound; and sound finally shapes itself into spoken word or song. To arrive at the truth, it is necessary in this process to work first through the breath in the body and so arrive at vocalized thought. The text is always the last to come. This is necessary because the storyweaver understands that often when men speak, there lies a profound schism between voice and gesture—word and deed. A cynical observer might point to the historical tendency for human beings to shape their breath into falsehoods and broken promises. A cynical observer might state that the spoken word is corrupted and carries no power; and such cynicism is, to a point, justified.

However, it is of crucial import to note that in ceremony often the spoken word, invested with the most breath and delivered with the most force, manifests the greatest power of all. The text, here, is the last to manifest itself, because it is the strongest manifestation of the power of breath; as such, it is held in reserve for the most solemn of circumstances and the most dire of needs.[12] For First Nations peoples who strive to follow the original teachings, words carry the power to reconfigure the universe. And to utter falsehoods is to defile the first gift of Creator—the gift of breath, the gift of life. To speak untruth is an abomination: it is a corruption of the first gift—it degrades and destroys life itself.

In Transformation Five, Mojica's Coyote in Drag shows up as "Storybook Pocahontas" to play out the separation of gesture from word, powerfully indicting Smith's misconception of the Algonquian "masque" in which he played such a pivotal role. In performance, she enacts a physical score without words; she then enacts the same score with breath (on guttural sound); and finally she adds the words that have been placed into Pocahontas's mouth—bastardized, misconstrued. We are confronted by the "Storybook Pocahontas" as a warped image, robbed of its original beauty by distorted myth, robbed of its power by the corrupted syllables that have been made to issue forth from its being, and robbed of life itself. The "gestic" score, enacted to assert and to preserve life, has been reduced to a series of febrile twitches enacted by the animated corpse of a foolish and wayward child.

"Where was her mother?" asks Contemporary Woman #1 (Mojica, *Princess* 147). And this is an important question. To those who have not grown up in a tightly knit community, surrounded by mothers

[12] In 1980, ethnomusicologist Marcia Herndon (informed by the late Tahquett Wallace) catalogued a series of Healing Rituals of the Eastern Cherokee related to spirit animals and the evil conjurers (ski li) who assume their shapes in order to harm members of the community. These curing ceremonies may be "thought, whispered, said…or sung" (180). If the case is a mild one, it is enough to think the ritual; as the degree of severity rises, so the effort invested behind the breath must increase; so that only the gravest of cases would require song as a vehicle for ritual. Note the gathering of power through breath at the end of Transformation Two: "They breathe energy downstage, upstage, stage left and stage right *until the breath becomes sound…*" (*Princess* 142, italics added). The storytellers gather energy here, and prepare themselves for a massive investment of that power—the invocation of the grandmothers.

and aunties, to those who have been taught to place themselves, as individuals, before the dictates of the social group, this question reads as a comical, vaguely rueful throw-away line. But Mojica issues a challenge here—a reminder to those who have grown up with a conscious awareness of our responsibilities within our communities of origin, imbued with the stories and traditions of millennia: we must first weigh what we *know* of ourselves against what we have been taught about ourselves. Only then can we make judicious decisions about who we were, and who we have come to be. Our stories and traditions have evolved, to be sure. But make no mistake, at their core, the foundational principles, ethics, and behavioral codes remain the same. Pocahontas's mother was most probably present at this ceremony, and if she was not, the teachers, Elders, and female relatives certainly stood by to watch this Beloved Woman carry out her sacred obligations. Would she have dared to flout her spiritual teacher, to endanger her community, to call attention to herself so blatantly and immodestly for even the most handsome of strangers? I think not. Where was her mother? She was there as a witness to her daughter's "leap"—a leap that would forge alliances, save the medicines, and birth new nations.

Just as the thirteenth moon heralds the coming of a new year, so Mojica's thirteenth Transformation marks the coming of a new era—"Una Nación"—and the conclusion of the ceremony. Here, the contemporary blue spot descendants stand up with the "word warriors" to assert our right to "carve and chisel my own face" (Gloria Anzaldúa quoted in Mojica, *Princess* 168). As we are called into the circle to stand shoulder-to-shoulder with contemporary word warriors of our nations, we are reminded of a sacred trust with which Indigenous women have been invested to witness, remember, and transmit our histories for future generations. Indeed, as the words and teachings of Paula Gunn Allen, Diane Burns, Gloria Anzaldúa, and a Kayapo woman are borne upon Mojica's breath, these and the historical grandmothers she has invoked towards the beginning of her play answer her invocation by calling upon us. And we, their blue spot descendants, indeed, as Mojica has positioned us, their blue spot "chorus," are enjoined to lift our hearts from the ground and continue the work to which these grandmothers have given themselves from the beginning of the beginning of the beginning... If we cannot, our nations will perish.

The task that belongs to us is as multi-layered as the journey it necessitates. On the one hand, it belongs to us to faithfully re-member, interpret, and disseminate our histories for ourselves and for the generations that follow us. On the other hand, Mojica and Allen add a second layer of endeavor, which complicates our task but which is crucial if we are to invest our labors with maximum efficacy: an assiduous investment of self to effect what I have come to think of as the "Red Reading" is required. Long time now, our words, actions, knowledge systems, and very persons have been read by the colonizing body and interpreted in accordance with that "body's" knowledge systems and metaphysical understandings. The descendants of those who wrote and interpreted our history have, for the most part, forgotten or chosen to discard the root systems and beliefs of their ancestors. Many no longer know why they believe what they believe, and yet their beliefs persist—unchallenged, unquestioned. And these unconscious belief systems continue to direct their attitude towards and treatment of the contemporary Indigenous peoples whose lands they occupy, even as they often direct our perceptions of and behavior towards ourselves.

Since the publication of her seminal text *The Sacred Hoop* in 1986, Word Warrior Paula Gunn Allen has continued to invest her intellect and investigative abilities to re-read and re-write the histories of Native peoples that we may better know ourselves. And she carries this work further by imposing a Red Reading on the literary artifacts of those who once read us, interpreting them through a Native lens and clarifying our understanding of the fears and fantasies that drove the colonizing body and that directed its documentation of our histories. Mojica takes up this work and deepens it with the added investiture of the physical, emotional, and spiritual aspects of her being. She tries on and tries out literary constructs that have been imposed upon us, exposing their senseless, ludicrous artifice. She engages directly with the words written about or attributed to Pocahontas, Malinche, and the other grandmothers who appear in *Princess Pocahontas and the Blue Spots*, revealing garbled translations and misconstrued meaning. Through this performative intervention, which is Mojica's Red Reading in action, a profound transformation occurs. At the very least, the offspring of the colonized and colonizing bodies who witness experience a transformational shift from a state of ignorance to a more profound and truthful intimacy with their own ancestors and the ancestors of the Others who sit beside them. And the possibility of spiritual transformation is also offered through the Red Reading in action, which invests the political intervention with spiritual efficacy.

Mojica likens our physical bodies to "a giant database of stories" in which are stored the collective knowledge systems of our ancestors ("Stories" 16). Encoded in our DNA are their experiences and wisdom; and it is against the wealth of knowledge stored in this "library" that Mojica weighs Eurocentric versions of our histories, as her body becomes the vessel within which the blue spot grandmothers interrogate the European-authored documents that have contained their lives and the lives of their grandchildren, long time now. (As a woman of Rappahannock ancestry through her maternal grandmother, Mojica may very well be an actual descendant of the central grandmother in her play.) The "red ink," which is Mojica's body, the information it carries in its very cells and the breath on which this information is carried, applies itself to the "black ink" of European history books, reconfiguring the one-dimensional characters on those pages and restoring their natural shapes and hues. Whether it is manifested as an intervention on the stage, on the page, in the classroom, in the town-square, or around the kitchen table, the Red Reading is a critical framework that could contribute enormously to the decolonization of liminal peoples caught betwixt and between cultural interstices, because it calls upon us to interrogate and set-to-rights the knowledge-systems of oppressor and oppressed and through such interrogations to re-configure multiple worlds as we relocate ourselves within the circle. And Mojica has developed this critical framework in a particularly exciting manner. Through a process of "transformational dramaturgy" that sits squarely upon the foundations of her own aesthetic inheritance, Mojica has converted the Red Reading into a performative intervention that facilitates both healing and transformation at multiple levels for Indigenous nations and the Indigenous women on whom their continued survival depends.

### The Blue Spots Re-member Themselves and Take Their Places in the Ceremonial Circle

*Princess Pocahontas and the Blue Spots* is more than a rousing exercise in storytelling, just as the Spiderwoman tradition is more than a rich exercise in storyweaving. This tradition did not simply begin with a theatre company in the latter part of the twentieth century. Its authors stand upon a tradition that pre-dates written history. As Paula Gunn Allen reminds us, this tradition emerges from primordial creative impulse (i.e., "the thought of Old Spiderwoman") and it engineers the bridges between all spatial and temporal interstices, drawing all of creation into a "seamless web of human and nonhuman life" (*Sacred Hoop* 100). And as it has ever been, *its primary function is to provide the gateway to ritual through oral tradition* (*Sacred Hoop* 100). Drawing from this tradition as she unites a scattered body politic within the four walls of a multi-cultural commercial theatre, Mojica lays out the medicines, invokes the grandmothers, and weaves the blue-spotted descendants into the story. A new generation is upon us. The Time of Transformation is at hand. The women are the medicine. But the heart of the medicine (Midewiwin) is on the ground, and the nations perish. We must rise from the ground; we must pick up our hearts—our medicines. That the nations might continue, we must leap into the dark, into the unknown, clutching our medicines and our faith.

As the "heartbeat of the round dance begins" (*Princess* 169), our hearts pick up its rhythm and rise to join in. And joyfully, miraculously, Mojica's final incarnation, "Blind Faith leaps in the dark" (169).[13] Is this a stage direction? Who or *what* is representative of "blind faith"? Who or *what* picks up the cue to leap in the dark? The *Blue Spots* who sit in the audience for whom this directive will not be articulated in the words that appear on page 169 of the published script, and who may never read these words, must pick up this cue. This is *our* directive: our cue to dance is unmistakable; those drums have been with us since the womb. "Blind Faith leaps in the dark," and we dance with our grandmothers—long time now. Listen...

*In the years that have followed Mojica's 1990 production, I have been finally and irrevocably orphaned, struggled with the despair engendered by self-hatred explicitly and subliminally imposed upon me from the forces that once sought to eradicate my ancestors and by a soul-numbing isolation I had imposed from within to protect the "shameful" secret that I still draw breath, despite their best efforts. Comfortably frozen within a liminal void that spanned cultural and existential states, I have struggled to seize hold of the faith required to blindly leap into an uncertain future—a future dearly paid for with the sacrifices of my ancestors. And seventeen years after I first witnessed Mojica's leap and responded to her invitation to embrace the "work to be done" and to accept my place within the circle, I begin to realize that I may now have finally grasped it.*

*I sit with Monique Mojica, in a trendy juice-bar in downtown Toronto to thank her for her teachings, for her commitment to healing and transformation, and for the work with which she has effected these in so many. As for me—an urban blue spot—I have been physically isolated from the community of Mishoomis ('my grandfather' in Anishinaabemowin). But I have come to an organic knowing that I still live on his traditional lands. And I feel my mother and my grandmothers beneath the concrete paths I walk. The stories I carry may rise from the towers of glass and steel, and they may find their invocation in the language of loss; but these stories rise to join the original canon of ancestral imagination and weave me inextricably into a timeless tapestry fraught with infinite meaning. And this understanding is part of my personal transformation.*

*As we sit trading stories, exchanging laughter, and sharing tears, Mojica, her eyes alight with purpose, tells me in compelling, musical tones: "As we stand up and pick ourselves up, we know we are the medicine. We get to say which songs we sing; we get to say how we are embodied; we get to say the way the story goes, and not get stuck in that story book."*

Of this, I have no doubt. This is our gift, our right and our responsibility. Today is a good day to *live!* There is so much good work that remains to be done!

[13] Mojica pointed out that this unseen and unseeing leap is the same movement (comes from the same place) as the transformation of "Somewhere Over the Rainbow" in Turtle Gals Performance Ensemble's *The Scrubbing Project.* (personal communication)

## Works Cited

Allen, Paula Gunn. *Pocahontas: Medicine Woman, Spy, Entrepreneur, Diplomat*. San Francisco: HarperCollins, 2003.

---. *The Sacred Hoop: Recovering the Feminine in American Indian Traditions*. 1986. Boston: Beacon, 1992.

Brant, Beth. "Grandmothers of a New World." *An Anthology of Canadian Native Literature in English*. Ed. Daniel David Moses and Terry Goldie. 3rd ed. Toronto: Oxford UP, 2005. 155-65.

Crestani, Eliana. "James Nelson Barker's Pocahontas: The Theatre and the Indian Question." *Nineteenth Century Theatre* 23.1-2 (1995): 5-32.

Herndon, Marcia. "Fox, Owl, and Raven." *Selected Reports in Ethnomusicology* 3.2 (1980): 175-200.

Howe, James. "The Kuna Portray Their Own Revolutionary History." *The Art of Being Kuna: Layers of Meaning Among the Kuna of Panama*. Ed. Mari Lyn Salvador. Los Angeles: UCLA Fowler Museum of Cultural History, 1997. 146-49.

Knowles, Ric. "The Hearts of Its Women: Rape, Residential Schools, and Re-membering." *Performing National Identities: International Perspectives on Contemporary Canadian Theatre*. Ed. Sherrill Grace and Albert-Reiner Glaap. Vancouver: Talonbooks, 2003. 245-64.

Mojica, Monique. *Princess Pocahontas and the Blue Spots. Staging Coyote's Dream: An Anthology of First Nations Drama in English*. Ed. Monique Mojica and Ric Knowles. Toronto: Playwrights Canada, 2003. 133-69.

---. "Stories from the Body: Blood Memory and Organic Texts." *Alt.Theatre: Cultural Diversity and the Stage* 4.2-3 (2006): 16-20.

Mojica, Monique, et al. "NAWPA Authors' Roundtable." March 19, 1999. *Native American Women Playwrights Archive*. 2007. Miami U, Oxford, OH. 3 Dec. 2007. <http://staff.lib.muohio.edu/nawpa/rt.php>.

Silko, Leslie Marmon. *Yellow Woman and a Beauty of the Spirit: Essays on Native American Life Today*. New York: Simon and Schuster, 1996.

Jill Carter would like to express her gratitude to Monique Mojica and the editors for the considerable time, energy, and thought each has contributed to this—an early project by an inexperienced scholar.

# Dancing with Tradition: Two Generations of Quileute Dancers in Preservation of the Culture's "Spirit Power": An Interview with Rochelle Warner and Bonita Cleveland, Members of the Quileute Tribe[1]

*Vessela S. Warner*

The mother and daughter featured in this interview are Quileute members who actively participate in the tribe's ceremonial dancing, song keeping, and business decision-making.[2] They have performed cultural dances all their lives, as their ancestors have done for centuries. Today, the Quileute Indians number approximately 800 members, of whom only 500 inhabit the Indigenous territory at the mouth of the Quileute River in the Northwestern Olympic Peninsula. Once great sealers and whalers, the Quileutes continue to make their living by fishing the salmon-rich waters of the local rivers and the Pacific Ocean. They use mostly modern methods of commercial fishing but occasionally, as part of cultural celebrations and competitions, they bring out their old and new dugout canoes. The Quileute reservation in the village of La Push has become an attractive center for out-of-state tourists, Olympic National Park hikers, ardent fishermen, as well as a few cultural anthropologists. The most extensive scholarship on the Quileute history and language has been completed by Jay Powell and Vicky Jensen. Their *Quileute: An Introduction to the Indians of La Push* and also Manuel José Andrade's *Quileute*, George Pettitt's "The Quileute of La Push," Leo Frachtenberg's "Eschatology of the Quileute Indians," and Albert Reagan's "Some Traditions from the West Coast Indians" constitute the major ethnographic studies of the Quileute tribe.

Historically, the Quileutes have been part of a larger northwestern Indigenous group extending to the Alaskan Tlingit on the north and the Nootkan groups on the south. They maintain their immediate boundaries with the Quinault, Makah, and Ozette peoples, with whom they have extensively interacted, intermarried, and exchanged culture and goods. Their relationship with the Whites started with skirmishes with Spanish and British conquerors in the late 1770s, continued through a process of perpetual Christianization and education in Anglo-American history in the early 1880s, and was sealed by a treaty with Governor Stevens in 1855 and the execution of President Cleveland's order for the establishment of a reservation at La Push in 1889.

The Quileute social structure consists of several house groups headed by a chief and a tribal council. The most popular tribal assembly—and, respectively, the most formal context of the Quileute dance—is the potlatch, a festival that could be reasoned by various occasions: name-giving, weddings, memorial ceremonies, and harvest celebrations. In the past, the host (sponsor) of the potlatch bestowed precious gifts upon the guests, the main purpose of which was to gain social recognition. As Jay Powell notes, "the greatest prestige [was] going to those who engaged in the most extravagant disbursement of possessions (including food stuffs, blankets and other goods, slaves, and strands of dentalium shell money). Rival families were then bound to repay the 'gifts' with interest that might amount to 100 percent per year or lose face and fall in status" (Powell and Jenson 23). The potlatch tradition is still powerful among the Quileutes, yet the economic function of this gathering has given way to the cultural and social ones.

[1] Originally published in the *Baylor Journal of Theatre and Performance* 4.1 (2007): 121-34; the journal is now titled *Ecumenica*.

[2] The name could also be spelled Quillayute. Both spellings are English language and reflect the Natives' pronunciation of the word, the meaning of which, according to Jay Powell, has remained unclear. For a full reference see Powell and Jensen, 15.

I interviewed Rochelle and Bonita in a series of e-mails and phone conversations. In the last ten years, I have been gradually introduced to their native village, its inhabitants and every-day life. The younger interviewee, Rochelle, is my stepdaughter, with whom I have numerous times discussed the limits and opportunities for someone belonging to two, somewhat opposing, American cultures. Rochelle and I had never talked in details about the character and context of the Quileute dance, in which she has been involved from a very early age. This interview became the first attempt for her, as well as for her mother and mentor Bonita Cleveland, to articulate their dance experience and reflect on its role in preservation of their communal and personal memories. In their own words and according to their own knowledge and value hierarchy, the two "artists by tradition" reveal details of the Quileute dance—its context, attributes, and audiences—while at the same time reaffirm the boundaries of their cultural identities. By paralleling the narratives of the two Quileute Indians, I hope to create a dialogue between the (self-) perceptions of two generations. The preferred language, cultural attitudes, emotional recollections, and critical observations of the interviewees debate the presence and purity of those spiritual forces which have for centuries upheld the Native American tradition.

Both Rochelle and Bonita respond to the same questions but often emphasize different aspects of the subject. In her answers, Rochelle prefers to internalize her dance practice, defining it mostly within her family boundaries of experience. Her narrative appears to be more fragmented, limited by the stories and memories recollected or by her role of a younger tribe-member who still undergoes the process of cultural learning. Rochelle's participation in the Quileute ritual is a personal journey of discovering and preserving her cultural heritage. Bonita, on the other hand, objectifies her experience, elaborating on the norms and values engaged in the tribal ceremonies. Her perspective is the one of a learned member who underlines the communal and historical extents of the tribal dance and repeatedly judges her performance according to the traditional code. Bonita's participation in the Quileute ritual, as well as in the tribe's leadership, determines the preservation of her personal experience through the collective cultural memory. In the repository of this memory lie the Quileute myths, religious beliefs, stories of survival, spatial self-awareness, and faith in the unwavering presence and guidance of one's "spirit power." Initially part of the religious rituals, the Quileute dance is a way of assuring "a correct relationship with [this] spirit power, without which even the most ordinary activities would be unthinkable" (Powell and Jensen 23).

**VW: Could you introduce yourself?**

RW: My name is Rochelle Lynn Warner. "Rochelle" is French for "little girl from the rock." The rock that I was named after, James Island, is located in La Push, Washington, home of the Quileute Indians. I was born in 1979 to Kevin Warner and Bonita Cleveland. On my mother's side, I come from the Ward-Woodruff-Cleveland

BC: My name is Bonita Rose Cleveland, with traditional (Indian) name Hah-Yeh-Letsa or "the setting sun." I was born and raised in the small fishing village of La Push on the Olympic Peninsula. Our family is the Ward-Woodruff-Cleveland family. I have two children—Zack, 33, and Rochelle, 27. I will soon turn fifty. As an enrolled member of the Quileute tribe, I once family. I am an enrolled Quileute tribal member and have resided in La Push all of my life until approximately one year ago, when I relocated to Lacey, Washington, in pursuit of more education and career opportunities. As a Native American, I maintain my rights to hunt, fish, and gather shellfish in the historical Quileute areas.

I have worked for the Department of Corrections since 1998 and continue to maintain employment with them as a Classification Counselor III. I earned my A.A. from Peninsula College, and I am currently attending Evergreen State College in efforts of earning a B.A. (Social Science). I like to compare myself to a steelhead because they originate in the ocean, travel up the pristine rivers of the Olympic Peninsula, spawn, and manage to find their way back home in the ocean. I too find myself frequently returning home. My immediate family continues to reside in La Push, and I remain active in the cultural events of the tribe.

held the position of Cultural Specialist. I acted as a "soul provider," which means having the duty of passing the critical values and ceremonies on to the next generation. I currently live in Olympia, Washington, and work for the Northwest Indian Fisheries Commission. I always visit home.

**VW: How did you start dancing? Who is included in your dance group? Do you have any disciples or younger followers at present?**

RW: Dancing is part of many ceremonies in the life of the Quileute people. I can recall being approximately three years old and participating in traditional dancing, songs, and storytelling through the Head Start program the tribe offers. In addition to this program, I have learned a significant amount about my culture from my mother, Bonita Cleveland, my grandmother, Shirley Cleveland, my late great-grandmother, Sarah Ward-Woodruff, various great-aunts and -uncles, as well as elders from the community. Indians say that it takes a village to raise a child, and this is very true.

There are about four or five main families in La Push. Each family holds songs and has a group of

BC: Traditional dancing has been a way of life for our people. We grew up learning all the different dances from our respected elders and, most importantly, from our grandparents, also known as the Wisdom Keepers. We listened to the stories and legends behind every dance, handed down to us from generation to generation. Our family holds several songs and dances: the Paddle dance, Welcome dance, Challenge dance, Whale dance, Elk dance, Gift-Giving dance, Dinner-Song dance, Song-of-Mourning dance, Power dance, and many others that we continue to dance today.

I really got into dancing when I was about five. My children were three when I made their first performers who dance to those songs. You must be from the family who carries the song in order to sing or dance to it. If you are not, you must have permission from the family that owns the song in order to sing/dance to it.

Everyone from our immediate or extended family, the Ward-Woodruff family, is welcomed to dance with us. If they are not members of our family, they have to be invited by an elder from our family or by my mom, who is the leader of our dance group.

Lots of the young children are encouraged to dance. My mom promotes that and teaches them right from wrong. For example, some of the kids think that it is acceptable to wear their shorts and tennis shoes when they dance. My mom watches for the strict dress code and behavior.

dancing gear. When our family gets ready to dance, we always have young and old alike asking and wanting to dance with our group. We have such a great power group, because we have the pride it takes to look good and we hold the clean path to carry this tradition on.[3] Our Ward-Woodruff-Cleveland family is a big and strong family. I consider our family group to be a very elite dance group that is respected by other tribes and communities up and down the coast.

It is not important what I do by being involved in our dance, but that it is our way of life. We live it day-in and day-out. When the time is needed, we know what we have to do and we just do it. We do not have followers, we have family. We always take the time to show and guide the young ones on a good path. We nurture them to become strong and to carry themselves in a good way. We will always uphold our way of life and the legacy it leaves for the generations to come.

**VW: At what celebrations and ceremonies do you perform? How does the specific context influence your performance?**

RW: Our family has participated in many dancing events. Oftentimes these events are traditional; however, occasionally we are asked to entertain the general public. Traditional ceremonies are typically conducted indoors, at the local community center on the reservation. A memorial service, for example, may start at mid-afternoon and last approximately the entire night and through the following morning. This is a result of the traditional protocol one must go through.

BC: Our family has performed at many elaborate tribal ceremonies (for instance, the First Salmon celebration, the Elders' week), potlatches, traditional name-giving, and traditional memorial services. Families often gather throughout the late night and early mornings in order to take care of business of the day. They also come to show the great gifts they have, or to show off the powerful songs, chants, dancers, and regalia in more ways than one. This ceremony is called

[3] On several occasions in our conversations both Rochelle and Bonita used the expression "clean path." As Rochelle explained, "clean path" refers to the choice of keeping away from drugs and alcohol, being a good member of the Quileute community, and representing a culture that promotes physical and moral health.

When we dance for the general public, we could be indoor or outdoors, depending on the event. Such performances are much shorter, lasting only a couple of hours and are often more fun than serious.

the "great potlatch." It involves the custom of bringing honor to your lineage through the great gift of giving. The family who holds the floor will give gifts to their guests.

We have also been invited to perform for many dignitaries such as the governors of Washington State, for Bill Gates's foundation, local colleges, universities, and schools, at the U.S. Coast Guard and Military welcoming ceremonies, city festivities, and many more. We dance upon invitations of other neighboring tribes. A family from another tribe will come to your door. They will drum and sing their family songs to invite you to the ceremony they will be hosting. This is done in a way that you cannot reject the invitation. You must honor it.

As you can see, we have danced at various ceremonies and no two tribal celebrations are alike. We have danced indoor and outdoor, night or day, along the water, around the fire, in the parades, in the canoes, and on stages under lights.

**VW: How is dancing for tribal audience different from dancing for non-tribal audience?**

RW: Traditional ceremonies are much more demanding than performances for the general public. For instance, if we are to hold a memorial ceremony in La Push, our group is the last to dance. We may find ourselves dancing at five or six o'clock in the morning and, by that time, we are extremely exhausted watching and listening to everybody, or sharing stories and legends. Nevertheless, when it's our turn to present who we are, we gather all our strength to perform well and not dishonor our family.

When I dance for the general public, I find that the "mainstream people" don't have an understanding

BC: Performing for the tribe is very serious since you are holding up your strong ability and your family name. Everything must be done in a traditional fashion and proper way. If you don't follow the traditional way, you will be corrected on the floor and this could bring shame to your family or indicate that your family is out of order. The elders or the one who follows the proper path will bring this to your attention.

In the non-tribal events, we always like to have fun along with the serious entertainment and, at the end of the program, we usually invite everyone to of who we are and what we are all about. This is our opportunity to share with them. I find myself having a lot of fun and interacting with the audience when I perform for the general public.

come out and dance with us. We might do a few more dances with members from the audience so that everyone can feel part of the program.

In traditional potlatches we try to dance only with members of our families, yet we may include extended family dancers from other tribes. When we dance for non-tribal audience, we often include other Quileute families in the dance group as well.

**VW: What was your first dancing experience? What was your last one? How were they different?**

RW: My first experience was for the Head Start program in La Push. My great-grandmother made my dress, along with one of my cousins. She also gave me an Indian basket, which was part of my regalia. She was a renowned basket-weaver.

My last performance was with the Alaskan Dance Group. We danced at the 2006 Commencement at the Evergreen State College. Despite of the similar use of drums and costumes, the Alaskan dancers differ from our group in their dance style. For instance, they do not imitate animals the way we do. There is a lot of strength in their dance though…

BC: My first dance experience was dancing at the 4th of July parade in Forks, a small, logging town about fifteen miles east from La Push. I was six years old. It was not at all a good experience. Our group had to endure many racial slurs such as "wagon burners," "squaw bait," and "salmon killers." I was carrying a beautiful Indian basket made by my grandmother that won us first place at the crafts fair. We won $10, a picture in the local paper, and a blue ribbon. Ironically, the baskets that our grandmother made were bought by the local townspeople.

The last performance was only a few weeks ago, on June 16, 2006. We danced for the graduation ceremony at Evergreen State College in Olympia. The commencement was attended by Governor Gregoire. It felt great to be asked to dance for our Governor and all the students, to feel respected by all the citizens who appreciated our presence and photographed our group.

**VW: What was your most memorable dancing experience?**

RW: My most memorable dancing experience was for my great-grandmother's memorial service. We prepared many months prior to the ceremony. We were introduced to the extended family from the Makah tribe at Neah Bay, shared songs, food, and exchanged gifts. Because my great-grandmother was a much liked and well-known basket-weaver, there were many people from various tribes who attended.

This is when we were first introduced to the Alaskan Dance Group. Apparently, my mom and grandma knew the Alaskans and invited them to attend. They were so well-organized, impressive in their regalia and powerful in the way they sung and danced...They were so proud...At that point in time, I was starting to get more into our culture and I thought, "I want to be like them." The Alaskans were a huge inspiration to me and to our dance group.

BC: My most memorable dancing experience was when I hosted a potlatch for my traditional name, Hah-Yeh-Letsa. I received this name from my mother Shirley Cleveland, who received it from her mother Sarah Ida Ward, who received it from her mother Mary Tyler Ward, who walked on when she was 101 years old. You can see that this is a very strong name, passed on to me from generations as I will pass it on to my daughter in time. During the name ceremony, my family was all in attendance and took part one way or another. My children made me proud when they danced. All my family and friends from the Makah tribe came and took part with their dancing. Everything went really smooth and it was a great potlatch.

**VW: What do your dances tell the audience? How do dancers interact among themselves and with the musicians and singers?**

RW: Because we are people of the land, all of our songs reflect our relationship with the Mother Earth. For example, we dance to the Paddle, Elk, Whale, Wolf song, etc. Our regalia symbolize all these characters. The Paddle dance is performed when we enter and leave a ceremony. A group of drummers sing the Paddle song, moving as if they are bringing us down in a canoe. Thus, we "paddle" into the ceremony. That's our opening dance. Since we perform six or seven songs in each ceremony, we need to change costumes

BC: The most significant dance of the Quileute people is the Sacred Wolf dance.[4] It's a mask dance representing animal spirits: the Kwakiutl dancers. The Quileute Indians believe that supernatural powers take over the bodies of the dancers and these spirits become alive. The dancers are fitted with prestigious headgear that belongs to the family and has lots of rich spirit. This mask is untouched by the head due to the protection of a sacred scarf. It's a great honor to become a mask dancer. This holds your family up high in

[4] According to an early myth, the first Quileute people were transformed from wolves and this is how the Sacred Wolf has become the tribe's totem.

and props. In the Elk dance, some of the dancers represent a herd of elk. They move as if brushing their horns or fighting like elk do. An Indian man, a "hunter" (my brother dances this part), comes out scouting: he is looking high and he is looking low, and he is looking at the elk of his choice. Then he throws his spear and kills that elk! Now that he has proven to be a successful hunter, he carries the "elk" (another dancer) off on his back. The "elk" will scream and the "hunter" will holler and celebrate his kill. The rest of the "elk" will then leave the stage. Indian women dance around, watching and protecting the "hunter." Our family holds a couple of different Wolf songs. In each of them, the wolf is represented as a very intelligent animal, the way it watches and dances.

For the tribal dance, it is essential to have several drums, strong singers, rattles, and the appropriate regalia (masks, paddles, robes, headband, and beads) to support the movements.

the community. Each mask dancer has to be able to dance the long song all the way through.

Additional to the wolf, the dance introduces other "spirit people" from the animal kingdom: raven, eagle, bear, and whale, whatever the crest of each family might be. These dancers move alongside the wolf dancer, taking special care and watching out for what they might have to warn the "wolf" about. Keeping in step to the beat of the drum, they all dance to the chant and the voices of the strong and powerful singers. You must have great stamina and agility, not to mention that you have to hold lots of strong powers, to dance in this fashion. In order to become a mask dancer, you also have to have a great family who is going to stand beside you when you bring out your sacred mask for such ceremonies.

**VW: Do you dance in a routine way? Do you ever improvise in performance?**

RW: Each dance is routine. All our dances come from our great ancestors. Each song belongs to a family. For example, my family sings and dances to several different Wolf songs, but other families hold other Wolf songs. Each song requires different movements, masks, and regalia; nevertheless, they remain routine.

BC: Each dancer has their own way of dancing according to how they feel the spirit taking their bodies. Our dance steps are routine, imitating the way a canoe glides, whales go up and down, elk goes all over, or birds fly...These are the movements the dancers perform, yet some of them do better then others.

Dancing also depends on the hand drum, our elaborate carved rattles, and the chants of our singers. The head singer will sing the story behind the dance and then the dancers will perform [the actions described by the singer]. When the singers sing really strong, the dancers dance strong and get into the transformation of a whale, elk, or wolf. I have to say my children really make the family proud because they can turn on the dance movements when they want to.

**VW: What is the meaning of your dance costume? How does it help you transform yourself?**

RW: My first dress had whales on the bottom, and my basket also had the whale design. This is because my great-grandfather, Fred Woodruff, Sr., was known to be a great whaler. Since my great-grandmother passed on, my mother and my uncle, Chuck Cleveland, who are very talented artists, have taken the initiative to prepare our family's regalia. My current robe is made of red, white, and black wool. It has the crest of the spirit wolf and the image of the totem man which my grandmother's uncle, Jack Ward, carved and painted long time ago. The totem's hands are raised up: a gesture, which for Quileute Indians means "welcome to our land." Around the trim, my costume has fish and birds. We are fishing people and in our mythology birds are known as messengers.

Wolf is our transformation crest. We believe that, while we dance, the spirit of the wolf goes inside us. These are the spirit powers we feel when we perform together.

Occasionally, I have danced with my brother's wolf mask. I feel so strong then. It's not very common for a female dancer to wear wolf gear. It is mainly an honor for a young man in the family to wear our wolf mask, because it's so old, passed down from generation to generation.

BC: We do not call it a "costume" but "traditional gear" or a "robe." Every robe has a different crest on the back depending on what family they come from. My first dance dress was red and black with the crest of the wolf on it, trimmed around the chest and bottom with olive shells and leather. I like to make all the dancers look outstanding from head to toe, really sharp to the eye. This gives the dancer the inspiration to perform well.

The wolf mask is carved out of red cedar tree, then painted with the colors red (for life), green (for the rivers and streams of our grounds), white (for purity), and black (for strength and wisdom). The wolf mask is a head gear which my son has danced with. In the Elk dance, the "hunter" is searching for the elk with cedar elk head gear on, holding a long pole…

The face mask, also carved from cedar, is fitted to the face of the dancer. Rochelle and I dance with a face mask painted with an image of Raven-the-Wise-One. In the whale dance, we hold rattles carved in the shape of a whale and dance in whale-like movements, up and down, shaking our rattles to the fast beat of the drum.

**VW: How do you express yourself in a tribal dance? How do you feel during and after each performance? Can you describe your feelings, thoughts, and mood during a dance?**

RW: I feel the spirit power when I dance for Indian ceremonies. These ceremonies require strong singers and drummers, and strong elders who share wisdom with us. There is so much strength from everybody there, that I feel a totally different person…I can feel the people around me…When we entertain the general public, I feel more like I am there to share who we are but I don't get into that spirit.

When I dance for a tribal ceremony, I have learned to be very serious. I have learned from my elders that we must respect our traditional ways: songs, dances, regalia, ceremonies, and people.

I only dance with my mom. If she is not present, I don't dance, unless my grandmother is there. My mom and grandma are usually together in that presentation. It's such a great feeling to be able to look at my grandmother when we all get to dance together. She has a twinkle in her eye, because she is so proud of us…

BC: When things go accordingly, I have a good heart and feel really happy about what we have just accomplished. I like to tell the dancers how good they all looked and what an outstanding performance they gave. It's really important to always give credit to the dancers and all the singers in order to stay strong and make everyone inspired for the next time we share our dances with others. When things get a little ruffled during performance, it is frustrating and sometimes it makes my heart feel heavy. It takes time to recover, time for everyone to condition themselves for the next time around. Tension is not good when you are going to dance; it puts everyone down and can really affect our hearts and the way we need to portray ourselves during our performance.

**VW: Do you remember your dance performances? How do you know if a performance has gone well or not?**

RW: Yes, I do remember my performances. Generally, I know it is going well if it feels good when I am dancing to the beat of the drum. If the drum has a strong beat, and the singers are giving all they got, I can dance stronger and longer. Oftentimes the audience is so fascinated with our performance, they ask questions regarding our traditional ways, and they always want to take pictures of our group.

BC: We seem to always have a very warm reception from the audience. Sometimes, we receive requests for more dances. After the performance, the viewers often come up to us to compliment us and ask questions about the different masks and gear. The times when we do not have the entire group or are missing a lead dancer, the dance does not always go as good as I would like it to be. Yet we still get good comments from our viewers.

**VW: Has anything changed in the Quileute dance tradition in the past years? Is there an aspect of the Quileute culture that is withering and, if there is, how could that process be reversed?**

RW: I don't think anything is changing for worse in our culture. I think we are only getting stronger. For me, it was harder to be so involved, to participate in the Quileute cultural activities when I was a little girl. At the time when I was going to school in Forks, it was somewhat embarrassing to show my Indian identity. My mom should say: "Rochelle, you are an Indian, and don't you ever forget who you are and where you came from." She always enforced [Indian culture] upon us. Even my dad [a non-Indian] would say: "You are a lucky girl, you should be proud of your heritage." As time went on and my grandmother got me into it, it became more a way of life for me. I knew that this is who I am and I have to learn that culture.

It is so different now. Evergreen [State College] has been so beneficial. The students, faculty, and staff there are so inquisitive of who I am and what I am. They promote me to American education.

BC: Many things have changed in our modern world. We have much nicer things to work with in order to create nicer pieces of carvings and robes. Tools have improved our abilities to sustain our traditional culture and way of life. Nevertheless, we must not forget that the most important thing for our culture's survival is to understand the true meaning and values of the songs and myths. The riches of material matter as much as the riches of the spirit inside each dancer. Dancers can bring to life the robes they are wrapped with through the goodness and physical endurance they carry in their minds and bodies.

I think the status of our tradition is dependent on the social structure. If the [Indigenous and mixed] communities are not standing united, then you see less elaborate [Native American] ceremonies. The culture of dance for our People depends on the perceptions of the surrounding communities. We were taught to be proud, but sometimes it has been difficult to show our pride through our cultural differences, because "mainstream people" didn't always understand or accept our ways of life.

Despite some changes, our culture is very much alive today. It will continue to stay strong if it provides in-depth education in Native history and brings more people together. It takes loyal and valuable advocates to not let the foundation of our culture break and to share it [with the rest of the world]. A clean path is needed in order to be a part of the dancing community. Strong orientation is given to each and every dancer to follow a clean path of life and it is left up to each dancer to learn where the line [of acceptable behavior] is and how not to cross that line.

## Works Cited

Andrade, Manuel Jose. *Quileute*. New York: Columbia UP, 1933.

Cleveland, Bonita. E-mail to the author. 14 July 2006.

---. E-mail to the author. 24 July 2006.

Frachtenberg, Leo J. "Eschatology of the Quileute Indians." *American Anthropologist* 22 (1920): 330-40.

Pettitt, George. "The Quileute of La Push." *Anthropological Records* 14.1 (1950): 1-120.

Powell, Jay, and Vickie Jensen. *Quileute: An Introduction to the Indians of La Push*. Seattle: U of Washington P, 1976.

Reagan, Albert. "Some Traditions from the West Coast Indians." *Proceedings of the Utah Academy of Sciences, Arts and Letters* 11 (1934): 79-93.

Warner, Rochelle. E-mail to the author. 15 July 2006.

---. E-mail to the author. 19 July 2006.

---. Telephone interview. 22 July 2006.

# SECTION II: *Honoring Spiderwoman Theater*

## Persistence of Memory[1]

*Lisa Mayo, Gloria Miguel, and Muriel Miguel*
Directed by Muriel Miguel
Performed by Spiderwoman Theater (Lisa Mayo, Gloria Miguel, and Muriel Miguel)

DIRECTOR'S NOTES:
It is important to build and support a generational memory.

This statement is especially true for us as Indigenous women.

Every day we fight to remember who we are, to hold on to the memories of our great-great-grandparents and the memories of their children, and to keep them fresh in our minds. This production is a gathering of energies and memories that Spiderwoman has collected over the last thirty-two years and through their lives. The theme is healing: of ourselves, our extended families, and our communities. The projections are a filmic tapestry of photographs and performance of former Spiderwoman members, of daughters Murielle Borst and Monique Mojica and of our immediate families, the people who have supported us over the years and to whom we pass on our legacy. We have told our stories over our kitchen tables, on our front steps, in our communities, on the stages of New York, Berlin, Auckland, and Beijing. It is important to be home again and connect our stories of the past to our future. Our future is the generations who will take their stories out into the world of the new millennium and who will create a new legacy for their future generations.

This is the "Persistence of Memory."

DEDICATION:
*Persistence of Memory* is dedicated to Ingrid Washinawatok EI Issa, Flying Eagle Woman, who will be in our collective memories forever.

*Persistence of Memory* is also dedicated to Josephine Mofsie Tarrant (Silvercloud) who inspired Spiderwoman Theater and her granddaughter Heino Josephine Eagle Eye Tarrant who is our inspiration and joy.

To all the women of Spiderwoman wherever they are, to all the women who have supported us over the years, and to all our relations.

In memory of Eva Bauman, Spiderwoman musician, who passed over in 1989.

And Sandy Crimmins, Spiderwoman stage manager, who passed in 2007.

THE SET:
The set consists of a series of hanging drops. USC hangs the Spiderwoman signature quilt, which is made from pieces of fabric that have been donated over the years by Spiderwoman members or collected from friends around the world. There is a peach-colored sheer curtain which can be opened and closed on a track, hanging upstage in front of the quilt. This curtain is used as scrim where action can be seen behind it. Two burlap panels are downstage and frame the quilt and sheer curtain. These provide separate areas for projections and can be used together to form a single large image. The stage floor is bare. US Curtain is closed at top of the show

[1] The DVD acccompanying this book contains a selection of the video clips projected during performances of *Persistence of Memory*, along with two clips videotaped during the performance at Miami University, February 20, 2007. In this text readers are cued to these clips at appropriate points, and words in the projected videos are enclosed in quotation marks to distinguish them from words of the live performers.

*Video Image: (full screen) Hortensia Colorado in profile blowing conch three times, fade to black and image of Elvira Colorado close up on beaded hair barrette, the image pulls out to wide view as Sandy Crimmins is heard in a voiceover.*

[See DVD, "In the Beginning"]

> "Working with a group like Spiderwoman can become all-consuming. The personal melds with the professional and life's stories. What I thought of as my own quite personal past and present concerns become part of a collective work. With Spiderwoman, because of this intimate use of storytelling, the blending of personal life and the professional life, and the intimacy required to make it successful, one begins to function within a realm that explores memory at the same time as fostering together new, now collective memories."

*Video Image continues: (full screen) Full body image of Elvira Colorado, "In the Beginning" from* Power Pipes; *her back is to the camera, hands to eyes, speaking.*

> "It was a long time ago
> Trying to remember. Una memoria. *(Elvira stands and faces camera, with gesture.)*
> Like looking into a mirror
> It was today.
> In the beginning
> Of the beginning
> Of the beginning
> Of the beginning. *(She circles around her stool several times. Close up on her feet.)*
> In the beginning, of the beginning, of the beginning, of the beginning."

*Video Image continues: (on two side panels) Muriel, Gloria, and Lisa performing "We Three" by the Ink Spots from the film* Sun, Moon, and Feather *directed by Bob Rosen. They play imaginary instruments, Muriel a bass, Lisa a guitar, and Gloria a clarinet. They sing "Plunky, plunk..." to mimic the sound of the guitar.*

*As the video ends, LISA peeks out of USL panel followed by GLORIA and MURIEL. They line up US center. Percussion music begins ("Ostinato Pianissimo," Henry Cowell) as they dance, as penguins. They look up and down, nuzzle each other, poke each other, and line up horizontally DS Center.*

GLORIA Do you remember?

LISA No.

MURIEL No.

GLORIA Neither do I.

MURIEL Think hard.

LISA It's coming to me. It's right on the edge. Wait, wait, wait.

GLORIA I remember that word.

LISA I remember that sound.

MURIEL Did you write it down? *(MURIEL pulls chairs out from behind panel.)*

GLORIA No.

LISA No.

MURIEL Doesn't this sound familiar?

GLORIA Not quite.

LISA Maybe.

GLORIA Somebody else will remember.

MURIEL I don't remember it like that. *(MURIEL places her chair SR.)*

LISA We don't remember because we don't remember. (*LISA places her chair CS and sits.)*

MURIEL Let's try to think about what we don't remember. (*MURIEL and GLORIA think hard like a squeeze, then sit.*)

LISA It sounds familiar.

MURIEL We did it somewhere.

GLORIA It's so easy to remember.

MURIEL BUUUTTT!!! *(MURIEL stands, lights fade.)*

LISA/GLORIA It's so hard to forget!

*Video Image: (full screen) Graphic of hand drawn poster with text "The Spiderwoman Theatre Group from New York." Cross fade to speaking and music from* Lysistrata Numbah. *Audience laughter on video. As performers sing "Mother of Daughters" (from "I Want You in the Home," lyrics by Brandy Penn, music by Jan Roybn), each ensemble member is introduced: Pam Verge, Naja Bey, Lois Weaver, Muriel Miguel, Gloria Miguel, Lisa Mayo.*

*Each sister goes to the chair she thinks is her place. The youngest sister, MURIEL, gets expelled from each chair by her older sisters until she comes to the last chair and sits. All speak at the same time.*

GLORIA I'm absorbed by my place.

I entertain, love, cry, heal in my place.

I dwell in my place for hours, days, years.

I love my place, it is clean, comfortably arranged and well equipped with works of art, photographs, books, music, a beautiful dining table, a large bed. Perhaps, I will die in my place.

LISA My comfortable, cozy place created from the memory of a ripe peach, an iridescent perfume bottle and a few yards of light green satin braid all given to me by my aunt who also taught me to draw, sew, bake and to write my name. It smells like me, it feels like me. I am happy, I feel secure when I am in my place.

MURIEL Sometimes that place is my place, but it's not my place. It's all right, I'll stay here. That place I'm not seen. That place isn't my place either. That's all right, I'll stay here. This will be my place. I'll stay right here. *(Lights fade.)*

*Video Image: (full screen) Close up on Hortensia Colorado in "Mexican, Mexican" from* Winnetou's Snake Oil Show from Wigwam City.

"Oh! *(She tears at her face with hands.)* Mexican! Mexican! Mexican! A surge of heat would rise up in my body and my face would begin to burn. I am an Indian woman. I speak Spanish and I am learning Nahuatl. Before the invaders, there were no borders. My grandmother married a man whose family came from Spain, and when they would come to visit they would lock her in a back room so they would not have to look at her. *(Image changes to full body shot.)* There is no going back to anywhere. I will stay here with this Indian face. *(Profile image of Hortensia)"*

*Baby photo of Muriel appears on SL panel; backlit shadow of GLORIA and LISA watching MURIEL appears on SR panel; MURIEL is DS curtain.*

[See DVD, "Birth"]

MURIEL White walls
White floor
White ceiling
White curtains
It's OK
It's OK to be in a white room.
I was born in a white room
Not in a white sheeted bed
But on a white floor
I almost had a white doctor
No, no I had a white doctor
'Til my grandmother took over.

I was told this story
Many, many times
I can tell this story like I was there
Well, I was
But I wasn't aware of the current events.

My mother was in the throes of birthing
*(MURIEL on hands and knees)*

My mother was on her hands and knees
In the throes of birthing
I was told this story
Many, many times
I can tell this story like I was there.
The doctor arrived and said,
"No, no this will never do.
What kind of woman are you?
Putting your daughter on her knees and hands."
The word "savage" hung heavy in the air.

I was told this story
Many, many times.

They put my mother on her back
That's the right way to do it
I was told this story
Many, many times.
"Savage" was murmured.
My grandmother, the midwife, said, "OUT! OUT!
This is my daughter, my grandchild; besides, it's not knees and hands, it's hands and knees!"

I was told this story
Many, many times
I can tell this story like I was there
Well, I was. *(MURIEL exits.)*

*Video Image: (full screen) Performers from* Lysistrata Numbah *with hands in air are singing "A Pretty Girl Is Like a Melody." Each one comes forward, smiling, to speak.*

[See DVD, "Introducing Spiderwoman Theater"]

"My name is Lisa and I have arthritis in my knees.
My name is Pam and I have a rash on my ass.
My name is Gloria and I have a scar on my belly.
My name is Lois and I have rotten teeth.
My name is Naja and I have hair on my face.
My name is Muriel and I'm too fat

*(They continue to sing and take a bow together; audience on video applauds.)"*

*Projection of their mother on SR panel. Music ("Some Are" by Philip Glass) as LISA enters with broom.*

LISA When I take care of my house, wash the floors, clean the carpets, especially when I use the broom
I think of her.
She often comes when I'm doing the floors.
She comes to take care of me, to tell me stories with special secrets in them for me.
She sings to me.
*(Singing "Persistence of Memory" by Becky Thunderbird)*
Hey Yah Na Hey
Hey Yah Na Hey
Hey Yah Na Hey Hey
Wey Oh Hey
Yah Wey Oh Hey,
My family, my nation
My Creator, my life
I sing for the next generation
Hey Yah Na Hey *(She transforms the song into "My Blue Heaven" by George Whiting.)*

*Video Image: (full screen) The three sisters performing "Tea Party" scene from* Rever-ber-ber-rations. *This image plays silently throughout this scene with live actors speaking.*

GLORIA Tea?

LISA Did you know pigs have orgasms that last three hours?

MURIEL Is that true?

LISA Scientific fact.

GLORIA It's not so bad being a pig. *(They all laugh, bending forward; they straighten up.)*

GLORIA He said, "I have to take Viagra now," and I said, "But you still have so much hair!" *(They all laugh, bending forward; they straighten up.)*

MURIEL I never buy generic juice.

LISA Pourquoi?

GLORIA Why?

MURIEL Because I'm not old enough

*Percussion music as before ("Ostinato Pianissimo" by Henry Cowell); LISA, GLORIA, and MURIEL dance as penguins.*

*Video Image: (full screen) Donna Couteau as The Radical Nun from* Women in Violence. *She wears a habit and has an aluminum foil halo on her head and clown make up.*

[See DVD, "Women in Violence"]

> "'Some of my friends are coming tonight to the evening show. Do you have that? Some of my friends are coming tonight to the evening show. Do you have that? Some of my friends are coming tonight to the evening show. Do you have that? SOME OF MY FRIENDS ARE COMING TONIGHT TO THE EVENING SHOW! DO YOU HAVE THAT? Some of my friends are coming tonight to the evening show. Do you have that?' *(Close up)*
>
> 'All right. I told him five times. He definitely knows. Then the afternoon show came around.'
>
> 'Hey! Where are your friends?'
> 'I told you that some of my friends are coming to the evening show.'
> 'You never told me that.'
> 'I told you five times!'"

*Percussion music transition ("Ostinato Pianissimo" by Henry Cowell).*

*Video Image: (full screen) This has a grainy old movie feel. Gloria is Demon #1 and Hortensia is Demon #2 from* Winnetou's Snake Oil Show from Wigwam City. *A home movie of the*ir father dancing, plays in the background of video. *DEMON #1 appears stage right.*

> "DEMON #1 EEEEEEEEEE. (*Two other demons appear center stage with the first demon joining them.*) Sulubevia. Oloindalgina, MatchYaapipi. My father believed in demons. Listened to Chief Nele and captured tortoise. At the age of thirteen, his body was covered with blue dye from the Poli Wala tree. And he slept three nights and three days alone in the rain forest. EEEEEE. He left Naranga on the San Blas Islands and became an able-bodied seaman. EEEEEEEE.
>
> DEMON #2 My father worked the fields, he washed dishes, he swept floors.
>
> DEMON #1 He traveled to Marseilles.
>
> DEMON #2 He paid his way.
>
> DEMON #1 Cologne, Monte Carlo, Paris, New York City. He still believed in demons. To chase away the demons, he gulped down a bottle of whiskey.
>
> DEMON #2 He followed the demon serpent, winding his way North. He followed the feathered serpent, Quetzalcoatl.
>
> DEMON #1 He never returned to Naragana. He still believed in demons. He believed in demons until the day he died."

*Lights up. GLORIA enters, dancing as she opens the sheer curtain. She dances to "La Cumparsita" by Gerardo Matos Rodríguez*

GLORIA I dance slowly, weighted down with the
burdens willed to me by my family
within me *(Dancing)*
behind me
above me
around me
beneath me.
*(She smiles.)* The dirty cuss.
*(She smiles.)* Are you leaving?
*(She smiles.)* I'm all alone.
*(Enraged.)* Give me that.
Give me that
Me, me, me, me.
*(Loud laugh, hits out, growls)*
*(Sighs, crying turns, emerges with smile; music fades up)*
I reach out to capture the present and
unknown future
I will to myself. *(Beat)*
*(GLORIA exits as MURIEL closes curtain.)*

*Image of Ginny Mayer with subtitle "Ginny Mayer, Stage Manager" appears on full screen. This fades into video Image of Sandy Crimmins. She reads from her essay, "A Stage Manager's Notes."*

"In many ways Spiderwoman is my writing program. With them I learned to look for the humor; it exists in all things that happen to women in this world—from love to abuse to child birth even dying. And I learned to look for the music running through our heads and, yes, I learned to be honest in my writing. If you aren't, no one else will be."

*Video Image: (full screen) Donna Couteau as The Radical Nun from* Women in Violence.

"'You know you always do this! You did the same thing in *Oklahoma!*'

Oh, and I grabbed her by the hair and I started to pull it down. I wanted to punch her right in the nose. No, I can't do that she'll leave before the evening performance. I'll punch her in the stomach. No I can't do that. I'll get her down, I'll kick her. I'll kick her fucking ass in–the bitch! I'll kill her! I'll–I'll give her street action—I'll…I can't do that.

I was so angry I had to take a walk around the block. I was so angry I couldn't even breathe, I can't breathe, I started to cry. Just calm down.

'Well, so do you hate me or what?' 'Oh, No.' 'And I'm so glad we cleared the air. I just realized I'm not afraid of you anymore.'

AHHH! *(Claps; makes sign of the Cross)*
AHHHH! *(Claps; makes sign of the Cross)*
AHHHH!"

*Fade to image of mother and father's wedding picture that appears on SL panel.*

LISA *(LISA enters from SR panel.)* Mama's beauty secret: To keep your skin wrinkle free always remove your make up at night with Pond's Cold Cream or Noxzema. And always color your hair if necessary. *(She dances.)*
Mama loved Tango. Mama loved Rudolph Valentino. Mama dances for me, Mama dances with me.
Down under all of our wrinkled and flabby skin, we are young and beautiful women, Mama. And even if you have arthritis, sore knees
Keep moving
Keep dancing.
Mama had suitors and gentlemen callers 'til she was over 86 years old.
*(She exits US.)*

*Video Image: (full screen) Lisa, Gloria, and Hortensia in "Mama's Caul" from* Winnetou's Snake Oil Show from Wigwam City.

"LISA She came into the world with an extra piece of skin covering her head. It was a caul. C-A-U-L. And Grandma said that she saved the caul and that one day she was going to give it back to Mama.

Grandma said, 'Your mother was born with a caul, so she has strong psychic powers. She can tell the future. She can see through anybody.' And Mama could tell the meanings of the symbols left by coffee grounds and tea leaves in the bottom of cups.

HORTENSIA And Grandma said...

GLORIA 'You have a gifted mother.'

HORTENSIA 'You should be thankful.'

LISA And Grandma had that gift, too. And all of my grandmother's children have that gift. And all their children's children have that gift, too. (*There is a continuous repetition of these lines as they all move together.*)"

*Music begins, "Oblivion" by Astor Piazzolla. LISA enters to stand in front of her chair SR, GLORIA enters to stand in front of her chair SL, MURIEL drags her chair on from SL to center. They all stand in front of their chairs and sit at the same time music goes out*

MURIEL I am one of three
I am three of one
1-2-3
I am the third
There are two more ahead of me
Three
Uno, dos, tres
1-2-3
You cannot have an equal part
You are always 1/3
There are two against one
There are three singles, 3 units, 3 ones
1-2-3
I am one of three.

LISA My mother became my sister. My grandmother became responsible for my sins. I am aware that the people here in this beautiful arena are studying me, gaining knowledge from me as they watch me.

MURIEL When those two met, they created me
No they didn't, yes they did
They created me, not from an egg
They took me whole
I am one of three
No, I'm not, yes, I am
I am the third
One, two, three
I look like them
No, I don't, yes, I do.

GLORIA *(Reading from book) Native American Postcolonial Psychology* by Eduardo and Bonnie Duran: "Once these children grow up with fear, rage, danger and grief as the norm, it is little wonder that family problems of all types begin to emerge within the family system."

*Video Image: (center screen) This is the first of three sections of Murielle Borst as Stephanie in* More Than Feathers and Beads. *She is lip synching to Pink Floyd's "Comfortably Numb."*

LISA Yes, I have a painful history. Impossible not to tell. I am a survivor still trying to survive. How can I tell my young niece about this? On the other hand, how can I not tell her?

GLORIA *(Reading)* "Inevitably, these children, now adults, have lived their lives with a series of perplexing questions and fragmented memories."

*Video Image: (center screen) Murielle says, "Yeah, yeah, I have a kid. I have a daughter. I named her Stephanie after me."*

LISA They called him Wahoo, a stupid Indian comic strip character. My father, broad shouldered, beautiful smile, glistening black hair brought a bright light with him when he entered a room. I know my own memories. I am an expert for only my own memories.

*Video Image: (center screen) Murielle says, "Sometimes at night I hear her crying and I look and nobody's there. Do I use drugs? Yeah, Yeah. Well, kind...I don't feel like I'm alive. I feel like I'm just here." She continues lip synching to Pink Floyd's "Comfortably Numb." At the end of this video, the music to "Comfortably Numb" continues through the rest of the scene.*

GLORIA *(Reading)* "The normal developmental tasks of growing up were mutilated beyond recognition by the traumas of loss and grief, danger and fear, hatred and chaos."

MURIEL I sound like them
I am one of three
I am them
They are me
No, I'm not, yes, I am
1, 2, 3
I model my role from them
No, I don't, yes, I do.

GLORIA *(Reading)* "We are presently in the time of the restoration of the hoop."
We have to make our own rules. Even if it starts just with the three of us. We have to change now, we have to start somewhere.

LISA Shame, anger, hurt. I must tell the youngest in my family about this. Elizabeth Ashton, my grandmother, hid from anyone who entered our house, hiding behind the parlor curtains where everyone could see her bare feet.

MURIEL I am melancholy
No, I'm not, yes, I am
I am joyous
Yes, I am
1 *( LISA stands.)* 2 *( GLORIA stands.)* 3 *(MURIEL stands.)*
I am one of three
*(Lights change to silhouette them and we hear the music to "Comfortably Numb" get louder. Blackout. Lights come up, GLORIA comes to center.)*

GLORIA Tea?

LISA *(LISA and MURIEL join GLORIA.)* When Gloria and I used to play fat and skinny, I played skinny.

GLORIA You did not, I played skinny.

LISA Ooo, that's even funnier. Well you used to be skinny.

GLORIA And you used to be fat.

LISA *(Looking at MURIEL and GLORIA)* You two played fat and skinny. Which one of you played fat?

*(To MURIEL)* The flowers are dead.

MURIEL Who told you?

GLORIA What flowers?

LISA There's no flowers. *(They exit.)*

*Video Image: (full screen) Monique Mojica from* Princess Pocahontas and the Blue Spots.

[See DVD, "Princess Pocahontas"]

"I remember my grandfather sitting in the sun of a soot-streaked city window, plucking whiskers, grazing his face with scissors, smiling at me from the side of his mouth. You smile a crooked smile, embarrassed that I see them in you—all my grandfathers. *(Home movie image appears of men in suits and ties, waving at the camera.)* Those short, dark men with broad shoulders and heavy muscled calves, with hard working feet that were made for climbing coconut trees and walking in the sand; their pigeon-toed gait out of time on the sidewalks of the city.

Iieeeee!

I remember my grandfathers sitting in my grandmother's front parlour, Sunday afternoons, playing the camu—blowing across the bamboo pipes. *(Home movie image of men dancing in circle playing pipes.)*

One of them would start to cry—
a high-pitched wail. The others would tease and laugh, but one by one they'd join his cry; a brotherhood of old, brown men mourning their lost home; a sorrowful sound whose bass note is a conch shell blown far out over the water.

I recognize my lifeline in your face when you bow your head in respect to hold a single kernel of corn in your hand; and Grandpa planted corn in the backyard. *(She plants seeds. Image of hands and feet, men smiling from before, and music of the pipes.)*"

*Side panels are back lit and show shadow of MURIEL drumming, which we can hear. LISA is behind SR panel in shadow. GLORIA is seen, CS with drum. MURIEL starts drumming, LISA starts to play the rattle. GLORIA starts drumming. Images of their father and uncles fade up on alternating panels of the scrims. The gobo of a palm frond fades up on the center scrim. GLORIA then completes whole phrase, MURIEL and LISA repeat.*

[See DVD, "I No Know Myself"]

ALL *(Using only the vowels of this sentence, then elongating the vowels , they find a rhythm and sound. Still using rhythm and sound, they start a harmony.)* I don't know myself, I don't know my self.

GLORIA I no know mysel', I no know mysel', I no know mysel', I no know mysel'.
*(MURIEL and LISA echo.)*
I no know mysel', I no know mysel'.

MURIEL and LISA I no know mysel'.

GLORIA I gather the words, I save the moment, I learn the lesson, I start the action
I no know mysel.' *(GLORIA single beat on drum, repeats.)*
*(MURIEL and LISA continue to echo, a drone.)*
My heart beats, searching for passion, a happy means to love.

I no know mysel', I no know mysel', I no know mysel'

Empower my song, my being, love, work, knowledge

Heal the generations of wounds.
Understand, not reject the pain and sorrow of our ancestors

I no know mysel', I no know mysel', I no know mysel', I no know mysel'

*(MURIEL and LISA accompany, no voice.)*

Three rivers, one rough, one calm, one winding.
They meet at the bottom of a waterfall, they join.
They mix in strength, they foam up, they travel on.
I no know mysel'.
Go back, change the rules, renew the old rules. There's no more time. Terror.
*(MURIEL and LISA drone begins again.)*
I no know mysel'.
Gather the words, save the moment, learn the lesson, start the action.
There's no more time.

I no know mysel'. *(Repeats. They end in a wail. MURIEL beats three times, GLORIA exits.)*

*Video Image: Photograph of Frank Harris, Lisa's son, on SR panel and photograph of David Harris, Lisa's husband, on SL panel*

LISA *(Enters from SR panel points to SR panel)* This is my son Frank Harris, he manages a bakery and lives in Los Angeles, California, and *(Pointing to SL panel)* this is my husband, David Harris. *(LISA exits.)*

*(David speaks on video.)*
"This is David A. Harris, Lisa Mayo's husband and Muriel and Gloria's favorite brother-in-law. I met them in their first out-of-town performance in Baltimore, Maryland, and I can remember then taking a three-day car ride from New York to Boston to do a performance. Now this is a four-hour trip, Spiderwoman does it in three days. Spiderwoman, they're funny, they're zany, they do so many great creative things that I'm glad they're finally getting a little bit of their due. These ladies are remarkable and amazing and I hope they keep going on, keep creating new things."

*Video Image: Photograph of Paolo Spano, Gloria's partner, on SR panel and photograph of Raphael Szykowski, Gloria's son, on SL panel*

GLORIA *(Enters from SL panel)* I have a grandson, Bear Thomas, he lives in Ottawa and he's a video artist. *(Pointing to SR panel)* This is my friend Paolo Spano from Italy, he's a fine artist and painter, and *(Pointing to SL panel)* this is my son Raphael Szykowski, he is a social worker and folksinger. *(He sings "Half Breed Blues," his own composition, on video.)*

*Video Image: Photograph of Racael Borst, Muriel's daughter, on SR panel and photograph of Deborah Ratelle, Muriel's partner, on SL panel.*

MURIEL *(Enters from SL panel and pointing to SR panel)* This is my daughter Calla Borst and she lives in Eugene, Oregon, and *(Pointing to SL panel)* this is Deborah Ratelle, Spiderwoman stage manger and my life partner.

*LISA, GLORIA, and MURIEL are discovered sitting US of sheer curtain. LISA is SR, seated; GLORIA is C, standing; MURIEL is SL, seated. MURIEL claps 4 times which starts the action. They all create personal circles. MURIEL begins large circle, walking clockwise in circle 1½ times. GLORIA enters circle, walking counterclockwise. They meet. MURIEL turns away from GLORIA, GLORIA follows her. LISA enters circle from SR, crosses clockwise. MURIEL meets LISA at SL, they both turn away and MURIEL meets GLORIA at DS, MURIEL turns away, GLORIA follows MURIEL, LISA turns clockwise, MURIEL and LISA meet and pass each other, GLORIA then passes LISA. This is all layered with avoidance and anger.*

MURIEL *(From SR)* You'll never do it.

LISA *(From SL)* Hey, cut that out.

MURIEL Well, you won't.

LISA *(They circle each other.)* I said I was going to do it, I will do it.

MURIEL Yeah, yeah, yeah.

LISA Why are you taking that attitude? *(GLORIA crosses outside of circle, going in the opposite direction.)*

MURIEL Because, you are not going to do it. *(Stares at her.)*

LISA *(They continue to circle.)* That's right, stare me down. What the hell does that prove?

MURIEL You're a bully!

LISA *(Makes a crazy face and sound)*

MURIEL Well, that's stupid.

LISA Don't you get it? It's a joke.

MURIEL It's not funny!

LISA You're not funny!

MURIEL You're not funny!

LISA Well, you're not funny either!

*(They are facing each other, they bump bellies. LISA faces DS, MURIEL dances a crazy tango-like dance as they step DS. They face US, looking at GLORIA as music starts, "Tanguera" by Mariano Mores. They dance an angry tango one against two, two against one, bouncing off one another. Using the tango as metaphor, they finally soften towards each other. As sisters, they come together and hug and kiss each other. They honor the four directions.)*

*Video Image: (full screen) Murielle Borst appears as Crystal from* More Than Feathers and Beads. *She is dancing to the drum and turning with a fringed shawl. She speaks as she continues to dance. LISA, GLORIA, and MURIEL can be seen sitting upstage of the center panel through the projection scrim.*

[See DVD, "More Than Feathers and Beads"]

"Hi yawl, my name is Crystal and I'm a fancy shawl dancer from Oklahoma... Then I put my dancing face; then the music starts. My first move is one of my fancy shawl moves and I use my shawl like this *(She demonstrates);* my second move is one of my pretty moves because that is a man judge *(She demonstrates)*; my third move is my spinning move and it goes like this *(She demonstrates)*; and my fourth move is one of my patented complicated fancy foot work moves and it goes like this—ready, step, step, step, step, hop—the crowd goes wild. Then I get in the middle of the arena and then the music picks up and I spin faster and faster until I can't stop because I need to be number one. Then I stop on the very last beat of the drum and I do my special stop. Then when I'm done I stroll over to line up so the judges take my number, and when they ask for another song I just say, 'She-it, I thought that was just a warm up.'"

*(They sing "Persistence of Memory". MURIEL begins, after one line GLORIA joins, and on the next line LISA joins.)*

Hey Yah Na Hey
Hey Yah Na Hey
Hey Yah Na Hey Hey
Wey Ho Hey
Yah Wey Oh Hey
*(The three together)*
My family, my nation
My Creator, my life
I sing for the next generation
Hey Yah Na Hey
Hey Yah Na Hey
Hey Yah Na Hey Hey
Wey Ho Hey
Yah Wey Oh Hey

*(GLORIA opens the curtain and crosses DS. She looks at MURIEL, LISA before she begins speaking.)*

GLORIA I didn't understand. I understood. She understands now.

LISA I understand now, but I didn't understand then.

MURIEL I understand. No, I don't understand.

*(MURIEL crosses SR to between LISA and GLORIA.)*

LISA *(As she begins to speak, LISA crosses DSLC, MURIEL crosses SR.)*

The Botanical Gardens in the Bronx. The sign reads: Before the arrival of Christopher Columbus, this area was inhabited by Algonquian Indians. They gathered herbs and collected water here. The rocks, spring, vegetation have been preserved in their natural state. Much of what is now New York City looked very much like this preserved area.

MURIEL *(As she speaks, MURIEL crosses CS, LISA crosses SL.)*

Are you ashamed of me? Are you?
Are you embarrassed?
Are you embarrassed by your mother, your grandmother?
Are you afraid I won't act right, wear the wrong clothes, just not fit in?

GLORIA *(GLORIA crosses DSC, MURIEL crosses SL, she and LISA hug.)*

On a bookcase in my apartment, there is a very old photograph, tattered and torn.

The photo is of me and my third grade class.

I'm sitting in the middle surrounded by thirty other children, the only dark one. I'm wearing a brown fur trimmed coat, my hair is in long braids. There is a faint smile on my face.

I didn't understand. I understood. She understands now.

LISA *(MURIEL crosses USR, GLORIA crosses SL.)*

I understand now, but I didn't understand then.

MURIEL I understand. No, I don't understand.

You picked your mother, you were hanging on the moon when you picked her. You came from far away just to be with her. Your grandmother and father crossed bridges and trails just so you can be here. Are you ashamed, are you?

LISA *(LISA crosses DSL, GLORIA crosses SR to MURIEL, MURIEL's back is to GLORIA.)*

It's warm today, in the Botanical Gardens. The sun is shining, here where our ancestors moved among the rocks and springs, gathering plants and herbs. I find a grassy spot and I completely surrender my weight to the earth. I fall asleep. When I awake, I know that something wonderful has happened to me today.

GLORIA *(GLORIA crosses SL to LISA, MURIEL puts her arm around LISA.)*

Visitors comment on the photo: "You haven't changed one bit, look at the braids."

My six-year-old grandniece was visiting me one day. I was washing dishes in the kitchen. She came up behind me holding the photo in the crook of her arm *(MURIEL and LISA follow GLORIA's action.)* and pointed to me in the photo.

GLORIA I didn't understand. I understood. She understands now.

LISA I understand now, but I didn't understand then.

MURIEL I understand. No, I don't understand.

LISA *(GLORIA crosses to USC, MURIEL crosses to USC.)*

Here, here this is the place where our sources and resources rest. Deep, deep down in time and memory. Available, connected, within; strength and power amidst calm and quiet.

*(LISA crosses SR.)*

MURIEL I understand. I was ashamed of my mother. My mother was ashamed of her mother. Are you embarrassed? Don't be.

GLORIA *(GLORIA crosses DS, MURIEL crosses DSL.)* "Is that you, Aunt Gloria?" "Yes, that's me." Looking up at me she said, "Then you know how I feel." Our eyes met for a moment. "Yes, Josie, I know how you feel." Three generations, three generations, and that knowing feeling is still present.

LISA *(GLORIA crosses SL; LISA sings verse from the traditional "Sometimes I Feel Like a Motherless Child.")*

Sometimes I feel like an eagle in the air
Sometimes I feel like an eagle in the air
Sometimes I feel like an eagle in the air
A long, long way from home.

*(MURIEL crosses to between LISA and GLORIA, LISA continues humming.)*

MURIEL We go back eons. Where you place your hand, your foot is padded with generations of us. We came from way, way ago to be here with you.

LISA I didn't understand then.

MURIEL I understand.

GLORIA She understands now.

*Video Image: (full screen) Josephine Tarrant singing "Persistence of Memory" by Becky Thunderbird.*

[See DVD, "Persistence of Memory"]

"Hey Yah Na Hey
Hey Yah Na Hey
Hey Yah Na Hey Hey
Wey Ho Hey
Yah Wey Oh Hey
My family, my nation
My Creator, my life
I sing for the next generation
Hey Yah Na Hey
Hey Yah Na Hey
Hey Yah Na Hey Hey
Wey Ho Hey
Yah Wey Oh Hey
*(Muriel's voice)* 'Very good, Josie.'"

*A terra cotta-colored silk drop drops from the grid over the center projection panel.*

*Video Image: (full screen) Music, George and Ira Gershwin, "Overture" from* Lady Be Good, *plays under a photo montage of the various performers who have been in Spiderwoman Theater. The first images are of Lois Weaver, Peggy Shaw, Naja Bey, Kachaka Snipe, Eva Bauman, Pam Verge, Sylvia Robinson, Lynette Yetter, and Kathy Gollner. The last set are photographs of the three sisters together, taken through their lives. The last image is of the sisters with their mother's wedding photo. The last image is the projection:*

"The End…for now."

[See DVD, "Retrospective," music not included]

*Persistence of Memory–25th Anniversary Celebration* premiered with the Aboriginal Arts Program at The Banff Centre, Rice Studio, February 2002.

Original Lighting Design: David Ingraham

Production Manager: Deborah Ratelle

Video Editor: Shawn Henry

In New York: Video Crew for Hortensia Colorado, Elvira Colorado, and Donna Couteau segments:

Camera : Xavier Henselmann

Camera Assistant: Lance Richmond

Sound: Tenolian Bell

Video Appearances

Hortensia Colorado, *Winnetou's Snake Oil Show from Wigwam City*

Elvira Colorado, *Power Pipes*

Lois Weaver, Naja Bey, and Pam Verge, *Lysistrata Numbah*

Donna Couteau, *Women in Violence*

Sandy Crimmins

Monique Mojica, *Princess Pocahontas and the Blue Spots*

Murielle Borst, *More than Feathers and Beads*

Josephine Tarrant

Frank Harris

David A. Harris

Paolo Spano

Raphael Szykowski

Racael Borst

Deborah Ratelle

Photo Collage Photographs by Jonathan Slaff, Martin Selway, and Martha Swope

MUSIC

Berlin, Irving. "A Pretty Girl Is Like a Melody" from *Ziegfeld Follies of 1919*. Various publications.

Cowell, Henry. "Ostinato Pianissimo." New Jersey Percussion Ensemble, *Percussion Music*, 1978. Elektra Nonesuch, 1987.

Gershwin, George, and Ira Gershwin. "Overture." 1924. *Lady Be Good: Selections*. Studio orchestra conducted by Eric Stern. Elektra Nonesuch, 1992.

Glass, Philip. "Some Are." *"Low" Symphony*. Brooklyn Philharmonic Orchestra, Karen Kamensek and Dennis Russell Davies, conductors. PointMusic, 1993.

Matos Rodríguez, Gerardo. "La Cumparsita." *Tango Argentino: Original Cast Recording*. Various singers and musicians. Atlantic, 1986.

Mores, Mariano. "Tanguera." *Tango Argentino: Original Cast Recording*. Various singers and musicians. Atlantic, 1986.

Penn, Brandy, and Jan Rybn. "I Want You in the Home."

Piazzolla, Astor. "Oblivion." *Todo Tango*. Various musicians. Milan Entertainment, 1994.

Thunderbird, Becky. "Persistence of Memory."

Waters, Roger, and David Gilmour. "Comfortably Numb." Pink Floyd, *The Wall*. Columbia, 1988; Capitol, 1994.

Whiting, George, and Walter Donaldson. "My Blue Heaven." Various publications.

PUBLICATIONS

Borst, Murielle. *More Than Feathers and Beads.* Native American Women Playwrights Archive, Miami University Libraries, Oxford, Ohio.

Mojica, Monique. *Princess Pocahontas and the Blue Spots. Staging Coyote's Dream: An Anthology of First Nations Drama in English*. Ed. Monique Mojica and Ric Knowles. Toronto: Playwrights Canada Press, 2003, 133-69; *Princess Pocahontas and the Blue Spots.* Toronto: Women's Press, 1991.

Spiderwoman Theater. *Power Pipes*. *Seventh Generation: An Anthology of Native American Plays*. Ed. Mimi Gisolfi D'Aponte. New York: Theatre Communications Group, 1999. 149-200.

---. *Reverb-ber-ber-rations*. *Staging Coyote's Dream: An Anthology of First Nations Drama in English*. Ed. Monique Mojica and Ric Knowles. Toronto: Playwrights Canada Press, 2003, 97-132; *Women and Performance* 5.2 (1992): 184-212.

---. *Sun, Moon, and Feather*. *Stories of Our Way: An Anthology of American Indian Plays*. Ed. Hanay Geiogamah and Jaye T. Darby. UCLA American Indian Studies Center, 1999, 287-314; *Contemporary Plays by Women of Color: An Anthology*. Ed. Kathy A. Perkins and Roberto Uno. London: Routledge, 1996, 299-309.

---. *Winnetou's Snake Oil Show from Wigwam City. Keepers of the Morning Star: An Anthology of Native Women's Theater*. Ed. Jaye T. Darby and Stephanie Fitzgerald. Los Angeles: UCLA American Indian Studies Center, 2003, 229-62; *Playwrights of Color*. Ed. Meg Swanson with Robin Murray. Yarmouth, ME: Intercultural Press, 1999, 69-105; *Canadian Theatre Review* 68 (1991): 54-63.

Many Thanks!!

The American Indian Community House, Rosemary Richmond, Marrie Mumford, Lance Richmond, David Harris, Paolo Spano, Mia Kemff, Harriet Nordlund, Robert Rombough, Tom Montvila, Luke Van Dyk.

Development of *Persistence of Memory* was made possible by funding from the Rockefeller Multi-Arts Production Fund, the 2002 Paul D. Fleck Fellowship in the Arts, the Canada Council for the Arts, and the Aboriginal Arts Program at The Banff Centre.

The production at Miami University (February 20, 2007) was funded in large part by the John W. Altman Humanities Scholar-in-Residence Fund, with further support from the Ohio Humanities Council, the Center for American and World Cultures, and the Miami University Libraries.

# Lousy Woman

*Marie Annharte Baker*

not polite to talk behind her back call her
a lousy woman and giggle suspend ourselves
in hysterical laughs Spiderwomen at play
trapeze together or solo each her worst word
about that woman's latest escapade did you hear
just how bad but she slashed tires on a car
of a minister who dumped her & that husband
she took off with was somebody else to figure out

a moccasin telegraph message system spreads
over continents linked by cruel conquests
didn't run the whole damn country for news
or see Manhattan Indian smoke signals nor
do I read Cree syllabics or gossip columns
because I am information my ears grow tufts

the FBI examined my disorganized purse
(a tongue depressor would work better
than frisking for weapons & for thrills)
could get arrested for Mukkytoon activity
when on political campaign a Jesse Jackson
visits the Village Voice but doesn't drop
into the Indian Centre to get our advice
(he'd see us jam frybread in deadly jaws)
like punctuation and exclamation signals
the right colour for my fry bread is done

last time I saw that lousy woman my back
covered she hovered but held her melba toast
elegant manner armed with a political elbow
drag across the chip dip sch-mooze-em black
fringed shawl all she has time for is network

(imagine a nation of lousy women doing damage)
who said witch art is in heaven which it isn't

For Muriel Miguel & Spiderwoman sisters

## What's an Indian Woman to Do[1]

*Marcie Rendon*

so the story with the poem is: spiderwoman was in minneapolis doing a theater residency at the playwright center, and i was lucky enough to be there for the two days they were leading it. i was brand new to playwrighting—early 1990s. i had not had a play produced. we spent the days doing improv; pretending we were trees, wind in the trees—and somehow the conversation got around to the appropriation of native spirituality, native life by non-natives... i went home that night and before i went to sleep the poem poured out of me, i got up, wrote it out, and the rest, as they say, is history—it is my most requested poem to date. Mark Anthony Rolo wrote a one-woman performance piece based on the poem that premiered at the Minneapolis Fringe Festival in 2005. My daughter, Simone Rendon, performed the piece.

what's an indian woman to do
when the white girls act more indian
than the indian women do?

my tongue trips over takonsala
mumbles around the word mitakuye oyasin
my ojibwe's been corrected
by a blond U of M undergraduate

what's an indian woman to do?

much to my ex-husband's dismay
i never learned the humble,
spiritual,
Native woman stance
legs tight, arms close, head bowed
three paces behind

[1] Previously appeared in *Native Arts Circle News* [Minneapolis], summer 1994; *Sister Nations: Native American Women Writers on Community*, ed. Heid E. Erdrich and Laura Tohe (St. Paul: Minnesota Historical Soc., 2002), 138-39; and *Futures* [Minneapolis] 2.19 (Oct. 2000).

my mother worked and fought with men
strode across fields
100-pound potato sacks on shoulders broad as any man
the most traditional thing
my grandfather taught me
was to put jeebik on the cue stick
to win a game of pool
so i never learned the finer
indian arts
so many white women have become adept at

sometimes i go to pow-wows
see them selling wares
somehow the little crystals
tied on leather pouches
never pull my indian heart

huh, what's an indian woman to do?

i remember Kathy She Who Sees the Spirit Lights
when she was still
Katrina Olson from Mankato, Minnesota
and Raven Woman?
damn, i swear i knew her
when she was a jewish girl
over in st. paul

as my hair grays
theirs gets darker
month by month
their reservation accents
thicker
year by year

used to be
reincarnation happened
only to the dead

hmmm?!?!?

what's an indian woman to do
when the white girls act more indian
than the indians do???

## Persistent Memories: An Interview with Spiderwoman Theater[1]

*Ann Haugo*

ANN HAUGO: Most of us in the room saw *Persistence of Memory* last night, and I thought perhaps we could start with that performance, but before we get to that, could each of you [Spiderwoman Theater performers] introduce yourselves briefly?

GLORIA: Well, I'm Gloria, and I usually go in the middle. [*audience laughter*] I used to be a faculty wife. Ow! [*audience laughter*] Every time I walk into a university like this, I think of my faculty days and my faculty kids. [*audience laughter*] Of Oberlin. We lived in Oberlin, Ohio. Monique hated it. And my son hated it, but they survived. [*audience laughter*] That was the sort of middle part of my life, and before that, and I had Oberlin, then I had Spiderwoman, and now I have old age. That's scary. That's me. That's all.

LISA: And my name is Elizabeth Elmyra Miguel. Elizabeth Miguel, Elizabeth Charentski, Elizabeth Harris, and somewhere along there I got the name Lisa Mayo when I was a Broadway baby walking off my tired feet. And who else am I?

GLORIA: Ola Na Dili.

LISA: Ola Na Dili is my Kuna name, and that name means "the first daughter to come from the stars," since I'm the oldest. Each one of us has a name, and it's a traditional name that comes from our great big saga. The daughters who come from the stars, the Kunas say, we came down to help things go right in the community, to fix the homes and make them comfortable, and to bring love to the children, and so on like that.

GLORIA: And to help men get along with women.

LISA: Yes, and help men get along with women. Okay. And I'm an actress. I always feel as though I started when I was two years old, and my family was on stage at our Methodist church in Brooklyn, and we were standing there as first families. I was confused, but I've been on stage since I was at least two.

And then Uta Hagen.[2] Uta, I do love you. [*audience laughter*] Yes, I love Uta Hagen. She was only looking for the truth and I didn't care if it was German, French, Irish, English, black, brown. I didn't care as long as it was the truth as best as I could get to it. I studied with her at the HB Studio, and if you go to the HB Studio, she's sort of a goddess. I relish her memory, and I am so happy that she saw my talent because I was what they called at that time an…not an "Indigenous," but what was that word they used? Anyway, not a white!

MURIEL: "Ethnic"?

LISA: Ethnic! I was a great singer and a budding actress learning my craft. I said, "Well do you think you can get work?" and an agent said, "You're much too ethnic. We couldn't even put you in the chorus. You stick out like a sore thumb." And I thought, "Ow! My God, how awful." So anyway I'm very happy to be here with my sisters as well as my nieces. My nieces have always surprised me, but this one [the performance by Murielle and Monique honoring Spiderwoman] is the topper! [*audience laughter*]

---

[1] This interview took place at the "Honoring Spiderwoman Theater / Celebrating Native American Theater" Conference on February 21, 2007, at Miami University. Because it took place in front of and with participation from an audience, the interview constitutes a performance itself.

[2] Uta Hagen (1919-2004). Well-known actor and master teacher of acting, Uta Hagen taught at Herbert Berghof Studio (HB Studio) with her husband (Herbert Berghof) where she trained generations of successful actors from 1947-2004. Her teaching is based on the work of Constantin Stanislavski, and her methods have been documented in her own books *Respect for Acting* (with Haskel Frankel; Macmillan, 1973) and *A Challenge for the Actor* (Scribner, 1991). http://www.hbstudio.org/.

LISA: Muriel Miguel, my baby sister. [*audience laughter*]

MURIEL: I'm not her baby sister. I'm her younger sister. [*audience laughter*] My name is Muriel Miguel. I came from the Open Theater, and originally I was a dancer—from a show dancer, moving into modern dance.[3] I studied at the Henry Street Playhouse with Alwin Nikolais, and then I studied with Jean Erdman.[4] Before that, well, at the age of thirteen, I met a woman that my sister introduced me to who just came from the Rudolf Laban laboratories in London, and from the age of thirteen and fourteen, I studied Laban.[5] I was taught that at a very young age and could see how that could be used for us, for Native people. I teach grass dance, I use Laban. I teach show dancing, I use Laban. It's a way of using a terminology that the student and the teacher both understand, as we talk to each other.

It's the same way that I bring Open Theater techniques. When I was in the Open Theater, Joe Chaikin discovered something called storytelling. It was one of those things where I said, "Oh yeah, I understand storytelling, darling." They did this whole thing about storytelling and then they say, "Geez, Muriel, you're such a great storyteller." But you know, growing up in a Native family, you knew how to tell stories from the bottom of your feet all the way up. You understood storytelling. When I left the Open Theater, I really was interested in and thought a lot about storytelling—like what exactly is the oral tradition, and where do you hear the stories? All the great stories that you learn from under the kitchen table, all the great secrets, all the juicy parts of your family that you hear from under the kitchen table where you've been hiding out listening to these stories. I was really interested in personal stories and how to tell personal stories, so I developed the technique about how to put together stories—storyweaving. Does a story necessarily have to start at "the beginning"? I've used that with what I call "organic continuity."

And then this is what happened to me. I had a very close friend growing up, one of my best friends. They were a Hopi/Ho Chunk family that lived next door. When I was looking for a way to develop these stories, I had many different groups of women that I would collect and work on stories with. Once, I asked my best friend, Josephine Mofsie, who did finger weaving, and another young woman to work on a creation story. I had Josephine on a very high mound of something. I suspended her finger weaving down, and she told the story of Spiderwoman as she did this finger weaving. I had just came from a sun dance, and I told the story of what happened at a certain section of a sun dance that I was at, and the other woman—a white Baptist

[3] Open Theater (1963-1973). This experimental New York theater company was founded and led by director Joseph Chaikin. The company was known for its collaborative methods in conceiving original work and its use of ensemble cast and improvisational techniques.

[4] Henry Street Playhouse (1893- present). This community center houses distinguished art programs for local youth and has become a founding site for professional companies, among them Alwin Nikolais' Nikolais Dance Theatre, an abstract modern dance company founded in 1958. http://www.henrystreet.org/.
Jean Erdman (born 1916) is a leader in the modern dance world; she worked with Martha Graham and then founded the Jean Erdman Dance Group in 1944. After teaching at several universities, she created the Foundation for the Open Eye in 1972 with her husband, mythologist Joseph Campbell. http://www.theopeneye.org/.

[5] Rudolf Laban (1879-1958). Laban was a founder and innovator of European modern dance. He is best known for creating Labanotation, a system of recording dance and movement that has been influential to dance educators, choreographers, and other artists. http://www.laban.org/.

woman from Virginia—told a story of making love to Jesus. I had a film of a river, and I showed this just on the floor. We were on different sides of the river, and I started to put this together where Josie would tell some of the story, and I would tell some of my story, and she would tell some of her story. Sometimes it was just one to two words, and then we would come back together again. Sometimes we'd talk together. So it was like the running of this river, this brook, but at the same time there were creation stories all happening at the same time. It was the first time I ever really tried that, and that was quite exciting.

From there I took all of that and went away and developed Spiderwoman. Josephine Mofsie, my best friend, had five children. The youngest one was Kevin, who married my oldest daughter Murielle, and they now have a child, which is my grandchild and my best friend's grandchild also. And it goes on like that. Indian country is more than small. So anyway, that's me.

ANN HAUGO: I wanted to ask if you would talk a little bit about how you started working on *Persistence of Memory*. How long has the process been to work on it? And what was the original—the spark?

LISA: Well, I think it began when we were invited to Sweden to a festival of people who were Indigenous people, people from Africa, people from Greenland, Sami people from Sweden...

MURIEL: Russian Indigenous...

LISA: Yes, yes, a wonderful storyteller, the woman who wore her dolls on her body. She was very interesting. She was Indigenous. She was interesting to watch. She was a white woman with blue eyes and beautiful blonde hair, but her features were completely Asian. She was interesting, wonderful to watch and to hear sing.

And I do think the name of the conference was *Persistence of Memory*. Is that right? Yes. And that's where it came from. We were talking. We spoke of Salvador Dali and the very famous painting of the melting clock ("Persistence of Memory"). Muriel, as I remember it, had the idea that *Persistence of Memory* would be our next piece. We had so many shows by that time that we could make an hour, two or three hours of the shows we had already created and so that was our next thing. Muriel really went out to look for venues for that show and we went up to Canada. Anyway, that's how it started for me and what *Persistence of Memory* was.

Of course, I had at that moment no idea that my wonderful nieces would be involved in it. My first little niece, when she first came in, the youngest one in the family who is thirteen now, and this was about, what, six years ago?

MURIEL: It was eight.

LISA: Eight years ago, so she was very young when she started to be with us and perform with us. That's how it developed, and then I took a turn for the worse I guess you want to call it. [*audience laughter*]

GLORIA: Well, I remember two or three things of when we were in Sweden. There was a Sami woman who did perform her show, and it was called *Persistence of Memory*...and then an African woman performed her show...and the women from Greenland performed their show, and we performed ours, and we were aware that each time each performer performed, she set out in a circle. Her show, her entire show, was performed in a circle. Every one of them, including our show. It was so obvious to us. We were saying that as Indigenous people we had something in common that came from waaaaayyyyy back and that also included the *Persistence of Memory*, of doing whatever it was it was in a circle. And that was one thing. We know we always perform in a circle. There's always a circle in everything we do, even the one-woman shows that we have. Whatever I do is a circle also. And then when we came home, and we asked the Sami woman if we could use that name "Persistence of Memory," which came from a painting by Salvador Dali, and she said, "Oh, yes, it would be wonderful to use the name." Then when we came home and started talking about it a couple years later, we thought, we will honor all the women from way back, whoever has worked with us since 1975, from our first rehearsal and the many women—some are dead and some are still roaming around the world. We were going to honor them when we do this new show. We wanted to think about what we would contribute.

The last seven years I have had a lifetime scholarship to Strasberg Institute.[6] That's a lot of fun learning the method and studying with young people from all over the world, which is very exciting. So, I was thinking about taking that method, which is included in almost everything I've ever studied even when we worked in Oberlin. When I studied theater, the method was there, but it was all little bits and pieces, from way back. And in Oberlin when we had classes, we did it in the circle. We did our exercises in a circle. When we told stories in the class, the circle was very important there, too. So I tried to think about what I learned in my classes lately, just like just taking a private moment or sense memory and putting it into what I was going to do in *Persistence of Memory*. I thought, how am I going to do this? What am I going to perform? I said I was going to give myself a song. I was supposed to give myself a story, and I was going to give myself a dance.

So I made my story. The story was in terms of "Persistence of Memory," and the one thought I had in mind was my grandniece coming to me and just by seeing the photograph in my house of me and my third-grade class and recognizing me and seeing me sitting there in the middle, she connected to what was going on in her life now. She used to spend the weekend with me. She just brought that photograph to me and said, "Is this you, Aunt Gloria?" and I said, "Yes." She said [*clap!*] she knew how I felt now! And that photograph was taken fifty, sixty, seventy years ago. I don't know. But she connected to that. My thought was she was on top of it. She was different in her group in her school, but *she* knew how to handle it. With me being the only dark one in the school, I became more inhibited and introverted, and it took a hell of a time in a lifetime to get a little bit out of it, because I'm still in it. I'm still in it, when I'm around people, I go like this [*hunkers down as if closing herself off*], and I have to force myself, my real self, out. So it's hard. So everybody looks at me and says, "Oh, you're the quiet one, AAHHH! Or you're the spiritual one, AAHHH!" And I'm frightened to death of people, and I have to AAHHH! myself to get out. So that picture was my story from the *Persistence of Memory,* and then I wanted to go into a song.

The song: I'm influenced by Philip Glass, I'm influenced by Mozart as well as the beautiful and powerful songs of the Kuna people that my father gave to me. All this music is in my body, and I think of it all the time. When I put a story together, I have the lights, the music, the sounds—it's all in there in one piece—and I have to put all the little people or whatever together in the story. So in my mind I have the Phillip Glass—noise, noise. I have Mozart—Da Da Da Dee Da. I have the Kuna song—la la la la. I have them all together.

I wanted to use the old men that I met as a child also because of the way they speak. They spoke differently, the men that came from Kuna Yala. They would use phrases that had a lot of meaning to us, just one or two lines like, as I said, "I no know myself." I would ask them a question, and maybe they knew the

[6] Lee Strasberg (1901-1982). The director of the Actors Studio starting in 1950 where he taught many actors. He is best known for his own unique American interpretation of Constantin Stanislavski's acting techniques. http://www.strasberg.com/; http://www.theactorsstudio.org/

answer, but maybe they didn't. Maybe they wanted to lie about it. Maybe they were being a little cagey. I would ask a question, and sometimes if they didn't want to answer, they would say, "I no know myself." I love that. I just love those words. So I thought I'd write a story about "I no know myself" and include in that story all the crap you go through in New York, all the crap you go through in this world, and how you fight it. I gathered words. I saved the moment. I learned the lessons, I started the action, and still, still, the quest goes on for the answers and the truth. Like "I no know myself!" And then to pray and ask for help, to give me strength to sing, to be a good person, to love and work and know and understand life and understand men in my life, and how to live with men and be happy because that's a hell of a job. It really is. I think that's the biggest, biggest job. [*audience laughter*] If you are a straight woman trying to...[*audience laughter*]

So I put that together with my song, and then the World Trade [disaster] came along, and I added all that, all those spirits that are flying through the air, in New York City. I tried to put all that in that song and then end up with the terror that's going on in the world—God there's a lot to fight against—and put it in a song and put all my feeling into it. So that was my song that was my Mozart requiem, that was my Kuna lullaby, whatever.

The other thing was a dance. I've always loved—all my life—the Tango, and I've always wanted to do the Tango, and I just didn't have the real flare for it. You have to feel like a peacock sometimes when you're learning that type of dance. I studied a little bit about what the Tango was like, and we all like that music. Elizabeth loves the Tango. The idea of the Tango came from the ghetto of Argentina, and it came from the people of Argentina. The classic people of Europe took it, and they did something else with it. Then it came back, but it was basically a dance of the people, the Tango. It's very spiritual, and it's always like a fight between a triangle. And *we're* a triangle, and, believe it or not, we fight a lot, the three of us. And sometimes I hate my sisters, and I don't want to be near them. I do. It's the truth. We are all very different. We are very different, believe it or not.

So my Tango was just carrying the burdens of my family with me all over and, and doing a dance with the burdens of my mother, my father, my grandmother, my grandfather, even the Elizabeth Ashton Moore back there—she was a nasty person. She was my grandmother. She was mean and nasty, and she used to try to beat me. She would try to beat me, and I said, "Don't you touch me! Don't you touch me!" I hated her! She tried to beat me up, and I said, "No woman has the right, no matter how bad I am, to touch me," and she said to me, "Gloria has the devil in her and I'll never touch her." So I protected myself from my grandmother.

Anyway, what I have to do as a woman is to reach out and capture the present and whatever future I have left that I will to myself, and to the music of the Tango. And so those are my three things put all together into this *Persistence of Memory* piece.

MURIEL: Well, yes, it did start in Sweden with this "Persistence of Memory" festival. What was so interesting was that there was a circle, but every one of these women did something to the four directions, which really amazed me. We were from all over the place, but we were all talking about residential schools. We were all talking about the same things, and then to see these pieces come on stage and even the woman from Russia who was from the back of the Ural Mountains.

She was really Indigenous. She came from an Indigenous village. So she went to Leningrad, and they said, "You are a Russian girl." And she said, "No, I'm not. I'm from the back of the Ural Mountains. I'm

Indigenous." And they said, "You are a Russian girl, and if you're not a Russian girl, you can go back. You can't study in our schools." And that was the end; she became a Russian girl. But she spoke her language, and even where she was, she came to Sweden to be with us, but she wasn't supposed to be out of Russia. She'd just left. So when she came back, she didn't even know if she had a job because she wanted to do her one-woman show so bad.

It was so interesting to watch all these women talk about residential schools and being denied and then to see them all go into four directions. I mean, that really hit me. When we came back and I was thinking about "Persistence of Memory," I really wanted to do a festival, I wanted to do a festival in New York, a "Persistence of Memory" festival, and ask all the women from Canada all the way down, women with one-woman shows or women just to bring things in because of that Persistence of Memory. I started to think about it, and I started thinking about the mothers that are crack addicts, the mothers that are whores, the mothers that are alcoholics, the mothers. Are they heroes? Are they anti-heroes? What are they? You just can't call them nothing. They did bring children into the world. And I can't...I can't say they are *not* heroes. I mean, they tried somehow to get a child or not to get that child someplace in the world. And somehow I had this question about whether these women are heroes or not, and in my mind somehow they are heroes some way, somehow, and I'm not quite sure why.

So thinking of that, I started to think about legacy, and I started to think about...where does that persistence come from, the things that you do in your house that you know that your grandma did, even if you hated your grandma? Grandma did it, and your ma does it, and so you do it, and so your child does it. Where does that come from? And does that mean that your great-great-great-grandma did it? You know what I mean? It's that sound in your ears all the time and that something that was implanted, somehow, that knowledge in your blood, in your blueprint of your family, of your tribe. Where does that come from?

And so that was the big question for me in *Persistence of Memory*. The "Persistence of Memory" doesn't necessarily have to be great, you know. It could be awful. It could be abuse. It could be alcoholism. It could be that, too. But we do carry with us, I think, like the animals, like people close to the earth, like birds, a "Persistence of Memory."

So with that, I did start to think very hard about legacy, and thinking about the legacy of Spiderwoman. I was working with Monique on her project; I directed her project. I directed Murielle's project. I think I went back and directed another piece of Monique's, and I started to really think that this is the legacy. Then hearing my grandchild sing and dance. Well, this is a legacy. And then it doesn't stop here.

That whole question about audience again comes back to me because I teach. In the last eight years I've been teaching quite a lot, and to just get these words out, just to get this communication between teacher and student. Having a methodology that's ours, and talking about a Native center, a Native core, having people think like this instead of in a linear line, pushing the envelope, [asking] so, yeah, you can do this? Well, suppose this was pushed this way? What would happen? Teaching that, with students, I realized that when we talk about audience, that student is an audience, and that student brings its own audience. That's what I was thinking about, that this student brings its own audience, and this student brings its own audience. So it's that ripple, that cliché ripple effect.

It does go out. I worked at Banff Centre for eight years, and I see all these dancers and playwrights emerging that I taught, that I worked with on a [Native performance] methodology that started at Banff with Floyd (Favel Starr) and myself and Monique and a group of us, trying to just grip it.[7] Then, thinking of all the women that did pass through Spiderwoman. So that ending [of *Persistence of Memory*], when we pulled down the curtain and you see all these pictures of Spiderwoman, the last thirty-one years was a tribute to all of them, that came through Spiderwoman.

That's where it started, and it doesn't end. I think it never ends. I heard a whole new section of *Persistence of Memory* from these two [Monique Mojica and Murielle Borst] today, and I really realized it when I saw the two of them singing together. Oh my god! This is really the beginning. A new creation story is being made. It's going again, and it doesn't necessarily mean that it'll be in our words or my words, but it goes on.

ANN HAUGO: Thank you. [to the audience] Do you have questions that you would like to ask, too?

AUDIENCE MEMBER: I'd like to ask about the Penguin Dance [in *Persistence of Memory*].

GLORIA: The Penguin Dance?

MURIEL: Oh! The Penguin Dance! It used to be the Flea Dance.

LISA: The Flea Dance—first we were fleas—

GLORIA: We were fleas, but it's hard to jump now-a-days. [*audience laughter*] Yeah, I saw this wonderful movie about penguins. There were two of them. It's fascinating about what they do and how they live.

LISA: And we can walk like them.

GLORIA: And we can walk like them, so we decided to change from flea to penguin.

LISA: Makes sense, doesn't it? It makes sense. We can't jump that way anymore. [*audience laughter*]

AUDIENCE MEMBER: I have a question. Murielle, you talked about in your presentation, and I've heard the rest of you talk about it at one time or another throughout the conference—this idea of always of going back to the core, to the kernel, to the center. I was just wondering if you could talk a little bit more about what that is for each of you?

LISA: I based it on an experience I had at the botanical gardens in the Bronx. I went up there one day because it's beautiful, it's inspirational. I would sit there and write or whatever, and I saw this sign. As I remember it, there was sort of a bridge. I heard this trickle of spring water and I looked down, and I saw rocks, and I saw vegetation, and I saw this sign that before Christopher Columbus came this area was used by Algonquian Indians. Well, my mother's people, there's a strain—I don't know exactly how it works—but we are descendants of some Algonquian nations. And I thought, "God this is really..." And I looked down, and I saw them. I saw them creeping and looking, gathering. There were men. They were, they were. It was summer time. They wore some little cloths around them or whatever, but they were carrying, talking, and playing in this water fountain. I walked further, and I found a little place. They have benches there. You're not really supposed to use the earth to sit, to sit down on or picnic on. I didn't eat. I just sat there, and I fell asleep. And I had this dream, and I thought this dream is telling me something. I'm really connected. I don't have to feel left

[7] The Banff Centre. Founded in the 1930s and located in Banff National Park at Banff, Alberta, The Banff Centre fosters innovative creative work across a variety of disciplines in the arts and sciences. It also hosts an internationally recognized Aboriginal Arts Program. http://www.banffcentre.ca/.

out in a country where I was born because that's always been a problem, not feeling wanted here because I was dark or different or I wasn't thoroughly a Christian. And I got it, here, in the earth, and just knowing about it gives me energy.

This is nourishing me, so I wrote about it. I never brought it to Spiderwoman until we were working on *Persistence of Memory*, and it's so strange because as great as it is for me, I knew when I awakened from that dream, that I was different than I was before. Not different from anybody else but different, different in terms of my understanding of myself. Where do I get my energy? Where does it come from? How does it enter my body? How do I use it artistically in a piece? And so I put it in this piece. And as it turned out the way the piece developed, I thought that when I mentioned it to my sisters that they would be thrilled by it the way I was. But they weren't, and it gave me anguish and I would keep talking about it, and I'd bring it up in the piece that I do two or three times, how it's there and all I have to do is touch it and it gives me strength. It feeds me spiritually to know that and I used it, I didn't try to change them, but I was persistent in talking about it.

GLORIA: My father and mother were in show business when we were little kids, and my father would do, in the thirties, a lot of Wild West shows, and Madison Square Garden, and rodeos. A lot of people came from all over the country, and some people were stranded. My father would see in the paper of a Native American family stranded, and he'd go down to City Hall or wherever they were and bring them home. And we lived with these people, many of them for years and months. My father realized, I guess, at some point that he could sing and he could dance, and they put all these different song and dances together, and at one time there was also a cowboy and Indian club in New York City, where cowboys joined us with their songs and dances and all the Natives. In our home when we were kids, at night in the evening or during the week people would come and sing and dance and we'd all be gathered together, so a lot of the songs that I know came from way out, from the Hopi or from the Navajo. At one point during the Depression my father needed money, so we used to go, the whole family, and do Indian family songs, Indian family dances for churches and places like that. And I remember...

LISA: Circuses.

GLORIA: One story in my mind...I guess had something to do with the flag. Our family was sitting on a rock in some big auditorium with the American flag and a light on the American flag and the wind blowing on the American flag and a chorus behind us. And our family was sitting there, and the chorus sang, "Oh, beautiful for spacious skies." I was six years old. I said, "I'm not going to do this anymore." I quit. I quit show business then, but I came back to it because performing was in my blood, but there had to be a different way. I didn't go back to it until I was thirteen years old, and I studied music, dance, and storytelling and worked with kids. I can't even tell you where it started, when it started, but it did. It was in my blood from day one that I can remember.

LISA: I always think of it in terms of some of the things that we are not really proud of. I mean, we were "showbiz Indians," right? That meant you really went out there and you did circus, you did side shows, you did the Christmas show, the Thanksgiving show, and the Columbus Day Parade and...

GLORIA: Pontiac Chevrolet.

LISA: Pontiac Chevrolet! You did all those shows. We knew all those people that did that, you know, and we use a lot of that in our shows, right? We do "Indian Love Call" in *Sun, Moon, and Feather*. In *Winnetou's Snake Oil Show*, we do all that stuff da da da da da da ya [stereotypical Indian music, sign language]. We can do the Lord's Prayer in Indian sign language, right, Muriel?

MURIEL: I can do "God Bless America." [*audience laughter*]

LISA: To me, those are kernels. You take that kernel, and you add another vegetable, and you put another vegetable, and you put another vegetable, and you add the water and—voom, voom—*Winnetou's Snake Oil Show*. So that's how I think about kernels, and sometimes it's not stripping away. It's adding to the kernel, but that kernel is not a nice place to go, you know what I mean? It's like we were a show biz family—like ugh. It's not a proud place to be, to know that your father was doing [stereotypical] things on a float or that you did…

GLORIA:…or making some kind of a thing in the bath tub…

LISA:…or that he sold snake oil on a street corner or any of them. I mean, I personally did the *Broken Arrow* and all those [shows], went from one movie house to another movie house. We did the ballyhoo or the broken arrow and gave out little charms during Thanksgiving. It's not a nice place, but that's a kernel. That's how I think about kernel.

GLORIA: It's core.

LISA: Kernel, core—it feeds you.

AUDIENCE MEMBER: I just wanted to say I was sitting here last night watching you, and really, one of the wonderful things about your performances is not just that you're sharing the performance, but that you're sharing yourself. I feel very fortunate. I saw you come here years ago, and I feel like the number of times that you been here now that you've really shared yourself with this community. I really appreciate everything that you've shared with us. One thing that I also notice that I really particularly appreciate about your performances is when you talk about memory. It's not just this kind of detached sort of photo-album memory, but you embody a real child-like quality.

GLORIA: God help us.

AUDIENCE MEMBER: I mean the way you know in *Sun, Moon, and Feather* when you're doing the dolls, but that you're not just acting like a kid. You're really embodying those children that you were.

LISA: We never grew up.

AUDIENCE MEMBER: Well I think a lot of adults don't do that, though. I think we let go of our childhood. We don't acknowledge that the children that we were are the people that we are. Is that something that has been mindful for you? Have you thought about that, connecting with your childhood in that way that it's a really central kind of thing, part of that core, maybe?

LISA: I'll speak for myself. It's changed somewhat, because I do have a craft, and I can go as far as I can, like Gloria uses an actual picture that was taken of her class. And it's a beautiful picture with all these nice little kids, and Gloria is right smack in the middle. And so obviously different from any of the other children. So that's not my picture, but I use that picture. I never told her I used it, but I use it because there's a lot of things open for me in that picture.

I also think of when we were thinking of *Sun, Moon, and Feather.* We were talking about how we survived as children in Brooklyn in an Italian neighborhood, and what did we do behind closed doors to make ourselves happy? We used to play fantastic games that went on for days and days, and my mother would let us. We'd set up chairs and put blankets over them. My mother let us keep those things out. We have wonderful stories of making ourselves happy, protecting ourselves from the cruel world out there and doing these stupid little things under the blanket and on the floor to make ourselves happy. That was like the core of *Sun, Moon, and Feather*, starting with what we did as children. One of the first things you do in those Strasberg classes also is go to sense memory. They say further than seven years. I can go way back, and I remember those little things that were so great and dramatic, you know, sitting on the steps for hours watching the little particles of the sun fall on the floor and wondering what they were as a child. You know, the stories that can come out of that. They're all like little, little, little girl stories. They're very dramatic, but they're juicy. You think of a story, and ordinary people maybe say, "That kid's nuts!" but to use them, to go back to sense memory, using them on the stage today...It is childish, but it's good...good material.

MURIEL: I think it's the chance, and that's what I think the bravery here is. I feel that I don't do it. I don't embody it right, but I do feel it from my sisters. It's that chance, that big jump, and to take that jump and to be able to do it. We can say all actors do it, but they're, they're like me. I'm not necessarily, I'm not childish, I don't embody childlike the same way, but they take that chance; they dare to; and I think that's the difference, you know, of all actors being able to do sense memory and you two being able to take the big leap. I think that's the big difference.

MONIQUE MOJICA: I just wanted to expand a little bit, when we were talking about legacy here, and Muriel was talking about legacy, and you're talking about legacy. We just had a little next generation moment here when you were talking about the uncomfortable place, about not being proud of the medicine shows, the snake oil shows, and posing in front of the American flag and knowing at six years old that you were never going to do that again. We're saying, well, we're not ashamed of that. I'm not ashamed of that, either, so it's like...

It goes on. It morphs into generations, whereas the way that I might carry that and say, Yeah, that, that's part of me, and that made room. That made Spiderwoman Theater possible, which made what I do possible, which made what Murielle does possible, which makes my son Bear a filmmaker doing a film on the family's migration to the cities, where for survival the family became performers. So the way that goes on, then, is that it becomes for us behind you [Spiderwoman] saying that it's not a shameful thing for us, because it's in us, and it keeps transforming.

LISA: As Uncle Joe would say, "make me feel shame."

GLORIA: I no know myself. [*audience laughter*]

MURIEL: You talk to different communities—the African American community had the Chitlin Circuit, Vaudeville. Jewish America had Vaudeville really. And we had Wild West shows. All those people who came out of Vaudeville and the Chitlin Circuit: The Marx Brothers came out of Vaudeville, and a lot of great comedians came out of the Chitlin Circuit, all of those type of performers, because you weren't allowed in anywhere else. Wild West was the only place where we could do it, and I think that is how we became performers. I think it's what paid the bills, or I think we would have been starving in the streets or begging for our supper. We decided to perform instead, and I always go back to that when things are bad. I think because of the snake oil shows we have grown up with—I grew up with—a big, big work ethic. And the work ethic is you gotta do what you have to do to put food on the table for your family. If you have to do show business to do it, you do it, and whatever you do, you do it seven days a week if you have to. Because of that work ethic, of the snake oil show and Wild West shows, it went into this, and you watched this your whole life so you feel when you go into it you know you have to work seven days. If you're going to do it half way, don't do it at all, I was taught. Is there an embarrassment of it? I don't know.

LISA: Whatever you do, whatever you do, you have the power. You have the power to change it.

GLORIA: I went to Spain to do a little movie, and they wanted me to be a Hopi spiritual mother. I said, "I'm not Hopi, and I'm not going to be a spiritual Hopi mother. But I'll sing a Kuna song." And they changed the whole thing around where I did a Kuna song written by a Spaniard. This all worked for me because I had the power to change it.

MURIELLE BORST: You gotta fight for your stuff. And I think that if one thing comes out of the conference it really should be that you need to fight for your stuff no matter what it is. I think that's one of the main things that I learned from Spiderwoman, other than the technique, that you need to fight. And you know what? Maybe you won't work. So what? You gotta make your own stuff. You gotta go in there. You know there's a thing called the glass ceiling that happens in corporate America? With Native people, it's the buckskin ceiling, and the thing is you got to tear it down, jack it down and go through it and go "laaa," because it's the only way it's going to work. You have to go against the norm because we are the counter culture. Native people are the counter culture, and when the mainstream likes it, you have to worry.

LISA: You have to worry. [*audience laughter*]

GLORIA: But you have to say, okay, but I have to stay in control of this always. I always have to stay in control of this. So that means that you figure out financial ways to stay in control of it, always, and when you go into mainstream, you go with your lawyers. Indians are good with the lawyers. You go in with your lawyers. You go in with your corporate tribe, and you go in and you do it.

AUDIENCE MEMBER: Well it's not really a question, but we're coming to a close and before you all leave... I told Muriel the story of how Spiderwoman began to affect me. But I just want to say that I appreciate so much everything you ladies have done for the conference, for Miami University, and the theater because you broke open the doors that allowed the rest of us to express ourselves in the way we needed to. For instance, a problem that many people have with my play is that it didn't 100% follow the Western format, and if I was going to follow Western format, then I needed to stay with Western format. You fight that when you're in theater because you're always in university settings, and you're always having to justify and answer questions and legitimize or take somebody down this long spiritual journey that shows that you fit the stereotype that they walked in the door with. And you and the women who have come from you have allowed us to say, "I don't have to fit your mold. Thank you, no, thank you. I'm doing what I want. If you don't like it, that's your problem." And we don't usually say it that way, but it's allowed us to be comfortable with how we're represented, using our art to represent stories that have come from our roots and our sisters and our mothers and our grandmothers and our grandfathers and all the way down taking it all the way down.

So often we see ourselves completely alone and completely scary, swimming in the center of a lake when you only know how to dog paddle. Reading about you, and different things that have been written about you, just knowing that you existed and you were out there, made it easier for me to keep acting and to keep doing this. And I just wanted to say that I appreciate it so much, and Murielle and Monique, you guys, you know I include you within that.

AUDIENCE MEMBER: I'm a mother. I have three daughters and six granddaughters, and everybody does some version of writing, acting, or whatever. If I write a piece, the actors are my daughters and my granddaughters. You guys talk about a lot about fighting amongst each other and arguing with other, so how do you keep working together? [*audience laughter*]

LISA: It ain't easy! I think the first thing is technique. We have a technique in theater. As an actor, you are acting, and even if things are personal stories we are performing, we are still actors acting. We had a big fight right before a show once, like a real hair-tearing thing, and the stage managers said, "Time to go on stage." (*clap!*) We were acting. I don't know how the hell we did it. But we have a technique. That's the first thing you learn. You're acting!

MURIEL: When I started Spiderwoman, I came from another group that I started. I started like three or four groups, looking for this idea of how to work on stories. There were three of us, again, but they were radical women. One woman just came out, one woman was a Weather Woman (from, remember, the sixties, the Weather Men?), and me, the Indian. And two of us did not get along. We were the same age, and we were born exactly a month apart. We fought consistently. We had a big fight, too. That whole thing, the clown, is my story. It actually happened. And I was the one going "hee." So we managed to patch it up, but we were still like siblings. There was a point in the piece that we did where I said, "I love you." That night we were on stage and, you know, I told her I loved her, and when we got off, she said, "You're such a phony. You don't love me. You're such a phony." And I was so shocked. I said, "I was acting!" [*audience laughter*] And, you know, it dawned on me that she wasn't acting. What do you do with that? You keep on going back to A. You never advance if one doesn't have any technique at all. So then at that point I realized that I really had to find a group of women, because that's what I was interested in, that really had some technique. That's what I started to look for when I started to look for other women to start Spiderwoman. My sisters were the best because they were both in theater.

LISA: We were phonies.

GLORIA: And we were all three phonies. [*audience laughter*]

AUDIENCE MEMBER: I think this one is for Lisa, although it's for everybody. I read an interview that was from a few years ago. This is going into technique again. I believe it was you who said that my writer artist is not my actor artist. I'm kind of like that too, I find. I used to beat myself up because I couldn't remember anything I wrote, so it was really empowering to me that I believe you were commenting on the same thing. I was wondering if you wanted to articulate at all what you think is the difference between the writer and the actor in you?

LISA: Yeah, in me? When I started to write I was surprised as a writer. I look at this material that's coming up to me, and then as I wrote sometimes I would stick to what had really happened, but sometimes I was...I would get ideas that never happened at all. Fantasy is what my niece [Murielle] was speaking of before. One thing would form with another on another level, which I had never done. It was fantasy, and I just allowed it to take its place. When I had to act that, I had to use all of my acting technique about who, when, why, where. Who am I? Where? What do I want? What do I do to get what I want? All those three separate things. The real truth was that it was fantasy. I had created something that understandably could have happened but never did. So that was one thing I acknowledged that I let that stay there, and I had to go at it as an actor. What do I really want from this person, or what do I want to really happen in this room? And that's what makes me an actor.

AUDIENCE MEMBER: Yeah, I studied with Uta, too.

LISA: You studied with Uta, too? I don't care if people don't like her. I love her. They all have seemed to share the technique. You write a story, whether it's true, a story that happened to you, or a made-up story. That's the story. Your story's ended. You have it, and then you approach it as an actor. But you have the advantage if it's your story of knowing all the emotional things. The other stories that you wrote, you have to add more to it, even if you did write it because maybe you didn't really experience it, but you still approach it as an actor with all those trimmings.

GLORIA: And it is funny because sometimes the actor is informing the writer, and then sometimes the writer is informing the actor.

MURIEL: I think there is big difference between if you are an actor and given a role from a playwright. It's quite different. That's really quite different than if you were writing for yourself. Just doing *Red Mother* with Murielle here and my daughter says to me, "Oh, it's really nice, Mom. It's very beautifully written. We're going to have to do something about that. [*audience laughter*]. It's so well written I can't do anything with this." I was going through the same process before she came in—all these beautiful words, but how do you act those? What did I write? It wasn't the actor informing. I was just writing, and so what happened? I stopped myself, and so when I gave it to her and I gave it to the director, it was like it's there. So she got out her pencil and she went zip zip zip zip zip. I had to start fighting for a couple of months there for something that I wanted to hold on to.

MURIELLE: I do I agree with that; like, if you do, like, stage readings and a playwright gives you something. A lot of times, you know, a lot of these actors get in and they say, "Well, I think you should change this and this and this." I always say, it's not your job to rewrite this. It's your job to act it.

LISA: That's right. It's for the playwright.

MURIEL: It's for the playwright.

LISA: If you're working with playwrights, it's totally different. It's different.

MURIEL: Well, that's different. She said something you wrote, right. Something you wrote yourself, so not taking from the playwright.

LISA: There's confusion going around. You have to respect the playwright. He wrote, she wrote it that way. You cannot change that. You can change how you get what you want. That's up to you.

GLORIA: You can't change it. You can't change it if the writer's in the room.

MURIEL: No, not in the room. You can ask a question. I heard movie directors say they took that, they took that story and they change it and the writer says, I don't know that story. You know.

GLORIA: The movies they do it, there; they're rotten in the movies, but you can make a lot of money, but you know.

AUDIENCE MEMBER: So do you two, Gloria and Lisa, do you two, at some point, give in to Muriel? For that control, as a third eye?

LISA: Do you mean as a director?

GLORIA: I do.

LISA: Of course.

AUDIENCE MEMBER: Does she take the red pencil, so to speak?

LISA: She certainly does to me.

GLORIA: Originally when we started Spiderwoman, we brought in our own stories, and we said it was an ensemble. Everybody was the same status, and Muriel would come in and put the stories in place. It was very difficult to change our precious words. It's very difficult. And so we gave in to some degree. And there was like a third eye, or she would take three different stories and mix them together. It's very difficult if you have an idea in mind and someone comes in and takes a word out that changes the whole idea of the story.

MURIEL: That's not true.

GLORIA: You have to fight to keep it that idea.

LISA: Muriel at one time called herself the third eye, the final eye. She was not called the director. She was the final eye, and that meant that if she came to you and said, "Look, we're gonna take this sequence out."

She says I fought with her, but I don't remember that. I thought I was a really good person at taking direction. [*audience laughter*]

MURIEL: It's so hard, you know? Yes, I was the final eye, the third eye, but I came in with the vision. Because I came in with the vision, it was hard to say that there were other directors. And we tried to have other directors, and it didn't work...

And so what happens when somebody says that they have this idea? You look at the idea and they say they want to do this and this and this with it. You say, "Fine," and then my job is to take it and to make it part of the whole, because I am the final eye. You see it from far away, that it's *this,* so sometimes this has to be altered. And when this is altered, it's not the individual we're talking about. It's that all of this adds to *this.*

GLORIA: What we wrote in the first place—we all had an idea on the subject, and we wrote concerning that subject. Usually it had something to do with what was going on. It wasn't like something would come in that had nothing to do with the idea away from *Persistence of Memory*. Something had to have some core of the idea of *Persistence of Memory* so that when that little story was put in, it filled the idea of the story. There are many, many, many different kinds of directors. Some directors come in and they tell you what to do, and some of them say to do what you want to do. So this whole ensemble, we started on a different premise. We all had different ideas of what we wanted to do, I think.

LISA: And that was also interesting because when we started out, we had different women, and each one of us had different ideas on, oh, many subjects. To take all of that and put it into one piece with all these different sizes, a hexagon type of piece—putting it all in that this person feels this way, that person feels that way. The interesting thing to me is to find the connections, all the connections. How do they segue? Where do they go? That to me is interesting. How does it meld? Then you start looking for the layers, the different layers, and then you start pulling it out there, the layer out there, or pulling it out here to get the whole feeling of it. That to me is a huge puzzle when you're working like this.

MURIEL: So, I guess to clear up what she's saying. It's like it's editorial. It's editing really. It's editing on a big scale, so when you talk about film editing, or you talk about writing editing, that's what it is. It's really editing. It's taking out with the same focus at the end, the same vision at the end, but you're editorializing what can go in and what can't. Editorialize is a terrible word, but that's the word. That's the word. That's the most academic word to find so it's not so vague. It's editorializing to get to the main point.

GLORIA: But sometimes it doesn't work at all. A lot of women we didn't work with or no longer work with had whole different concepts of what they wanted to say and how they wanted to say it. We couldn't work with them. They're no longer with the group because they had to start their own group. They had other concepts, so they started their own group.

LISA: Like Split Britches.[8]

GLORIA: But we couldn't work with them.

LISA: Split Britches was a part of us...They really wanted to do lesbian theater...which is wonderful!

MONIQUE MOJICA: I just had a thought on this comment about the writer and the storyteller. When you're talking about editing and the difference between

---

[8] The Split Britches Lesbian Feminist Theatre Company was founded by one-time members of Spiderwoman Theater. http://www.splitbritches.com/.

director and third eye and final eye. What Muriel does in my experience with working with her is kind of become all of the above. That role that the dramaturg would play in conventional theater, Muriel does that also as you go along so that's the red pen and why we don't have anything to do with that process—because usually that's between the playwright and the dramaturg. But if we're the playwrights and the actors, Muriel does that, too, and she kind of takes up all that space with her big red pen.

MURIELLE BORST: Everyone was so shocked that I asked my mother to dramaturg a novel and to do a whole novel, but she used the same techniques of Spiderwoman, and she used the same red pencil.

MONIQUE MOJICA: But also what I think is unique about the way that Muriel works with actors is that she also helps to generate the material. Right? So, it's not just bringing her your pieces of paper and then gone. She's there to get the story out, and if it's not coming out, what's wrong with it and what layer is missing and what dynamic is not working right?

GLORIA: More is better than less, and that's what she always says.

MURIEL: And then you, then you take it out. Yeah. More is better than less. Come with more because then I can take it out. Come with less, I can't help you. If you give me two pages and expect an eight-page play, we both have to do work, and if you have twenty pages, we can cut it down to eight.

MURIELLE: You have to come in knowing that you have let it go.

GLORIA: Yeah, yeah you have to come in knowing you have to let it go.

LISA: You might have to let it go.

ANN HAUGO: Thank you, Spiderwoman Theater!

## Spiderwoman Theater's Legacy[1]

*Murielle Borst*

Thank you, Ann Haugo, for that introduction. As Ann said, my name is Murielle Borst. I did my undergraduate studies at Long Island University, but I did my internship with Spiderwoman Theater. I could have done it at Oxford or I could have done it in Italy or with the National Shakespeare Company in New York, but I decided to do it with my family. I felt if I could survive that, I could survive anything [*audience laughter*], and I learned a lot. I learned about technique, and this technique is what I want to emphasize in talking about Spiderwoman's legacy—the technique through which they combine storytelling, acting, and writing to create their kind of theater. I've interviewed each one of these women individually and collectively over the years, and I spent ten years of my life before then, too, living within family stories and theater stories. When I interviewed the three ladies—I tried not to think of them as my aunts and my mother, which is easy to do when they start to talk about Spiderwoman Theater—I really wanted to know how they worked and how they brought together European concepts and Native concepts and European civilizations and Native civilizations.

One of the first things to talk about is the oral tradition and how important it is. If you can say that in Western civilizations storytelling started with Greece, then I can say that storytelling started here in the Native country on Turtle Island. I think of Native people as a civilization. Storytelling is an Indigenous art form. In European cultures, with their kings, queens, and emperors and with their physicians and their actors, they reached out to the people, they reached people through storytelling. In Native culture storytelling is extremely important. In Native communities we have our leaders, our medicine people, and then we have our storytellers. The storytellers are the rememberers. They are the ones who pass on the oral traditions and who pass on the oral history. So if we take oral history as seriously as written history, then we say this is something that we need to do as scholars, to collect all their stories together across the United States. That has been my work for the last ten years, trying to put this together and compare Native storytelling techniques to European techniques.

One of the main sources of the oral traditions in my family is my grandmother, who was a storyteller. I bring it up because my daughter was looking at the *Prince of Egypt*. She was looking at it and she knew all the stories. Now, I don't go to Sunday school and neither does my daughter, yet she knew all the Bible stories. I said, "Where did you learn that?" And she said that my Aunt Gloria took her to see the *Prince of Egypt*. She knew all the background to all the stories. Then she asked me, "And how do you know all the stories?" and I said, "My grandmother taught me all the Bible stories." So I can tell you about Moses and the plagues and every Ten Commandment. When Easter came, it was great because Grandma would go into full swing. Bible stories were used as a basis in my family because of their Southern background and their sometime Christian influence.

Why do I bring this up? Because storytelling is storytelling, no matter what the subject is, from Bible stories to creation stories. It is the basis of the craft of theater. Storytelling is a key aspect of Spiderwoman's technique, whether traditional or non-traditional. I grew up not only with storytelling from my grandmother but also watching the technique of sharing stories with Spiderwoman in rehearsal. Telling the story and then

[1] Ms. Borst's unscripted talk about the legacy of Spiderwoman Theater was recorded, transcribed, and then edited, but the flavor of her own performance of storytelling and stand-up comedy has probably been sacrificed to retain her informed comments about technique.

taking the story and having another tell it her way. This technique was used with several topics, such as violence and women, the sexual power men have over women, and romance. These techniques were used in three specific plays that I talk about later, but they can be used in developing any theater piece to get to the core or the root of emotion. And when I talk about storytelling, especially with Spiderwoman Theater, I also inevitably talk about feminism, about "herstory" versus history.

I first saw the development of their technique in *Women In Violence*, Spiderwoman's first piece. I was only seven or eight years old. It was the 70s, and it was in the bottom of the West Bank Theatre. Everybody was sitting in a circle. There was Aunt Elizabeth, there was Aunt Gloria, there was my mother and two other women who were in at the beginning of Spiderwoman, and it was a huge studio. Everyone started talking about men and violence and why violence happens to women. All these stories started to come to them, and each, individually, of these women started to tell their story. The one I remember most was about cat calls; they started talking about cat calls. Do you remember walking across the street and there was a cat call? So my mother got all the women up on their feet and said, "Okay, now let's act like all the men." So they started to throw things at her and called her "Whore! Slut!" as she walked across the street. Then my mother turned around and said, "Okay! Now let's sing, 'We're wishing, we're wishing / For the one I love.'" And they all said, "Jeeez," like that, and they turned around, and a man was put in the women's position. I always go back to this technique. I always go back to Spiderwoman. I always go back to the source. I always go back to the core.

I was working with Shakespeare, working with *The Tempest*, and was sitting in as a Native consultant with a director who really wanted to put Native influence and dance into this piece. A lot of the actors weren't getting the story and were having trouble with the syntax, so she said, "Is there anything you can do to you get them going?" So I sat them around in a circle, and I had them start talking about the core of *The Tempest*. We were talking about Prospero's world, and we started to talk, and everyone talked about their individual ambitions, and then I told them to get up from what they were talking about. They got up on their feet and looked at our particular production, and everyone got it, because we already had an idea of this technique, and we got up and started doing it, and then the words started to come easier for the actors.

I also used this technique when I was working on my first book. My mother was helping me edit this book, and I thought I should read parts of my book aloud, but she said, "No, you have to *listen* to it." So *she* read *my* book to *me*, so I was able to hear the dialogue in someone else's voice. I asked her later, "Where did that come from? Did you create it?" She said it really had come out of feminism, herstory versus history. A lot of women told stories, they knew stories, but they never got to hear their *own* stories. And from there, from the feminist movement, from telling women to get up and tell a story, came the exercise that I was taught. Someone goes up and tells a story; another person comes up, and they take something from that story and they add a piece to it, which is their favorite part of the story. They tell someone else to come up, and the third person comes up and tells a little piece of that story. Then there's the fourth person, and then they all go in movement and the person who wrote the story sits there and looks at their story in four dimensions. And this is storytelling, this is Native storytelling, but taking it and putting it into a modern form.

There are three Spiderwoman plays that have been great influences on my work: *Women and Violence, Lysistrata Numbah*, and *A Night of Disgusting Songs and Pukey Images*. The reason they are great influences is partly that I grew up when they were being written and being produced. It was in the height of feminism. Women and violence, it wasn't spoken about. There were things that weren't spoken about. Spiderwoman's *Women and Violence* gave women permission to react to violence among themselves. You saw that it was okay for men to tell dirty jokes about women, but it wasn't okay to tell a dirty joke about men. It was a danger still. Women were getting raped, women were getting beaten, but no one was talking about it out loud. *Lysistrata Numbah* was about sex and control. *A Night of Disgusting Songs and Pukey Images* was about romance. My mother said she thought it was important to talk about romance, for she felt it was a trap for women. Romance was an illusion. For me *A Night of Disgusting Songs and Pukey Images* made it okay to think outside the box because that particular play was Spiderwoman's brand of musical theater since it was a musical but not in the standard sense. You didn't have to think in the norm of musical comedy or musical theater.

My mother, Muriel, talks about a formula: Storytelling x Acting=Theater. She has an organic explanation of the formula: A tree trunk grows straight; the branches veer off but the trunk continues the journey. The creative process, whatever you get, you get organically. That's the only way to talk about this creative process. It's the organic continuity, the kernel, the source, the objective of the work. A harmony that comes together from single notes that start in different places. There are different sides to the same story. A three-part harmony worked into one voice to make a chorus. Three voices going and then get to one voice—but anything can happen during the process. It looks simple like Native beadwork, just as all Native process is thought of simplistic but is not. In Native thought and European thought processes both minds are complex, both are trying to get to the common goal. There is sound, there is movement, there is gesture, and then there is building on it and making it three-dimensional. We're back to the three-part harmony and the original formula, Storytelling x Acting=Theater.

And we talk about arcs. My mother hates to work in arcs, but I do. I have my arc, because I write from my arc, because I believe Native storytelling has an arc, because all storytelling has an arc if you want to compare Native and European civilizations. In the academy they base all of this on Euripides and teach about arcs: there is the comic arc, there is the tragic arc, we got this from the Greeks. But I say, No, this is our Native arc, and we didn't get it from the Greeks; we have an arc, but it doesn't look like everybody else's arc. We sometimes start with the arc up here, and then we go down this way, and they say, "Do you have an end?" And I say, "Oh, yeah, we'll have to think about it, let me go to a different key." And that is how it is organically formed, because it is formed in the same way if you look at it. It is the same when they talk about Greek myths. If you can compare a Greek myth and you compare Native myth, you'll come up with the same outcome with the same heroines, the same villains. I do believe that. It's all a three-part harmony. It's different sides of the same story. Greek chorus. There's the three sides of same story. Three people working at the same time. The same time, the same way. In Native storytelling, there are three stories. You have continuity and you have creative arc, each coming to the same objective. I believe a theater piece that works is like a journey on a ship. The actors or storytellers are the shipmates, the director the captain, but the playwright is god. And the currents are the outer voices that stir the ship to get to the right position. They all need to be in unison. The ensemble. They all need to work together. To work in one voice. One harmony. One movement. So it starts with a journey and listening to different stories to get to the final journey. It doesn't have to be linear. You can start from A, you can start from C, but you need to get to D. This is what she means when my mother says, "Theater is storytelling on an epic scale."

The one question I asked all three of the ladies at different times is, How does one take this process and use it for a standard play? When I interviewed Aunt Lisa, we talked about how as an actor she got to a character, what technique she used to get to a character, and how her sense memory reaches so far back. With my aunt, we always had a relationship where I went to her about my work, so I was able to create an oral history of what she told me—how it was with acting. We both studied acting with the same teachers, we both studied at Herbert Bergdorf Studios. Then I was talking with Aunt Gloria and asked her about the process: "When you take this particular process, how do you use it with another technique? Does it ever get confusing?" She was working on *Macbeth*. We had a discussion, and she said that she was using all of these things from the Actor's Studio, where she had studied, to do the monologue. But she realized that she didn't have to imagine spirits. She didn't have to really think about it. She used all that from her center organically to bring the scene home. She understood what it meant, spiritually, which is the most important thing about *Macbeth*. She did not have to follow a literal way of thinking; clinical acting technique and the Spiderwoman technique both work from the inside out.

I asked my mother, Muriel Miguel, who worked with the Open Theater and studied the Laban Technique, "What would you do if you were to play Blanche Dubois, from *A Streetcar Named Desire*? What would be your first work?" Standard: she would read the work, get it down. Then she gets the Laban of the character. She identifies the movement from heaviness to the lightness, the Laban of movement. A rhythmic voice has them floating and then from there, and that is the beat, standardizing, there's a beat, which is always technical, how you get to the beat. She gets into the character's head and into her body. And then she puts in the personal stories on the next layer. She said it was like Native bead work. It looks very simple, but when you look at it more closely it has all these different layers that go in and out and zig zag. And then she gets the moment-to-moment of the personal stories of this character. The Native method is no different than the European method: both can be used; both are working in layers for the actor; both are looking for organic continuity; both are looking for the kernel, the source, the objective. So she, my Aunt Lisa, and my Aunt Gloria, they all get to the same place, to the core of the story and the core of the character. European and Native methods are similar but use different terminologies. As in creating their own work, they use the same technique when acting in another play. I mean, is it important that you know who your great-grandfather is when you are studying Ibsen? Maybe not, but it helps. You never know where you might strike gold. The personal story is the most important at times, other than the text.

And that brings me to the techniques of writing and of developing your own piece. There is storytelling, there is acting, there is writing, and that makes the theater piece. I'd also like to talk a little bit about *More Than Feathers and Beads*, my one-woman show, and how I was taught to write with Spiderwoman. I do not write in first person at all. I don't take personal stories and I don't tell my own personal stories. That's not how I work. I'm interested in characterization, taking a character and changing the person around a thousand different ways, and then making a completely different character of two or three or four fictional people. I always work in fours for some reason. So I take that, and I develop it.

When I did my one-woman show, there were three one-woman shows that had a huge influence on me. The first one is *My Sister Ate Dirt*, a musical comedy written by Lisa Mayo. Again Spiderwoman taught me about how you can get somewhere through music and telling a tale to music in the musical theater genre. Another very important piece was *Jealousy*, which my Aunt Gloria Miguel wrote. She told me, when I talked to her later about it, she started with three lights of different colors and within these lights she had different feelings that went into these lights. Ironically, she told me the colors of these lights were green, red, and blue, the colors I used for my characters for the one-woman show, and I didn't know that until I got into the conversation with her. And then the third one-woman show is *Hot 'n' Soft* by Muriel Miguel, where she took coyote stories and made them into erotica, teaching me you can take stories and flip them around and change them. That is the idea of storytelling, to take the story and then tell it your way. And I'll add a fourth important piece, *Princess Pocahontas and the Blue Spots*. I loved the idea that my cousin Monique Mojica didn't use her personal stories; she took characterizations of different women, and she performed them on stage using the method of storyweaving.

So when I developed *More Than Feathers and Beads*, it was these plays that influenced where I wanted to go. I asked Muriel Miguel to direct it so I would have that flavor of something that was off center, off the norm and yet within the standard of my text. Most importantly, what I learned form these pieces was that I had the permission to ask "why" on certain things, on the incest, the rape, the racism, not only as a woman but as a Native person and Native mother living in this country. Storytelling is a sacred gift. A lot of times we are the mirrors to the communities. Spiderwoman gave me that permission to ask questions, to ask the whys, to speak within the silence, and to take no prisoners when it comes to the vision of your work.

When I became a writer, fantasy for some reason spoke to me. I realized that I first learned to write in the genre of fantasy from Spiderwoman actually, which always surprises them. My first opportunity to work in fantasy was in their *Power Pipes* when I interned for the national tour. It was basically about goddesses and deities on stage. I wrote a piece called *Windhorse the Spirit Warrior*. I wasn't sure how to get there. So I called up Aunt Lisa, and I said, "Well, I have no idea how to do this piece. I don't know how I'm going to do it. I don't know where to start." So she said, "O.K., let's get it down to, Have you had a dream recently?" And I said, "Yes." "What did you dream about?" "I dreamed I was in this room," and I gave her the colors, "and I was with all these dead people and all these spirits. They were all talking to me, and they all said you are a warrior." And she said, "O.K., take it from that. Write that dream down and then you elaborate on it." And from that technique, I was able to elaborate on that dream, and from that came my character in the play, and I was able to write it from that dream, from the center and the core of myself. And, so I've always taken that technique: whether it's a song or, usually, a dream, I take it and I build on it as a writer. One of the biggest influences was *Princess Pocahontas*, as I said; my cousin was the first to actually talk or write about her in my family.

I would like to read some of my writing today since Spiderwoman is my influence also outside of theater. Let me tell you a little bit about this first piece. Recently when the movie *The New World* came out (New Line Cinema, 2005), I was beyond appalled to say the least. To say I hated it was an understatement. But I needed to do something. I thought I could either get naked in front of The Gap or the movie theater...but instead of getting arrested, I wrote a piece after I had a dream about Pocahontas. I wrote about her story, not history. I made up this story the same as the movie made it up, but I made Pocahontas ambitious. I investigated the "what if?" Always work with the "what if." What if Pocahontas was no-good, ambitious, wanted trade, and wanted colonization? But not a victim. Like Cleopatra when she had to deal with the Romans. But at the end of Pocahontas's journey there is downfall. Ambition is a human quality. I felt that she is dehumanized because she is made so unearthly, pure, untouchable, the stoic virgin...almost an idiot. This is my take on her, a short story called "The Death of Pocahontas."

*(Reading from "Death of Pocahontas")*

The ship was smelly of the whites' unwashed bodies but there was one who stood out like no other. Captain Samuel Argall. Not a young man, a man of middle years into maturity. Not smelly like a wet dog like most whites, dark brooding eyes, black graying hair neatly tied in a nap at his neck. A fine long nose, a strong chin, his teeth straight, not rotten. Clean shaven not bearded. A single pearl earring. A sword on the hilt of his hip. Not a handsome man but appealing. Even attractive for a white. I knew he had no problem getting any woman he wanted. And I knew that was my maneuver with him. His dark eyes blazed into mine. Not soft eyes but smart eyes. I touched his barriers with my mind as all Star Carriers could. Not a weak soul but an ambitious one. I meekly lowered my eyes and trembled my lips, knowing that this type of man liked a damsel that he could save, but also a woman who had intellect. That was what he longed for and craved most of all.

I put my hand out to him, as it was deemed proper for high ladies to do. It was then I created the myth of myself, the legend, the stoic lie.

"My Great Lord, I am the Princess Pocahontas, the daughter of the great king Powahatan. My father is a mighty king. His wealth is beyond any in the realm. Take me to the fort, my Great Lord, and the rewards shall be thus of good and plenty from him for me."

Samuel bowed low as one from a lower rank did to any from royal blood and kissed my hand.

"My good Princess, I am no great lord or lordling. I am a common sailor that comes to this fair land under the laws of King James of England. Please, my good lady, let me see what can be found for comfort among the gruff men on this ship, for the journey is long till we reach the fort."

He then escorted me to his lower quarters. We ate the pitiful rations together. We drank red liquid from a goblet of wood. It was a smelly and foul-tasting drink, but I had heard of it from John Smith. I knew it was proper to sip the drink evenly, even though he drank his down quickly.

We talked politely; I saw his brows rise at how well I spoke the language and knew his English history. I mostly listened and gauged the man before me. He told me of his wife and children back in his home. I also had seen the loneliness of a man out at sea far too long without a female companion on his ship. I found him intriguing—and I found myself in a debate with him about the reasons the English were here. Debate was not a new thing to me since I had done with my father and older brothers all of my life.

"You must understand King James seeks to better the world, my good lady. To embrace all nations and make them into one."

"But, good sir, do the English embrace? I think not. Control is the word you seek. Are you not a student of war? Those who come from your teachings do not come to embrace. Am I wrong, my good sir? "

He made a small, real laugh for the first time. A true smile of enjoyment came to his frowned lips.

"But, Princess, you must understand that without the might of the sword there is no justice at all. Blood unites all men."

"And women?" I said with a cocked brow. He cocked his brow back at me sternly.

"I have seen my fair share of ambitious women, my good lady. There are no ambitious men without ambitious women. Women and men are the same in many ways."

"But different…at least bodily," I said very low and precise.

He cleared his throat nervously and swallowed as if there was not enough air in the rocking cabin. He shifted in his chair. I knew I had him.

"And the world, my good sir? What of the world you seek?"

"Yes, fortunes favor the bold, if I may quote from

my student teachings of war in your presence," he said in amusement and hand over his heart in jest. I tossed my head back and laughed.

"Ah, my good sir, are you the bold that this fortune shall seek? Is that not why you saved me so heroically from my father's enemies? To seek the good fortune it will reap? As any good knight would do for his king?"

Our eyes locked in understanding. I eased back in my seat and knew from his reaction that we could be on the same side.

"Let us understand one another: you have made yourselves into guests in our home who became very comfortable. Do I understand it? No, I do not. Do I respect it? Respect is another matter. But I can. If you are here to unite as you say, would it thus be favorable to all who were the first to unite those riches? The very first to take to your king from this fair land the goods of prosperity?"

He tilted his head and I knew I had all of his attention: "Continue, Princess."

I sipped the red liquid and licked the flame tasting liquor from my lip. I saw the cords on his throat tighten. I knew that for a man such as himself this talk was just as arousing as foreplay. I folded my hands on my lap.

"It is simple, my good sir. The first to take the gold to your king is the first to garner the reward."

"Gold? There is none here. We have plundered many here and found none."

I made a giggle that turned into a deep, throaty laugh. I saw the cords go tighter to his throat. "What I can provide can turn into gold, my good captain. You have the ship to deliver it to your king. We have the goods of trade. Isn't your very harbor of the great England just like the one here? We will provide, and you shall sail it away. Can it not be done, my good Samuel?"

I shrugged and turned my head, making believe I was no longer interested in these intrigues with him when he gave me no outward reaction.

"Maybe I sought the wrong man for this purpose. Maybe it shall be another I seek when I arrive at the fort. Maybe one with common links such as yourself would not understand."

Then I leaned my body over the table that separated us.

"But are we all not servants to the common good of the worlds to come? Servants do reap just as many rewards, my good sir, do they not? Titles, are they not bought from good fortune in your English land? Maybe my studies of the English virtue are wrong."

I saw the intelligence gleam and glare into mine. He seized the handle of his wooden goblet as if grasping the future in his hand. I wasn't sure if I insulted him or charmed him.

"Yes, there is a way for it to be done. The Virginia Company."

He waved his hand in the air in a dismissal. "We will talk more on it in the morning."

I knew at that moment we met each other's destiny. He suddenly got up, but staggered from exhaustion. It was morning when I arrived on the ship and it now was late night.

"That is enough of this talk, my high lady. You are under my care and protection with oath and sword to the king. It is time for us to go to bed."

I laughed at him, and he gave me an exhausted look.

"Why do you laugh, my lady?"

"Do you not mean for me to go to bed, my good Samuel?"

He smiled that true smile once again at me. And took my hand in his.

"No, Princess, I never fault my words."

We exchanged smiles, and we became allied lovers that very night. The nightly dalliances were a small price to pay to forge the alliance needed.

In fantasy, one of the main things that I'm always interested in is ideas I get from Spiderwoman. I have spent plenty of time talking about human nature and hierarchy and manipulations. You know, if you look at the *Sopranos*, you see these characters in your communities a lot of times, you see them in any family, and I decided to go into dark fantasy at this moment. In this particular story I used my own traditional language, Kuna, and I took it from some of the traditional stories of Kuna Yala. Again I worked on the "What if?" What if Europe was called "The Three Kingdoms," and they came to this hemisphere during the height of civilization? What would happen? I made up long-lived races, you know, people who could live 500 years, and I developed these types of concepts to make an alternative universe. This particular piece was done when I hated all men in every form. It's called "The Betrayal." And I also based it on my four very good friends. Every year we go to the beach, sit in the sand, and we talk. And we notice that each one of us came from one of the four directions. One from the East, one from the West, one from the South, and one from the North. You know, like the good witches. So this is called "The Betrayal."

*(Reading from "The Betrayal")*

The Volcano Queen from under the Veiled Sea fell in love with the Shark Prince. They met every night on the island Nula Yala. The Volcano Queen got with his child, but he had to return to his wife. The Volcano Queen sought the oldest, the albino Jaguar who knew the magic of the ancient appliqué. She asked him for a special weave to get her lover from his wife. Jaguar told her to think of him day and night and weave a tapestry of his face from layers of cloth. For nine months she weaved the tapestry and thought of nothing but the Shark Prince. He left his wife and returned to her. When the Volcano Queen gave birth, the wife of the Shark Prince came. She was the great enchantress, Oloburdili, from the underwater invisible island. She threw her own appliqué made from blood of sorrow and betrayal. It seeped inside the girl child. She put a curse on the Volcano Queen's female bloodline. All of her female line would fall in love and from that love would come a great betrayal. The Volcano Queen took her child and brought her to Nula Yala. She placed her as the Eastern Empress. The Volcano Queen gave her intelligence. So the curse would not come to pass. But every generation a great love came to an Eastern Empress. In every generation they seek to be free. This all happened thousands of moons ago, our great grandmothers say.

—From the Oral History of the Nula Yala

*The Nula Yala Empire in the year of the XXII$^{th}$ Dynasty of the Eastern Empresses*

The azure water of the Veiled Sea shined like cut obsidian, and the night sky black as multi-layered velvet. The heated air softly breezed through the several lighted cities by the bay harbor. The palm trees swayed, the monkeys screeched, the jaguars roared from the rainforest. The pink dolphins jumped in the water. A cry of rejoicing came from the harbor cities. From the four-story cliff citadel came the scream of a tortured man inside the dungeon, the Eastern Citadel that housed the Great Eastern Empress OloNelee. The citadel carved from red bloodstone and embossed in an appliqué of gems. The citadel representing the Four Sisters of creation, the daughters of Palewala.

The Empress OloNelee stood under the body of the suffering man in the torture chamber. Rivulets of red poured down his naked body, his hands and feet tied in back of him as he hung down from the rafter.

She grabbed him by his bloodied hair, her long black nails digging into his skin, her golden eyes furious. His head hung unconsciousness. She motioned for her guards; they rubbed the sea salt into his ripped, open genitals; and he wailed.

"How long?" she demanded.

"A-a century...My...Great One."

She sliced the knife across the veins of his throat; the hot blood made jets in the air. She drove the knife in a single stroke down to his loins, his entrails spilling onto the cobbled dungeon floor, and the water rats ate his remains.

The next thing I would like to read to you also has a great Spiderwoman influence. I spent six years of my life writing a book, writing a series called *Starcarrier Series*. It started as a historical novel and turned into a fantasy series, but I got these things from being a Southern Indian and collecting these stories from my family, from my grandmother, from my Aunt Gloria, from my mother, from my Aunt Elizabeth. I went to Westmorland, Virginia, and I spent time down there, and I got a feeling of what it means to be a Southern Indian rather than a City Indian, and I took that and developed, again, a "What if." The main "What if" is, What if Indians have money? I've spent a lot of time with Native people who think when they get money, things are going to be better. They don't realize that when you move into the upper classes, when you become upper-middle class or whatever, you still come up with the same problems. This particular selection is at the end of my book. It is based loosely on a story my Aunt Gloria gave me a very long time ago that I took and wrote in a different way. I wanted the Indian to win, I wanted the Indian to leave in triumph, and I wanted the Indian to be the one that persevered at the end. It is based on my Aunt's Indian name, Moon Woman, who has now come to the Earth and is a great Oracle, but she is being punished. She, the great oracle, is now trapped in a human body. This is after she goes to France and she adopts another Indian child and she goes away. It is sort of a creation story. [Ms. Borst then read from her "Indian Manor" but the excerpt has not been included here.]

This last thing I would like to do is a small piece that I wrote last night after the discussion I had with my cousin Monique about showing how you take all of these techniques and put them together on your feet. It is five minutes. The title is "A Valentine to My Grandmother," story by Murielle Borst and song by Monique Mojica. It starts with a song by Sam Cooke, "A Change Is Gonna Come."

A Valentine to My Grandmother

MONIQUE (*Singing "A Change Is Gonna Come"*)
I was born by the river
In a little tent
And just like the river
I've been running ever since

It's been a long long time coming
But I know a change gonna come
Oh, yes it will.

It's been too hard living
But I'm afraid to die
I don't know what's up there beyond the sky

It's been a long long time coming
But I know a change gonna come
Oh, yes it will.

Then I go to my brother
I say brother help me please
But he winds up knocking me
Back down on my knees

It's been a long long time coming
But I know a change gonna come
Oh, yes it will.

There's been times that I thought
I wouldn't last for long
But now I think I'm able to carry on

It's been a long long time coming
But I know a change is gonna come
Oh, yes it will.

MURIELLE
I fell to earth
I crashed
The otters took me to the river
The whale guided me to the land
I planted the seed
I made the hope
I made the first generation.

MONIQUE (*Singing*)
I was born by the river
In a little tent
And just like the river
I've been running ever since

BOTH (*Singing*)
It's been a long long time coming
But I know a change gonna come
Oh, yes it will.

MONIQUE
My name is Felicia Moore
I'm from Turtle Clan
I'm a medicine woman
I know the old medicine,
The medicine's been given to me by my great-, great-, great-grandmother, and her grandmother before her
I'm the last to know the old ways
Things are changing
Must run soon.
Don't know which way to go

MONIQUE (*Singing*)
I was born by the river
In a little tent
And just like the river
I've been running ever since

MURIELLE
My name is Elizabeth Moore Ashton
My mother came from Turtle Clan, the last midwife in these parts
My daddy's a slave master
I'm leaving these parts, war's over now
War had nothing to do with it, he was broke anyway
I'm going north, get married right
I'm going to get an educated man, that's what I'm going to do
Give my kin a good start.

BOTH (*Singing*)
It's been a long long time coming
But I know a change gonna come
Oh, yes it will.

MONIQUE
My name is Ellen Moore Ashton Spencer
I come from Turtle Clan
My great-grandmother was the last of the midwives in Virginia
I married a young man, a mighty powerful man
I hear voices in my head
In my mind's eye are voices from the other side, coming, changing

BOTH (*Singing*)
I was born by the river
In a little tent
And just like the river
I've been running ever since

It's been a long long time coming
But I know a change gonna come
Oh, yes it will.

BOTH
We are descendents from the river and the stars
We are the of the eternal Turtle Clan
We are the next rememberers
We carry the songs in our hearts
We carry the stories in our blood,
The hope in our souls
We are the past, the present, the future
Take this story and hear the hope.
Take this story and hear our voices of our nations.

MONIQUE
I was born by the river
In a little tent
And just like the river
I've been running ever since

MURIELLE
This to my aunts,
This is to my mother
This is to my great-grandmother
This is to those who will come after us
This is to my grandchildren
This is to my great-grandchildren
This is to Gloria Miguel, to Lisa Mayo, and to Muriel Miguel.

BOTH *(Singing traditional Native American vocables, Monique and Murielle gesture with their hands as they sing. They come to the same harmony together in song as they gesture to the right and left and then to the middle, to the audience.)*

# SECTION III: *Voices*

## Weaving the Rain: A New Play [excerpts][1]

*Dianne Yeahquo Reyner*

SYNOPSIS: The Two Crow family must unravel the wall of silences and secrets that prevent them from taking their place as a family. They are called to the hospital as the father is brought in by ambulance. These trips have become routine because of the father's physical deterioration from cirrhosis. However, this will be his last trip to the hospital.

Trapped in the waiting room, this family is also trapped by history and the choices they have made. Each person feels isolated and angry in the life they feel forced to lead. As the night progresses, they are guided by the spirit of the Old Man and the spirit of the oldest son, Roy. As the family begins to purge the poisons from their lives, they realize that they are never alone, and never forgotten. The family comes to understand that their survival is founded in the strength of the land and their culture.

CHARACTERS:

OLD MAN: Elderly man of indistinct age. Tall and slight of build. His clothes are old and ill fitting, seeming to be made for a much larger man. He wears a white, long-sleeved dress shirt buttoned to the neck, khaki slacks, and a mismatched sport coat. He should present the calm, dignified demeanor of a man comfortable in any situation.

MARGIE: Woman in her 60s. Conservatively dressed in muted colors. Her attire is fashionably outdated. She carries a Bible with her at all times, but it appears to be more of a prop than a comfort to her.

EVE: Thirty-four years old, well educated. Dressed in casual office attire. She is the middle child in the family and the only girl.

MICHAEL: Twenty-five years old, the youngest son in the family; he has never lived away from home. He maintains a childlike demeanor, making it hard to determine his age.

JOHN: Thirty-six years old, he is the oldest child in the family. His clothing is rumpled and hair is unkempt, but his demeanor does not reflect the same disinterest as his appearance.

ROY: Early twenties. Handsome, slight build, athletic. He dresses casual, but neat.

SCENE: An Indian Health Service (IHS) hospital waiting room.

TIME: Present

PLAYWRIGHT NOTE:

There are four songs written into this script: a mourning song, an honor song, a family song, and a song in celebration of children. Each tribal nation has its own version of these according to language, culture, and tradition. The location of the production should determine the song selection. Care should be used to guarantee permission is obtained. Songs often belong to a person, family, or community and should not be used without permission.

SETTING:

We are in a hospital waiting room. Furniture is worn, and the room reflects a sterile atmosphere. Two chairs are positioned in line at center stage; additional chairs of waiting room style; and newspapers are scattered atop two tables. At the start of the first excerpt, MARGIE has been onstage as EVE enters the waiting room; they are unaware of the OLD MAN who has been onstage since the play's opening.

[1] Color photos of the cast and final scene are included as a slide show on the DVD accompanying this book.

### *EXCERPT NO. 1*

Act One

EVE Okay, I'm here. What's up this time? Dad get a hangnail?

MARGIE Is that any way to greet your mother?

EVE You're right. I'm sorry.
*(EVE moves to take the seat next to her mother and gives a curt kiss.)*
Hello, Mother.

MARGIE I guess that's better. Where have you been? I've been calling and calling. They brought your father in here over an hour ago, and you were nowhere to be found.

EVE You know I had that meeting in D.C. We're trying to get funding for that new housing project. Now, what's going on with Dad?

MARGIE You'd know if you were where you were supposed to be instead of always running around.

EVE Mom, I just flew in. My office got hold of me the minute my plane landed. I haven't even been home yet.

MARGIE Well, there you go, off in Tim-buck-too, takin' care of everybody's business but your own.
*(MARGIE waves her hand in the air as if her point has been made.)* Must be nice. Coming and going without a care in the world. I have to be here, taking care of things. People depend on me.

EVE People depend on me too, Mom. I can't always be here.

MARGIE You don't have to *always* be here, but you should be here when you are needed.
*(MARGIE reaches into her purse and takes out a Kleenex. She begins dabbing invisible tears before lifting the Kleenex as if making an offering.)*
No one knows everything I have to put up with. Now you come in here and start picking a fight at a time like this.

EVE Mom. I am not trying to pick a fight. I am trying to find out what's going on. Okay? Now, why is Dad here?

MARGIE *(Regaining her composure)* Your father had an episode and they had to come get him.

EVE *(Distracted, EVE begins to look for papers in her briefcase.)* Episode? What does that mean? What kind of episode? Is he all right?

MARGIE Of course he's not all right. He wouldn't be here if he was all right now, would he?

EVE Mom! Please not now. I'm tired and I don't want to fight.

MARGIE You always fight. I think you live for it. Stubborn, just like your Dad.

EVE Please, don't compare me to Dad.

MARGIE Why not? You act like that's something to be ashamed of.

EVE I'm not ashamed. I just don't think we are anything alike. Let's talk about something else.

MARGIE The two of you are more alike than you think. That's why he always favors his baby girl.

EVE Mom, why is Dad here?

MARGIE Your Dad fell and I couldn't get him back into bed. That's all there is to it. I'm too old to be lifting anything heavy. Used to be I could do just about anything. The doctor told me I needed to be careful of my back. *(MARGIE sighs and begins speaking more to herself than EVE.)* I couldn't do it, couldn't even help him. I can't do anything anymore. I'm old, old and used up. (*Becoming angry*) It's a good thing Michael was with me. He didn't leave me all alone. Thank the good lord at least one of my children cares what happens to me. Michael was where you should have been. Not traipsing around the countryside.

EVE Here we go again. I wasn't traipsing around. Oh, never mind. He fell. What exactly does that mean? Is he hurt?

MARGIE Of course he's hurt. He wouldn't be here if he wasn't hurt now, would he? I swear; wasting all that money on a college education didn't make you any smarter, did it? You'd think...

EVE Fine! You're right, mother. You wanted me here; now I'm here. Are you going to tell me why, or should I find the doctor?

*(Enter JOHN)*

JOHN Hello, hello, hello. This must be the place. *(Laughing)* Sounds like home.

MARGIE John!
*(JOHN crosses to MARGIE as she reaches to embrace him. JOHN bends to kiss his mother.)*
Thank God you came. I've been so worried.

JOHN No need to worry about me. I'm at your beck and call. Heya, Sister. I thought you were off saving the planet or something.

EVE What, you farm your kids out again?

JOHN At least I got some kids.

*(EVE appears wounded by JOHN's remark.)*

MARGIE John, leave your sister alone.

JOHN *(Feeling appropriately rebuked, JOHN tries to redirect the conversation.)* So, how's the ol' man doing?

MARGIE Not good. He's...he's in a coma. The doctors say he'll be lucky if he is with us in the morning.
*(MARGIE expertly removes a tissue from her purse and begins to dab her eyes.)*
I don't know what I'm gonna do when...

EVE Wait a minute. What are you saying? When what?

JOHN *(Obviously uncomfortable by the news)* Ah, he'll be okay, Mom. You know he always pulls out of it. Last time it was what...a week before he came out of it? He's a tough old bird. I wouldn't worry too much about him. Like they say: "Only the good die young." *(JOHN begins laughing at his own joke.)*

EVE Oh, please. Who says that? You, and your buddies down at the Hide-a-Way? When are you going to grow up? Can't you see Mom is upset?

JOHN All right, all right already, geeze. It was just a joke. Don't get your feathers all ruffled up. I was just trying to lighten things up. You know, ease the tension. *(Checking his watch and looking for an excuse to leave)* Look, Mom, I'm sure he's fine. He always is.

MARGIE No, this time was different. 'Bout two o'clock he was getting up to watch his show. You know that show he likes to watch? The one with that woman judge...anyway, he was getting up. He got this really funny look on his face, like...Then his face got all white, and he just fell down. There was blood all over the bed. The doctor said it was because he was hemorrhaging inside. If it wasn't for Michael, I don't know what I would have done. He made the hospital send an ambulance. *(Angry)* It took those people an hour to get to the house. Your Dad could have died and they were driving around, lost in the country. Act like they know it all. Live in town and think they know everything. It just goes to show; they ain't as smart as they think they are. *(MARGIE begins talking to herself.)* Treat us like we're a buncha dummies, and they're the ones who are lost.

EVE Mom, why didn't you tell me all this was going on? You only told the office that he fell. I thought you were just overreacting again...

MARGIE I'm not telling the whole world my business. If you had been where you were supposed to be you would have known what happened.

EVE Jesus Christ! I was where I was supposed to be. *(Looking accusingly to JOHN)* I was working. How was I supposed to know this was going to happen? I'm not psychic, for God's sake.

*(OLD MAN stands up abruptly, disgusted. The family finally realizes that they have not been alone. He gathers his things before leaving the room.)*

MARGIE Lower your voice.

EVE I was only trying to say...

MARGIE Hush! You can't be taking the Lord's name in vain, little girl. You should be thanking him for making sure your father is still here.

EVE Thanking him, for what? For this?

JOHN Eve, come on. Just chill, will ya? *(Mocking EVE)* Can't you see Mom is upset? She doesn't need your attitude right now. So save it, okay?

EVE Attitude? What attitude? All I've tried to do since I got here is find out what happened to Dad.

JOHN Well, you found out. Mom just told you. So now what's your problem?

EVE No, John, she didn't tell me, she told you.

JOHN Me. You. What's the difference? You heard her, didn't you? *(JOHN jokingly reaches to pull EVE's ear.)* Clean your ears out, girl.

EVE Quit that, you moron.

JOHN Don't you worry about a thing, Mom. I got it all under control. I'll take care of everything. Where are they keeping him?

MARGIE He's in room 225.

JOHN I'll just go and check things out for you.

MARGIE They won't let anyone in right now. They chased Michael and me out. Said they had to do some tests. That doctor they brought in can hardly speak English. He's one of those foreigners the IHS brought in. Guess we don't rate a real doctor. I don't think he even knows what he's doing.

JOHN I'll go find out what's going on. You just relax, Mom. Ah, maybe I better call some people while I'm at it. Tell them what's happening. You got any money, Mom? I'm kinda short right now.

MARGIE *(Reaching for her purse)* Sure, honey. How much do you need? *(Pulling out a couple of bills from her wallet)*

JOHN That should do it for now. I'll bring your change back. *(Quickly pocketing the money)* Say, where is Michael?

MARGIE He's waiting outside Dad's room. I told him to stay there and make sure he kept an eye on those people. You have to watch them all the time or they won't do anything. Let your Dad just lay there.

JOHN Well, if Michael's got things covered I'm going to use the phone. I'll be back later. Don't you fret about a thing.

*(JOHN exits.)*

EVE You don't need to be giving him your money. You know what he's going to do with it.

MARGIE What I do with *my* money is *my* business.

EVE I just...*(Taking a deep breath)* At least don't get all upset about Dad. Everything is going to be fine. Just like before. In a day or two Dad will be back to raising cain with everyone. They have some fairly decent doctors here. They just got their degrees in a different country.

MARGIE Well, it's probably some type of Voo Doo medicine he's practicing, making us leave like that. *And*, he can't be much of a doctor if he's working in this place. I don't trust these doctors. People come in here and before you know it they're gone. You know that's just what happened to your Aunt Evelyn. Her daughter made her come in here for a check up, just because she was tired. Next thing you know... she's gone. Evelyn never came home again.

EVE Mom, Aunt Evelyn had to have open-heart surgery. All the arteries to her heart were blocked. When Peggy finally talked her into seeing the doctor it was too late. There wasn't anything they could do.

MARGIE Just don't you start thinking about putting me in here. Oh, you'd like that, wouldn't you? Get me out of your hair. Well, I might be old but I still get around just fine. I don't need no doctor poking around and stirring up trouble. I put my faith in the Lord. He'll take care of me just the way he always has.

EVE Sure, Mom. Just the way he always has.

MARGIE *(Missing the sarcasm in EVE's voice)* The only thing that gets me through all this is my faith. That's the one thing I have to hold on to. No one else around here seems to care about all the things I have to put up with. It's Job all over again.

EVE Oh please, you know that everyone cares about you.

MARGIE And, how would I know that? *(Pulling her wallet out of her purse)* You need to go down and get Michael something to eat. Poor thing hasn't eaten all day. He's been busy fooling with your Dad. *(Handing money to EVE)* Here, take this.

EVE That's okay, Mom. I've got money.

MARGIE No, you take this.

EVE I said I've got it. I'll get him something at the snack bar. I could use a cup of coffee anyway. What about you? Do you want me to bring something back for you?
*(MARGIE has opened her Bible and is engrossed in it as she silently moves her lips while she reads.)*
I imagine you haven't eaten either. Have you? Mom, have you eaten? Would you like some coffee?
*(MARGIE continues reading and distractedly waves EVE away.)*
I'll get you some coffee and something to eat. I'll be right back.

*(EVE exits, leaving MARGIE alone again. MARGIE stops reading and looks up. She stares at the door EVE has just gone through. Reaching into her purse, MARGIE pulls out another tissue and begins to wipe her eyes. Without an audience, her tears are real. Looking up she sees the pinkish glow of sunset filtering into the room. MARGIE sets the Bible down and crosses to the window. MICHAEL enters; his appearance is casual. MICHAEL takes pride in his appearance but is obviously ruffled from the long day. Seeing his mother with her back to the room, MICHAEL pauses in the doorway.)*

***EXCERPT NO. 2***

*(MARGIE storms into the room in a huff. EVE follows closely behind.)*

EVE Mom, you can't act like that!

MARGIE I can do anything that I want. If they can't do their job, they need to have someone tell them how to do it.

EVE You can't insult the doctor like that.

MARGIE He insulted me! How dare they treat us like we're nothing but a bunch of dumb Indians. Did you hear him? Talking that sticky sweet talk. Like I was a child. *(Imitating the doctor)* There there now, Mrs. Crew. Calm yourself. We wouldn't want to have to get a bed for you, too.

EVE I heard him, Mom. He was just trying to be nice.

MARGIE He didn't even know my name! Doesn't a doctor read a chart? How difficult is it? Two Crow, Two Crow. Two words, spelled exactly like it sounds.

EVE They're simply doing their job. You have to let them…

MARGIE My husband is lying there hooked up to all their machines, and they keep telling me everything is going to be all right. It's not. It never will be. Didn't you see him? Did you look at him? He doesn't even know where he is.

EVE Telling the doctor that he's one damn fool isn't going to help matters.

MARGIE I want that doctor to tell the truth. Just tell me the truth. Does he think I'm too stupid to understand? *(Imitating the doctor)* Mrs. Crew, just leave everything to us. We know what's best for your husband. *(Challengingly)* They know nothing. And they don't know a damn thing about your father. They never will. How could they? Were they there when he was struggling, fighting to stay a man? They only see what happened after his spirit was crushed and he gave up hope. Those people treat him like he's a drunken bum on the streets. He deserves respect. Damn them all.

EVE I've never heard you curse before.

MARGIE I don't care. I'll say it again. Damn, damn, damn, damn.

EVE *(Grabbing MARGIE by the shoulders)* Mom, stop!

MARGIE You remember, don't you? You've got to remember. It's all up to you. You have to be the one. Eve, what are we going to do? Please, tell me. I'm tired. I'm so very tired.

EVE *(Gathering MARGIE into her arms)* I know, Mom. I know.

MARGIE I can't do this anymore.

EVE You don't have to. I'm here. I'll do it now.

MARGIE *(Pulling away, MARGIE begins to collect herself.)* Go to the house while your Dad is sleeping. He likes to have his own things about him. He'll see them when he wakes up. Get his quilt for him. The one his mother made for our wedding. I think he's cold in there. He feels cold. They keep it so cold in this place. How can people get well when it's this cold?

EVE *(Guiding MARGIE toward chair, center)* Mom, please sit. Rest for a little while. It will be okay.

MARGIE How are things ever going to be okay?

EVE I'll leave and get everything Dad needs in a few minutes.

MARGIE It just goes on and on, doesn't it? It never stops. It's never gonna stop.

EVE It will. I promise.

MARGIE Don't forget Dad's slippers. When his feet get cold, he gets cramps. His sweatshirt. He likes that blue one. You need to get him in something warmer than that thin gown. Thank God he doesn't know they put him in a dress.

EVE I will.

MARGIE His lips are chapped.

EVE I've got some lip balm in my bag. I'll take it in to Michael.

MARGIE Good. Good. That will help. Michael is such a good boy.

EVE Yes, he is.

MARGIE I don't know what I would do without him. He's all I've got left.

EVE *(EVE is visibly shaken by MARGIE'S comment.)* I'm here.

MARGIE You'll leave just like you did before. It's only a matter of time. Everyone leaves.

EVE Why do you keep saying that? I came back, didn't I?

MARGIE Did you?

EVE I'm standing right here. Tell me what you want.

MARGIE I want you to be a *daughter.*

EVE I am your daughter.

MARGIE There is more to being a daughter. You never understand.

EVE Obviously not. Besides, you apparently don't need a daughter. You have your precious sons.

### *EXCERPT NO. 3*

Act Two

*(The waiting room is empty. The sound of rain and rolling thunder cuts through the silence. The OLD MAN enters pulling his watch out of his pocket and checks the time. It still doesn't work so be begins to shake it.)*

OLD MAN This thing never did work right.
*(Flash of lightning can be seen through the window followed by rolling thunder. The OLD MAN crosses and stands watching the rain.)*
The rains are starting to get harder.

*(JOHN rushes in.)*

JOHN Mom? Eve?
*(Seeing no one, JOHN begins pacing.)*
God damn it! This can't be happening. It's not time. He can't...

OLD MAN You okay, young fellow?

JOHN Gawd, you scared me. Who the hell are you?

OLD MAN You look kinda upset.

JOHN You think? Who wouldn't be? *(Making an effort to compose himself)* Breathe, John. Just breathe. No, I'm fine, really. It's jus...

OLD MAN Your Dad?

JOHN How'd you know?

OLD MAN I'm waiting with your family.

JOHN Waiting, all we ever do is wait. *(Beat)* There are tubes, machines, and...Dad is just...there. It looks like some damn science fiction movie.

OLD MAN Not too good, eh? Maybe you need to go back.

JOHN I can't. Not yet. Not now.

OLD MAN When?

JOHN Later. I need to think. I need to...to...

OLD MAN To what?

JOHN I don't know. Why are you asking me all these questions? Who are you, anyway?

OLD MAN Just an old man.

JOHN Well, grandpa. This is none of your business. So butt out, will ya?

OLD MAN Yeah, I always seem to be buttin' in where I'm needed. *(Begins digging in his bag)* You hungry?

JOHN What?

OLD MAN Eat. You want something to eat?

JOHN No, I don't want anything to eat.

OLD MAN *(Pulls out an orange and hands it to JOHN)* Here. This will help you feel better. Something a bit sweet always helps.

JOHN *(Staring at the orange in his hand)* My Dad loves these. When he was a kid, these were his candy.

OLD MAN Go ahead, eat.

JOHN *(Begins to peel the orange)* Thanks.

OLD MAN You need to keep up your strength. Our old chiefs used to love these too. *(Begins peeling his orange)* That was when men knew how to be leaders.

JOHN What chiefs?

OLD MAN The ones the army sent to that prison in Florida. They thought if they rounded up all our leaders and shipped them off the heart would go out of the people. But they were wrong about that. The heart beats in us all.

JOHN Fort Marion.

OLD MAN That's right. You know that story?

JOHN They kept our leaders there for years. Sent to prison for trying to feed our people. Everyone knows the story, but I didn't know they ate oranges.

OLD MAN Everyone knows the story, but do they remember? *(Beat)* Hard, annit?

JOHN What's hard?

OLD MAN Waiting. Knowing there's nothing you can do to help. We waited for those chiefs too. It was a long time before the army let them come home. But they finally made their way back. You've been waitin' a long time.

JOHN What are you talking about, now?

OLD MAN You. I'm talkin' bout you. Everyone is waiting for you.

JOHN Crazy old man. What do you know?

OLD MAN I know you're a good man, with a good heart. Just got your feet off the road, is all.

JOHN Oh yeah? And what road is that?

OLD MAN Your road. Your people's road. The one you're supposed to be on, remember? It's time for you to take the lead.

JOHN Oh, now I get it. The Good Red Road, right. Great, you're one of those. This is just what I need.

OLD MAN And what kind of those am I?

JOHN Born again Indians. Walk the sacred path of the medicine wheel, all things in balance types. They're everywhere these days. Crawling out of the woodwork. They don't live up to their big talk. They put a price on being Indian, and those hungry white people are all too willing to pay the big bucks for a "real" Indian ceremony.

OLD MAN *(Laughing)* No, I was never born again. Just born once. Once was enough.

JOHN Well, keep your sacred circle talk to yourself, okay? It's all a buncha bull. It only impresses the wannabes.

OLD MAN You don't like these…wan-na-bes?

JOHN Hell no. They took everything we had: our land, our language, and our souls. Now they're back for more. They aren't content just taking anymore. Now they want to *be* Indian. You tell me, what makes them think they have the right to something they will never understand. It's all a game to them, a hobby. Let them try living it, day in and day out. Damn hobbyists. They think that playing dress up is all there is to being Indian. I even had one jerk ask me if I'd let him visit my Tee Pee.

OLD MAN What are you so mad about?

JOHN I'm not mad. I'm just sick of it. They come swarming in here every summer with their goddamn cameras. Worse, are the ones that want to help out all us poor Indians. Or they keep trying to convert us. A free ticket to heaven. That's all we are to them. They travel in packs, like wolves.

OLD MAN They sound like a dangerous bunch.

JOHN Don't let them fool you. They're only out for themselves. They give us their old clothes, and the rest of their trash, so they can feel forgiven. Then we're supposed to kiss their ass. They give with one hand and take away with the other. And they keep on taking. Do you know how many books are written about Indians?

OLD MAN How many?

JOHN Tons, I can tell you that. University people make their careers on us, but can we get a job? Hell no. We're nothing but a fucking project to them. They think because they decide to study Indians we should be honored. There's no honor in being a God damned specimen. I'm proud of what I am, and the next one that wants to interview me and tell my story, I'm gonna beat the crap outta them. I can tell my own damn story.

OLD MAN *(Amused)* That's a whole lotta anger you got there.

JOHN Hell yeah. Aren't you pissed?

OLD MAN I was, once. No one ever taught those people how to behave. They move outside of themselves. They have to take from others to fill their own emptiness. You should pity them.

JOHN You want me to just let them take everything? I can't do that.

OLD MAN That's not what I said. You have to let the anger go. It will make you crazy.

JOHN You know what's worse?

OLD MAN I have a feeling that you're going to tell me.

JOHN Those damn tribal administrators. They don't stand up for the people. They walk around like they're some big Indians. Going to meeting after meeting so they can hear themselves talk. Selling out their own people to line their own pockets. As long as they are doing well to hell with the rest of us. And my sister works for those crooks.

OLD MAN You don't like that?

JOHN They'll eat her alive. Just like they do anyone who tries to make a difference.

OLD MAN Maybe you should do something about it.

JOHN Right. Like anyone would listen to me.

OLD MAN Anger can focus you, pump your heart up and get you ready to fight. But you have to control it for it to make a difference. You have to let the anger move you forward, not hold you back.

JOHN *(Taking in OLD MAN'S words)* You're kinda creepy; you know that?

OLD MAN *(Explodes into laughter)* You remind me of my grandson. That boy's always saying whatever pops into his head.

JOHN He must be a pretty great kid, then.

OLD MAN That he sure was.

JOHN Was? I'm sorry I didn't realize…

OLD MAN No, he ain't gone, just grown up, is all. Got his feet off that road you talked about. He lost hope, thought he was alone. He got angry too. He started drinkin' his anger.

JOHN *(Becoming uncomfortable)* You don't say. That's too bad.

OLD MAN Forgot who he was. Where he came from. You know what that's like, don't you?

JOHN I don't know what you're talking about.

OLD MAN Sure you do. I could smell the beer on you when you walked in. Look at you, all rumpled up. Part of being proud is taking care of yourself. Heck of a thing to go drinkin' before you come to the hospital. You talk big, but you're drinkin' to find courage.

JOHN Look, old man. You need to lay off. You know nothing about it.

OLD MAN I know more than you think. I know those people you talk about. They been around a long time. Always asking their questions. Recording everything. Telling us they wanted to help, to save us. Guess they thought we were fool enough to believe them. They even brought a new god with them when they came. We took a good look at their god. You know what? It was the same god. They just couldn't see it. They owned god like they wanted to own the land. Those people didn't treat him right, either.

JOHN Don't let my Mom hear you talk like that.

OLD MAN You think she don't know that? She knows.

JOHN You're wrong on that one, gramps. She carries her Bible around like it's made of gold.

OLD MAN You ever take a look in it?

JOHN I don't need to look in it.

OLD MAN Of course not. Why would you want to learn something?

JOHN I know enough.

OLD MAN Is that so? My grandson started drinkin' when he lost our home. He tried as best he could. Couldn't make enough to feed his family and sold the land. Some white man bought it up. Used the house to keep his hay in. It used to be a good house. It's still there if you want to take a look at it. Course, it don't look the same. That's where my boy grew up. There's a big tree sits behind the house. In the summer we'd sit under that tree, tell stories for days. People came from all over to sit in the shade of that tree. All our folks are buried up there, now.

JOHN That's an old story. Everyone 'round here's got the same story. You hear it every day. People are always talking about what they used to have, and what they ain't got now. It's a waste of time. It's never going to get any better.

OLD MAN That's just the kind of thinking that gets you in trouble.

JOHN It's the truth.

OLD MAN Lots of things change. Some things stay the same, like this land. It's waiting. It can hold you close and cradle you. Just because someone puts a fence around it don't mean it ain't still there for you. You should look deeper. Under all that concrete it lays waiting for us. *(Beat)* How's your headache?

JOHN What? Oh, it's gone.

OLD MAN Good. That's good.

JOHN My old man drank. Drank all the time. That's why he's here. His liver is shot.

*(OLD MAN walks over to the window and watches the rain falling.)*

Oh, he wasn't wild, didn't run around or anything. He just drank, beer mostly. Man, he could sure pack it away. He only drank on weekends at first. Then it got to be every day after...well anyway, he lost his job. It wasn't much of a job, but it put food on the table, and clothes on our backs.

OLD MAN Your Dad tried, really hard. It musta' been rough on you after he lost hope.

JOHN Hey, I'm not looking for any sympathy. I was just telling ya. It's no big deal. Like I said, everyone's got the same story.

OLD MAN Is that why you drink? 'Cause your Dad did?

JOHN I don't drink. Well, not anymore. I'm on the wagon.

OLD MAN That wagon seems to have a busted wheel.

JOHN It was only a couple of beers, for gawd sake. I wish everyone would get of my back. A man's entitled to a couple of beers once in a while. I can handle it.

OLD MAN That's just what my grandson used to say. I can handle it.

JOHN Don't preach to me, old man. You don't know anything about it. You don't know anything about my life, or what I have to deal with.

OLD MAN What are you afraid of, John? Sometimes men can't face pain.

JOHN I'm not afraid of anything. People are afraid of me.

OLD MAN There's no shame in it, only in what you do with it.

JOHN I feel my headache coming back. Look, old man. I don't mean to be disrespectful. It's just ...I have a lot on my mind.

OLD MAN Sure, sure. I know. It's hard to see the people we love hurting. It is never easy. Seems like I spend all my time in this room.

JOHN I know what you mean. I hate hospitals. *(Pause)* My Dad is disappearing. It's like there's almost nothing left.

OLD MAN There's always something left.

JOHN He could have been something, you know? But, they wouldn't let him. Every time he tried they just kept pushing him back down until he couldn't breathe. You know they called him chief? They didn't even give him the dignity of knowing his name. He deserved better.

OLD MAN He has something better.

JOHN Oh yeah? Like what?

OLD MAN Like you. Like your sister, and your brother. It isn't only the land that makes us strong. It's us, all of us. Family. You carry us into the future.

JOHN Now there's a bargain for you. Dad would be so proud of us.

OLD MAN I know that he is. He always has been.

JOHN He's not proud. We haven't done anything we were supposed to do. Now, my brother, Roy, he was different. He was going to rock the world.

OLD MAN Really, how's that?

JOHN He could do anything. All state champion: football, basketball, baseball. You name it and he could do it. Dad was in hog heaven when the scouts came courting. Everyone loved Roy. Yeah, he was gonna bust outta here, show the world.

*(The lighting changes as the OLD MAN turns his back. JOHN doesn't notice the change in lighting.)*

OLD MAN You talk like he's not around.

JOHN He isn't.

OLD MAN Where is he?

JOHN *(Uncomfortable)* I see him, ya know? All the time. I can't get away from him.

OLD MAN Why is that?

*(OLD MAN has moved to the doorway and motions someone in.)*

JOHN He died a long time ago. Nothing was the same after that.

***EXCERPT NO. 4***

*(JOHN and MICHAEL exit after embracing EVE. EVE lingers not certain of what to do in the quiet of the waiting room. MARGIE sits, begins to softly sing as she removes a small medicine pouch from her Bible).*

EVE Mother?

MARGIE What is it now, Eve?

EVE Nothing, it's just all such a waste.

*(MARGIE begins to stare at EVE as if attempting to dissect her.)*

I mean everything could have been so different for all of us.

MARGIE Different? How could things have been different?

EVE Well, we wouldn't be here for one thing.

MARGIE Where should we be, Eve?

EVE Safe and warm in our beds, not sitting in this cold room in the middle of the night.

MARGIE Is your life so terrible you would wish it away?

EVE You have to admit, it didn't get a good start.

MARGIE I worry about you.

EVE You? Worried about me? John is the one you need to be worried about.

MARGIE John will do what he needs to do. He's almost ready.

EVE Will you stop making excuses for him? John isn't ready to do anything but slide down with the rest of them.

MARGIE I make excuses for all my children.

EVE Excuse me?

MARGIE Do you ever see anything good? In your life, is there anything good?

EVE Of course. I've worked hard to make it good.

MARGIE It takes a lot of work to build walls. You have to become a rock so nothing can touch you.

EVE Let's not do this. I get along just fine. I'm just trying to get through this night.

MARGIE What happens when this night is over?

EVE We go on. That's all. We just go on.

MARGIE What do you remember, Eve?

EVE Remember?

MARGIE From your childhood. What do you remember?

EVE Oh, God. As little as possible.

MARGIE That's a problem.

EVE That's salvation.

MARGIE Is it?

EVE What do you keep dancing around? Why is it so important to you that I remember anything? Do you want me to tell you that I had a wonderful childhood? Well, I can't. There wasn't anything wonderful about it.

MARGIE It was a time this family had hope. We had dreams that could become true. Some of them did, for a little while. We have to hold on to those moments. Cherish them.

EVE You can cherish them if you want. I'd just as soon forget every minute.

MARGIE You have to remember everything the way it was. You have to see things clearly to understand.

EVE I understand perfectly. We're here because Dad wouldn't stop drinking! This is all his fault. He could have stopped and he chose not to. We could have grown up feeling like someone gave a damn about us. Instead, we were always afraid of saying or doing something that would set him off. We couldn't do anything right, nothing was good enough. Even Roy couldn't satisfy him. If it weren't for Dad, my brother would still be alive! I hate him. I hate him! He deserves this.

MARGIE No one deserves this.

EVE Why do you always take up for him?

MARGIE I'm not taking up for him. You always want me to choose sides and I can't, I won't.

EVE You already chose sides, Mama. You've made that clear enough.

MARGIE I chose this family. That's what I chose. You expect everyone to walk some line you have in your head. When we can't you get angry and shut us all out. You pretend we don't exist.

EVE I'm trying to fix this mess of a family. Everything I do is to make things better for all of us, and do I ever get a thank you? I didn't become a drunk or a good for nothing. I made something of myself, but none of that matters to you. I should never have come home. I don't know what I was thinking.

MARGIE Thank you? Is that what you want? Well, thank you for setting yourself up as our judge and jury. Is this what we're here for, the execution? Your father would be so happy that he could finally please you.

*(MARGIE begins digging in her purse and pulls out a checkbook, begins filling it out.)*

EVE Mom, what are you doing?

MARGIE Here, you want your money back? Take it, we don't need your money. I saved it all for you. It means more to you than it ever did to us.

EVE No, Mom, I don't want it. That was for you.

MARGIE What did you think you were buying, Eve?

EVE I wasn't trying to buy anything. I was just… I was trying to make things better.

MARGIE Money doesn't make things better.

EVE Well, it certainly helps.

MARGIE Your father thought money would make our life better and he was just as wrong as you are. Ranchers flashed a big wad of money in front of him for the land belonging to his family, and he took it. Said everything was going to be better for us. But it never was. When he realized what he had done, he tried to give the money back. Those men had what they wanted. They just laughed at him and said he was just another stupid Indian. He lost it all, everything he was supposed to protect. He was shamed. And that shame set him on the path that led him right here.

EVE But he took us all with him, Mama. You're right, I do remember. I remember when home was the safest place on earth. That's what I was looking for when I came home. I had this stupid idea that when Dad quit drinking things might be able to be the way they use to be.

MARGIE Nothing will ever be the way it used to be. Never again.

EVE Why didn't you just leave him? Anything would have been better than what we had to go through.

MARGIE You want such simple answers to everything. Life is not so simple. I don't know, maybe it was because in the beginning I loved him too much. I thought he would find his strength. But, it was too late, too late. Then he needed me too much. Leave, it's easy to leave.

EVE We needed you, Mama. We needed you.

MARGIE There just wasn't anything left to give. I'm sorry.

EVE Sorry? Sorry? What am I suppose to do with that? Are those the magic words that make everything right again?

MARGIE You are always so angry. It shadows everything else. You better put that away or anger and disappointment will be all you ever see. I tried to make you hard enough to survive. But I see now that I only hardened your heart.

EVE My heart is not hard. If it were it wouldn't break; it wouldn't bleed. God, how I've prayed for our family to be whole again. Somehow we could finally allow some peace into our lives.

MARGIE I know how you can find the peace you are looking for. See your father for who he once was, and who he was meant to be. Let him leave this world as the warrior he is. You have to release him. Forgive him.

EVE How can I forgive him? After all these years the pain is too deep.

MARGIE Eve! Do you want to move forward or just keep complaining about how hard your life is? When are you going to be ready?

EVE Ready? For what?

MARGIE To take your place as part of this family.

EVE I wonder if I have a place in this family.

MARGIE Oh Eve, stop it! Of course you do. Without you there is no balance.

EVE I just don't want to feel so alone anymore.

MARGIE My poor baby. Don't you see that we are not alone? We are never alone.

*(MARGIE embraces her daughter, cradling her like a child.)*

Now, you need to go to your father. He is waiting for you.

EVE I need you, Mom. I don't know how to do this by myself.

MARGIE *(MARGIE takes the small pouch and caresses it.)* I have what you need. This belonged to my grandmother. She gave it to my mother. Now I give it to you. Take this. You are the woman now, Eve. You are the heart.

*(EVE tenderly takes the pouch and begins to leave. Turning, she reaches for her mother. MARGIE takes her hand and they exit together as the stage slowly fades to black. Overlaying their exit is the mourning song that MARGIE was humming at the beginning of the scene. A center spot comes up as JOHN moves into the circle of light.)*

OLD MAN *(An Honor Song begins as the OLD MAN speaks and is sung softly throughout the remaining lines.)*

Each generation carries our people to the next, if we can see beyond the dust that tries to bury our hearts. Our memories are in the air, they are everywhere. As one moves, others carry us into the future. Remember, we continue not as one, but as many woven together. Those who came before live in our breath and they are always with us, just as we will be here for our children.

*(The OLD MAN begins to gather the father's spirit and move slowly upstage.)*

EVE *(Entering the spotlight)* Are you all right, Johnny?

JOHN He's gone, Eve.

EVE I know. We're here for you John. We are here for each other.

*(JOHN reaches out, gathering his sister in his arms.)*

MICHAEL Last night, I had a dream about Dad. There was a bunch of other men with him. They were dressed ol' style, and they were all on horseback. As they started to ride away he turned and I saw him. Dad was with them. He was wearing that old blue sweatshirt he likes so much. He looked tired, but he wasn't sick anymore. He was sitting strong with his head held high. Roy was by his side.

MICHAEL There's something else. I knew he looked familiar when I met him. You know that old man that was in here?

JOHN It was the grandfather.

MICHAEL He was holding the reigns to Dad's horse, and he was leading him away. At one point Dad turned to me and waved. He said goodbye, but I heard it in my mind. His lips never moved. "Watch out for each other," he said. As I stood there I saw them ride away. I felt something I can't remember ever feeling before. I felt peace.

*(The rain has ended. All characters remain frozen as the lights begin to fade on the family. The honor song is replaced by a family song. Upstage lights focus on the OLD MAN and ROY, viewed in shadow, leading the hunched over figure of a man, the father. As ROY removes the father's hospital gown the father begins to stand erect, his back remains toward the audience. The OLD MAN and ROY prepare the father for his journey. Using their hands they use red earth clay to paint the father's body. With an eagle fan the OLD MAN blesses the father. After they have completed the ritual the light changes to the color of a new dawn.)*

***THE END***

*(A song in celebration of our children is sung as the houselights return and continues throughout the curtain call)*

## Friends

*Marcie Rendon*

SYNOPSIS: Three generations of women have a conversation about friends, motherhood, and lice.

CHARACTERS:

SUSAN RED HORSES: Grandmother

KASHII: Granddaughter, 10-12 years old

LISA: SUSAN's daughter, 25-35 years old

Scene opens on a room where granddaughter is seated on chair, with grandmother behind her combing through her hair with a fine-tooth comb looking for lice. Daughter is seated nearby. Present day.

KASHII Grandma, how come we get lice?

SUSAN (*Rolls her eyes and pushes down on KASHII's head*) Hold still.

KASHII These things are nasty; why would god make lice?

SUSAN Why not?

KASHII You're pulling my hair.

LISA Listen to your grandma.

SUSAN Where'd she get these anyways? School?

LISA Yeah. I told her not to be using anyone's brush, but she doesn't listen.

KASHII Did too. They jump.

LISA Right, they jump.

KASHII I think they're from Bacardi.

SUSAN Bacardi?

KASHII She's my friend.

SUSAN Now what kind of parent goes and names their kid Bacardi? Spose her brother's name is Jim Beam.

KASHII No. Everyone calls him Whiskey.

*(Grandmother and mother laugh in disbelief.)*

KASHII I think his real name is Waylon though. Bacardi's my best friend.

LISA Well, you don't need to be sitting head to head with her.

SUSAN Lisa, hand me that red pen over there so I can part her hair.

(*Pause*)

Names like Bacardi…and what? Jim Beam?

KASHII Whiskey!

SUSAN …shouldn't be sitting with her at all if you ask me.

KASHII Grandma! Don't draw red lines on my head.

LISA She's only making a part so she can find them better.

KASHII I don't want to go to school with red ink all over my head.

SUSAN Red line down your middle part, you'll look like a traditional dancer.

LISA You should charge for this, Ma.

KASHII I jingle dress.

LISA I'm serious, Mom, you could make at least twenty bucks a head for cleaning out all the nits. No one picks them all out anymore. They try to kill them off with chemicals. Now the little bugs are just immune to Quell, Nix. They're like cockroaches, they've mutated and just drink the poison like it's water.

KASHII Bacardi says her mom dyes her hair. She says that's the only way to kill them.

SUSAN Sounds like you better stay away from that kid.

LISA So you knew she had lice and you still sat by her?!

KASHII Can I dye my hair blond?

SUSAN Yeah right. I don't think so.

KASHII Mom?

LISA Listen to your grandma.

KASHII With a blue streak down the side.

SUSAN Yeah right. And I'm going to tattoo Bugs Bunny on my forehead. Put your head down.

KASHII Did you ever have lice, Grandma?

LISA One time your grandma had a boyfriend.

SUSAN Shush.

LISA We're all sitting around the table eating supper and he says, "Susan, I think I have friends." Your grandma says, "That's good, we all need friends."

SUSAN Nah. knock it off. Keep your head down.

LISA He says, "No, little friends." And starts scratching his head.

SUSAN Says he caught them riding the bus to and from work. Must have been mutated bugs. Took me I don't know how many bottles of Qwell to get rid of them. All you kids had 'em. Was doing laundry for two weeks straight.

LISA Was he the boyfriend who went to get cigarettes and never came back?

SUSAN No…

LISA Or the one who went to do laundry and never came back?

KASHII Went to do laundry?

SUSAN Yep, walked out of the house with a black plastic garbage bag tossed over his shoulder. I said, "Where you going?" He said, "To do my laundry."

LISA We had a machine in the basement.

SUSAN That one must still be out there panhandling for quarters.

KASHII He never came back?

(*Pause*)

KASHII Grandma!!! That hurts.

SUSAN Be quiet now. Sit still. Anyways, that wasn't the one with bugs.

LISA Remember when we saw him at the Indian Health Board pow-wow and you told Chuck to run over and ask him if the dryers broke? Too funny.

SUSAN What about the time you sent Kashii here up to that old boyfriend of yours up at the Cass Lake pow-wow?

KASHII I remember that. She told me to run up to him and say, "Daddy, Daddy, where you been?"

LISA Except you ran up to the wrong guy!!

KASHII I didn't know. I just grabbed on to his arm and said, "Daddy, Daddy," and he started swinging me around in circles trying to shake me loose.

LISA Total stranger. He was looking around all crazy.

SUSAN Looking to see if his past finally caught up with him!

LISA Hoping his new girlfriend wasn't around.

KASHII I don't get it.

SUSAN Nothin to get—hold still.

KASHII Then he saw you and Grandma trying to hide.

SUSAN We tried to duck down under the picnic table. God, that was funny.

LISA You know what your grandma's name is, Kashii?

KASHII Susan.

LISA Susan what?

KASHII Susan Many Red Horses.

LISA It's really Susan Many Red Husbands.

KASHII What?

SUSAN Knock it off.

KASHII What do you mean, Mom? Red husbands?

LISA Your grandma had lots of husbands.

SUSAN Red Husbands! Was never married to no communist.

KASHII Communist?

SUSAN Hush, you're too young to understand.

KASHII No I'm not. What's a communist?

SUSAN Kinda like an Indian but from Russia. Believes everyone should share everything.

KASHII What's wrong with that?

LISA Your grandma's just telling you stories.

SUSAN You're telling stories.

LISA Ain't no story. You had so many husbands we don't even know who our dad is.

SUSAN I know who your dad is.

LISA Or which dad belongs to which kid.

KASHII Is that why I got so many grandpas?

SUSAN *(Getting angry and upset)*
You only got one grandpa. And your mom only has one dad. If she don't know who her dad is by now, I can't help her.

LISA Lots of boyfriends since then.

SUSAN I was only married once.

LISA Come on, Mom, I was only teasing.

SUSAN Only one father for all you kids.

KASHII Oww—Quit pulling my hair, Grandma!

SUSAN Sit still, I'm almost done, then you and your fatherless mother can go home.

LISA Mom!

KASHII Why you mad at me, Grandma? I didn't do nothing.

SUSAN Not mad at you.

KASHII You're pulling my hair like you're mad.

SUSAN Just tired of your mom's stories.

LISA I was just joking.

SUSAN Right.

LISA Come on, Mom, I'm sorry. So who was the guy with the bugs?

SUSAN Don't matter.

KASHII Grandma, are you ok?

SUSAN Yeah, I'm fine.

LISA Come on, Mom, I was just teasing. (*Long silence as SUSAN combs out KASHII's hair*)

LISA Remember when you almost hit the dead end sign down by Julie's house?

SUSAN Didn't. I knew where I was going.

LISA What about the time you almost ran over my boyfriend in eleventh grade?

SUSAN Should have.

KASHII You tried to run over someone?

SUSAN More of your mom's stories.

LISA Uh uh, you better be careful not to get your grandma mad.

KASHII She don't ever get mad at me.

LISA That's cause she's not your mom.

SUSAN Enough.

LISA Then there was the time your grandma left her shoes in Perkins.

KASHII You did what?

LISA It was summer, and you know how your grandma always goes around barefoot. She slipped her shoes off in the restaurant and then forgot to put them back on. We get home and she started yelling at us, asking us what we did with her shoes. Yelling around. Finally, Chuck says, Mom, maybe you left them in the restaurant. She says, No! He said, You want me to call? So he finally calls for her and sure enough, the manager says there's a pair of shoes at the restaurant, under the table.

KASHII Did you go get them?

SUSAN Ummph.

LISA She made me go in and get them. What about the time we went shopping in that big old green Buick? At Wal-Mart? It was around Christmas time and when we came out we had our arms all full of bags.

SUSAN It was cold that year.

LISA And we were rushing out to the car, freezing. We all jumped in the car.

SUSAN I put the key in the ignition. *Tried* to put the key in the ignition.

LISA And it wouldn't go. You started to look mad, and us kids started to get worried.

SUSAN Then Chuck said, Mom, how come we have a Bible in the car?

LISA And we all looked around and damn, it wasn't our car.

SUSAN We all jumped out. From the outside, it looked just like our car.

LISA The Salvation Army guy was looking at us like we were crazy.

SUSAN I looked at the car. It was the same old green Buick. Never thought anyone else would drive a car that ugly.

KASHII You got in the wrong car?

LISA Us kids went running through the parking lot until we found our car.

SUSAN We all hopped in and drove off laughing.

LISA I was so embarrassed.

SUSAN You? I was the mom. Lucky we didn't get arrested for attempted carjacking. See, Kashii, that's why the creator gave us lice.

KASHII Huh?

SUSAN To make us pay attention to the little things in life.

*(You hear a snap as SUSAN squashes a lice egg between her fingernails.)*

***The End***

## Cannibal Woman Camp Out

*Marie Annharte Baker*

THE SETTING: *It is springtime in British Columbia Lower Mainland in year 2007. A Wreck Beach sign reads* CLOTHING OPTIONAL. *One particular bush is wiggling. (Loud male scream) A woman emerges out from behind the same bush with small feathers scattered through her hair. She is partially nude except for large frame sunglasses. Her bare breasts and crotch may be hidden by twig and reed constructed dream catchers. She is an older First Nations woman with long hair.*

OWL WOMAN
Did you notice a naked guy running out of this very bush holding his privates? That was prime Sir Loin but, damn, he had to be a vegetarian to run like that. Too damn fast! He was so sinewy. I just want to drool thinking about what I just missed. Yummy yum yum.
*MUSIC: Inuit Women throat song. Scary sounding modern kind.*

*OWL WOMAN appears apprehensive and returns to the bush hiding place.*

*SOUNDSCAPE: Police car siren but music goes back to erotic like sounds of Women song but mixes with hip hop beat and then rattle sound followed by a west coast canoe song.*

*A NATIVE LADY COP enters talking on her cell phone. She is semi-nude but has a jacket and cap on.*

NATIVE LADY COP
I just talked to this guy I found huddling, covering himself with a face cloth size towel. No sign of his attacker so far.

*NATIVE LADY COP walks up to bush to put a yellow tape over it. Tape reads:* KEEP OUT–CRIME SCENE. *Documentary video shot appears on the rear wall. The image is a crowd of naked men gathered and huddled together with trembling bottoms.*

*A NATIVE WOMAN JOURNALIST arrives to interview the NATIVE LADY COP. She holds a mike and speaks to a camera.*

NATIVE WOMAN JOURNALIST
Wreck Beach has been hit by a stalker. A young man was forced to leave the beach area without his clothing. He was attacked by a vicious older Native woman. He was so scared he confused the on-duty Security Personnel by calling his assailant a cougar. The Stray Animal Patrol was then alerted. Eventually, the mix up was explained. Cougar is a name used to describe an older woman who preys upon or chases younger men. Something to look forward to in one's old age, I guess.

NATIVE LADY COP (*Butts in*)
There were scratches not immediately visible except around the genital region.

NATIVE WOMAN JOURNALIST
Rrrrrrrrrr! Ev-rrr nasty!

NATIVE LADY COP
I didn't manage a closer look but the hand towel he used to cover his injury looked pretty nasty too. There has been a rash of random reports. Usually the beach is peaceful and men enjoy the company of each other blissfully without anticipation of attacks by women, never mind Native women. Since the dawn of time, men have been allowed a rape, a pillage, and a sack without undue consequences. I am now referring to the dominant statistics of male perversion.

NATIVE WOMAN JOURNALIST
This reversal of violence is definitely premeditated. If this reign of terror continues, a task force will need to be formed. I would recommend, though it is not really my place to do so, that this group be controlled by Native women and that we especially include our

women elders. We have to be fair even though there are those out there in ndn country all too ready to pay back society for past wrongs. I won't get into any detail about that except to say that just because I am expressing a personal view, I am not on a soap box or preaching dissent. If this had happened on Canada Day, there might have been strong support for the predator, especially if she was an easily identifiable ndn.

*Next morning at an apartment. Doorbell rings. OWL WOMAN enters and gropes about as she has just been asleep. She brushes feathers from her hair and spits out one or two. She peeks out the door peep hole.*

OWL WOMAN
The Police! (*Pause*) Okay, okay. Give me a few minutes. I'm still in my jammies. (*She grabs her cell phone and dials while she puts on a Chinese robe.*) Police just showed up. What a mess. I just woke up with all these feathers from my pillow on me. I look like I'm molting. (*Door bell rings and then door pounding with voice yelling, "Open up. Police"*) Right away, Officers.

The gathering? When? (*Pause*) I'll be there but on ndn time I guess. Damn, I have to get the door. Hey, maybe they will frisk me! (*Laughs*) Laters. (*Puts the phone down and walks to the door*) Hey, just a minute. (*Starts singing*) Hold on, I'm coming. (*Dancing*) Hold on, I'm coming. (*Changes tune*) Heya heya. Heya heya.

*SECRET LOCATION OF CANNIBAL WOMEN CAMP where OWL WOMAN is interrogated by her peers. Lamp is turned toward her face.*

OWL WOMAN
He got away. I couldn't help it. I didn't have enough traction in bare feet. It was a nude beach and I had to remove my runners.

CANNIBAL WOMEN VOICE OVER
No excuses. You were put in charge of the entertainment. You have to take it seriously. Get out there and get us a man!

*Afternoon on a street corner. A priest stops to solicit hooker. He approaches and digs into his pocket. He bends his head down in front of her. She grabs his cross and fondles it. Then she bops him on the head. He falls. He grasps her hips as he goes down to the pavement. She signals to other women who surround his body. She gets the car keys out of his pocket. She jingles them in the air. She takes his money and puts it in her bra.*

OWL WOMAN
Tie him up good. Put him in the back seat. I'll take him over to the camp. I hope none of these do gooders around here saw us take him down. It's broad daylight even. Too many street missionaries trying to drag women off to a soup kitchen. Sorry. I'd have to say, I'm on a special diet. No, maybe I could say I got a dinner date. Heh heh.

*TIPI SECRET LOCATION. CANNIBAL WOMEN CAMP. Signs read:* WELCOME DELEGATES. REGISTRATION. *OWL WOMAN stands in front of tipi entrance holding the priest collar in her hand, which she then holds above her head. She lets out a big whooping yell.*

OWL WOMAN
I remember when the residential school closed down this old bugger had to go someplace else for sex. I got him! I collared him! Let's have a good time and defrock him.

*SOUND: Cheering. More whoops.*

*OWL WOMAN puts on the collar. Then she immediately starts choking. She holds her throat and motions for help. She struggles to remove it. She coughs.*

OWL WOMAN
Damn. Enough of that. Does someone have any ndn medsin to share? That thing was toxic. Maybe I got an allergy to that regalia thing. I should get compensation for that! Anyone got any spare root?

*MUSIC: Donna Summer's "Bad Girls."*

*Documentary shot of women sitting around in a large circle. Behind them is a large tipi.*

*SOUNDSCAPE: Blend of the disco, eerie throat singing, and pow wow.*

OWL WOMAN
Welcome, sisters. I am so glad we were able to stop all our predating acts. Let us set aside our selfish interests to join together. We were able to operate on our lonesomes before so we could be more on the undercover. (*Laughs*) No, I don't mean that kind of undercovers, either. We are in great danger of becoming more extinct than we already are. Our people don't remember us. They don't warn their children to stay away from the rivers. When it's getting dark, the mothers are forgetting to tell the kids about us. Crying shame. They end up letting the social workers take their kids. The neglect of us is disgusting. We are being upstaged by punks, no name brand poseurs…we were the original bad girls. (*Cheers*) If we don't organize to protect our professions and careers, we are all going to be has-beens. I am so used to terrorizing the West Coast by myself but from now on I definitely will need more help. I have to raise money for my legal defense fund but I want to hear from you women from all the four directions. Next to me is the one and only Windigo Annie. I want to listen to what is happening in her territory. We got Slug Woman from California to show up. She came up with Llorna from East L.A. Hey, is Malinche in the house?

*SOUND: Murmurs. Chit chat sounds then calls for shush. Sh. Sh. A cell phone rings and announcement is heard to please turn off all cell phones.*

WINDIGO ANNIE
Boo joo, Sisters. Miigwiich for the heartfelt welcome, girls. I can hardly say I am representing the East anymore. The Cree and Ojibway people hardly talk much about me to their children. Sure, they say Windigo now and then. But it is so impersonal. They don't sound too scared anymore. No more, watch what you say, she could be listening. No, Native kids even dress up like me for Halloween. It's all about the witch bitches! I am tired of being overlooked. No special mentions. They are talking gangs all the time. All hoes. Street mamas. Even when I hang around bars and pubs, they just look past me or through me. I'm here to help my sister Owl Woman and all of us who are taking a beating from sheer neglect. No more abuse.

*SOUND: Chanting:* No more abuse. *Crescendo and laughter.*

SLUG WOMAN
I will speak next. Though I am out of turn. I back up what both my sisters are saying. There was not much back up for Owl Woman at Wreck Beach when she went out all by herself to get a trophy for our gathering. She got some help from me and our southern gang, Llorona and Malinche, to bag that priest. He was not exactly on the Most Wanted list for us but it's a start. I slithered in here so to speak to join your posse. I like to hang with home girls but what if we don't have a home anymore? My Latino sisters know what it is like to get blamed for everything especially that Cortés dude. Now that was slime ball. Now we know more about his sneaky ways. Now all these guys act like him. Making conquests, hah. Right! They aren't doing anything for our profiles, doing that bragadisamo. Keep in mind though the older we get,

the more they don't want us. Now that we are ancient, it is getting worse. We need to stand up to these damn gangstas in the hood. Sure they might want older women when they know we got pensions and they want to buy drugs. It's a damn shame. They got their welfare mamas but they are coming after us too. It's too much. I'll pass now.

SASQUATCH SALLY
I'll give it a try. I'm Sasquatch Sally. I usually roam the north but I have been working a lot on the West Coast though some sisters don't always catch my presence. Like my presence is my smell. (*Laughs*) Hey, don't mention it. I am not the only one that is high tonight. Phewie! I think some of you ladies have been washing up and trying out deodorants. All you gotta do is use more rotten fish oil! I don't think it is necessary to mask our scents. Why do we think our stink is so bad? Slug Woman always leaves a bit of her glossy self on the trail. It's sparkly and maybe could cure cancer. Some research is pointing that way. I always rub myself on the trees and bushes. Get used to it. We are women of odor.

OWL WOMAN
Okay, Ladies. We got the basic introductions done. Let's take a quick energy break. Some necessary entertainment. When we come back, we can break into small groups.

*Outside Tipi. Each woman is given a long narrow branch. Two women with hand drums sing. The women form two lines facing each other. The priest is released although still bound at the hands. He runs the gauntlet with the women hitting him as he staggers and runs between them. They scream with joy and laughter.*

*Lights Down. Slight Flicker.*

## Chocolate Woman Dreams the Milky Way[1]

*Monique Mojica*

I have been thinking for quite awhile about knowing and not knowing. What we know and *how* we know it. There's a saying in Spanish–*saber sabiendo*–literally "to know knowingly." But it also carries the connotation of knowing the unknown, the intuitively known or what we don't know that we know.

Most of the work that I have done over the past two decades reflects tapping this kind of knowing. I haven't always done it consciously and I haven't done it alone. Since 1991, I have collaborated with Floyd Favel and Muriel Miguel, among others, in performance research and laboratories searching out how to do consciously what we do *un*consciously. This work has resulted in studio investigations and produced performances that aim to identify and hone a methodology that Floyd has called Native Performance Culture. These two visionary directors have had an enormous influence on me and I will talk more about them later.

So, I have been doing this performance thing for a long time. It has been fifty years since I first started training (!), twenty-seven years since I first worked with an all Native theatre company: *Indian Time Theater*, directed by Bruce King, out of the now-defunct Native American Center for the Living Arts in Niagara Falls, N.Y. It has been twenty-four years since I moved to Toronto to be one of the early Artistic Directors of *Native Earth Performing Arts*. Those were the times just preceding the infamous "Native theatre explosion" in Toronto when our small circle included the Highway brothers Tomson and René, Billy Merasty, Makka Kleist, Maariu Olsen, Gary Farmer, Shirley Cheechoo, Graham Greene, and Doris Linklater. Over the years, I have accumulated quite a bit of material. Some there is no record of; some is in the form of drafts lost on floppy discs that my computer can no longer read. Some drafts hide in my not-so-organized filing cabinet, and still others are scraps of paper folded into notebooks: fragments of stories and notations of improvisations. As someone whose writing process includes doing laundry, making lists, and sifting though papers, I excavated some two-decade old writings, dusted them off, and had a look. What I found is that not only could I recognize recurring themes and imagery, but I could also trace a trajectory, a personal transformation as an artist and as an Aboriginal woman. This trajectory transforms amnesia through stories drawn from conscious memory, muscle memory, blood memory, then births organic texts, allowing me to emerge trusting the Indigenous knowledge encoded in my dreams, in my waking visions, and in my DNA.

I have organized this chronologically, so I am going to begin with some fragments from a writing exercise written during the development of *Princess Pocahontas and the Blue Spots* (1988), dramaturged by Djanet Sears. When I uncrinkled this and read it, it occurred to me that it contains many of the themes that I have worked with since and that it is something of a prophecy for my life's path.

[1] This essay is a revised version of two oral presentations, the first offered at the Distinguished Lecture Series, University of Toronto, in January 2006, and the second at the Honoring Spiderwoman Theater/Celebrating Native American Theater conference, Native American Women Playwrights Archive, Miami University, in February 2007. It was revised and updated in January 2008 and has been published in *Collective Creation, Collaboration and Devising*, ed. Bruce Barton (Toronto: Playwrights Canada, 2008). An earlier version will appear in a forthcoming volume of essays on North American Native performance, edited by Steve Wilmer, to be published by the University of Arizona Press.

Once upon a time there was a little girl who lived in a stone cave, not entirely by herself—but almost. She lived that way, away from other people, because she was not entirely invisible—but almost (maybe about half). It made other people very uncomfortable that they couldn't see the other half of her even though she referred to it often and insisted that it actually was there and that it would bleed if she scraped it, and even scab over and get well.

One day, the girl got tired of waiting in her stone cave for someone to believe her and she decided to leave. But she didn't know where she was going so she didn't know how to get there. So, she called to the spirit of heartbreak and sadness, the spirit of blood and rebellion, the spirit of back-breaking endurance and the spirit of transformation to help her make a map.

(The part of the story that follows has been lost but this is the next recovered fragment:)

"Easy for you to say," said the girl, "but I only have one foot!"

"Ah, ahhh," said the Grandmother spirits, "but just because other people cannot see your other foot doesn't mean it doesn't make an imprint when you walk. One foot in front of the other. Follow your own path, which is ours."

So she did.

This is how elements from this exercise appeared in the final *Princess Pocahontas and the Blue Spots* script:

CONTEMPORARY WOMAN #1:

No map, no trail, no footprint, no way home

only darkness, a cold wind whistling by my ears.

The only light comes from the stars.

Nowhere to set my feet.

No place to stand. *(Rising)*

No map, no trail, no footprint, no way home.

*Sees basin of water; brings it to center.*

He said, "It's time for the women to pick up their medicine in order for the people to continue." *(Washes hands, arms)*

She asked him, "What is the women's medicine?" The only answer he found was, "The women are the medicine, so we must heal the women."

*Washes from basin head, arms, legs, feet. Tiple theme begins.*

*Squatting over basin in a birthing position, she lifts a newborn from between her legs, holding baby in front of her, she rises.*

When I was born, the umbilical cord was wrapped around my neck and my face was blue.

When I was born, my mother turned me over to check for the blue spot at the base of the spine—the sign of Indian blood.

When my child was born, after counting the fingers and the toes, I turned it over to check for the blue spot at the base of the spine.

Even among the half-breeds, it's one of the last things to go. (19-20)

"No map, no trail, no footprint, no way home" is a refrain echoed by the character, Lady Rebecca, as Pocahontas was renamed when she was converted to Christianity and then taken to England's Elizabethan court as an advertising gimmick. The theme of being lost in my motherland, finding no trail to follow because my grandmothers and great-grandmothers left no written records of themselves or their experiences, weaves through my early work. Narratives of wandering without a map, having forgotten my way, evolved to another recurring theme: memory/remembering/memorializing.

The following text fragment is from a writing exercise on "amnesia" from *Un(tit)led* (1993), a piece co-written with Djanet Sears and Kate Lushington that explored the borders and boundaries of race and women's friendship. It was presented by Nightwood Theatre as a workshop production, facilitated by Clarissa Chandler, animated by Bañuta Rubess, and directed by Muriel Miguel, with a set designed by Teresa Przybylski.

***Amnesia fragments***

Amnesia.

Long nightmare hallways,

lost, wandering.

Memory just slipped away.

All recognition of myself,

who I was or am or might be.

Where does the spirit of an amnesiac go to find refuge?

Does it hang around waiting to be recognized, brought home,

fed and warmed as the relatives on the other side do

when we forget to acknowledge them?

Plastic Halloween costumes,

remnants of some vague need for ritual,

walking in the night—not to wander

nor to play but to be fed—Day of the Dead.

Sacred time to eat,

to celebrate,

to consecrate,

to pacify,

to subdue.

Smoke filled hollows of spaces long neglected needing

to be filled and fulfilled with the brimming nurturing

sustenance of food

of flavors on the tongues of we who are we who are we

who make fire,

who plant,

who hands in the cornmeal bless the masa dough

facing East.

I forgot.

I forgot the ant spray.

I forgot where I've been.

I forgot where I walked

I forgot what it's like to walk on sand,

to be in the ocean every day,

to sleep in a hammock,

to wake at dawn and go with the other

women in dugout canoes to the mainland

to get water from the river in the forest.

I forgot what it's like to climb coconut trees and

to know the jaguar watches over us.

I forgot to remember.

The following is the piece that was actually scripted from this exercise and presented. It began as a monologue that I wrote, and then we broke it up and Djanet and Kate added some character-specific images.

***Forbidden Territory***

MONIQUE: In this forbidden territory, the landscape itself is treacherous.

DJANET: No Exit.

MONIQUE: No entrance.

KATE: No admittance.

ALL: *(Whisper)* Only, only us.

MONIQUE: White lies in twisted words of "Discover America!" *(Singing) "See the USA in your Chevrolet!"*

KATE: Poor Dinah.

MONIQUE: Twisted words of nice hiding behind a Sunday school smile.

DJANET: Sssh, it's a secret.

KATE: *(Singing) "Someone's in the kitchen with Dinah."*

MONIQUE: I always thought that meant Dinah Shore.

KATE: Poor Dinah.

MONIQUE: In this treacherous landscape where we by our natures are forbidden.

KATE: In secret we meet.

DJANET: It's a secret manoeuvre.

KATE: Sssh.

MONIQUE: Covert operation. Undercover. Under wraps. Under the stars, under the cover of night.

DJANET: Dinah never fooled me; I always knew she was Black.

KATE: In the shadows, in the margins...

DJANET: ...our spines pressed flat against the wall, bellies pushed against our spines...

KATE: We gasp for breath to fortify us in our vigilance. Vigilance, unless I keep constant vigilance, I will forget everything.

DJANET: ...like a flower, a Black Cosmos, pushing up through the concrete.

KATE: I have forgotten who I am, I have forgotten who you are, I have forgotten why we are important to one another. The stars are going out inside my mind. I used to remember; how to dance, Pythagoras theorem, the capital of Australia.

ALL: We who are we who are we who are we... (*Continues under*)

DJANET: ...we who jump the borderline into this forbidden territory. Clandestine.

KATE: Clandestine.

MONIQUE: Clandestine mass graves—bones of my ancestors, bones of my ancestors, bones of my ancestors.

KATE: *(Singing) "Dong dong bell, bodies in a well! Who put them in?"*

DJANET: Sssh, it's a secret.

MONIQUE: The souls of amnesiac Indians on the land roam like trick-or-treaters on a Halloween night in the suburbs.

DJANET: *(Singing) "See the USA in your Chevrolet!"*

MONIQUE: White lies fall apart, shattered into millions of metallic mirrored pieces only to reproduce as mutant thoughts in the bodies of our unborn children.

| | |
|---|---|
| KATE: | Poor Dinah. |
| DJANET: | Incognito we advance. Masked, veiled, disguised and hidden. |
| KATE: | Subversive. |
| MONIQUE: | We meet with a password: |
| ALL: | Now! |

The voice in the previous piece became a character I named Rebelda. Here is Rebelda's story:

> There once was a woman named Rebelda. She has a plan. She has a memory. Rebelda knows they will come knock on your door, take you away and kill you. Rebelda knows they will burn your homes. Rebelda has no time to cry. Rebelda plans. Rebelda makes allies. Rebelda strategizes. Rebelda will not be wiped out.
>
> She carries memorized in code: a recipe for cornbread, a song for birthing babies while under fire. Propaganda in her hand and propagation on her mind. A baby on each hip and a weapon in her hand. Rebelda has no time to cry. Rebelda plans. Rebelda makes allies. Rebelda strategizes. Rebelda will not be wiped out.
>
> Like the coyotes, they haven't built a trap that will hold her. Like the raccoons, Rebelda spreads her brood. Rebelda steals. Rebelda eats garbage. Rebelda will not be wiped out.

Another one of the recurring images in my work is the bag-of-bones-carrying girl/woman. A character I will refer to as Bag of Bones/Rebecca first appeared in an early Native Earth production, *Double Take/A Second Look* (1983), written by Billy Merasty, Gloria Miguel, Maariu Olsen, and myself and directed by Muriel Miguel. Rebelda is another aspect of the same character. In retrospect, they are both early versions of Esperanza, my massacre-collecting atrocity tour guide from Turtle Gals' *The Scrubbing Project* (2002 and 2005). My original inspiration for this character came from Gabriel García Márquez's *One Hundred Years of Solitude*, which I read for the first time at age sixteen. This is a passage from García Márquez's magical novel: "That Sunday, in fact, Rebecca arrived. She was only eleven years old....Her entire baggage consisted of a small trunk, a little rocking chair with small hand-painted flowers, and a canvas sack which kept making a *cloc-cloc-cloc* sound, where she carried her parent's bones" (47). I carried this bag of bones around for a long time—these "bones of my ancestors"—and with the bones, the history of Native women on this continent. The history of being the sexual commodities for the conquest, the stories from the female side of the colonization experience, were not being told in the course of the "Native theatre explosion." I wanted to work with other Native women who felt the void and who had the courage to tell their own stories.

Jani Lauzon, Michelle St. John, and I first worked together in 1990 on the set of a CBC mini-series, *Conspiracy of Silence*. At that time, during pre-dawn conversations on the way to the set in sub-zero temperatures, we discovered a common interest in a theme that had left its mark on us all. Each of us had, or knew some one who had, tried to scrub off or bleach out her colour. These conversations and recognitions were the first seeds of *The Scrubbing Project*. It was not until nearly ten years later that we gathered to create the work.

In 1999 Turtle Gals Performance Ensemble was formed. Its founding members included Jani Lauzon, Michelle St. John, Sandra Laronde, and myself. For the first two workshop presentations in Nightwood Theatre's Groundswell and Native Earth's Weesageechak Begins to Dance, *The Scrubbing Project* was performed by a four-woman ensemble. By our second Groundswell presentation in 2000, we had become a trio.

In *The Scrubbing Project,* the Bag of Bones/ Rebecca/Rebelda character was fully developed and her story expanded to include the massacre imagery that I had been working with since The Centre for Indigenous Theatre's residency at the Banff Centre in the winter of 1995. This was a program that Floyd Favel and I co-directed that included Muriel Miguel, Pura Fé, Michelle St. John, Archer Pechawis, Maariu Olsen, Jennifer Podemski, Alex Thompson, and others. There were several questions from this residency that carried over into the creation process of *The Scrubbing Project.* They were 1) What are the consequences of creating art out of atrocity? 2) Is there such a thing as internalized genocide? (If so, what does it look like?) A question from a subsequent research project on memorials I did with Floyd Favel was, How do we create memorials to the holocaust in the Americas? To which Turtle Gals added 1) Once Native women have put down the bundles of grief and multi-generational trauma that we collectively carry—then what? And 2) How do we get from victim to victory?

*The Scrubbing Project* is a study of the manifestations of internalized racism and genocide. Esperanza, my Earthplane character, is a persona formed from my deepest victimization. She carries with her at all times a bag of bones she recovered from a clandestine mass grave: bones which she scrubs, feeds, and cares for. She also carries a bag filled with shoes she collected from massacre sites, which she treats as prayers and offerings, which the play's three characters transform into tobacco ties, to honour them—to memorialize.

Esperanza was further informed by this quotation from a document entitled "Guatamala: Memory of Silence: Conclusions and Recommendations" from the Report of the CEH (Commission for the Clarification of History) in 1999 (see Tomuschat). This is an excerpt of testimony made by a witness to the commission who arrived carrying human remains. I put these words in Esperanza's mouth:

> It is very painful to carry them...it's like carrying death...I'm not going to bury them yet...Yes, I want them to rest, I want to rest too, but I can't yet...they are the proof of my declaration...I'm not going to bury them yet, I want a paper that tells me "they killed them"...and they had committed no crime, they were innocent. Then we will rest.

In contrast, my Starworld character, Winged Victory, was created from my strongest vision of victory: the huge copper and bronze winged beings, round breasted and full in the thigh, who crown the tops of the triumphant neo-Greco/Roman statuary our colonizers have erected in order to commemorate *their* victories. She is also rooted to the knowledge that the Kuna Rebellion of 1925, led by Nele Kantule, and the Mayan uprising of 1994, led by the Zapatistas, are evidence that sometimes we get to win.

This is an excerpt from *The Scrubbing Project* where Esperanza crosses a threshold into a "Massacre Portal" and tells the story of the recovery of the bones. By the end of the story she cradles the bones in her arms and addresses them. When Turtle Gals performs this, there are pieces of text woven into the story and the character Ophelia's "Passion Portal" unfolds out of the "Massacre Portal" like a kaleidoscope before its conclusion. Here, I've put the sections back together in order to read it as a whole.

***Massacre Portal***

ESPERANZA: Crack! Thud! Crack! Thud!

*BRANDA tries to hang on to tradition. DOVE spirals down to Earthplane, back to OPHELIA.*

ESPERANZA: It's that once you see you can't ever pretend you don't see.

And I see,

I see the men lined up on one side, the women trembling on the other. I've never witnessed a massacre/I see them all the time.

I see the soldiers raise their rifles—

I see

Skulls shatter

I see

Bodies fall:

Friends

Companions

Husband

Crack! Thud! Crack! Thud!

I've never seen a body fall under the crack of

Bullet splintering bone/I see them all the time

And once you've seen, you can't ever pretend you don't see

And I see...

ESP & OPH: Little rivulets of blood...

ESPERANZA:...soaked up by the thirsty earth.

ESP & OPH: All the colours of the rainbow...

ESPERANZA:...dried to a rusty brown crust.

I've never seen my relatives' bodies piled on the

blood soaked earth/I see them all the time.

Spit on blood fades the stain.

But once you've seen, you can't ever pretend you don't see

and I see.

*(As she gathers up bones)*

I will carry you, I will care for you, I will feed you, and I

will sing you songs of comfort.

I will wash away the dirt, and the ragged flecks of flesh and skin

And you will be warm

And you will be loved

And I will build memory.

I am very grateful to the process that Turtle Gals went through diving headlong into the dark places of our victimization. The willingness to go there has allowed me to use those depths as a springboard—a trampoline that offers me the possibility of grounding myself in another place: a place where I cease to identify with my own victimization and no longer recognize my reflection as "the victim."

I would now like to talk about two veteran theatre directors whom I consider to be light-bearers in our movement. They have consistently held up a beacon, shed light on the path and given me a direction through their incredible vision. They are Floyd Favel of Takwakin Performance Lab on the Poundmaker Reserve in Saskatchewan and my aunt, Muriel Miguel of Spiderwoman Theater in New York City.

I will start with this equation that Floyd created, and although it is somewhat-tongue-in-cheek and pseudo-scientific, I think it works.

TrAd (social/ritual) x M = NpC

Or, Tradition, social or ritual x Methodology = Native Performance Culture.

Instead of trying to interpret what Floyd means, I will offer a quotation from an article he wrote called "The Shadowed Path":

> One of the ideas of Native Performance Culture is to search for accessible ritual and social structures that can act as a catalyst for creative action. I believe that there needs to be a bridge from a ritual and social action to the professional stage. Tradition needs to be filtered and transformed for the objective needs of the theatre. Without this bridge, theatre risks presenting "Artificial Trees"

> on stage. "Artificial Trees" is the superficial or clichéd presentation of ritual and social structures on the professional stage.

In another article entitled "Waskawewin," published in 2005 for *Topoi*, an international philosophy journal published in the Netherlands, Floyd defines the concept of "Artificial Trees" this way: "to take the traditional sacred dance as it is and transplant this to the modern stage. This process I feel turns the dance into folklore, or an 'artificial tree.' A tree cut off from its roots, a facsimile of culture and sacredness" (114).

He describes the methodology for Native Performance Culture he has been searching for in these words:

> One would have to isolate the technical principles of the dance and use these as starting points for contemporary performance. What is meant by technical principles is: the position of the body to the earth, the relationship of the feet to the ground, the head to the sky, the different oppositions in the body, balance. It is the enigmatic relationship between these technical principles that create the dance. These enigmatic relationships are the shadow zone where ancestors and the unknown dwell, and this is where creativity is born, where the impulse is born. In Japan, they call this the Ma, the pause between beats and notes. In my tradition, they say the ancestors dwell in the space between the dancers. (114)

One of the things that I love about Floyd is that he doesn't get stuck in his own dogma. He warns against his equation being applied as a formula, saying that each artist must work from his or her own equation. In a recent phone conversation he also said, "'Artificial trees' is its own valid form." And that is true. It is what my grandpa did performing Indian medicine shows—it is the "Lakota" commercial. Which provides the perfect segue to...Spiderwoman Theater.

I have known Muriel Miguel all my life; she is my mother's younger sister. I grew up watching her, my mother, Gloria Miguel and their older sister, Lisa Mayo, perform long before Spiderwoman Theater was founded. They are my lineage and I am proud of the precious gifts that I have inherited from them.

As the director that I have worked with most consistently over the past two decades, Muriel has truly been the one to mold the raw material of my writing into performances. This is how she describes what she does. It is from the director's notes from *The Scrubbing Project* program.

> As Indigenous people, we see all disciplines as interconnected, with roots in traditional forms of storytelling. As the artistic director of Spiderwoman Theater, I have, over the past 30 years, been using a methodology called storyweaving to entwine stories and fragments of stories with words, music, song, film, dance and movement, thereby creating a production that is multi-layered and complex; an emotional, cultural and political tapestry.

I have been thinking about the way Muriel works when she directs. She helps generate materials, she dramaturgs that material and weaves it together in a way that is very intuitive—not at all an intellectual process. In fact, it is a mistake to even try to justify something to her intellectually. She will wave it away with her wrist and say, "That sounds very intellectual"—as if to also say, "I can't do anything with that, Dearie—you're going to have to go deeper." Muriel does not allow an actor/creator to stay in her head. Muriel works from that place of what is unconsciously known, intuitively known—*saber sabiendo*: to know knowingly. Nor is she satisfied for a piece of theatre to be one or two-dimensional when it could be three-, six-, nine-, or even twelve-dimensional. And dynamics!—do not play her the same note!

Then I had a brain flash. Maybe it was just menopause, but I could see, I thought, what Muriel does. She makes *molas* out of theatre. *Molas* are her palette and her dramaturgical tool. *Molas*: the art of Kuna women. *Molas* are the traditional textiles of the Kuna nation from the autonomous territory of Kuna Yala, in what is known as Panama. Kuna women are renowned for their skills in creating their designs and combining colour. Originally the designs were painted and tattooed on our bodies. Kuna women wear two *mola* panels—front and back—sewn together to form blouses. Each *mola* tells a story. Each story is a layered narrative. When the women walk it is said, "We are walking stories." Kuna perception, Kuna cosmology, Kuna identity are encoded in the layers of our *molas*.

*Molas* are made by the combined techniques of reverse appliqué, appliqué, and embroidery. They require several layers of fabric and the designs are cut out free-hand to allow the colours from the layers underneath to show through. Stitching the edges of the designs with the tiniest of stitches is the most fastidious part because it is what connects the layers. The *mola* gets thicker and thicker. Sometimes a corner will be torn apart and another colour or pattern of cloth will be inserted. Some areas will be built up with appliqué and details embroidered on. There are no even edges and although symmetry and duality are central principles, even two panels of the same blouse will not be exactly the same. Ironically, sewing machines were introduced to make Kuna women's work faster, a more economically sound enterprise. They did make the work faster but these *molas* are thin with square edges to their designs and inferior overall. It is possible to trace the design of a *mola* and reproduce its outline but it would lack the multi-dimensional layers of meaning that make it Kuna. I have never made a *mola*, neither has my mother nor my aunts, but we all grew up living with them, touching them, tracing their texture and designs, smelling them, sleeping on them, and wearing them. It is this thickness, this multi-dimensional knowing applied from the principles of Kuna women's art, that I believe is my inheritance from Spiderwoman's theatrical methodology. And I want that thickness in my work.

I still have a *mola* that was my mother's since before I was born. When I was very small I used to put it on to dance around our apartment. It was too long and fell almost to my knees; it would slip off my shoulders. I always wore it accompanied by a little red ballet tutu, and I would dance and create performances all by myself. I would spend hours dancing in my *mola* and red tutu to Tschaikowsky, Mendelssohn, Rimsky-Korsakov. I have not thought about that outfit in fifty years, but I can feel myself going back to where I began, only now with more experience and more information. *Saber sabiendo*.

In November 2007 I had the unique opportunity to try these ideas in a studio/laboratory setting starting from a clear premise and intent. *Chocolate Woman Dreams the Milky Way* is a multidisciplinary collaboration among three senior artists: myself as writer/performer, Floyd Favel as director, and Kuna visual artist Oswaldo (Achu) DeLeón Kantule as painter, designer, and cultural consultant. Our proposal was 1) to collaboratively create a multidisciplinary live theatre piece that integrates traditional and contemporary art forms and incorporates visual imagery with text and performance, and 2) to build on a methodology of Native Performance Culture by applying principles and structures from traditional visual story narratives to script development. We also wanted to explore a) how organically generated text and story narrative can support (not explain) the visual image and b) how a performer can embody the visual image such that it can be used as the framework for a narrative structure.

The first three days of the workshop process were spent looking at paintings from Achu's considerable body of work—stunning contemporary paintings rooted in the aesthetic of *mola* designs and pictographic writing. Then we poured through piles of ***molas***, with Achu making us familiar with the principles in ***mola*** art from the most abstract (most traditional) to the most representational or figurative (most modern). We studied the ***molas***' dissection of designs, their dualities, multiples of dualities, and thematic abstractions. We then turned to the pictographic writings that notate the chants of the traditional Kuna healers and identified the literary structure of the chants: a repetition that builds through the accumulation of verbs—dramatic action.

From these principles, rooted in an Indigenous cosmology, identity and aesthetic, we employed abstractions (a process Achu has been using in his paintings for some time) to create the beginnings of a form and a structure for *Chocolate Woman Dreams the Milky Way*. We also used the Kuna principles of presenting image and story metaphorically as if through the smoke screen of Chocolate Woman's smudge in order to protect its true meaning by encoding it.

We knew from the first improvisation on my feet that we were onto a process that worked; however, we were quite astonished when I was instructed by Floyd to notate that first improvisation using the process, and my text emerged as pictographs written from right to left, then left to right[2]. We have now taken a first step towards developing a dramaturgy specific to an Indigenous aesthetic and literary structure—in this case, one rooted in the principles of traditional Kuna visual art and literature. In Achu's words, "We are reclaiming cultural history." What is more, this same model could be adapted and applied by an Ojibwe artist investigating the bark scrolls, an Inuit artist examining the syllabic writing system, a Pueblo artist looking at rock paintings, or a Mayan artist deciphering the glyphs.

This collaboration also gave space to a discussion about the evolution of Floyd's "formula" for Native Performance Culture. He has grown away from the term "methodology" as connoting something too fixed and product-oriented. He now prefers to call the transformative journey to the stage (and back to our origins) simply "process." So the "formula" now looks like this:

Tradition⇔Process⇔Performance.

It is a fluid, multi-directional continuum where the three elements all relate to each other in an equal manner.

Tracing the themes in my work over the past two decades has allowed me to see up close my trajectory from victim to victory. Returning to the fragment from the development of *Princess Pocahontas* noted at the beginning of this piece, I can say that today I am no longer willing to call to the "spirits of heartbreak and sadness, blood and rebellion, or back breaking endurance." I spent a long time digging around in massacre imagery and now I must call out to other spirits because transformation is a continuum, and I must conjure myself into another place on my map. My writings and the theatre I create from them are my offerings, my prayers, my healing chants, my history, my identity—my ***molas***. This is what the stories in *Chocolate Woman Dreams the Milky Way* are about.

*Siagua*, cacao beans, are what chocolate is made from. In the central part of the Americas (from Mexico south) they are very important. They are used as currency, they are burned as smudge to purify, pray, and heal and they are an important part of the traditional diet. *Siagua*. Without it many Kuna have developed diabetes and high blood pressure. I have started eating these beans. In Kuna culture all the medicines are

[2] For much of the public reading of this work-in-progress presentation my text was read from pictographs.

women, so *siagua* is referred to as Cacao Woman—*Puna Siagua*. Intrigued by the yummy image of a chocolate woman I began calling to Cacao Woman just as *Ixquic*, Blood Woman from the Mayan creation story, did when, bereft and alone, she cried out for help. This title piece of a new multidisciplinary collaboration evolved, in part, from a dream I had about ten years ago.

***Chocolate Woman Dreams the Milky Way***
***an invocation***

In this time when my blood is held inside,
the cries of my dolphin children are carried farther out to sea into the arms of
*Muu Bili*, Grandmother Ocean.

Now that my blood is held inside,
Purified by the smoke of Red Cacao Woman's beads—*siagua*—here on *Abya Yala* Land of Blood.

*Puna Siagua, Siagua kinnit!*
*Be an anwe be sagua waale waaletgine*
*Wrap me in the arms of your purifying smoke*

*Olowaili*, the morning star is the sister of the sun.
My grandfather whose broad chest was tattooed with an eagle's wingspan open full,
saw *Olowaili* fall to earth over New York harbour and named me for her.

*Olowaili*, swirl and dance!
Spiral and place your feet in mine!
Fill my belly with starlight!
*Olowaili guile birya birya!*
*Be nak odoe an nakine!*
*Be an saban enoge nizgana guallu gine*

In heavy chocolate dreams I swim to shore
I am naked as the warm turquoise water breaks over my face.
I can see the shoreline. There are houses made from cane stalks lashed together
their palm-thatched roofs hang low.
Swaying and rebounding in the sea breeze are the palms themselves.
The beach burns brilliant.
Sand blinding white. *Kuna Yala!*

I stand and walk out of the sea. Salt water slides off my naked skin.
Against the starkness of the sand there are *molas* neatly laid out.
A blanket of red layered and encoded with meaning.

To my left, a few steps away from the *molas*, stands a beautiful young woman.

She wears the clothes of Kuna women: a red *mola* blouse, sarong skirt, a red and gold head-scarf, winis—beads wrapped tightly around her wrists almost to the elbow, adorning her ankles almost to the knee, a gold nose-ring, and a gold necklace that falls over her entire chest like a breast-plate. A delicate line of blue-black paint traces the centerline of her nose. Her round cheeks are shiny with moisture and stained achiote red. Her black hair cropped short frames her face. There is something on her head like...a golden bowl whose sides undulate in constant motion.

She is smiling. Smiling at me. Her arms outstretched, fingers spread wide. She shows me her *molas*, neatly arranged in rows on the sand. She is proud of her work. She begins to spin and spin and spin. Faster and faster.

*Olowaili, guile birya birya!*
*Be nak odoe an nakine!*
*Be an saban enoge nizgana guallu gine*

*Puna Siagua! Siagua kinnit!*

*Be an anwe be sagua waale waaletgine*

Let my smile mirror the spinning girl on the beach!

Full moon hangs low over the Ocean.

It is December. The air is humid and night cocoons the narrow thread of highway.

Sugarcane fields whip past.

Shards of moonlight like fragments of broken disco ball bob in the black water—laying a path of stars to the Milky Way—*negaduu*.

If I could place my feet upon those stars like stepping stones, I would follow them to visit my ancestors. And we would drink cacao—*siagua* mixed with ground, roasted corn from gourds. We would smack our lips; wipe our mouths on the backs of our hands and talk. Wouldn't we talk! *Tegi*!

I, too, am a granddaughter fallen from the stars

I call to Sky Woman: send me your courage!

The courage of the valiant Morning Star, Olowaili, when she rises each morning to greet her brother, Ibeler, the sun, at daybreak

And there, for some moments, we hang in the liquid pigment of a watercolour sky.

(2006-2008).

## Works Cited

Favel, Floyd. "The Shadowed Path." Unpublished.

---. "Waskawewin." *Topoi* 24.1 (2005): 113-115.

García Márquez, Gabriel. *One Hundred Years of Solitude*. Trans. Gregory Rabassa. 1970. New York: Avon, 1971.

Mojica, Monique. *Princess Pocahontas and the Blue Spots*. Toronto: Women's Press, 1991.

Tomuschat, Christian, Otilia Lux de Cotí, and Alfredo Balsells Tojo. "Guatemala: Memory of Silence. Report of the Commission for Historical Clarification. Conclusions and Recommendations." February 1999. 23 Jan. 2008. <http://shr.aaas.org/guatemala/ceh/report/english/toc.html>

[See DVD for photo of Ms. Mojica wearing a *mola* and holding cacao beans.]

# Pushing the Bear: A Script about the 1838-39 Cherokee Trail of Tears

*Diane Glancy*

Author's Statement, December 2007

I knew about the Trail of Tears since I was a girl and we visited my Cherokee relatives in northwestern Arkansas. My mother was of English and German descent. My father was an undocumented Cherokee, because his grandfather was not in Indian Territory at the time of the Dawes Rolls. I grew up with the maternal side of my family. Once in a while, we made visits to my father's people. Something not talked about was there. Attention was paid to ripples on a lake. The clouds. The leaves. The way something moved was taken notice of. When I moved to Oklahoma after college, I began to feel again the presence of that unknown history. I remember driving to Tahlequah, Oklahoma, when I lived in Tulsa, to see an outdoor presentation of the Trail of Tears at the Cherokee Heritage Museum. Afterwards, I visited research libraries and eventually drove the 900 miles of the trail, from New Echota, Georgia, to Fort Gibson, Oklahoma, which was called Indian Territory at the time. As I researched, I found information before and after the trail, and there was a line linking the two—"and they walked 900 miles." Wait, I thought, that is what I wanted to know—the spirit, the emotional journey, the heart-beat during the march. Three major themes became evident: a) political issues (a few chiefs signed away the land without agreement from the rest), b) religion (Christianity vs. the conjurers), and c) gender (uprooting is usually more difficult on the men; the women continue to prepare the meals and take care of the children—thus their lives do not change as radically). I think it was in passing over the land that I began to hear the voices of the people in my imagination, and began to think how they could fit together. I am interested in giving voice to history. It takes many voices to tell the story of a nation.

From October 1838 through February 1839, some eleven to thirteen thousand Cherokee walked nine hundred miles in bitter cold from the southeast to Indian Territory (later Oklahoma). One fourth died along the way.

*"I suggest, for your consideration, the propriety of setting apart of ample district West of the Mississippi, and without limits of any State or Territory, now formed, to be guarantied to the Indian tribes, as long as they shall occupy it."* Andrew Jackson's address to Congress, December 8, 1829

There are as many stories as there are people who walked the trail.

CHARACTERS[1]

KNOBOWTEE

MARITOLE: Knobowtee's wife

O-GA-NA-YA: Knobowtee's brother

REVEREND BUSHYHEAD: a Cherokee minister

ANNA: an old woman

A SOLDIER

[1] A photo of the cast of the Miami University reading on February 20, 2007, is included on the DVD accompanying this book.

KNOBOWTEE
There was at first *advantage*. We traded deerskins for kettles and metal pots. We built mills and trade stores and taverns in New Echota. We built a ferry and newspaper office. Men wore turbans and coats. Our women wore calico dresses.

REVEREND BUSHYHEAD
We became like them.

O-GA-NA-YA
It was called—assimilation.

KNOBOWTEE
It was called—survival.

O-GA-NA-YA
But how do we stay who we are while taking their ways? Is it possible to remain who we are?

KNOBOWTEE
I say we return to our ways. Fight for our land.

REVEREND BUSHYHEAD
We're outnumbered, Knobowtee—

KNOBOWTEE
I don't want to be swallowed by the new ways.

REVEREND BUSHYHEAD
We already are.

O-GA-NA-YA
What to do with us? That is their problem.

KNOBOWTEE
How to get us out of the way so our land can be theirs.

REVEREND BUSHYHEAD
There is the moral component.

O-GA-NA-YA
What they do will be in the root of their nation.

KNOBOWTEE
It will be our nation, too, O-ga-na-ya, my brother.

O-GA-NA-YA
They know removal from our land is wrong, but a new nation is being established.

REVEREND BUSHYHEAD
They are struggling with these ideas.

KNOBOWTEE
I don't think they are struggling at all, Reverend Bushyhead. They just want us gone.

REVEREND BUSHYHEAD
Anyone able to think this way has to know the ramifications. They have to see the long run.

KNOBOWTEE
The long run has been decided: Removal.

O-GA-NA-YA
We see government as federal, state, and Indian. But they see only national sovereignty and state sovereignty.

KNOBOWTEE
We're on our way out, aren't we?—Pick up your metal pots and kettles, Maritole—Here they are. Soldiers with bayonets at our door.

MARITOLE
Give me the seed corn to carry.

KNOBOWTEE
I'll carry it in my tunic.

O-GA-NA-YA
There's Bushyhead dismantling the church—

SOLDIER
Move. Get to the stockade—

O-GA-NA-YA
They'll only let him take the room beam in the wagon.

MARITOLE
We are sick and despondent in these close quarters.

REVEREND BUSHYHEAD
There are men in Washington arguing for the Cherokee to stay on their land. There are Cherokee cooperating with the government to remove the Cherokee. None of the boundaries are clear. There are fractures and inconsistencies everywhere Chief John Ross turns. He said he tried to explain the complications, but President Jackson sat at his desk thumbing through a newspaper. Jackson didn't want to hear. Sometimes the government would not recognize him. John Ross! Principal chief of the Cherokee nation. An educated man with the same responsibility for governing his people as Jackson has. In the end, Chief Ross asked for funds for removal. In the end, he argues for anything that will get our people out of the stockades before we die here. How many voices are there making nothing clear?

MARITOLE
My mother holds my baby. It cries until it is too weak to cry. Then it sleeps until it wakes to cry again.

O-GA-NA-YA
What does a nation do when it arrives in a place where there is another nation? Do they just walk over them and establish their land on the land of another?—Take the present occupants and move them to new land far away in the west?

KNOBOWTEE
Only three chiefs sign away all our lands. We are more divided than the nation that drives us to the new territory. I would not want to be those chiefs when we arrive there.

ANNA
Remember the eclipse of the sun several years ago? We knew it was an omen.

KNOBOWTEE
The conjurers said a frog was trying to swallow it. The conjurers beat their drums to scare the frog away.

REVEREND BUSHYHEAD
The Christian ministers explained how the moon got between the earth and the sun.

O-GA-NA-YA
Are there always two ways to everything?

KNOBOWTEE
The soldiers outside the wall of the stockade line up the wagons for the march. We will leave, but we will stay. Both are true. We go on the forced march. But the soldiers do not know we are the land. Our voices are the corn tassels in the wind. Our roots entwine.

MARITOLE
In one of our old stories, a woman named Selu was killed. Where her blood fell, corn began to grow. Our life comes from blood.

REVEREND BUSHYHEAD
There's another blood, the missionaries tell us—the blood of Christ that gives another life—one that does not die.

MARITOLE
Some of us believe.

KNOBOWTEE
Some of us spit on the ground in front of Reverend Bushyhead.

MARITOLE
At dawn there's a shot. Drizzle begins to fall. The sky is hard and gray.

ANNA
The hills are so quiet, I can hear a dog bark from the distance.

MARITOLE
The soldiers hand out rations of flour and bacon. We have to cook our breakfast and prepare one meal to carry with us. My father, Knobowtee, and O-ga-na-ya hold the blanket over us while my mother and I cook the bacon and make a lump of bread from the white flour we are not used to.

ANNA
Reverend Bushyhead leads the camp in prayer. His voice carries over the stockade. He asks forgiveness for the Georgia Cherokee in the hearts of the Tennessee Cherokee who signed away the land.

KNOBOWTEE
I can't forget.

MARITOLE
The conjurers hiss. Reverend Bushyhead asks for the Maker's blessing in getting us to the new land. The soldiers ride back and forth. Their voices are confusing.

ANNA
We start walking slowly. Some of the old women climb into wagons. I shiver as we begin to move. The rain soaks through the blanket around my shoulders and runs down my neck.

MARITOLE
I don't want to go, Anna.

ANNA
Listen, Maritole. What do you hear?

MARITOLE
Nothing.

ANNA
What else?

MARITOLE
Babies crying.

ANNA
Listen again.

MARITOLE
What's there, Anna?

ANNA
You tell me.

MARITOLE
Someone's sick.

ANNA
Listen again.

MARITOLE
Soldiers talking to a girl.

ANNA
Not that.

MARITOLE
The trees?

ANNA
What else?

MARITOLE
The river. Yes, the Hiwassee. It says we're moving now, too, just as it moves.

SOLDIER
This is the way we will travel:
North through Tennessee
Kentucky
Across the Ohio River
The southern tip of Illinois
Across the Mississippi River
West across Missouri
Then a corner of Arkansas to Fort Gibson, Indian Territory

MARITOLE
I slip in the mud in my moccasins as we walk into the Hiwassee—Knobowtee!!

KNOBOWTEE
I hear Maritole call my name, but I'm helping an old man across the Hiwassee. The rush of cold water around his legs and hips paralyzes him. The man's turban falls, but I hold his tunic. With one hand, I pull him, trying to keep his head above water, with the other hand, I hold the pouch of our seed-corn in the air.

MARITOLE
A soldier dismounts. He pulls me up. He motions, I can ride his horse, but I refuse. Knobowtee is looking. Anna helps my mother. I hold the baby high against my chest as we wade through the waist-high water.

REVEREND BUSHYHEAD
I carry my terrified child and guide my pregnant wife through the river.

ANNA
A horse passes me, its ears thrown back, its eye wide as a full moon. The bit jerks in its mouth. A driver is trying to get the wagon across the current.

KNOBOWTEE
This new nation is in a clamp. What they do is not right, yet it is expedient for the nation they are establishing. That's what takes precedence.

ANNA
On the other side of the river, we build a fire and dry our clothes.

O-GA-NA-YA
We are in the clamp if you ask me.

KNOBOWTEE
Somewhere north of the Cumberland Mountains in Tennessee, rain turns into snow and snow into a blizzard. We huddle under the wagons or on the ground without fire. I hear the conjurers working their magic against the storm. I hear Reverend Bushyhead praying.

MARITOLE
In the cold dawn, I see more people have died in the night. I see my mother does not stir. I know she is dead. My baby also in the crook of her arm.

SOLDIER
Leave the dead unburied beside the trail.

KNOBOWTEE
We bury our dead. Otherwise their spirits will wander without rest.

SOLDIER
Here's a shovel. Dig the frozen ground.

KNOBOWTEE
We carry the bodies in wagons until we find ground that is not hard as the new nation that is being formed with this in its history.

SOLDIER
You're going to freeze. Put these on.

MARITOLE
No! They are clothes of the dead.

SOLDIER
You want to live?

KNOBOWTEE
Stay away from her—

MARITOLE
When Knobowtee is not looking, I put on the clothes of the dead—trousers under my skirt—another jacket.

REVEREND BUSHYHEAD
We camp for the night by a road under a severe rainfall with heavy winds, with a canvas for a shield from the weather and the cold wet ground for a resting place. I perform the burial for Maritole's mother and baby. The soldier helps dig the graves. Several are ill and in the last struggles of death.

SOLDIER
1300 Indians march.
There are 80 wagons
800 horses
60 oxen
A line 10 miles long.
We make a journey of 10 miles a day and bury 14-15 at every stopping place. Look how quietly the Indian woman mourns her mother and baby. Look how she sits with the older woman while her husband looks away.

MARITOLE
I feel I am pushing a bear along the trail we walk. At first, it is the discouragement I push against each day. Then the bear is the sorrow I feel for my baby and mother. Then I remember an old story: A long time ago, the Cherokee forgot we were a tribe. We thought only of ourselves. Our hair grew long on our bodies. Claws grew on the ends of our fingers and toes. We crawled on our hands and knees. We forgot we had a language. We forgot how to speak. That's how the bear was formed.

REVEREND BUSHYHEAD
I remember something about the year of Jubilee—I look through the pages of Leviticus—A drop of snow or cold rain from the trees spots the pages. There it is—in the 25th chapter, 23rd verse. The land shall not be sold forever: for the land is mine; for you are strangers and sojourners with me. EVEN THE LORD WAS A SOJOURNER? What ideas the white God has. What does that mean? I have trouble thinking in the cold. The land is returning to the white man? No, it wasn't his to begin with. It means nobody owns anything permanently. I can say the Cherokee are going through a year of Jubilee—giving our land that isn't really ours back to God. Now we can travel. Maybe that is the idea. If it will help the people walk, then I will tell them.

KNOWOWTEE
The snow is a helper. The snow is a spirit being. Speak to the snow. Ask it for help.

REVEREND BUSHYHEAD
I remember the little table in the church we left—the bottle of anointing oil on it. How I need the oil as I listen to my young daughter cough. Behind the table was a white wall—white as the Kentucky fields we walk—And as pure. How can that be? Does everything come from the spirit?—Even this? My wife can't keep up with the walking line as she grows heavier with our second child. She can't bear the bouncing of the wagon. A soldier puts her on his horse for a while.

O-GA-NA-YA
Despite the trips to Washington, the hearings, harangues, pleadings, petitions, accusations, resolutions, prayers, divining stones, conjurer's spells, we're walking, aren't we?

ANNA
The land got tired of listening and drove us away.

REVEREND BUSYHEAD
Hold to your hope.

KNOBOWTEE
I sit in the woods calling a bird. I whistle the way I remember my father did. But the bird just sits there on the branch of the tree—I'm hungry for you—anything but this salt pork and white flour.

O-GA-NA-YA
Bird, my relative, come into our hands.

KNOWOBTEE
Maybe we can make a blowgun.

O-GA-NA-YA
The soldiers won't let us have any weapons.

KNOBOWTEE
Maybe I can turn myself into a bird. Or if I think I am a bird, maybe I can become a bird spirit. It's the way my father hunted. It's the way he became another. If only I could remember how he did it.

O-GA-NA-YA
Give yourself, bird. I honor you with song.

KNOBOWTEE
Yet the bird flies away.

ANNA
Now we come to a wide river.

SOLDIER
The Ohio.

MARITOLE
I've never seen such a river—Wide, turbulent and full of ice.

SOLDIER
Here's another jacket—

REVEREND BUSHYHEAD
Another minister who leads another detachment rides forward in the line. He says the Cherokee will freeze here beside the river. It is time to cross. He orders the soldiers to start three wagons loaded with the old and sick on an ice floe. One wagon almost makes it to the other side before it tips and the three wagons overturn, dumping their passengers into the river.

ANNA
We hear their screams and watch them flail in the water before they sink.

MARITOLE
O-ga-na-ya jumps in the river to save them, but they are gone, and Knobowtee throws him a rope to pull him out.

REVEREND BUSHYHEAD
Build a fire—

KNOBOWTEE
I don't want you near us, Reverend Bushyhead. It was one of your ministers who ordered this.

ANNA
More people die in the cold waiting to cross. Even the pack-dogs die of hunger.

SOLDIER
Several days later, when the ice chunks are smaller, the Indians begin crossing slowly on the ferry, the rafts, and small boats that come for them.

REVEREND BUSHYHEAD
The conjurers say, the water spirits will pull us into the water, just as it did the old ones. But I say, God will help us across.

ANNA
For long nights afterwards, I see the dead dance in the river, the cold water making them rigid, soaking their lungs until they sank like sacks of the white man's flour.

SOLDIER
Ride with me.

MARITOLE
I can't.

SOLDIER
Then get in a wagon.

MARITOLE
They are for the old and sick—and the children who can't walk.

KNOBOWTEE
Leave her alone—I tell you, Maritole, we will walk and not fall.

MARITOLE
At night, I dream a bear is eating me. Inside, it is warm. I gain its strength. The conjurers suck me out of the bear. I am able to walk again.

ANNA
I walk as if on a white field of clouds, my feet not touching the ground. I am so cold I feel warm. Still I walk beyond anything I could endure. O mystery. O unexplainable God.

O-GA-NA-YA
There's an old story of two turtles—how they challenged a deer to a race—one turtle started out, but another turtle stepped out of the woods before the deer and crossed the finish line first.

KNOBOWTEE
We are two nations now—The Cherokee who walk west, and the Cherokee who ran into the mountains and will remain east.

O-GA-NA-YA
We joined the British during the Revolutionary War. What did we expect?

KNOBOWTEE
Gold was discovered near Dalonagah in Georgia, and farmers wanted our fertile land.

O-GA-NA-YA
What is a title to the land to an Indian? The land is for hunting and growing corn. No one has ownership of the land.

SOLDIER
But you're acting possessive of the land you had to leave.

KNOBOWTEE
The United States acknowledges us a sovereign nation. This march runs contrary to the binding treaty they signed.

REVEREND BUSHYHEAD
How much wrong can right absorb?

ANNA
The conjurers work their magic over a family. They spit into the snow. Smoke rises from it. I'm not afraid of their magic—they couldn't do anything when smallpox came—What can they do? Call the sky down to hide us?

KNOBOWTEE
I call a meeting. Few men come. My throat is sore, but I talk as though we have a council. I remember Wilson Lumpkin's speech—the Commissioner to the Cherokee. *The earth was formed for cultivation and none but civilized men could cultivate it.* Wilson Lumpkin, Commissioner to the Cherokee, made a speech like that. But Lumpkin said the heathen should be treated with *magnanimity.* That was his word. Therefore we would be removed to the west. I felt my anger. How could we deal with men who thought like that? My fist pounded something—the side of a wagon until the sick ones cried out. Then I pounded something else—

O-GA-NA-YA
Get away from the oxen, Knobowtee, you're hitting the animal that pulls the wagon.

ANNA
Now this is the story of our baskets. Some think the idea for weaving baskets came from the earth, which is the holder of our cornfields, the holder of our lives.

MARITOLE
Yes, some say the baskets just copy the land.

ANNA
Others think the idea for weaving baskets came from the sky—an upsidedown holder of the rain. So it falls back to us. But I say the ideas for baskets came from our stories. The baskets hold fish and corn and beans. Just like our stories hold meaning. Yes, I say the baskets copy our stories.

REVEREND BUSHYHEAD
The soldiers need to know that men are woven from the land. Hollow as a basket with a hollowness that pulls things into it. Because its purpose is to hold things, like the stomach, I think, feeling my hunger. But how much more like a basket are our stories? They hold our fear and hurt and resentment and anger. They give us a place to order our disorder; a direction for our *directionlessness*. They give us a place to argue with ourselves. Not because soldiers took our land, but because they took the order that couldn't be seen. They open us up to the old disorder, and we will have to build the world again—and that takes so much time and energy. They are unweaving the weaving that we have taken generations to complete. And what is wrong with that? What if we are hollow like our baskets? Nothing remains empty. That is the horror of the trail—we see beyond our cornfields and villages into the west where the sun disappears. And worse—we know the black space inside our heads is only a copy of the nothingness itself. And because of the hollowness, we are meant to hold things, and will always hold things, as long as there is something to hold.

MARITOLE
One day we come to another huge river.

SOLDIER
The Mississippi—We've reached the edge of Illinois. We will cross it into Missouri. We camp under the cover of brush and watch the ice float by Green's Ferry landing.

MARITOLE
The people cry, remembering the Ohio where some drowned.

REVEREND BUSHYHEAD
The earth and sky are ghost white in the frozen air.

ANNA
Look at that terrible outcropping of rock upriver.

SOLDIER
It's a bluff.

MARITOLE
The hills are higher than they had been when we crossed the Ohio, and the trees shorter, allowing the heavy sky to push us down.

REVEREND BUSHYHEAD
Many die while waiting for the ice to pass.

ANNA
That bluff is where the earth steps up to the sky world.

MARITOLE
I feel my fear of the river grow. How can we cross the water? We'll die. We'll drown like the others. Look at it, Anna. It's a spirit river. I watch the river pass for a few more days. Then one morning I wake with the taste of peaches in my mouth. I hear the soldiers preparing to cross the river. We will be among the first to cross. My heard pounds wildly. The bear camps before me as usual. I try to push him away, but he does not move. Old bear, I say, today we cross the river. I pat his hide. Move over. I go, even if it is to the afterlife with Mother and the baby. We cry as the soldiers herd us toward the landing. I feel a tightness in my chest. My arms hurt. Surely the land and the trail

we walk will fold under the earth with the sun. I hear the trees mourning for us. Above us the clouds wear my grandmother's bone-carved hairpin. I call to her and she smiles. Her face is now gray and lovely above the wind that snarls upriver. I see the spirits eating from my feather-edged dishes. I hear them in the wind. They put down their knives and forks. They come and hold the sides of the tossing raft as we step onto it, some of us falling, others crying out. The spirits wear bright tunics and turbans, and I can't see beyond them as we cross the river. They hold the raft steady as it jerks between large pieces of ice. I spoon more cornbread to them, more squirrel meat and peach cobbler. I cooked it just this morning in my dream. Hold on. Hold on. I hear them say as we cross the river, their ghost voices laughing to the freezing wind.

REVEREND BUSHYHEAD
My second daughter, Elizah Missouri Bushyhead, is born Jan 3, 1839, in a clump of trees after we cross the river.

KNOBOWTEE
Stay away from that soldier, Maritole. He looks at you.

MARITOLE
Have you helped me like he has? Did you comfort me when my mother died? Our baby? When have you helped me on this trail?

ANNA
You're growling, Maritole. You turn Knobowtee away.

MARITOLE
In the cold, I hear someone snore like a bear's growl.

ANNA
Maybe a conjurer killed a field mouse, eating it with his beak. Or maybe it is someone dying in the wagons. Sometimes death-breathing and snoring sound the same. How can anyone sleep? It is so cold.

MARITOLE
My hand twitches. Is it the bear gnawing my bones again?—Giving me its strength, or taking it from me with its greed. Go on bear, I snap. You are nothing but part of myself. Get moving—You are a part of everyone. Why else do we march? No one is free of the bear.

ANNA
I am part of the earth as I walk. I am the harvested crops. I should not mind the trail any more than the corn minds the harvest. When I hear the voice of the corn, I know I am part of the earth. Not the stalks, or leaves, or kernels, but a will to live that walks of its own accord. It doesn't matter if I walk, or cause the walking.

SOLDIER
How can you say that?

O-GA-NA-YA
She's mad with cold.

KNOBOWTEE
Everything is broken. Even my wife looks at a soldier. I cannot stop her with my anger. She is broken for me too—We're all torn and hurt. I cannot forget those who signed the treaty giving our land away—But we're nearing a place where we have to start over.

O-GA-NA-YA
We push south through Arkansas in the late winter. Now it is mud that slows us. Where are the three who signed away the treaty? We haven't seen them on the trail. Did they go by keel boat up the Mississippi and across the Arkansas rivers? Join us, Knobowtee. We have to take revenge. We'll wait until they build their cabins and think they are safe.

KNOBOWTEE
We'll just set more wrong into action.

ANNA
I am a spider now. Don't I walk even when I can't feel my feet?—Not the two feet I started walking with—out of North Carolina into Tennessee and Kentucky—Across Illinois into Missouri. I walk through the fall and into winter. I walk nearly into spring. I walk into Arkansas. I walk toward Indian Territory.

MARITOLE
I sit on the cabin steps in the new territory. The cabin was built hurriedly. It leaks. The place is silent—except for the birds—though once I think I hear the distant growl of a bear. Sometimes at the orphan school, I tell the story of the two turtles who tricked a deer into a race. There was a turtle at the starting line in the old territory. There was a turtle at the finish line in the new. Our Cherokee nation had become two to survive. At night the children slept against us, crying sometimes in their sleep. Knobowtee and I held them between us. Maybe someday he would touch me. Maybe someday love would come.

# SECTION IV: *Community and Collaboration*

## Theatre in the House/Raving Native Productions

*Marcie Rendon*

*"Can you believe you exist if you look in a mirror and see no reflection? And what happens when one group controls the mirror market? As Native people, we have known that in order to survive we had to create, re-create, produce, re-produce...The effect of the denial of our existence is that many of us have become invisible...the systematic disruption of our families by the removal of our children was effective for silencing our voices...however, not (everyone) can still that desire, that up-welling inside that says sing, write, draw, move, be...we can sing our hearts out, tell our stories, paint our visions...we are in a position to create a more human reality...in order to live we have to make our own mirrors..."*[1]

The first time I saw a Native woman on stage was 1991. I was stunned. It was not anywhere on my radar that we, I, Native folks, could, would, should do theater. I grew up in northern Minnesota where live theater was not part of the cultural landscape. The biggest drama we saw were high school basketball games, fights among town drunks, and parades down main street. But once I saw what was possible—thank you, Margo Kane—I was hooked.

Stage moves a people from invisible to visible. From silenced to vocal. From stoic to the broadest range of emotions possible. Once I saw the possibilities, I wanted this for myself and for my community. With encouragement from Juanita Espinosa of the Minnesota Native Arts Circle and then with mentors from the Playwright Center, I started to write for stage. The first scripts were bad. Truly. With no formal training either as a writer or a theater professional, it was only a life-long propensity to put pen to paper that propelled me forward.

While I knew how to write, with some writing published, I had no idea how to write for stage. To learn, I took workshops and classes at the Playwright Center in Minneapolis. One workshop was with Spiderwoman. To spend a weekend with this incredible group of Native women, who dared to be bold, loud, and outrageous and who were so confident this was exactly the right thing to do, was further confirmation that theater was something to remain engaged in.

Whenever possible, live productions became my classroom. Once, sitting in Penumbra Theatre, a nationally known African American theater that produces August Wilson's plays, and more recently, William S. Yellow Robe's *Grandchildren of the Buffalo Soldiers*, my youngest daughter said in a loud stage whisper, "Mom, we're the only Indians in here." Moments like that convinced me to continue doing what I do. I really believe Native people belong everywhere. Everywhere. I wanted to be sure that my daughter and my grandchildren knew they had a right not just to be, but to be fully present, everywhere.

So, I kept writing, trying, creating, making mistakes, junking scripts, and starting all over again, submitting scripts, being rejected, and, eventually, seeing my work produced.

---

[1] From "my own grandmothers..." by Marcie R. Rendon. Previously published: "Opening the Door," *Colors* [Minneapolis] 1 (Jan.-Feb. 1992); *Sweetgrass Grows All Around Her*, ed. Beth Brant and Sandra Laronde (Toronto: Native Women in the Arts, 1996), 46; *The Colour of Resistance: A Contemporary Collection of Writing by Aboriginal Women*, ed. Connie Fife (Toronto: Sister Vision, 1993), 127; *Speaking in Tongues: An Anthology of Poetry and Creative Prose by Selected Participants and Their Mentors in the Loft Inroads Program*, ed. Ellen Hawley and Carolyn Holbrook-Montgomery (Minneapolis: Loft, 1994), 55; and Jim Northrop, Marcie R. Rendon, Linda LeGarde Grover, and Denise Sweet, *Nitaawichige: Selected Poetry and Prose by Four Anishinaabe Writers* (Duluth: Poetry Harbor, 2002), 5.

In early productions of my work here in the Midwest, theaters could not find Native actors to perform. And there were certainly no Native producers or directors. I realized early on three things needed to happen. First, I had to tell my story. Second, I had to try create an environment that made it possible for folks to want to participate in live theater, to want to become actors, producers and directors, playwrights, at a community level. Third, again, live theater is not something most of our community members are familiar with or have the money to attend. Most see theater as a white activity and have not been brought up valuing theater as something to see, participate in, or support. So, I realized if I was writing with the hope of creating a mirror for Native people, I had to build audience. There was no point writing for theater if my people are not included in those invited to fill the seats.

For many Native people, our exposure to theater is limited. We tend to think of theater as Shakespeare, white culture, and inaccessible to us. While it is true that Western theater was introduced with European contact, Native people have always told stories and performed stories for the community. However, our reservation and urban communities have limited access to stage, props, and costumes. We have small numbers of playwrights and few trained actors at the community level.

Shortly after seeing Margo Kane perform, I took a workshop at the Playwright Center facilitated by New York playwright Ellen Maddow. Maddow gave us exercises and writing assignments to create a site-specific theater piece at a private home in Minneapolis. The process was fun, inspiring, accessible, and uncomplicated. After participating in Maddow's site-specific workshop, I made the decision to adapt, refine, and expand on the process to create Native theater projects as a way to involve Native people in creating scripts from idea to production. I created a workshop format called "Theatre in the House/Raving Native Productions" to encourage folks to write and act to produce shows at the community level. Guerilla theater. Initially, this meant productions at people's houses, in parks, and in Native-owned coffee shops. We would do our show and then pass the hat to pay the actors. In the ensuing years I have used the simplest formula of this process to help high school students create three-minute scripts and perform them in class during a one-hour classroom experience. In longer and more intense residencies for Project Hoop I have conducted three-week residencies for community participants to create theater pieces in their communities. The workshop can last for one hour or three weeks, but the goal is to keep everyone involved—creating character, writing script, performing, and helping with stage production needs.

At the residency at Lac Courts Oreilles Ojibwa (LCO) Community College in Hayward, Wisconsin, Native people who had never written for theater or been on stage became engaged in the process. Together we created an hour-long script they performed at a community Diabetes Prevention conference, then outdoors at the tribal center's picnic spot, and finally at a community pow-wow during supper break. Another small group, at the Anishinabe Cultural Center in Detroit Lakes, Minnesota, created a ten-minute script in Ojibwe. We first met on Friday late afternoon and by Sunday afternoon they performed their piece, in Ojibwe, to a small audience.

As facilitator of these workshops I hold out the idea that, "Yes, we can do this." I begin the process by saying, "We are going to use a fast and furious process to create a script that you will then perform at the end of this workshop for the people of your community. It doesn't matter if you have never written or acted before. We will create this together, and the script will come from characters and dialogue you create. You will know exactly what to do during each stage of the process and by the time you get up on stage, everything will be right there for you because you will have created it. It will be your character, saying words you have written, behaving in ways that you determine." I remind them that we are engaged in a process that is purposely intended to be fast, with not much time to think. When people think too hard, they get worried and scared. This is an exercise, in a spirit of fun, to give them a positive outcome. They can use what they learn during this process to write a more polished script or performance at a later date.

As facilitator I try to remain aware of the cultural background of the participants. Cultural traditions vary from tribe to tribe, and questions need to be asked to clarify the traditions of each group worked with. It's important to consider if there are elders in the community who should be invited to give prayers for the work you and the community are doing. When creating the script and characters, I encourage participants to incorporate their tribal stories—past and present; to utilize their songs, whether traditional or modern; and to be consistent with the spiritual teachings of their people out of respect for their community. For example, when working with Ojibwe people, they cannot tell Wanabazhoo stories unless there is snow on the ground. This is a cultural belief. Other tribes will have other beliefs. When working with one group of younger students, they used a pow-wow drum to do "street dance"—a form of pow-wow breakdancing. When I asked another group from another community to try the same thing, they were offended and refused to do so. They did, however, add hand-drum music to some of the more traditional scenes of the piece they created.

When first meeting with participants, I ask, Who dances at pow-wows? Who sings at the drum? Who knows yoga? Who can tap dance? Our communities are filled with people who have traditional talent, and then there are surprises, like the young person who plays classical piano and the 30-year-old champion polka dancer. It is a great challenge to help them merge the old with the new, the traditional with the modern. I do not encourage any group to put ceremony on stage. One piece that a community group created had a closing scene where the characters made offerings at the river. Rather than show actual offerings being made, they created a stylistic movement that symbolized the offerings being made, and, because the audience already knew the river was a part of the production, it all made sense without crossing cultural taboos. We are a ceremonial people. We create and love ritual. Through dress, song, movement and lighting, we can create the essence of this ceremony in ways that do not offend our elders.

Some of the harder stories of our struggles as Indigenous people always come through in each production, it seems. Someone always dies. People fall in love. Stories of alcohol and abuse, including rape, are often central themes. Participants should be encouraged not to shy away from these stories. The group can be encouraged to shape these stories in ways that add growth to the community and strength to the participants, while using real-life tension to create the drama of a piece.

The "Theatre in the House" process I developed is very streamlined. Each person creates a character—they create a move specific to that character, and they write their own dialogue within the parameters of the "theme" the group chooses to focus the script on. Each character has a sound or music theme specific to that character. A portable CD player often is used as a sound system. Where and when to utilize the song is left up to their imagination and where it will have the most impact. Each person chooses one prop for their character. This can be a coffee cup, a cigar, a cell phone—something that signifies who their character is. Each character has one costume item that defines them, like a long skirt or a beaded headband. Early in the process everyone identifies who their character is by showing us their character's move, prop, costume item, and their song. They also read their monologue.

This familiarizes everyone with the characters who will inhabit the story.

The next step is to create the story. What brings all these characters into the same space? What events occur? Will this be a comedy? A love story? A murder mystery? A tribal myth? As participants brainstorm, stories emerge, drama occurs, and the ideas are written down. The participants create the storyline, decide the tone of the script (serious, comedy, dark, etc.) while I ask questions to help them shape their story and write down their ideas as fast as I can. Participants must continually be writing down their thoughts and lines of dialogue as well.

The facilitator is the story shaper, the one with the knowledge of how to create a storyline with dramatic action that moves a story forward. The facilitator asks questions, which by their nature require a dramatic response so the characters' answers will create a sequence of events that move the story forward. Participants, in the persona of their character, answer the questions as their character would. They write the dialogue down in notebooks, which are clearly labeled by character. Question after question is answered to acquire pages of dialogue related to numerous events that could possibly occur between the characters. The questions are all related in some manner to the storyline the participants have agreed on. This very fluid process requires quick thinking, flexibility, and a determination to keep encouraging people even when they feel like nothing is happening.

Finally, an outline for the story is typed and then all the lines of dialogue are entered either by character or by scene. By working from beginning of story to end, each scene gets fleshed out and completed. In the next dialogue-creating session, they create the next scene, and so on, until the closing scene. By having each scene typed, the actors each day have a script to begin memorizing. Because they wrote the lines of dialogue, it is easier for them to learn their lines.

Once we have the entire script written, rehearsal begins in whatever building or room is available. At this point the facilitator becomes the director—encouraging, shaping, suggesting tone of voice, facial expression, blocking for each scene. Again, the idea is to make this as organic to each person as possible. It is important to follow the lead of the participants at their level of readiness and always to be encouraging and supportive of their efforts while pushing them gently to move way beyond their initial comfort zone.

At each "Theatre in the House" residency or workshop there are people who want to be part of the production but do not want to act. I encourage them to be production personnel, such as the sound tech carrying around the CD player or the lighting director. This has involved carrying around a flashlight to light the way for actors in the dark. Sometimes it has meant carrying a flashlight to focus on one scene or to create a visual effect.

The facilitator often has to improvise the staging. For communities with an available stage, whether that is a theater house or a school gym stage, approach whoever needs to be approached about the availability of that space for the time you need it and work from there. In communities without a stage, look for a natural setting that has space for audience to view the production. In one production the story took place in the middle of the college campus with a gazebo being main stage, the steps to a library another stage, a darkened delivery area another stage, a tree another, and a lattice-work concrete wall was the "spirit" house. Students carried signs saying "Follow Me" moved the audience from stage area to stage area. At LCO when the production was staged during the pow-wow supper break, we utilized the tribal art gallery. We used tables and the natural shapes in the space for each different scene. We set up folding chairs for the audience in a semi-circle where all staging areas were then visible to them.

Theater on stage is a fairly new art form for our communities. Part of our job in creating Native theatre is inviting the community to be audience and making the production accessible to them, both in space and affordability. I mention to the participants the importance of being an audience member. I remind them that theater is for entertainment and audience attention fuels the drama on stage. Without an attentive audience, the actor does not feel compelled to give a peak performance.

Send out flyers, put up posters at churches, schools, health clinics, gas stations. Have the tribal radio station do an interview with the actors and talk about the process while inviting everyone in the community to the show. Ask the local newspaper to run a press release. Get photos taken. Have the participants invite everyone in their family to the show. Have opening night in conjunction with a community pow-wow, conference, or school event where a ready-made audience is already gathered. Rather than charge admission, pass the hat and then divide the take among the cast members.

The key idea is to give the participants a positive experience. This is not about creating fine art (although it can be) or the next play that will run for five years on Broadway (although it can be the seed for such a reality). This process is to build the heart, soul, and enthusiasm for a community to want to continue this process once the exercise is finished. The goal is to leave the community with replicable tools and the fire inside to want to do it again.

# Thunder Road Theater and Community-Based Native American Theater: An Interview with Julie Pearson-Little Thunder and Jana Rhoads

*Vincent Scott,* National Museum of the American Indian

VINCENT/NMAI: I'm here in Tulsa, Oklahoma, in the winter of 2007 with Julie Pearson-Little Thunder and Jana Rhoads, founders of Thunder Road Theater, formerly known as Tulsa Indian Actors Workshop. I have just had the honor to direct a production of Drew Hayden Taylor's *Someday* for the company and wanted to take time to interview Julie and Jana to share their story with our colleagues in Native American theater.

Allow me to begin by asking each of you, why and how did you get involved in drama?

JANA: I first got involved in drama when I was in the ninth grade attending a small Oklahoma high school. The English/Speech teacher was a dedicated, somewhat formidable woman who seemed determined to make her students into "silk purses" having come, almost literally, from a "pig's ear" vis-a-vis their rural and farming backgrounds. I was somewhat out of place in that small town, having mostly grown up in small cities, but I definitely found a passion in theater that has continued throughout my life. My maternal grandparents owned and operated a drive-in theater in Anadarko, Oklahoma, and spending time in that environment colors many of my childhood experiences. I reveled in the multitude of movies I saw and experienced as a child and adolescent, and I was enthralled with the fact that my grandmother regularly read the movie magazines, which my mother considered somewhat "trashy." It was my pre-adolescent guilty pleasure to read these "forbidden fruits" and discuss them with Grandma. As I continued my participation in drama, I truly found my home with other students who shared my ideas and adolescent dreams in that weird and bewildering world of high school.

JULIE: I didn't discover drama till college. [I] don't even know if my high school had a drama department. Sometime between the ages of nine and sixteen, my Dad (who doesn't like plays, but loves music) took me to see two musicals, *Oliver* and *Man of La Mancha.* I guess those two musicals worked on me because among my first courses in college was a drama course, and I declared myself a theater major towards the end of my first year of college.

VINCENT/NMAI: Describe the history of Thunder Road Theater and its predecessor.

JANA: Julie and I first met when I was in a production of *The Cuckoo's Nest* produced by the American Indian Theater Company (AITCO). Later on that year, she served as interim director for AITCO, and our friendship was forged by our association with the company, with Julie as artistic director and me as a board member/actor. I continued acting with AITCO for a few years although on a fairly limited basis. I also participated in several local community theater acting workshops for a few years. It wasn't until my late 30s that I realized theater had to be a part of my life and that I needed to continue developing as an actor.

Over the next few years, Julie and I began to tentatively discuss forming our own theater company; finally, one day we wrote down our individual goals and objectives for doing this; our responses were complementary, and we thought, "It's a fit!" Along with Merlin, Julie's husband, we decided to focus strictly on plays by Native playwrights, as well as on training Native actors, techs, etc. During the first couple of years we definitely learned from our mistakes. We learned quickly that funding was always a problem and pursued state arts grants, which continue to be our major funding source.

Also, in the mid-1990s, it was not easy to find material we wanted to produce. Of course, we were lucky to have

Julie serve as artistic director and playwright, but we were constantly searching for contemporary plays by Native playwrights, plays that focused on contemporary Native issues, concerns, and experiences—"more than bows and feathers," so to speak. After the first couple of years, we had a core of actors, numbering about seven to ten, who were involved with our group on an ongoing basis, some serving as board members, as well as those who participated less actively. Some of our actors had community and/or college theater experience while others had none. I think one of the most satisfying things for me has been to watch different actors developing and growing in their skills.

The Indian community's response to our productions has always been positive; we often hear comments such as "I'm so glad to see something like this…I've never seen anything like it before," or, "That really told our story," etc. However, it is a constant struggle to maintain and to increase the numbers of our audiences. The non-Native audience members seem to enjoy and learn from our plays although, again, it's been difficult to have attendance numbers at the level we would like them to be. Our Guest Artist program has been helpful in raising public awareness about our productions and theater company, and the company has benefited tremendously from the experience of working with successful professional artists, actors, musicians, poets, and directors.

We began to offer summer workshops for children taught by company actors several years ago and have continued to do so. Initially, we produced the majority of our plays at the local performing arts center in their smaller stage venues. After a few years, Julie and I decided this venue seemed somewhat removed or perhaps even inaccessible to many Indian people. We had performed some plays while still in the rehearsal stages at several area Indian communities. We both felt strongly that this was the direction we wanted to go. We wanted to focus on bringing theater to communities that might not otherwise have access to this experience; to highlight the connection between oral tradition and theater; to foster a feeling of inclusiveness in this process; and to present live theater in an atmosphere where people would feel welcome and comfortable. Currently, we produce one play a year at the performing arts space, or in smaller local theaters, but we would like to focus on outreach/performance in smaller communities. We're still working on finding the most effective and successful ways to do that.

JULIE: Thunder Road Theater's predecessor was Tulsa Indian Actors Workshop. Jana and I met initially through American Indian Theatre Company where I had worked as Administrative Director from 1980–83 under J. R. Mathews. When Mathews left AITCO in 1985, I spent a number of years doing freelance articles on Oklahoma Indian artists for *Southwest Art* and *Oklahoma Today* and got away from theater entirely. The same with Jana—she had done no acting since the company disbanded. We were both missing Native theater in our lives, and we realized with Merlin (my husband), who had painted and designed theater sets a bit in college, that we could cover the artistic bases necessary to start a new group.

We called our group a Workshop because we wanted to emphasize the process aspect of it. We often gave ourselves six to eight weeks to put a show together, especially if it was one of my scripts. I gave free acting classes at one of the city parks, and with the exception of Joann Whitecrow, who never came to any of the classes, we had Indians turn out who were brand new to acting. At our most expansive, we had about twelve trained actors, men and women, from their 20s–50s, who were working with us on about two shows a year. We also began to offer summer acting workshops for youth and to draw upon our actors to help conduct these workshops. This was also the period when we had a board comprised solely of actors—another feature unique to our company, I believe.

VINCENT/NMAI: Julie, you've mentioned to me that you have founded a community-based theater, not a community theater. Please explain what you mean.

JULIE: Community theater and community-based theater have different histories. Community theater is of course a product of the Little Theater movement. By my definition, it most often stages ready-made scripts by white playwrights. And community theaters take the same basic production approach to these scripts, regardless of the geographic locale in which they are staged or the [lack of] ethnic background[s] of the actors. In community theater, the text pretends to stage universal experiences for the entertainment and consumption of the audience, and there isn't much social critique. Whatever social critique the text might contain is undone by the way the play is produced. It's what Bertolt Brecht calls "culinary theatre."

Community-based theater comes out of popular, grassroots theater efforts that began in the 1970s and 1980s. The production of community-based theater texts varies widely because the *process of production* requires using authenticating and rhetorical conventions in the text that are drawn directly from the lives of the community being performed for. The audience sees itself and its material realities as the subject of the stage representations and thus is highly aware of its influence in shaping the material of the play. Community-based theater emphasizes localized, highly specific values that allow the community to differentiate itself from others, to do what Bruce McConachie calls "the work of including and excluding that constitutes a community" (38). In the case of Native theater, then, community-based theater is shaped by a specific Native audience in a specific locale at a specific time period, often through the presentation of tribally specific material which builds both tribal and intertribal community and identification.

VINCENT/NMAI: Jana, any thoughts?

JANA: I *really* like Julie's answer; and she is the one who exposed me to this particular differentiation. However, that's where I was heading ideologically, so to speak. To bring a sense of connection, involvement, identification to the theater experience—that's what makes it so very powerful. And to have Native experiences expressed by Native writers is so much more meaningful than to have these stories told by a person not familiar with or a part of that culture or experience. Two years ago we presented a play written by Julie at two tribal community centers that included a shared meal following the performance. I remember thinking, "I wish more people were here; I know they would have enjoyed it." That is what I hope we will continue to do—present these experiences to increasing audiences along with their involvement in the process.

VINCENT/NMAI: Your passion is evident. I can tell you not only feel strongly about what you do but also enjoy it. What do you find most rewarding in reflecting on the work you and TRT have done over the years?

JANA: What I've found the most rewarding is not only my own growth as an actor but also watching other actors grow in their skills. I have found my understanding of and confidence in my acting skills continue to grow and improve, as well as my knowledge in both the technical and business end of theater. It has been exciting to see artists participate in a medium they had no experience in—we have had a couple of visual artists design our sets who had no previous experience in stage design. It has been a rewarding journey, if not just a bit challenging, to find plays we thought depicted and reflected the experiences of Native people. There have been people who have been involved in our productions who had never had any theater experiences before; to see them committed, as well as changed, by their participation with our theater company was quite rewarding. And, then, there are the audience responses. To hear laughter, comments of acknowledgement and murmurs of like experiences, and to see tears of sadness and joy and appreciation, these have definitely helped make our efforts and struggles worth it. I just thought of something else: it has definitely made me feel more connected to my grandparents and to my ancestors and that means so much to me—it feels as though I carry parts of their stories within me.

VINCENT/NMAI: How about you, Julie?

JULIE: I think the rewards have occurred at two levels: individual and collective. Some of our converts to acting or playwriting or technical work have found a new creative outlet for their talents. They may already sew or dance or bead, but they've found another source of enjoyment: working collaboratively with other Indian people to tell Native stories on stage. Watching these people grow as individuals and artists, and then watching that growth reach down intergenerationally through their families, so that we have the grandchildren of some of our actors wanting to do Native theater, has been incredibly rewarding.

It has also been incredibly rewarding to see audiences from different tribal communities respond in a positive way to theater, making the connection between Native theater, Native languages, and the oral tradition and the ability of this process to combat stereotypes and misconceptions about Native cultures. They often say that they never thought of using theater in this way, for this purpose. Especially underserved rural communities—it completely changes their preconceptions of what theater has to be about or what it has to look like.

VINCENT/NMAI: In addition to the rewards, there must be challenges. What are the challenges you encounter in successfully keeping alive a Native theater company for almost fifteen years?

JANA: Number one is funding. It seems we're always functioning on a shoestring budget. The other, which is predicated on the first, is being able to pay guest directors, artists, techs, etc., appropriately and *on time*. Luckily, when I felt like throwing in the towel, Julie was there to reassure me, and vice versa. We were also encouraged by our actor/board members who constantly reminded us that our company provided a voice for the Native community. I think that is what has kept us going—providing a voice for Native experiences from a contemporary perspective.

VINCENT/NMAI: Talk about those voices for Native experience from a contemporary perspective you mention. Describe examples of plays by contemporary American Indian playwrights as well as workshops you provide in Native communities.

JULIE: In presenting plays by contemporary Native playwrights, we look for plays that are not didactic or preachy. We look for both humor and substance—plays that will provoke people to think about issues or simply about the representation of tribal peoples on stage. In doing workshops within communities, we are focused on process and on teaching and empowering participants to *make their own theater*. Sometimes we are teaching acting skills to young people or helping young or older people stage their own stories.

In our summer youth work, we have done a number of acting camps with different themes: growing up stories adapted from elders, stories with urban ecological themes, animal stories, language preservation through puppet plays. In the latter, we used cultural consultants to help us translate traditional stories into Muscogee phrases, alternating with English, and the students memorized these stories and performed them with puppets. Everything we do involves being sensitive to community protocols, getting permission from elders and involving elders in our work, adapting to the community's sense of itself. We don't market ourselves to communities; we wait to be invited.

JANA: In presenting plays by contemporary Native playwrights, we are never surprised by the reaction from Native audiences and constantly surprised by the reaction from those who are non-Native. Ignorance of Native experiences by non-Natives seems so unlikely in this day and time, but it is what we've come to expect. Comments such as "Did that really happen?" and "I had no idea that happened" are what we have now come to expect rather than to be surprised at. Plays such as *Rez Sisters* (Tomson Highway), *Evening at the Warbonnet* (Bruce King), and *Indian Meadowlark* (Julie Little Thunder) have served as a source for comments like these. Our workshops have usually focused on youth theater and acting skills. We have focused on stories from our elders, tribal languages, and telling stories from our own experiences. When we worked with Spiderwoman Theater, we were able to bring our individual stories into a central theme of family—most specifically, stories from our grandmothers. And, as Julie mentions, getting permission from elders and those people who are involved with their communities is utmost in developing our presentations.

VINCENT/NMAI: Julie, you are also a playwright. What have you learned as a playwright from running a Native theater company?

JULIE: I've learned a tremendous amount about playwriting from working with TRT. It's a playwright's dream to be able to have actors read your work as you're trying to get it on its feet and figure out what works and what doesn't. I've learned it's not about the words but about the action and that this action can be much more free-form than I used to think, reading the "classics" in college. I have also tried to write in a more scenario-like manner that allows for localized groups to adapt or change the phrasing or staging of some moments of text. I used to think the text had to remain inviolate and now for me, that's almost the least interesting part of writing.

More interesting is how much can others coming into the work change for themselves without losing the action of the script. I had never taken a directing course until recently (in grad school), although I read a number of directing texts and tried to watch other directors work whenever I could. Mainly, I learned to direct by directing. This meant learning how to talk to actors in a variety of ways, because each actor is an individual, while respecting the actors' impulses and often, letting them do some of the problem-solving. I bring with me ideas of collective decision-making and consensual decisions that I think reflect Native values and of course, there's lots of laughter in rehearsal. Without that, we couldn't get through a single rehearsal session.

VINCENT/NMAI: And Jana, you are an actress as well as a producer of Native theater. What have you learned from the plays you have acted in with TRT?

JANA: Primarily, I have learned so much more about the acting process. When I look back at some of our first productions, I can see how I would now be able to bring much more to each character I played. I have learned that the rehearsal process is a journey, a journey that is shared by cast and crew alike. I can't imagine not having this as a part of my life. I have also learned how a script comes to life—from read-throughs of works in progress to the final drafts—to cuts and changes of lines while in rehearsal—we actors always hated that part! I have learned much about the histories and culture of Native people, not only from the scripts but from people who have served as our cultural consultants in the majority of our productions. I have learned that when people can identify with and relate to the stories we have shared, they can feel a powerful sense of connection to their theater experience.

VINCENT/NMAI: And who comes to your plays? Who is your audience? How have they responded to TRT over the years?

JANA: Our audience is largely urban Indian and interested or curious non-Native audience members. At times, there have been Native audience members who have never been to a theater production before and are there because a friend or family member is a part of the cast or crew. Their response has been one of surprise, and then enthusiasm for what they've seen. Humor has long been a way Indian people have of coping with difficult situations, and our plays always have some of that "Indian humor," whether it is a drama or comedy. There have been many times I've noticed that our Indian audience responds well to this kind of humor—laughing at just the right times and commenting how much they enjoyed our plays to cast and crew. As I mentioned earlier, it hasn't been easy to maintain the numbers of audience members we'd like to have, but just hearing and seeing their response to our productions has been very rewarding.

JULIE: I also see our audience as a largely urban Indian audience, a mixture of grassroots Indians and Indians who work in a professional capacity. Often they are the kinds of people who are active in other Indian organizations—but sometimes they are just salt-of-the-earth people whose lives we've touched in outreach work who keep coming back to the theater. I think the non-Indians who attend our plays are often people who have an appreciation of Indian culture already and who might go to some Indian social events like pow-wows or go see Indian movies and who are curious about the culture. Because Tulsa has such a large Indian population and because there are always so many events going on at the same time, while at the same time, we are very much a face-to-face community, our attendance will often vary depending on what weekend we are performing and who's in the play. Almost every week, however, someone will call and ask to be put on the mailing list or ask when our next show is, so while attendance fluctuates, the level of interest, I think, has remained high, and may be even higher than ever just because the accumulating years have given us more visibility.

VINCENT/NMAI: What is the mission of TRT? What are you hoping to accomplish with your work?

JANA: Our mission is to train Native actors and techs, to present contemporary Native theater—to present the human experience from a Native perspective. I think we continue to work on these goals on an ongoing basis, as well as finding new approaches to do so, e.g., presenting plays in community settings. We have been able to produce plays written by Native playwrights, which has always been a part of our mission. It's an exciting time in Native theater because there is so much more material we can choose from now as opposed to when we began.

JULIE: That's exactly it: to train Native actors, playwrights, and directors, to make Indian audiences aware of the accessibility of live theater and its power to communicate their stories through live performance.

VINCENT/NMAI: Tell us more about this power in communicating stories. Do you encounter audiences (Native or non-Native) changing misconceptions they may hold of themselves or others?

JULIE: (*referring to the play,* Someday, *which the interviewer recently directed for TRT*) I told you the story about the white usher who asked if there really had been a "round up" of Indian children by social workers who had these children taken away from their families because the family lived in a traditional house with a dirt as opposed to linoleum floor, etc., because of ethnocentric value judgments that had nothing to do with the welfare of the children. Perhaps because our scripts are Indian-authored, we have never had Indian spectators disagree with a representation or say it was misrepresented—at least to our faces. Often we incorporate a sense of dialogism in our work (or I do in my texts), e.g., where someone telling a story will say, that's not the way I heard it. That opens up the representation, lets people know we're not positing this or that story as the only version of say, a Cheyenne ghost story about the woman who was captured by ghosts, or the origins of the Gourd Dance or any cultural phenomenon. One Native cultural value is tolerance—this is the way I heard it. Indians were perhaps the first post-modernists, willing to acknowledge multiple and often opposing explanations or stories, or ways of viewing things.

JANA: I've mentioned some things earlier regarding this. Some of my own misconceptions have been changed by our plays. I have learned more about the allotment process, about issues affecting funereal repatriation, boarding school experiences, the appropriate use of tribally specific songs and dances, to name just a few. I feel certain that our audiences have been able to learn some of these things as well. If my experience can serve as an example, Native people often have to go through a process of "re-education," discarding stereotypes and misconceptions they have been taught in school or seen in movies or on TV, etc., and have subconsciously internalized. Some of my friends have said when they were young, they sometimes had the wish to be white, even though they may have had strong cultural ties. So, I feel misconceptions/perceptions are not only changed in our non-Native audience, but in our Native audience as well.

VINCENT/NMAI: That is really exciting. We all know that to do theater that makes a difference we need money. How is TRT funded?

JANA: Mostly through grants from the Oklahoma Arts Council. Over the years, we have had donations from a few corporations and individuals, as well as the Muscogee Nation, but these haven't been a significant source of overall funding. We have had garage sales, dances, T-shirt sales, Indian taco sales, and these functioned mostly to keep us afloat for short time periods—and keep us from writing bad checks… ayeeee! This past year our board president was able to obtain donations from his tribe's casino. Unfortunately, we haven't been successful in having other casinos do the same—yet!

VINCENT/NMAI: If TRT was your dream company with all of the resources you needed, how might it look differently from what is now?

JANA: There would be something to look *at*! In other words, we'd have a space of some kind, preferably an office and a black box theater. We'd have paid staff—an artistic director and office assistant at the very least. Then we'd actually have our very own rehearsal/acting class/and performance space! We would have the monies to sponsor our own outreach programs and performances, and we would also be able to bring in guest artists on a more regular basis. We would be able to bring in other Native companies and host their performances. We would provide workshops for writers, actors, and directors in order to develop new works for production. Sounds like a great dream, doesn't it?!

JULIE: We would have at least two paid personnel—an office manager and an artistic director. We would have our own rehearsal and office space. We would have an ensemble of ten well-trained actors on retainer for any given show. We would tour about half of the year each year, mostly in Oklahoma to start with, and perhaps after that, to other cities or regions. We would host touring shows of Native theater productions as well and offer workshops by other Native actors, directors, movement coaches, etc.

VINCENT/NMAI: What would you like folks who don't know about TRT to know about it?

JANA: (*laughs*) That they've been missing out on a lot by not knowing about us! Seriously, folks, I would love to have more Native people aware of our existence. Whenever I've told people I've met about our theater company, especially if they're Native, their responses have been interested, pleased, and even proud to learn of it. It's as though they somehow share in our dreams, knowing that we are working to share all our stories and experiences. I want people to know that we offer something that is unique at this point in time: a chance to see the kind of material that has virtually not been seen before. I want them to know we work at the grassroots level—in Native communities as well as featuring Native work from different areas of the country.

VINCENT/NMAI: Let's conclude by moving our conversation from the local to the national level. What would you like to see differently with the national Native theater scene? How might we get there?

JANA: First of all, why aren't more people aware of Native theater? I think of other ethnic theater groups, plays, directors, actors, etc., and the recognition so many of them have received, regionally and nationally. It's as though most people don't even know contemporary Native theater exists. "Beads and feathers" unfortunately remain in most people's minds. With all that being said, I know there are so many more Native scripts out there, more and more Native writers who have begun to tell their contemporary stories. We do have our own August Wilsons out there. This has to be nurtured, along with nurturing Native actors, directors, techs. Associations with larger institutions such as the NMAI, the Autry, or colleges and universities are definitely moves in the right direction. Exchanges between Native companies from around the country would strengthen connections and access to new material and artists. I know there are networks of Native theater out there; these resources need to continue to be accessed. I know Julie has been good about using some of these networks, but I've been less inclined to do so, one reason being I don't have a computer at home, but that's another kind of funding problem!

JULIE: I would like to see more federal funding made available to small companies like ours that slip through the cracks because our operating budget is less than $50,000 a year. I would like to see producing organizations like Native Voices at the Autry, or what had been Project Hoop, or the National Museum of the American Indian spend some of their funding helping the plays and playwrights they produce tour their work to our part of the woods. I would like them also to think in terms of touring works that can draw some of their cast members from the places they are touring to. Finally, while it is great that actors in these works can receive their Equity card, for companies like us it means that, without exemptions, we can't afford to bring these actors in as guest artists at the very moment in their careers when they would be a draw for our group, and when the opportunity to work for us might also benefit them. I would like to see exchange residencies between groups and artists—you come out here for two weeks, and we'll go out there for two weeks. These moves would go far towards giving Native theater more visibility around the country and introducing the kind of work that is out there to wider and more varied audiences.

VINCENT/NMAI: Thanks very much, Julie and Jana. It's been a pleasure.

## Work Cited

McConachie, Bruce. "Approaching the 'Structure of Feeling' in Grassroots Theatre." *Theatre Topics* 8 (1998): 33-53.

# "Forceful yet transitory and fragile": An Interview with Victoria Nalani Kneubuhl

*Ann Elizabeth Armstrong*

This interview is based on a telephone conversation from August 3, 2007. It represents the culmination of the two authors' discussions throughout January and February, 2007, leading up to and during the NAWPA conference "Honoring Spiderwoman Theater/Celebrating Native American Theater." During this time, Ann Elizabeth Armstrong directed Victoria Kneubuhl's *The Conversion of Ka'ahumanu* for Miami University Theatre's season and the NAWPA conference. That week, Kneubuhl gave a number of presentations and pre-show talks including "Hawaiian History and Ka'ahumanu's Legacy," "Feminism and *The Conversion of Ka'ahumanu*," and "Performing History: Identity and the Politics of Interpretation in Theatrical and Living History Performances" (this last with Carlyle Brown for the Miami University Women's Studies conference, "The Power of Intersections").

ANN ELIZABETH: I wanted to start with this beautiful statement you wrote in *The Quietest Singing*. I really thought it summarized a lot about the power of your work. "Theatre is a conduit into our everyday world through which mystery and magic may still enter. At the same time, theatre can serve as a powerful platform for examining the social and political issues of our time. I am extremely proud to be part of a craft that is forceful yet transitory and fragile" (Lum, Stanton, and Enoki 218).

VICTORIA: That about sums it up. I wrote that when I won the Hawai'i Award for Literature in 1994. It is the highest literary award in our state. I had to write an artist's statement to go on the program, and so I did think very hard about what I wanted to say. Now that I hear it again, I realize that I still feel that way about the theater, although sometimes I am disappointed because most theaters producing plays aren't looking for the same things. Theater is a business, and people want what's popular and what sells tickets. I think for people who look at theater as an art form, which I certainly do, it's a little harder because being popular isn't the primary goal.

But I knew that when I got into it. [*laughter*]

ANN ELIZABETH: I really like how you say it's "forceful yet transitory and fragile." This seems particularly relevant to the way you explore the contradictions of particular historical moments. You've done this in your work that crosses over both living history and theater, like *January 1893*. That project is a good example of how theater's connection to its audience makes it forceful, yet transitory.

VICTORIA: Let me to tell you more about how the whole 'Onipa'a Centenial Pageant came about. Well, in 1992, the Hawai'i State Legislatures decided that the one hundreth anniversary of the overthrow of the Hawaiian monarchy had to be commemorated in the following year, 1993. The governor formed a blue ribbon committee to oversee the event. At that time sovereignty was a big issue. In fact, I think it was more of an issue then than it is now. Groups were active, and the idea of some form of independence for the Hawaiian people had taken hold. Independence was something that was being explored in other island groups in the Pacific that, like Hawai'i, had been colonized in the eighteenth and nineteenth centuries. It was an idea that was in the air. People were excited about it. I think it coincided with the recognition of the unjust way in which the Hawaiian Nation had been usurped. The sequence of events that led to the overthrow had been forgotten and certainly glossed over in history texts. Several generations had grown up not knowing this history of injustice. Today, there has been a lot of focus on the Akaka Bill and there's some controversy about whether that's a good thing or a bad thing.[1] The Office of Hawaiian Affairs has initiated its Kau Inoa program to register Hawaiians and hold a convention about sovereignty, and that seems to be the only thing that's gathered any momentum. But let's go back to 1993.

There were many groups formed that were interested in some form of independence. Hui Na'auao was one group that was an umbrella group for all kinds of Hawaiian organizations. Its purpose was to bring groups together to talk about sovereignty education. There were radical groups in it at one end of the spectrum and at the other end were old Hawaiian civic clubs and Hawaiian societies that had been around forever. It was a great organization. And they got some money from the Governor's committee to do some kind of educational program for the commemoration. Dallas Voegler, who was part of Hui Na'auao, had come to the downtown walking tour that the late Glen Grant and I used to do about the overthrow. She had been a theater director in L.A., so she was very excited about performance and how it could be used to get people interested and thinking about sovereignty. It's funny, because Glen and I used to have these—we thought they were pie-in-the-sky—schemes about reenacting the overthrow on a big scale. [*laughter*] So when Dallas came and asked me if I would write a script for a pageant for the commemoration, I automatically agreed.

I didn't really realize what a huge project I had taken on until I had to sit down and write the script. I wrote the script, and I had envisioned all of it happening at one time, but she decided to break it up into three days. I think I did a little rewriting to accommodate the shift. Then, at the eleventh hour, we realized that we needed someone to bridge the different scenes because the audience might be constantly changing and building. So Dallas asked Glen Grant to come act as the person who would fill the audience in on what had happened before. Glen pretty much provided summaries of the previous scenes or the events of the previous day. These summaries were improvised and not part of my script, and of course, being himself, Glen couldn't help but interject his own comments, which were mostly sympathetic to the monarchy. Glen was a historian and a gifted living history role player. He had a great love of history and Hawai'i.

Our backdrop for the pageant was the downtown area around 'Iolani Palace and Ali'iolani Hale. Many of the real events of the overthrow took place in this vicinity, and we tried as much as possible to do our scenes in the places where they actually occurred. The performances were moving events for those who assumed roles and for those who observed. I think it was the personal investment of the performers and audience, the particular occasion, the emotional and volatile nature of the subject matter, and the physical space of the performance that created a powerful, unrepeatable chemistry for everyone involved. This, for me, reaffirmed my conviction that theater and performance can be forceful, fragile, transitory and can create a space for real communal magic. The pageant reviewed the events that led up to the overthrow of the Hawaiian monarchy and, in particular, the three days that preceded the queen yielding her authority to the United States of America. The events included political intrigue, reports from the queen and her ministers, rallies of Hawaiian patriots, rallies of annexationists,

[1] In 2000 Senator Daniel Akaka (D-Hawaii) introduced a bill (identified as S. 310 and H.R. 505 in its current form) that would establish a Native Hawaiian governing body legally empowered to negotiate with the U.S. and State governments. Proponent and opponent sides both include bipartisan, Native Hawaiian, and non-Native members.

and the landing of the U.S. Marines. The pageant concluded at dusk on the final evening with a speech from the queen from the steps of ʻIolani Palace. It was followed by a torchlight procession.

Throughout the script for the pageant, I had pretty much stuck to the historical record, used a lot of primary source material, and interjected as little of myself as possible. But when it came to the last speech, I knew that I would have to find a way to bridge the past to the present moment. My great-grandmother and her husband were confirmed royalists, loyal to the monarchy and the Kingdom of Hawaiʻi. I tried to put into words the things I thought our queen, Liliʻuokalani, would have said to her people on this day and things that my own family would have wanted me to say. When the speech was delivered at the end of the pageant, Leo Anderson Akana, who played the queen, delivered it from the palace stairs to an audience of over 10,000 people. You could have heard a pin drop. It was so quiet. As the writer it was a little scary. That's when I realized that performance can have real power, and that we, as writers, should consider what we write and leave behind us in the world. It was a very powerful performance experience but, again, it was fragile, too. We had a lot of people there and anything could have happened.

ANN ELIZABETH: Because the audience is on both sides of that historical moment, the present and the past, they know what's at stake so that they really feel that fragility of what is happening moment to moment. The growing size of the audience speaks to the force of history that draws them together. I think it's wonderful how you created the group of historical characters that responded to the political situation of 1893, but also you have the audience there and they are deeply connected to that same group of characters. I'm always thinking about the relationship between a social movement and a performance event, how there can be a profound resonance between the two. As I read the pageant and as I imagined Liliʻuokalani on the steps of the palace giving her speech from that location, that has such power and resonance. It's more than just the power of reenactment.

VICTORIA: I think resonance is really what the living history experience should strive for. As a person who has worked a great deal at historic sites, I know how a sense of place is a large part of creating resonance. People respond on an emotional and intuitive level to physical places and spaces. And as I said previously, we tried as much as possible to perform events where they actually took place. For instance, we had the reading of the declaration of the Provisional Government scene at the side steps of Aliʻiolani Hale. This document, in effect, just declared that there was a state of emergency and that their Committee of Public Safety was taking over the government—declaring themselves the government. [ANN ELIZABETH: Is that the part that's at the Post Office Courtyard?] It's just across from the Post Office. Aliʻiolani Hale is just behind the Kamehameha statue. What is totally ironic is that they basically read it to themselves. There was nobody else around, and as soon as they read it they had somebody run over to John L. Stevens, the American Minister, to sign it. His signature meant that the United States recognized their Provisional Government. After that recognition, the Provisional Government could call on support from the U.S. Marines who just happened to be aboard a ship, the USS ***Boston***, in the harbor. In our scene, they read the proclamation to each other as they smoked cigars, drank brandy, and congratulated each other.

ANN ELIZABETH: Yes, it was very ironic. There are all these interesting self-conscious "performances" throughout the entire story that make us aware of how reality is being constructed. The queen swears allegiance to the constitution, and then, when her proclamation is misinterpreted, the members of the Provisional Government move the rhetoric around until they can call her revolutionary. Then *they* start making proclamations, but when she tries to rescind her proclamation, they don't accept it. And they say, hypocritically, "We judge by deeds, not by word alone..." (*January 1893* 63), and yet this entire thing has been just this whole rhetorical...[*laughter*]...sliding of words!

VICTORIA: I know. It was an excuse. They were looking for an excuse. They thought they found a good one, and they ran with it.

ANN ELIZABETH: And it is all about a performative agreement, and it becomes a game to get what they want. [VICTORIA: Oh, yes.] That makes seeing this history in performance very significant, creating a space for reflection on those very same tactics.

VICTORIA: I think a lot of people didn't realize how much of a little word-and-paper game the whole thing was. I was surprised at how it was such a back-door takeover. It was really about how much power was available to a certain group of people at a certain time. If the Marines had not been in the harbor, they might not have dared to go through with it. Some events from the history, we had to leave out. For example, supporters of the Provisional Government, I think they called themselves the Honolulu Rifles, went to Ali'iolani Hale, and they hung out there with their guns. They sang these American patriotic songs. They perpetuated the phony idea that there was some kind of danger to American life and property. That was a sick fabrication, a sick spin. Some things don't change much, do they?

ANN ELIZABETH: I know, we're still living it, aren't we?

VICTORIA: When you look at the newspapers of the time, it's easy to recognize the incredible spin that the Provisional Government overlaid on events. My particular favorite included a pirate motif. They compared the government to a ship that had been taken over by pirates—meaning the queen and her supporters, the *Hawaiian* people: "It might be compared to a ship at war which has been captured by pirates" (*January 1893* 42).

ANN ELIZABETH: The pirate, yes, and, Hawai'i is the bride waiting for her engagement. Thurston says, "Let us think of Hawai'i as a bride whose marriage day is not definitely fixed, but who will go through with the ceremony whenever the signal is given" (*January 1893* 44-45).

VICTORIA: Yes. Both the bride and the pirate metaphors came from the newspaper in 1893. Isn't it incredible?

ANN ELIZABETH: Tell me a little bit more about how the other performance aspects of the pageant, the participation of other civic groups that may or may not have been reflected in the script.

VICTORIA: Dallas Voegler was the person who was the director of the production. She was the one who got the cast together, but also there were so many groups that wanted to be part of this in some way. A lot of them weren't Hawaiian groups. We had a Japanese-American group of participants. Marcus Oshiro, who is now a legislator, brought the group in. We found a historical note that a group of Japanese plantation workers decided to march into town to support the queen, so we included a scene that gave voice to their concerns. An elementary school group wanted to participate with a song. We had a group of people who were interested in military history come in costume as the Marines. A hālau hula participated by chanting and dancing. Members of the Royal Order of Kamehameha, a very old civic club, escorted the queen from one building to another. The Royal Guard participated. I think Dallas did not turn down any group that asked to be a part of the commemoration. We had incredible community participation.

ANN ELIZABETH: It's so rare to have such a broad kind of civic level of participation, just to mobilize that many people. It tells you what that significance is to the people who just want to be a part of it. No one's getting paid. It's only for that sense of trying to be a part of this history and commemoration.

VICTORIA: We were not the only event in the commemoration. There were other people and groups doing all kinds of things, too. There was a high level of participation across the board for all of the events.

ANN ELIZABETH: Now I remember from our discussions before that there was some danger involved and some controversy in the audience reaction to retelling this history.

VICTORIA: I didn't find out until after everything was over that during the pageant members of the National Guard had been hiding in the State Archives building. It's a small building right next to 'Iolani Palace. And the only reason I found out is because my boss's husband happened to be one of those weekend National Guard members, and he was one of the soldiers that was hiding in the Archives. I guess some people were afraid of the whole idea of commemorating the overthrow. I think some people thought that it would incite violence. I remember being at a dinner with some woman, and, when I told her about the pageant script, she said things like—*Why are you doing that? Don't you know that there are people who say they're going pick up cane knives and come to town?* She had what I would call the "natives are restless" syndrome…[*laughter*]…hate to say it, but I think some people are still afraid of what people of color might do if they get angry.

ANN ELIZABETH: What about within the Hawaiian community? Were there any internal conflicts about what was represented or who was representing them?

VICTORIA: There was some competition within the Hawaiian community about who should have the attention on that day, about which group should have the most attention. Dallas did tell me that somebody did threaten to do something to our actors because they were jealous or perceived us as "competition." So there were people that escorted the actors from the changing area to and from the scenes. It was Dallas's decision to make, and she wanted to be sure the actors were safe—not just from the people who made the threat but from anyone who might not want us to tell this particular story. I think it turned out to be a good decision just because the crowds that turned out were so large. Ann Elizabeth, I thought we'd be lucky if we had forty or fifty people for each one of these scenes. The first couple of scenes that were really early in the morning started out that way, but by the end of the first day there were hundreds of people, which then turned into thousands the next day. I know Dallas wanted to make sure that everybody was safe. Listen, we still have people in our community today that don't want Hawaiians to have a single thing. They'd like to dismantle the Office of Hawaiian Affairs. They'd like to dismantle the Kamehameha Schools. They'd like to see any program that benefits Native Hawaiians gone, and they're persistent.

ANN ELIZABETH: Like the situation with the National Guard, that's really extreme. It's almost a suggestion that emotions will be aroused, causing something to happen. It says something about the danger and the power of performing this outside of the theatrical context. It's not contained by the frame of art. Because of that, it is a threat.

VICTORIA: I went to a seminar shortly after the pageant, at the East West Center. There was a woman from South America, and she said to me: in her country when they performed political theater on the street, the police were always there. She said sometimes they were there to break them up. Because, she said, because the Government realized that artists have powerful messages that people listen to. We're not used to hearing that in America.

ANN ELIZABETH: Yes, a public space is very fraught territory. Now, tell me about the reactions of audience members and how the pageant might have influenced or changed perceptions within or outside of the sovereignty movement. What were the repercussions after 1993?

VICTORIA: Well, for one thing, I think, and I have no way measuring this, but I think people were much more aware of the overthrow of the monarchy as a blatant act of injustice. I went to a really good private high school, and there was not one mention of this history. I think people who saw the performance were inspired to learn more about our history and the events that have brought us into the present. As I look back through my files, I have so many newspaper clippings, and I'm looking at this one that accused us of being biased and Glen Grant's response to that accusation. Here Glen says, "One hundred years ago many sentiments and emotions were expressed in support of the queen. And to people who say, 'shouldn't we hear two sides of the story,' I'd like to say my role is complex. The play is written from a point of view sympathetic to the Lili'uokalani. My job is to serve as a bridge to those feelings. The other side's story has been told for 100 years. They had 100 years to tell their story. I'm proud to be a part of this telling" ("Play about Takeover"). That's nice, yeah.

ANN ELIZABETH: So, you were really filling in a gaping hole in the telling of this history.

VICTORIA: There were all kinds of controversies surrounding the commemoration. There was a squabble about removing the American flag from 'Iolani Palace. They took down the American flag and only flew the Hawaiian flag during the 'Onipa'a observance. Some people were really upset by that. And one newspaper article reporting on our pageant questioned whether the things we were doing was based on "reality." As it turned out, *he* hadn't done *his* homework.

ANN ELIZABETH: "Reality," that's interesting. There is the ability for something like this to build upon what's going on in the current moment and hit a nerve causing folks to ask: What is our reality? People discover our reality is not what we thought it was, is it?

VICTORIA: Well, our reality was definitely not his. We did actually have an impact that resulted in some modestly measurable results. A few months after the centennial activities, one Hawai'i state senator spoke to Hui Na'auao about the large number of bills regarding Hawaiian issues that were introduced to the legislature after the pageant. They included a bill for sovereignty referendum and a bill that created tuition waivers for students of Hawaiian ancestry attending the University of Hawai'i. The senator reported that he thought the introduction of these bills came in response to the overwhelming interest in the centennial activities and, in particular, the historical events that were portrayed during the course of the pageant. I wrote about this with Dolly Strazar in *History News*, a publication of the Association for State and Local History (Kneubuhl and Strazar 14). We also received an Award of Merit for the pageant from this national organization.

ANN ELIZABETH: That's wonderful! It sounds like it's hard to say whether or not the pageant contributed to the legislation, but it certainly paved the way for the timing of it. It seems quite significant that the pageant coincided with a moment when people are ready to take political action in response to this history.

VICTORIA: I'm sure when Dallas came to ask me to write a script, she knew that this kind of intersection would be taking place. She had that kind of intuition. She believed in the goodness and the determination of the Hawaiian people and really wanted to contribute to the movement toward sovereignty. She passed away a few years after the pageant, and we miss her.

ANN ELIZABETH: Well, let's switch gears and time frames now. I'd like to talk about your play *The Conversion of Ka'ahumanu*. What does it mean to take a production away from the audience it was originally written for? That's something I've been reflecting on since directing the production of *The Conversion* at Miami University in Ohio, and I'm always asking myself,

How much is a performance about the perception that the audience brings with them and how much is it what you can influence through a production?

VICTORIA: I have seen other productions of *The Conversion* outside of Hawai'i. On tour we performed in Edinburgh, Washington, D.C., and Los Angeles. Let me say first, that the most important thing to me is that people learn something about our history no matter where this play is performed. I think that for people in Honolulu the issues that *The Conversion* brings up might be more immediate and emotional to them than for an audience that's not from Hawai'i. But when we performed the play in Edinburgh, I had an eye-opening discussion with one of the reviewers. He wanted to talk to me about the play, and he wanted to tell me that so many of the issues that were brought up in the play were issues that were issues for Scots after colonization by the English—having their culture degraded, having subsequent problems with alcoholism, disease, and poverty. I was quite moved to see that someone so far from my own home could make this kind of deeper connection to the issues of the play.

I also hope that when people see that play, they are inspired to think critically. People have so many stereotypical ideas about both missionaries and Hawaiians. It was such a complex time, and there are still complex issues from that time that plague us today. I'm not sure if any of them will ever be resolved, but it's much better to think critically and to look at things openly than it is to think stereotypically and rigidly about the past. I hope that the play opens up avenues for wider thinking. And then there's the issue of women in history, and what kind of roles women played in history and how their important contributions always get swept under the carpet. We've had centuries of men writing history and men recording their actions as central, leaving women out on the periphery. As far as the mission in Hawai'i goes, I think it was really the women who won everyday people over to Christianity. When you start to look at people in history as individual people instead of "the missionaries" and "the Hawaiians," that's when you really gain personal insight into the past. When we think of people in collective ways, we fall back on collective ideas, and we miss all the nuances in the individual experiences of life. People's individual lives in the past and present are much richer to me than the collective experience. I don't know, maybe God *is* in the details.

ANN ELIZABETH: Yes, that's an interesting point. There's definitely that relationship between that individual and collective, and I think this drew me into the play. Of course, as audience members, we identify with individuals, and you present five characters that have their own thoroughly un-resolvable conflicts. Today, we still haven't resolved these issues, from class differences to gender roles to breast cancer. We're still trying to grapple with how we survive in the face of the destruction and inequity that's been thrust upon us. Do you think it was dangerous to allow the missionary women to have an arc?

VICTORIA: It's much easier and safer for us to think in the collective and to experience controversial issues in the collective because it's easier for us to categorize and to say, especially if you have a political agenda, it's much easier to say, "Oh, these people were bad and they did this, and these people were good and they did this." When you start looking at individuals and individual experiences in certain situations, it's harder to do that and everything gets gray. It's harder to say what's good and what's bad. One of the things that saddened me about some of the leaders of the sovereignty movement is that on a certain level they didn't encourage critical thinking. I guess when you are promoting an ideology sometimes you're afraid of looking at things critically. It doesn't matter to me. I mean the overthrow was wrong—whether Sanford Dole had an adopted Hawaiian daughter he was totally devoted to or not, the overthrow was still wrong. Whether the missionaries were good or bad, the overthrow was still wrong. Confronting controversy in history is scary.

When I was working at the mission house, we were engaging with controversy, dedicated to the idea of looking at the controversy of the mission. We were open to talking to people about it and seeing how people felt about it. As museum educators, we felt that museums and historic sites could be great community platforms to openly discuss the controversies of the past and their impact on the present. We had some big ideals. We thought living history (our version of it) would inspire and create critical thinking. I wrote *The Conversion of Ka'ahumanu* while I was participating in that living history program, *Honolulu, 1831.* Much of the material in the play came out of my research for the program and my experiences performing. We performed every Saturday, and even though people were given a good orientation to the program and the process, some visitors still got upset about nineteenth-century attitudes and language. Some people still felt they had a stake in some of those issues. So for us as performers it could be intense, sometimes frightening, but at the same time we were providing this safe space where the audience could externalize, discuss, and examine issues. When things got intense, we learned the most about the issues, about our visitors, and about ourselves. As time went on we developed a depth of understanding about the past and the present that we could not have learned any other way. It was one of the best learning experiences I have ever had, and I think the other core role-players in the program would say the same thing.

One interesting note about *The Conversion*: a few people were upset because the missionary women characters weren't knee-jerk stereotypical missionaries. Along with wanting converts, they are concerned and want to help. They want to improve the health of the native people, provide education, and generally improve their welfare, which as far as I can tell is true. Those women were, when you look back at nineteenth-century history in America, the social reformers of their time. They were educated. Some of them were teachers. At that time in America, women were starting to form societies that were interested in temperance, female education, and prison reform. They were looking at the way children were raised and trying to develop a system or way of bringing up a child that was more beneficial. Those were the kinds of women who became missionaries. Many people today don't want to hear that. They just want to hear that missionaries came over and they made all these rules. But talking about missionaries in an open and not stereotypical way is not popular when there's a certain agenda.

ANN ELIZABETH: Right. Would you say that you are without an agenda? As a writer?

VICTORIA: No. I'm not without an agenda. And I think I've discussed this with you before: one of my agendas was to write a play that was modeled on some of the feminist plays that we were reading in Juli Burk's class at University of Hawai'i, "Women and Theater," where women had major roles, where women from different classes were represented, where it was an ensemble, where it looked at social issues and it looked at the contribution of women and their own struggles with them in the bigger context of history. And one of my other agendas, as I said before, was to look at the women in the play as individuals, and that includes the Hawaiian women also. I didn't want to portray Hawaiians as people who were led around by the nose, people who were easy pushovers for missionaries. I wanted intelligent Native Hawaiian characters who could think for themselves, who saw clearly, and not people who were waiting around for Westerners to come and tell them what to do.

ANN ELIZABETH: In many of your plays, you use a chorus or an ensemble. Tell me a bit more about that choice. It's a distinct aspect of your writing style that allows for a fluidity of space and time that is nonlinear.

VICTORIA: The idea to use a chorus for my first play, *Emmalehua*, came from my uncle, who was also a playwright. I can remember the moment he suggested it. He was staying in this apartment. He was cooking something on the stove, and we were talking. He said: "Why don't you have a chorus of Hula dancers in your play?" I thought it was a great idea. My playwriting teacher, Dennis Carroll, really encouraged us to look at plays that were structured in non-traditional ways. I found alternative structures much more exciting, much more creative, than the well-made play structure. There is something much more creative and free happening for me when I use a more "open" structure. It opens up a bigger space for my imagination to play in and offers so many different ways to think about staging. And I think with the popularity of film, which does reality so well, that the strength of the stage today is its theatricality. Use a camera if you want to peek through the fourth wall. It works better. Another practical advantage of having a chorus is that you can use the actors of the chorus for multiple roles. I really like to see actors changing roles.

ANN ELIZABETH: It's the theatricality of it.

VICTORIA: Yes, I think it gives them the opportunity to show off and to stretch their talent. I love to see actors practicing their craft in creative ways.

ANN ELIZABETH: And it's pleasurable for the audience, too, to see that transformation in front of them.

VICTORIA: I hope so.

ANN ELIZABETH: Yes, and I think you really do address the collective through the chorus or choral elements. I think it is a reminder of that collective.

VICTORIA: And a reminder that the theatrical production is a collective endeavor. It's a bunch of people pretending together. When you use a chorus, when you draw on the chorus for multiple characters, you also call attention to the artificiality of the theater. I like including that awareness, or trying to include it. I think it adds a little more tension, a little more excitement to the experience of watching.

ANN ELIZABETH: Yes, we've talked before about the importance of the collective process of making theater for you. I know that Honolulu's Kumu Kahua Theatre company has been really important for you in this respect.

VICTORIA: I don't think I could have become a playwright without Kumu Kahua Theatre. Right away there was a theater that was hungry for what I was writing. My first play got a production, and everything else I wrote after that was produced.

ANN ELIZABETH: That's incredible.

VICTORIA: Right from the beginning, I was able to see my work go through the process of production. There's nothing better for developing as a playwright than following your play through that process. I can imagine what a struggle it must be for playwrights who don't get productions—how heart breaking it must be. You have to spend so much time writing a play, even a bad one. Kumu Kahua has been essential in my development as a playwright. When a playwright has a theater that they have a real relationship with—it's a tremendous opportunity to grow and to develop your craft. Kumu Kahua has been doing community-based theater for over thirty-five years. They only do plays that reflect our Pacific Island community and our local experiences. Consequently, they do a great number of new plays every year. They support the craft of playwriting and have wonderful roles for performers of all ethnicities. Our community is enriched by this theater.

ANN ELIZABETH: So, this brings me to the question: How do you identify yourself in larger communities? You've been published in collections of Native American plays, Asian American plays, post-colonial plays, local plays, and Hawaiian literature so—Where do you fit in?

In terms of your voice, where would you place yourself among these labels and where do you speak from or whom do you speak to?

VICTORIA: First of all, in all of those contexts, I am a playwright. A playwright who can't afford to turn down the offer of publication. I haven't given myself or my plays any of those labels. They've all been labels that educators, theorists, editors, and publishers have created. All I want is to get published and produced. The academic community has a great affinity, perhaps need, for labels and categorization. But if I had to give my voice a label, put myself in a category, I would call myself a Pacific playwright, a Pacific Island playwright. When I started writing, there was no such category or label, so I was thrown in either the Asian Literature category or the Native American category. In the long run, it's not that important to me. What's important to me is that people read my work and discuss it and talk about it. I feel the same way about theory. We can all watch theory come and go. The business of labels and theory is not the business of the writer. I don't sit around thinking about theory and labels when I'm writing. Writing is a totally different experience. I'm not an academic. I'm a writer, but I'm very happy that people debate and discuss and talk about my work in an academic context.

ANN ELIZABETH: These labels set up certain kinds of expectations. Perhaps they serve certain marketing tasks in the grouping of ideas but, obviously, as you're saying, they also narrow our thinking. I think it's just a wonderful sign that you have crossed over all of these areas simultaneously, and that's really unusual.

VICTORIA: I've noticed that even in the early development of Pacific Island literature as its own category, people are creating expectations and vying for authority. I have a big distrust of canons. We've all seen how women writers over the years have been marginalized and discriminated against through a canon.

ANN ELIZABETH: Yes, inevitably even feminism gets to a point where there are gate keepers, and suddenly you have to be feminist enough to enter. It replicates the whole system, it's true.

VICTORIA: Sad but true.

ANN ELIZABETH: But there are also productive things about mobilizing, codifying, and identifying who the group is and why their traditions are important. So it's just that constant negotiation between keeping a soft boundary there, not making it a gate-keeping task.

VICTORIA: Which some people can do, and some people can't because they need power and authority to be happy. I guess my bottom line as a writer is that I didn't develop a skill so that someone else could tell me what to write.

ANN ELIZABETH: Right.

VICTORIA: I have this thing about my personal freedom as a writer and my personal space as a writer. I'm ferocious about it. I had to work very hard for this place in my life, and nobody else is going to protect it for me. At the same time, I want to be a sensitive writer, sensitive to the needs of others.

ANN ELIZABETH: Tell me more about the traditions you build upon. I know that you often talk about your uncle, John Kneubuhl, who was also a playwright.

VICTORIA: Well, have you read my uncle's plays?

ANN ELIZABETH: I saw you perform in his play *Think of a Garden* at Kumu Kahua when I was in Hawai'i in the 1990s.

VICTORIA: John was born in Samoa in about 1922. He came to Honolulu to attend Punahou School, and, when he went on to Yale, he wanted to be a concert pianist. He wrote this libretto for his teacher, Paul Hindemith. Hindemith told him he should be a playwright, and he sent him over to the Yale 47 Workshop. He was the only undergraduate in the program. After he graduated, and after World War II, he came back to Honolulu as the Assistant Artistic Director of the Honolulu Community Theatre. And he started writing local plays. His slogan was "Pacific Plays by Pacific Playwrights," and he wanted to develop a regional Pacific theater here. He used Pidgin English in his plays, and he caused some excitement in the community with his ideas. And then my grandfather told him that if he was going to be a writer, he had to support himself (and his wife and three children). Somebody offered him a job in Hollywood writing for television, which was fairly new then. For twenty-something years he wrote over a hundred television programs. I'm sure you know the *Wild Wild West*. Remember that midget genius? That was his character. I think he wrote one *Star Trek,* but he wrote several for the *Wild Wild West.* He wrote for *Medic, Rawhide, Dr. Kildare, The Fugitive*, and *Hawai'i Five-O* and many, many others. One day, I think he was in his mid-forties, he said I can't stand this anymore, I have to get out of here, and he moved back to Samoa. And started writing plays again.

He taught English, and he helped start the Community College of American Samoa. He was a brilliant man. He was a passionate man. He had great theater values. He wrote a series of early plays in the 1940s, and then he wrote three or four more plays in his post-Hollywood days. He was a wonderful writer, although I don't agree with some of his politics. He was from a very different generation. He was really excited that I was part of the theater, but I couldn't really talk to him about my work specifically because he could be very opinionated and overwhelming. But we did talk about theater in general, which was great.

ANN ELIZABETH: So tell me about the letter. I know you said that he wrote you an important letter about the ancestor's voices.

VICTORIA: When he first heard that my first play was going to be produced, he was so excited that he wrote me a letter. He was in Samoa, and I was here, in Hawai'i. In fact, I have it right here. I keep it by my desk. He wrote, "Today we seem to be disloyal and amoral camp followers who will sleep with armies of either side"—he's talking about being a playwright—"but remember that we began as oracles and priests and as conjurers of our dead ancestors' spirits. We are essentially holy. So although they may love us for our bodies, it is really for our voices they yearn for. What begins with pleasure ends in awe. What is manifest play is latent mystery. Find your own voice and honor it. The words that give it body are sacred so don't let the good fun of doing a play allow you to be seduced by others, directors, actors, well meaning friends, into easy compromises. Remember that your play is always at the bottom an act of worship. Your act of worship, it's your voice, sing your song." That was a really wonderful thing for a new playwright to hear from someone who had already been around the block.

ANN ELIZABETH: Oh, I'm so glad you read the whole thing. It's really very powerful, and the idea of "manifest play is latent mystery," that's so true.

VICTORIA: Because I have had this person in my life, in my family, who felt like this about writing, because he validated the idea that writing is a sacred and transformational act, I have always felt that I have a foundation for my vocation. I am part of a family tradition, and my ancestors, distant and not-so-distant, stand behind me.

ANN ELIZABETH: Is there anything else you would like to say about what it means to dedicate yourself to that creative voice?

VICTORIA: I still am a little amazed about what I do. When I was younger, I never dreamed that I would be a writer or be a playwright. I didn't go back to school until

I was almost in my thirties. I had my kids when I was very young. I had a really tough adolescence—almost no adolescence, and I never thought of myself as very smart. It's taken me a long time to acknowledge that I can do this. It's taken me a long time to say to myself and to other people that I'm a writer. Sometimes, I'm amazed at what comes out of myself because I'm not quite sure where it comes from. I'm just happy that it happens. I look back at some of the things that women have written over the centuries, and I'm inspired by them. I think it's such a miracle that I can hear these voices from the past and that when I read these words I can I can hear this person talking to me. It's an amazing transference, leaving your tracks in the scrawl of words as you pass through life. I feel really honored to be part of that tradition, that tradition of women writers.

## Works Cited

Kneubuhl, John. Letter to Victoria Nalani Kneubuhl. 17 Apr. 1984.

Kneubuhl, Victoria Nalani. "Feminism and *The Conversion of Ka'ahumanu.*" Miami U, Oxford, OH. 23 Feb. 2007.

---. "Hawaiian History and Ka'ahumanu's Legacy." Miami U, Oxford, OH. 21 Feb. 2007.

---. *January 1893.* Ts, 1993. Native American Women Playwrights Archive, University Libraries, Miami U, Oxford, OH.

Kneubuhl, Victoria Nalani, and Marie D. Strazar. "January 1893: The Overthrow of the Hawaiian Monarchy Relived in History." *History News* 49.1 (1994): 12-15.

Kneubuhl, Victoria Nalani, Carlyle Brown, and Ann Elizabeth Armstrong. "Performing History: Identity and the Politics of Interpretation in Theatrical and Living History Performances." The Power of Intersections conference. Miami U, Oxford, OH. 23 Feb. 2007.

Lum, Darrell H. Y., Joseph Stanton, and Estelle Enoki, eds. *The Quietest Singing.* Honolulu: State Foundation on Culture and the Arts, 2000.

"Play about Takeover Criticized for Bias." *Honolulu Star-Bulletin* 18 Jan. 1993: A7.

# Native Drama in the Mainstream: A Case Study of the *Te Ata* World Premiere[1]

*JudyLee Oliva and Christy Stanlake*[2]

*The drum is full of dreams*

*The drum is full of memories*

*The drum sings for me, the song of olden things.*

*I am very small, as I dance upon the drum-head: I am very small...*

*I dance upward with the day; I dance downward with the night...*

*Someday I shall dance afar into space like a particle of dust....*(Oliva 2)

With this recitation, the *Te Ata* World Premiere opened the night of August 5, 2006. An historic production, *Te Ata* became the first professionally produced, mainstream Native American play to be financially supported by an Indian Nation, the Chickasaw Nation of Oklahoma. The production's significance and its biographical focus on Te Ata Thompson Fisher, a Chickasaw actress who achieved the honor of becoming Oklahoma's "First State Treasure," inspired the state to name the *Te Ata* World Premiere the inaugural event of Oklahoma's centennial celebrations.

The same year of the *Te Ata* World Premiere, Gigi Bolt wrote in the December issue of *American Theatre*, "How wonderful it would be if more artists came home and put down roots in Oklahoma or North Dakota or Iowa to tell the remarkable stories of those places" (8). The world premiere of *Te Ata* accomplished just that when its national production team, under JudyLee Oliva's artistic direction, united in Chickasha, Oklahoma, to stage the play in the very theater where Te Ata Thompson Fisher first performed. From the start, the project's objective was ambitious: to produce a mainstream, Native American play in a region where such Broadway style productions are not the norm. For the purposes of this article, the term "mainstream" refers to the large scale and professional production of the play, not the plot's content or focus. Oliva believed that Te Ata's life created a powerful story that deserved to be staged using all of the theater's available means: equity actors, professional lighting, highly technical stagecraft, period costumes, and full sound. She aimed to reach the widest audiences possible and to use the theater's magic to inspire those viewers. In one interview, Oliva explained, "I just think Native people, as well as other cultures, need to see that we can tell our stories in mainstream theatre. We don't just have to have a small set and tell stories and play the flute. We can have an orchestra, and the play can be about Native people" (Stanlake 116).

Such grand visions for Native American productions in the United States are rare. While various theaters and organizations are working to develop Native plays, their productions tend to be limited by the staging venue or the producing organization's means. Professional theater companies with the revenue and

---

[1] Color photos with captions from the premiere production are included as a slide show on the DVD accompanying this book. For the play's text, see: JudyLee Oliva, *Te Ata: A Play with Music, Footpaths and Bridges: Voices from the Native American Women Playwrights Archive*, ed. Shirley A. Huston-Findley and Rebecca Howard (Ann Arbor: U of Michigan P, 2008) 200-68.

[2] We chose to write this article from one perspective voice. Our association as playwright and dramaturg on the development of this play has exceeded a decade, and our observations and insights are firmly grounded in our shared experiences.

Young Te Ata (DeLanna Studi) in pose that was featured on Te Ata Fisher's publicity materials.

space capable of mounting large-scale, professional productions remain skeptical about producing Native American plays, often fearing that they might not sell tickets, cannot find professional Native actors to cast, or could face political and cultural conflicts. In order to stage *Te Ata* in the highly theatrical, technically demanding way that Oliva scripted it, the World Premiere was produced in a non-traditional manner. Instead of having a professional theater company sponsor the play, the Chickasaw Nation with other financial supporters formed a temporary partnership with the common objective of producing *Te Ata*. As Native American playwrights continue to stage mainstream productions in the United States, such unusual producing arrangements might offer a way for Native plays to reach wider audiences.

The goal of this article is to use the *Te Ata* World Premiere as a case study for examining Native Drama in mainstream theater. The authors offer personal insights, struggles, challenges, and accomplishments deriving from the production. These include discussions about working without a traditional theatrical infrastructure, as well as reflections upon how important communication becomes when a production team, cast, and crew are assembled from various organizations. As with any production, the more people who work on the play, the easier it becomes to lose sight of the original vision expressed in the script. Accordingly, the authors relate stories of how the production of *Te Ata* sometimes struggled with maintaining the script's authority. To help readers imagine the play script and its production, several visual images from the world premiere and excerpts from the text accompany this account of staging *Te Ata*. The article ends with a section devoted to strategies for the future, information that might be helpful for those interested in producing Native American plays in large, professional theater venues.

Playwright JudyLee Oliva began her research on Te Ata, a Chickasaw actress and storyteller, over thirteen years ago when she happened upon ninety-one of Te Ata's files housed at the University of Oklahoma's Western History Collection. Oliva, who also came from Oklahoma, had never heard of Te Ata, the legendary figure who ultimately changed Oliva's life. Te Ata was a classically trained actress who performed a one-woman show for over seventy years. During her professional career, from the 1920s through the 1980s, Te Ata performed all over the world for all kinds of audiences, including special presentations at the White

House and for the King and Queen of England. The play *Te Ata* chronicles the actress's remarkable life.

Oliva's research enabled her to meet Te Ata before the actress passed away in 1995, just shy of her one-hundredth birthday. Oliva grew to become close friends with Te Ata's extended family over the thirteen years she researched, wrote, re-wrote, and workshopped the play three times, twice in Oklahoma and once in New York City. Te Ata's family allowed the playwright access to rooms full of Te Ata's personal letters, pictures, and performance notebooks, materials that Oliva viewed over a three-year period. Te Ata's remarkable letters were a rare

Young Te Ata, as college student, performs in the Chautauqua as Elder Te Ata (Donna Couteau Brooks) remembers.

source of information, both personally and historically; Oliva incorporates several elements from these letters into her dramatized portrayal of Te Ata's life.

In shaping Te Ata's biography into a theatrical script, Oliva faced many issues. The playwright questioned how she could best tell the remarkable story that spanned almost a century. To resolve the challenge of covering such a long period of time, Oliva chose to use two Te Atas. The dramatic action is sequenced by Elder Te Ata's perspective, as she remembers her life. This arrangement of the storyline allowed the playwright to use a storytelling medium that would foster a less linear plot, as Elder Te Ata's memories transport the audience back and forth in time. Young Te Ata's actions appear in a more linear structure as she enacts the life that Elder Te Ata remembers. The connection between Elder Te Ata and Young Te Ata is continuously maintained because Elder Te Ata remains onstage most of the time, watching, remembering, and often enacting the same movements and saying the same words as Young Te Ata. At the end of the play, the two characters become one, completing the circle of Te Ata's life.

Oliva was also concerned about how to create other biographical characters, the close friends who played a large part in Te Ata's personal and professional life. The research issues were ongoing as Oliva uncovered the real-life stories of the many biographical characters in the play. Like Te Ata, many of these people had remarkably full lives. Although it was important to the playwright to maintain historical accuracy, Oliva did not allow biography to overshadow the play's theatricality; she took artistic liberties that helped highlight important relationships and events. For example, the playwright combined two of Te Ata's dearest friends into a single character, Margaret Ball. Oliva met the real Margaret Ball before she passed away. The playwright also performed extensive research into the life of Te Ata's husband, Dr. Clyde Fisher, the Head and Curator of the Hayden Planetarium in the New York City Museum of Natural History. In other instances, when Oliva could not find much public information, she read letters to glean an understanding of characters such as Ataloa, another contemporary Chickasaw performer and a distant relative of Te Ata whom she called "cousin." Oliva simplified the women's relationship by creating Ataloa as a more direct cousin. Over two hundred personal letters from Te Ata, her husband, and her beloved teacher, Francis Davis, helped Oliva construct dramatic characters from the lives of Te Ata's contemporaries.

Dramaturg Christy Stanlake collaborated with Oliva over the years as the playwright refined the text and prepared to communicate its intricacies to a production team. Stanlake views *Te Ata*'s dramaturgical style as a script that has a very simple storyline but a theatrical structure that is quite complex. Time in *Te Ata* is fluid. Elder Te Ata greets the audience using direct audience address, and then the play unfolds through her memories that are ordered by associated thematic shifts rather than a chronological unfolding of events. Because Elder Te Ata is a character who transcends time, she can step into Younger Te Ata's past and actively affect events. The plot's layered use of time, place, and character demands *Te Ata*'s productions to incorporate various levels of reality that should, ideally, shift the actors' playing styles.

Stanlake identified four levels of reality working within the script: presentational scenes, shared scenes, metatheatrical scenes, and scenes of heightened reality. The presentational scenes are those that merely break the fourth wall, as Elder Te Ata directly addresses the theater's audience. Shared scenes are those that are played realistically. These include many of Elder Te Ata's memories played through the character of Young Te Ata. However, Te Ata's memories also depict moments from her performance career. During such metatheatrical scenes, the audience views short performances within *Te Ata* and witnesses Te Ata's growth as a performer. The playing style of the metatheatrical scenes is complicated because it blends the two distinctly different performance traditions that marked Te Ata's performance career: Native storytelling techniques and Francois Delsarte's style of declamation, a popular acting technique practiced by Te Ata and other classically trained actors who performed at the turn of the twentieth century.

In a surreal scene, members of the chorus (Terrance Wright, Robert Cheadle, and Julie Ray Burwell) yell rumors about the death of Native American film star Long Lance.

Finally surreal scenes, or scenes of heightened reality, complete *Te Ata*'s challenging dramaturgy. In these scenes, the internal world of Te Ata drives the action, the spirit world becomes palpable, and characters transcend their physical boundaries. These scenes must play magically. The tension between *Te Ata*'s playing styles and the liquid way in which scenes transition from one style to another create a feeling of limitlessness, an extreme freedom that promises that something magical might occur at any moment.

When the *Te Ata* World Premiere production team first met to discuss how to stage the play's unique dramaturgical demands, Oliva learned that some of the dramatic conventions she had originally called for actually hindered the designers' ability to create fluid scene changes. Bob Cothran, the production's set designer, voiced his concern that stage directions calling for slide projections that detail the time and place of various scenes might detract from the plot's motion. He also worried that printed titles might obscure the symbolic Oklahoma sky that serves as Te Ata's background. Oliva eliminated the projections and replaced them with stage directions calling for actor-generated transitions that would work to successfully shift between scenes without pausing the play's internal rhythms.

Although the production team worked successfully to solve the fluidity of scene transitions, one aspect of the dramaturgy that got lost in the play's production was the juxtaposition of *Te Ata*'s various playing styles. For example, after Young Te Ata's performance for the Roosevelts in Hyde Park, a scene that should end in a highly theatricalized Delsarte pose, the action shifts to a surreal moment that depicts Te Ata's doubts about her career choices. Oliva's stage directions state that after the performance, "the sun is almost down and for a moment the stage is empty. Then from different areas Margaret and Dr. Fisher enter first followed by Kuruks and then Te Ata" (70). The momentary silence, followed by four characters entering the vast stage from different areas, is intended to draw the audience into Te Ata's aloneness and self-doubt. However, in production, the juxtaposition and disorientation of these vastly different playing styles were lost when realism replaced the transition. After the Hyde Park performance, the characters walked the circle of the stage until Te Ata's three friends remained together in a downstage right grouping. Upon Te Ata's reentrance there had been no silence and the group of three did not convey a feeling of isolation. Rather, the scene played as a realistic gathering of friends after a realistic play within the play.

Beyond the challenge of physicalizing Oliva's complex dramaturgy, other pre-production issues faced the *Te Ata* World Premiere's production team, the most significant of which was producing a large-scale professional play at a venue that had no real theater infrastructure. While the production team functioned as a professional theater organization with union designers and equity actors, the theater venue was the main auditorium at the University of Science and Arts of Oklahoma, a very small liberal arts university with a one-person theater department. The production team's goal was to premiere the play at USAO because Te Ata had attended school there, when it was still Oklahoma College for Women, but USAO had no box office and no established personnel for mounting productions. Additionally, most of the production's artistic staff came from out of state. Thus, almost every technical aspect of producing and promoting the play proved to be a problem to solve.

Young Te Ata (left) writes a letter to Miss Davis as Elder Te Ata (center) recalls her days at Carnegie Tech.

A further complicating factor was that, in order to produce the show, several different entities that all functioned in different ways had to find a way to work together. The Chickasaw Nation, the production's major sponsor, had established ways to conduct business that often did not comply with USAO's business practices. Added to that incompatibility were the regulations stipulated by Actors Equity and to a lesser degree the design unions. Since USAO was the hiring organization, the school's name was on the contracts; however, as a small university, it did not have the traditional mechanics of a professional theater, such as required insurance or personnel familiar with union requirements. Luckily, such challenges were addressed successfully, but they often forced delays of hiring and caused a great deal more work for many people.

Even auditions proved to be somewhat challenging, but for a different reason. In addition to playwright, Oliva also served as the artistic director, though she resided in Albuquerque. The production manager was initially the only production member working on site at USAO, so it fell to the artistic director/playwright to create and send out all of the preproduction publicity information. A statewide cattle call audition was announced with the goal of hiring as many Oklahoma actors as possible. The funding and Equity rules limited hiring to only three professional actors, who would likely come from out of state. Oliva sought out and identified one thousand potential sources for actors in Oklahoma and mailed audition announcements to talent agencies, theaters, tribal headquarters, dance studios, high schools, and colleges. About one hundred actors auditioned, and over half were Native. Unfortunately, most actors were unfamiliar with the audition process and did not come prepared with the required monologue and sixteen bars of music. Because *Te Ata* was such a unique play, storytelling and a cappella singing were allowed. However, such changes to the audition process made it difficult to evaluate actors' abilities to memorize text, sing with accompaniment, or read music.

While most of the actors came from across the state of Oklahoma, Oliva also needed to hire a full, professional artistic staff: director, set designer, costume designer, lighting designer, choreographer, stage manager, and others. The team was very qualified, but all members came from different parts of the country; therefore, communication was a constant challenge throughout the production process. Maintaining a cohesive artistic vision that honored the play was in some instances lost in the individual artists' goals of getting their aspects of the production done and within budget.

Budget was also a constant concern, something that Oliva was uncomfortable dealing with because there was no real structure for the production budget, which was constantly in a state of revision. The Chickasaw Nation gave $100,000 toward the production, and the USAO foundation contributed some additional funding through grants, though most of that funding was earmarked to renovate the hundred-year-old auditorium. It became apparent early in the process that the partnering institutions' agendas were often a stumbling block and that the play was often used by various entities for a variety of purposes. As the play entered production, the artistic team desperately needed additional funding for set, lights, and costumes, and although the university was applying for grants in those areas, it was more experienced seeking funding for the physical needs of the institution than for artistic productions.

While funding issues are often part of professional theater, there were unique challenges in presenting a Native American play in Oklahoma. Many of these complexities arose once the production team, cast, and crew were onsite working in Oklahoma. Oliva was not a constant presence during the rehearsal phase; the director had requested time with the actors without Oliva's presence in order to establish a strong, trusting relationship with them. The director's request was understandable; however, as rehearsals developed, it became apparent that the playwright was often viewed as an outsider to the process of play development. As dramaturg, Stanlake spent more time in Oklahoma during rehearsals but found that the director preferred her working as an historian, rather than as an expert in the unique dramaturgical aspects of the script. Oliva's absence and Stanlake's limited role resulted in a rehearsal environment in which there were few opportunities to advocate for text of the new play.

One of the greatest textual challenges that *Te Ata* presents to an artistic team is the way in which the play stages multiculturalism. *Te Ata*'s cast calls for a multicultural community comprised of both Native and non-Native characters. Within those Native American roles, multiple Nations are represented. Te Ata and Ataloa are Chickasaw; Kuruks is Pawnee; and chorus members mention being part Cherokee, Seminole, and Potawatomie. Like many Native American plays, the casting of *Te Ata* also reflected multiple Native Nations, so, for instance, DeLanna Studi who is Cherokee played Young Te Ata; Donna Couteau Brooks who is Sac and Fox played Elder Te Ata; and Sarah D'Angelo who is Mohawk played Ataloa. Holding open auditions in Oklahoma created the opportunity to cast a range of actors from different Native Nations. Keenly aware of their Nation's producing *Te Ata*, a significant number of Chickasaw performers auditioned. Since Te Ata and Oliva are both Chickasaw women and because the Chickasaw Nation is actively developing a performing arts program, it was important to include a substantial number of Chickasaw performers in the premiere.

Professional actors from out of state played the leading roles of Young Te Ata, Elder Te Ata, Ataloa, and Dr. Fisher. Many beginning actors from the Chickasaw Nation filled several of the chorus roles. The remainder of the actors had varying degrees of theatrical experience, ranging from university theater majors, to professional Native storytellers, to first time performers. The differences among cast members created a community where newer performers looked to more experienced performers for mentorship and where cast members often looked to elders to learn about cultural issues. These differences created various approaches to the rehearsal process. Some actors viewed the production process as primarily business, others as cultural, and yet others as summer camp. Sometimes actors felt insecure about their theater experience; other times, actors felt insecure about their knowledge of various Native American traditions that ranged from Chickasaw culture, specifically, to the different Native cultures that were represented by members of the cast and that varied not only across but also within Native cultures.

Similar to the ways in which *Te Ata*'s cast of characters represents the many different people who shaped Te Ata's life and who were touched by Te Ata's performances, the play's set also had to be expansive enough to reflect not only the many places where Te Ata performed but also the many places that influenced how she experienced the world. The vastness and importance of the natural world is such a key component of *Te Ata*'s dramaturgy that it shapes the play's language. For example, Act One ends with a monologue that Oliva developed from one of Te Ata's letters to Clyde Fisher. On a literal level, the letter allows Oliva to focus the play's dramatic action on Te Ata's marriage and her successful career's demanding schedule; symbolically, the monologue conveys the significance of the natural world within the play's dramaturgy. Young Te Ata states:

> 28th Sun of the Hunting Moon. On the High Seas. 1936.
>
> Dear Clyde. Three years of togetherness on the trail—and we have known the tang of the desert sage-brush and seen the gnarled strength of piñon and cedar. We have walked together under green hemlock boughs and marveled at the dignity of the northern pine. We have sailed "big waters" and have felt drawn and fascinated by the knowledge of the Ancient one. We have loved the smoke and the beauty of the campfire and have felt the warmth that comes from companionship and real friends. We have felt our aloneness and the sadness of parting—but always knowing we would feel as much. The keen joy and the sweetness and strangeness of coming together again—and—we have caught a photographic cloud or two and had an occasional dance among the stars!
>
> The 28$^{th}$ Sun of the Hunting moon and an Indian on the Atlantic sailing back to you! (Oliva 63)

The monologue reflects the incredible scope that *Te Ata*'s stage must convey to its audiences. Not only does this play range almost a century in time;

spatially, the play transitions from Oklahoma to New York to places of the spirit. To portray *Te Ata*'s wide world, Robert Cothran[3] began his design concept with the image of the Oklahoma sky, the limitlessness one senses when she lies in a field looking upwards. From such a perspective, the sky appears as a circle shaped by the horizon. To represent Oklahoma's big sky, Cothran stretched a circle of sky onto a frame of birch saplings. This "drum sky" served as his central metaphor.

Cothran's magical night sky.

Cothran carried the circle onto the stage floor's three major playing areas. The central space was the highest level on stage, perfectly circular, covered with Plexiglas, and ringed with beadwork. The space could be lit from below to suggest water, sky, or sacred places of the spirit world. Surrounding it, the middle ring was a colorful path of terracotta, ochre, and blue, representing Te Ata's path, originating in Oklahoma's red earth, grass, and stones. The outer ring possessed the most distorted circularity. Composed of staggered, angular chunks treated to look like concrete, brick, wood floors, rugs, and asphalt, this manmade ring signified Dr. Fisher's world and the sites of Te Ata's professional career. This space was intensified when Cothran flew in horizons of skyscrapers that blocked the big sky. Cothran's design depicted both the tensions and interconnections between seemingly disparate worlds. The three different circles were physically connected, allowing Te Ata and other characters to seamlessly cross boundaries of time and space. Sometimes characters stood in two contradictory areas simultaneously.

Te Ata's Oklahoma sky was also the basis for Cothran's portrayal of Te Ata and Dr. Fisher's marriage. At the bottom of the stage was a silver band marking declination, part of an astronomer's system of locating celestial positions. Cothran explained, "This silver, mechanical gauge running around the very outside [of the stage], way down from Te Ata's sky, is an indication of Dr. Fisher's sky, as a scientist" (production meeting). In Cothran's design these seemingly separate skies actually mirrored one another. Te Ata's drum sky held the constellations that directly aligned with the measurements on Dr. Fisher's band. Cothran's set design worked beautifully to support the dramaturgical movements and ideas inherent within Te Ata. Moments in which the set was not as effective often occurred when realistic staging elements were added to scenes through directing or lighting elements. For example, for one scene that occurs in Te Ata's New York apartment, actors brought in a table, a couch cushion, and other realistic props. The set change created an unnecessary break in the fluid plot, while the props detracted from both the dramatic action and set by forcing an added layer of realism that was unnecessary in the brief shared scene.

[3] Cothran's career as a scene designer extends over fifty-five years. His credits include productions on Broadway and professional theater across the United States, including the original workshop production of *Sugar Babies*. His lithographs are in the permanent collection of the Library of Congress, the Smithsonian Institution, and the Ammon Carter Museum, as well as in many private collections.

Costumes and choreography posed interesting options. In terms of costumes, Designer Mike Buchwald,[4] who is head of the University of Oklahoma's School of Drama's Design Area, felt that because the play spanned nearly a century, it was important to be period specific. He agreed to remain within budget, but he felt strongly that every period should be reflected in the costumes. The artistic staff supported Buchwald's position. The playwright's original thinking had been to use pieces of the actors' clothing to mark time shifts, similar to the way in which the set conveyed shifting places through suggestive changes. Buchwald's costumes were lavish and beautiful; they reflected Cothran's colorscape from the sky and land. Costume changes, however, were a challenge since there were so many of them. Compromise was also necessary, especially in terms of the cast members. In one dance number, Buchwald suggested that rather than have the entire chorus dancing in tuxedos and ball gowns, it might be better to have just one couple dancing. The other couples could be dressed the same, but they would stay stationary due to their inability to move elegantly in the costumes as dancers should. Buchwald's suggestion was honest and appropriate.

Beth Shumway[5] created choreography and movement. In discussions with Oliva, Shumway agreed that most of the play's dancing would be suggestive or stylized, and for the most part that was accomplished. For example, the "Corn Dance" presented a stylized version of a traditional corn dance. As with other elements of staging, the artistic team remained sensitive to tribal rituals and boundaries, as well as the limitations of the cast and the various levels of the set. One dance that was unable to achieve the original idea expressed in *Te Ata*'s script, however, was the "False Face Society Dance," in which Oliva borrowed the Iroquois notion of False Face Masks to create a world where Te Ata moved out of her Oklahoma surroundings into the unknown, surreal world of New York. The dancers wore half-masks that allowed them to look normal from one side and then grotesque from the other when the dancers alternated profiles. When Young Te Ata walked into the dance, the choreography of the dancers in two-sided masks was intended to convey how Te Ata felt caught within two cultures. Unfortunately, the composed music didn't serve the dance well and the set offered additional challenges making back and forth movement difficult. Because of these technical limitations, neither the director nor the choreographer was able to realize the image of being caught between two worlds. In the end, the entire dance was cut the night before opening.

Lights were often stunning and served the play; however, there were several instances where the work of the lighting designer did not comply with what the script called for. It seemed that lighting functioned to make the set "look beautiful" rather than to push dramatic action forward or to support the playing style of a particular moment. Two strong examples of this conflict between text and lighting relate to the symbolic meanings associated with *Te Ata*'s sky. The first example, as seen in the photographs of the set, has to do with Cothran's drum sky. The script calls for Elder

[4] Buchwald has designed over three hundred plays, musicals, operas, and ballets for University of Oklahoma productions, and he has been recognized with the Regents' Award for Superior Teaching, the Associates' Lecturer of Excellence Award, and as the Rothbaum Presidential Professor of Excellence. His extensive body of work as a guest designer for commercial theater, television, and film has kept him in constant demand.

[5] Shumway, who holds a Master's degree in theater from Catholic University, founded the Prairie Dance Theatre, a company of Native performers that she has directed for over twenty-five years.

Te Ata to "walk out of the sky" (Oliva 1). Though clearly it should be a powerful moment, that image exists not only for theatrical reasons but also for important dramaturgical meanings. Her entrance through the sky establishes that Elder Te Ata is a spirit, that she has powers to do, and say, and be anywhere. Cothran supported this dramatic concept through his design of an infinite sky with a cut out hole, which—if the lighting was balanced properly—could not be seen by the audience. Lighting on a backstage cyc would blend with the drum sky, making the image appear whole when Elder Te Ata walks out of the drum sky and onto the stage. Instead, the lighting designer emphasized Elder Te Ata's entrances and exists with white light that intensified when Te Ata moved through the sky. The lighting choice revealed the hole, and the theatrical magic was gone.

The second example of lighting difficulties concerned the use of stars. Cothran created an exact replica of the Oklahoma sky, with a perfect alignment of constellations. Oliva's script specifically calls for the stars throughout the play in the various scenes that emphasize transitional moments in Young Te Ata's life. In production, however, stars did not appear during all of these moments. The lighting designer and director explained that they wanted to save the stars for dramatic effect. Otherwise, the lighting designer thought, the stars would lose their magic for the audience. Others on the production team disagreed with this view and felt the play suffered by not having the magic of stars when and where the script called for them. Dramaturgically, the elements of the natural world are a significant metaphor for the entire play. This conflict over the stars serves as an example of where the production team could have returned to the play's text. In the world of *Te Ata*, stars are intended to be magical every time the characters see them.

One of the areas of tension that arose in final production team meetings concerned the marketing of *Te Ata* after opening night. The *Te Ata* World Premiere was an historic event for Native American theater, the Chickasaw Nation, the state of Oklahoma, and women's history. The commemoration of the event took different forms. For the Chickasaw Nation and Te Ata's family, the play was celebrated by community gatherings. For those marketing the play to the public, commemoration went hand-in-hand with business. At first, the Te Ata gift shop was going to sell three items: a framed and signed print of Cothran's set design, a poster, and a T-shirt. However, those in charge of marketing the play soon wanted to sell anything associated with the play: extra programs, costume cards, T-shirts, large and small posters, prints of Cothran's set design, the press kit book, and ribbons used in the play's private opening ceremony. This tension mirrored some of the uncomfortable rifts that occur in commercial theater. Are plays for artistic and cultural expression, or are they for profit? Who owns the play's images once producing organizations get involved? Is the product for sale the event, the play itself; or is the product for sale a souvenir, the material proof that one attended the ephemeral event? As Native American theater crosses into mainstream theater, the issue of the commodification of artistic/cultural expression will likely become ever more contentious.

Another conflict between cultural perspectives and marketers concerned advertising. Part of the *Te Ata* press kit was a six-minute DVD that included an introduction to the play, discussion of the World Premiere's significance, bibliography of Oliva's work, and commentary on Te Ata Fisher's life. It was beautifully arranged with interviews, historic photographs, and a voiceover from a local anchorwoman. The DVD had one glaring mistake, however. During two separate moments when the voiceover mentioned the Chickasaw Nation and Te Ata's "making her people proud," the image that appeared on screen was of a mid-nineteenth century group of Plains Indians standing in front of teepees. The inaccuracies were obvious and inadvertently offensive. Te Ata lived from 1895-1995, in Oklahoma, where she resided with her Chickasaw—not Plains—family.

Beyond being wrong, the photo went against everything the play and Te Ata's seven-decade career worked to address. Stanlake called, e-mailed, and harassed the publicist, so that he would understand the gravity of the error, how such an image could undermine the entire production. The publicist agreed to fix the error. After a couple of weeks, during which many people were the recipients of one of the bulk mailings advertising the play with the faulty DVD, Stanlake received an "edited" version. The first picture had been removed, but the second one remained. The voiceover and the images were no longer aligned. It was a gesture to appease the dramaturg, as if to the marketing world, the artists' request to redo the DVD displayed a lack of business sense, a waste of time and money to marketers who did not see the error as significant. In other ways, however, the marketing embraced the soul of the play and the project. The press kit, constructed by using leather and the round shape of a drum, was filled with professional publicity information about the show; it served as the basis for almost all media information about the premiere. The publicity team hand delivered over one hundred fifty press kits to newspapers and media agencies across the state of Oklahoma.

As the production neared opening night, it became clear that the more people who were involved in the production of *Te Ata*, the more difficult it was to keep the play's script in the forefront of everyone's mind. The play became a thing to be marketed, designed, and directed. Sometimes "realizing" the script became an afterthought, even for those most intimately connected to the original text. When a production team premieres a new play, Native or non-Native, the text and the playwright's vision for that text needs to remain central to the production process. Later in a play's production history, there is room for reinterpreting and re-envisioning the multiple ways in which the play can function, but the premiere of a production is unique. It represents the first, and perhaps only, opportunity a playwright will see her work staged as closely as possible to her original text.

Like the work of many playwrights, Oliva's writing is as scenic as it is verbal. Often she includes stage directions detailing rhythmic, imagistic, and aural aspects of the play that function to provide additional levels of emotional and analytical meaning. When the stage directions were incorporated into the staging of the production, the audience experienced the play that the playwright had scripted. For example, in Scene Ten, titled "Coming Together," Te Ata performs for a group of Campfire Girls on Iona Island in New York, while Dr. Fisher presents a lecture to Catholic schoolboys visiting the Hayden Planetarium. Oliva's stage directions state, "We should see a few stars just beginning to show.... Music underscores the whole scene, [which] is done [entirely] in mime. It should look like a duet, danced far apart, as Te Ata and Dr. Fisher tell the children about the moon, and Indians, and explain their various props. At times their gestures are exactly the same, other times in complete opposition" (88). In the moments that Dr. Fisher's and Young Te Ata's gestures mirrored and contradicted each other, the physical juxtaposition of the Hayden planetarium and Iona Island lectures worked. Audiences saw Te Ata and Dr. Fisher separated by distance but held together by their common passion for teaching others to marvel at the world around them. The stars that illuminated Te Ata's drum sky not only served as a literal setting for Te Ata's outdoor presentation and Dr. Fisher's indoor planetarium lecture, but they also portrayed the couple's intimate relationship across the physical distance. During the scene, the stars grew brighter, foreshadowing magical transformations that occur in the following scene.

In moments when the stage directions were not privileged by the production, not only did theatrical meanings get lost, individual interpretations led to conflict among the cast and crew. *Te Ata*'s "Dance of Youth and Age" symbolically portrays the merging of Young Te Ata into Elder Te Ata and her subsequent passing away. To create the transition, Oliva envisioned the entire stage space, Te Ata's world, functioning as a shawl that protectively wraps Te Ata's body in preparation for her journey toward the next world of existence. The stage directions state that in addition to Young and Elder Te Ata, there are three couples, each representing a younger and an elder self. From the shawl that each couple carries, to the surreal lighting that splashes upon the sky, vivid colors dominate the scene. The text reads, "While Te Ata and Elder Te Ata are moving in a traditional, round dance, step dance, the couples are doing a more stylized version incorporating the movement of the shawl.…The three couples look like flying birds [as]…shawls are flying and lilting and floating in the air, [and] the beat of the drum gets louder and more intense. It is both ominous and beautiful.…At the end of the dance, [the couples] have somehow swept up Young Te Ata, and she, along with the [younger] half of each couple disappear from the stage" (Oliva 106).

The imagery and purpose of the scene reside in the stage directions; however, the stage directions soon became secondary as choreography, directing, and costuming began to dominate the rehearsal process. As this happened, the stylization of "The Dance of Youth and Age" got lost; in its place arose a fancy shawl dance that made a few of the men uncomfortable. Solutions made the matter worse because they did not stem from the intended stylized image of a colorful shawl wrapping around Elder Te Ata; rather, they intensified an association with the literal fancy shawl dance and made realistic shawls, not Te Ata's transformation, the focus of the scene. With the playwright and dramaturg out of town during that phase of the rehearsal process, and no one thinking to return to the stage directions that could have spoken in Oliva's absence, the director felt caught in a cultural dispute about gender roles and fringed shawls. The final performance resolved the issue, by using blankets instead of shawls, but Oliva's theatricalized metaphor never materialized. Nothing surreal could transcend the literal staging and choreography.

There is never a time when all aspects of a production are realized as the playwright or even the director would have wanted. But the *Te Ata* World Premiere, despite its challenges, did accomplish its most important goal, which was to share Te Ata's story and secure her place in history. When Oliva tells her story about discovering Te Ata's papers, she often explains that discovering Te Ata's story changed her life. Likewise, those who worked to produce *Te Ata* and those who attended the production, expressed a similar notion; the play altered many people's perspectives about Native American performance and Native American history.

Indeed, one of the play's major themes centers upon Te Ata Fisher's own transformation from a shy girl in Indian Territory to a globe-trotting actress who used theater to bring cultures together. Te Ata's "Loon Island" scene presents Te Ata's shift from worrying about her personal choices into accepting her unique professional calling. In a realistically played, shared scene, Young Te Ata confesses to Miss Davis how her father's death in Oklahoma has made her question her commitment to performance. She explains:

> When I come here, to Loon Island, I always leave feeling so torn. I can find solitude here, and pinecones, and rocks, and wild asters and…here I don't have to perform for my supper. Here I don't have to justify my choices. I lose all obligation…My mind can just slumber. No Ataloa reminding me of what I should do; no Kuruks reminding me

> of what I haven't done…mainly for him. No CF, who just by his presence reminds me that…I wish I were more like Margaret. She never looks back. And you, you are always so sure. Sure footed, like a deer. I live in the hard brick buildings of New York, with a white man and I only wear my buckskins for performance…And…on the phone…when Ataloa called me to tell me that Father…She said…his last words…he spoke in broken English like the old people…like, she said… the way I do when I…He thought Ataloa was me…he tried to tell her the story of the owl and the rabbit…Then he…She laughed at his confusion…I think of myself like a paper doll, with paper clothes and depending on what clothes are put on me, that's the way I must behave and that's who I must be for a day, or an hour…I don't know who I am, except when I am here, or when I'm home, in Tishomingo, picking up handfuls of red dirt to remind me where I come from. Spirits are calling me, calling me, all the time…in the loon's cry, in the moon's light, in the wind's path…(Oliva 81)

Soon after Te Ata shares these anxieties with her teacher, the dramatic action shifts into a scene of heightened reality. Elder Te Ata joins Young Te Ata, dresses her in a new buckskin, and imparts knowledge that allows Young Te Ata to embrace the complicated, sometimes contradicting, elements of her life. The scene encapsulates the challenge Te Ata faced in attempting to honor her Native heritage while daring to tread an independent trail as an actress. The universal core of Young Te Ata's conflict is how difficult it is for anyone to follow her dream.

It was interesting that both Native and non-Native members of the cast discovered various connections to Te Ata's struggles. In the end, many felt that this Native American production was also an American play. Terrance Wright, an African American chorus member, wondered about the lack of Native American representation in American theater:

> From my perspective…Native Americans and African Americans have a lot in common… having land taken away from them, having us taken away from our land. People saying that Native American theater isn't mainstream or that it's hard to cast Native characters is pretty much like saying to me it's hard to have Black American theater or cast African American people. I find it really stupid that America is so uptight about a lot of things…so concerned about audience reception when we are all the same people. (personal interview)

DeeDee Beard, a theater major from USAO who played Te Ata's theater teacher, Miss Davis, discovered that there was much about the region's history and culture that she did not know. She explained, "I'm viewing Native American culture very differently…. [There are] more stories than I could ever have imagined…stories told in a different way that I didn't know" (personal interview).

Many of the Native American cast members remarked that they enjoyed creating a Native theatrical production with people from various Native and non-Native backgrounds. Several mentioned that learning about Te Ata's career introduced them to a story that they did not know. Robert Cheadle, a Chickasaw chorus actor who did know Te Ata's story before joining the cast, said that he enjoyed the way theater allowed him to turn the tables of performance traditions; he played several different white characters in the play. Cheadle spoke about the challenges and rewards of Native American productions in mainstream theater:

> It's very difficult for the reason that all tribes are unique and every individual of each tribe is unique. The level of tolerance about speaking about Native American

> issues, Native American ways of life, Native American beliefs is a challenge, even among Indians. So it's difficult to maintain [a production]. Still, I really hope Native people, Native artists, continue to provide commercial works for every audience...I would love to see [Native theater] expand, go to Broadway. (personal interview)

While the *Te Ata* World Premiere never set out to be a model for producing large-scale, professional Native plays, the production team did encounter and learn from the many issues that arose during the production process. Oliva and Stanlake offer this account in the hope that the *Te Ata* World Premiere will serve as a case study for others who choose to build from this project's successes and failures. Strategies that the authors feel would be most helpful for future premieres of Native American mainstream productions include: increasing table time with the script for the artistic team and actors; having an advocate for the script present during all rehearsals; discussing openly everyone's role, artistic, cultural, political, or financial; and maintaining control of materials used to publicize the play, before and after production.

The most important lesson that the *Te Ata* World Premiere production team learned was how necessary it is for playwrights to hold on to their visions. Most of *Te Ata*'s difficulties arose when the words and images expressed in the text became overshadowed by production choices. As a play nears production, it is normal for the artistic staff to become more focused on their particular responsibilities and deadlines. The original text can get lost easily in these frantic days leading to opening night. If the playwright and/or dramaturg can remain present throughout the rehearsal process, an advocate for the script can remind a busy production team to return to the text when concerns arise. Not only does a playwright enter the production process knowing that she is giving her script to an artistic team responsible for creating a physical production, but the artistic staff should also commit to realizing the new script in material form. A premiere is not the place to reinvent images; it should create a close interpretation of the script so that a playwright can see how her text works on stage. To this end, allowing the playwright and artistic staff adequate time—possibly more time than a production team feels is necessary—to communicate early in the production process about how the play functions dramaturgically could help ensure that all artistic staff members are working with common images and interpretations.

In a similar way, table time focusing on the new script becomes more important among the director, dramaturg, and playwright, as well as during the rehearsal process with actors. Because Native American plays often incorporate dramatic conventions (such as *Te Ata*'s use of several levels of reality and their different modes of performance styles), it is necessary that the playwright, dramaturg, and director have a clear sense of how all the dramatic conventions are intended to communicate meaning in a Native American play. As the actors begin to study the script during their first group readings of the play, it is important to talk through the dramatic conventions and to allow time for actors to ask questions about their characters and the scenes' intentions. A lengthened period of table time will ensure that everyone has analyzed the play, understands the text, and has had a chance to work through intercultural concerns. Because new plays do often change, sometimes immediately before opening night, the director should also prepare the actors to expect change as part of the production process.

If a Native American play relies upon nontraditional partnerships to produce a large-scale, professional production, its production manager and artistic director should have a plan for working with the supporting organizations' various styles of management. While obtaining funding from a range of institutions provides a wide, supportive base for the production, unforeseen complications can arise when the sponsors disagree about hierarchy and methodology. When such entities unite to finance a play production, open communication about procedures, deadlines, and hierarchies is paramount. The artistic director should ensure that all of the institutions understand both the necessary timeline and process of producing a professional production, such as adhering to Actors' Equity rules. The supporting institutions also must find a way to coordinate their various internal procedures to meet the collective goal of producing the play. Related to the conversations of producing the play, the financial entities and the playwright will need to negotiate the differences between owning the script and owning the production. Tied to those financial discussions should be detailed conversations about how the production will be marketed, before, during, and after the production. A production team might want the dramaturg or a designated cultural advisor to approve all materials used to market the play. Similarly, all of the financial backers and the artistic director should agree upon what mementos from the production are appropriate to sell. Such questions of appropriateness should address not just financial but also cultural concerns.

*Te Ata* concludes when Elder Te Ata crosses over to the spirit world. In direct address to the audience, she states:

> I do not wish to have small thoughts behind big words...One day I was young and the next day I grew old...I am old now...All my people have left me...I am tired. My dreams are confusing. I wish to be on the last trail for I can no longer see with insight. I can no longer hear with understanding...The sounds I hear now are of long ago. I hear the weeping of the Choctaw women on the Trail of Tears; I hear the Loon mother wailing for her mate, I hear the cry of the hunted doe. My maker is calling for me. (Oliva 107)

She then turns upstage to step through the sky to embark upon a new journey.

Audience reception was extraordinary, as were the theater critics' reviews. *Te Ata* was staged in the newly renamed and renovated Te Ata Memorial Auditorium on the campus of the University of Science and Arts of Oklahoma in Chickasha from August 5-13, 2006. The USAO Foundation, Chickasaw Nation, and East Central University jointly sponsored the play with generous support from friends of USAO and Te Ata. The *Te Ata* World Premiere website records that:

> Nearly two hundred cast, crew, and staff members from across the nation worked together to bring *Te Ata* to the stage. The cast included actors from ten states and eight Native [American Nations]. More than 3,300 audience members from thirty states enjoyed eight performances[; these viewers included] state and federal officials and a dozen reporters for state and national publications. Opening night was preceded by a gala event hosted by Governor Bill Anoatubby of the Chickasaw Nation and a host of Chickasaw legislators. Eighty-six members of Te Ata's remaining family attended the performances, which were made possible by twenty-eight corporate, foundation, and individual sponsors.

It is important to keep in mind that a world premiere of a play is a rare event in Oklahoma. Many who attended *Te Ata* had never seen a play or had only seen high school productions. It was very heartening to see so many Native people in attendance. Theater for Native people in Oklahoma is not a common event. Significantly, it was Te Ata's story that resonated with the audience, especially with Native people, yet her story is also universal. The World Premiere's goal was to present Te Ata's story to a large audience through a mainstream theatrical medium; that goal was achieved and, perhaps, laid the groundwork for other such plays and events to celebrate Native heritage.

## Works Cited

Beard, DeeDee. Interview with Christy Stanlake. 10 Aug. 2006.

Bolt, Gigi. "Wishing Well." *American Theatre* 23.10 (2006): 8.

Cheadle, Robert. Interview with Christy Stanlake. 10 Aug. 2006.

Oliva, JudyLee. *Te Ata*. Ts. 2005. Native American Women Playwrights Archive, Miami U Libraries, Oxford, OH. Quotations in the text are from the typescript. See also the published version: *Te Ata: A Play with Music, Footpaths and Bridges: Voices from the Native American Playwrights Archive*. Ed. Shirley A. Huston-Findley and Rebecca Howard. Ann Arbor: U of Michigan P, 2008. 200-68.

---. *Te Ata*. Dir. Sherry Landrum. Set Robert Cothran. Perf. DeLanna Studi. Te Ata Memorial Auditorium, U of Science and Arts of Oklahoma, Chickasha, Oklahoma. 5-13 Aug. 2006.

Stanlake, Christy. "Interview with JudyLee Oliva." *Baylor Journal of Theatre and Performance* 4.1 (2007): 109-20.

*Te Ata* Photographs. Aug. 2006. U of Science and Arts of Oklahoma Archives, Chickasha, OK.

*Te Ata* World Premiere Website. U of Science and Arts of Oklahoma. 2006. Chickasha, OK. 21 Apr. 2006. <http://www.usao.edu/teata/>.

Wright, Terrance. Interview with Christy Stanlake. 10 Aug. 2006.

# *Contributors*

# CONTRIBUTORS

**Armstrong, Ann Elizabeth.** Associate Professor, Theatre, Miami University. Besides having directed Victoria Nalani Kneubuhl's *Conversion of Ka'ahumanu*, Armstrong co-directs a university-wide project about Freedom Summer 1964, has co-edited *Radical Acts: Theatre and Feminist Pedagogies of Change* (Aunt Lute 2007), and has published on community-based theater and feminist theater.

**Baker, Marie Annharte** (Saulteaux Ojibway). Poet, playwright, performer, and activist now at the University of Manitoba, Baker's most recent book is *Exercises in Lip Pointing* (New Star 2003) and recent performances include "Raven in the Hood," "Granny Bootcamp" (2006), and her one-act "Mischief in Her Eye" (2007).

**Borst, Murielle** (Kuna, Rappahannock). BFA, Long Island University, followed by internship with Spiderwoman Theater. Borst has won a Native Heart Award from Native American Music Awards, performed internationally, and directed Muriel Miguel in *Red Mother*. Her one-woman show *More Than Feathers and Beads* was nominated for a Rockefeller Grant and produced by Sydney Opera House and at the 2002 Olympic Games. A fantasy writer, she has completed three volumes in her series *The Star Song Carriers*.

**Carter, Jill** (Anishinabe and Ashkenazi). Doctoral candidate at the Graduate Centre for Study of Drama at the University of Toronto. A performer, director, and dramaturg, Carter teaches performance and Indigenous theater and is a teacher and adviser in the University of Toronto's Aboriginal Studies Program.

**Glancy, Diane** (Cherokee). Long-time professor of English and Native American Studies at Macalester College and awarded the Richard Thomas Chair at Kenyon College in 2008 and 2009, Glancy has an extensive bibliography of poetry, fiction, essays, and plays, including two collections of plays, *American Gypsy* and *War Cries*. Her *Stone Heart: Everybody Loves a Journey West* was premiered by Native Voices at the Autry in Los Angeles and performed at NMAI in New York and Washington; the Autry International Center also produced her *Jump Kiss* (2001) and *Salvage* (2008). In addition to her Trail of Tears project, she is working on *The Reason for Crows*, a play about 17th-century Mohawk Kateri Tekakwitha, a collection of voices of Biblical women, and a novel about BTK called *One of Us*.

**Haugo, Ann.** Assistant Professor, Theatre, Illinois State University. Haugo teaches theater history, literature, and criticism, courses on American Indian theater, the literature of decolonization, gender and performance, and race and nationalism. She has published on American Indian theater in *American Indian Theatre in Performance* (UCLA 2000), *The Color of Theater* (Continuum 2002), the *Cambridge Companion to Native American Literature* (2005), *Companion to Twentieth-Century American Drama* (Blackwell 2005), and academic journals.

**Johnson, Kelli Lyon.** Associate Professor, English, Miami University. The author of *Julia Alvarez: Writing a New Place on the Map* (University of New Mexico Press 2005), Johnson has also published on Native and Latina women writers.

**Kneubuhl, Victoria Nalani** (Hawai'an, Samoan). Writer, performer, and playwright in Honolulu. Kneubuhl's plays have been collected in *Hawaii Nei: Island Plays* (University of Hawaii Press 2002) and have been widely performed. Winner of the Hawai'i Award for Literature, she works with Native stories and historical events and characters and has recently published *Murder Casts a Shadow: A Hawaii Mystery* (University of Hawaii Press 2008).

**Knowles, Ric.** Professor, Theatre, University of Guelph. Besides having published extensively on Shakespeare, Canadian and modern theater, and performance studies, editing *Canadian Theatre Review* and *Modern Drama*, and directing Playwrights Canada Press, Knowles has published on Native theater and with Monique Mojica has edited *Staging Coyote's Dream: An Anthology of First Nations Drama in English* (Playwrights Canada Press, vol. 1, 2002; vol. 2 in preparation).

**Mayo, Lisa** (Kuna, Rappahannock). A performing member of Masterworks Laboratory Theatre of New York, Mayo studied at the New York School of Music and is a classically trained mezzo soprano. She has also studied with Uta Hagen, Robert Lewis, and Walt Witcover, as well as Charles Nelson Riley for Musical Comedy, and at The Actors and Singers Academy with Susan Slavin. Mayo has created two one-woman shows, *The Pause That Refreshes* and *My Sister Ate Dirt*. She taught theater crafts and acting to young people as part of the Minnesota Native American AIDS Task Force and has directed the Native American Actor's Showcase at the American Indian Community House, where she has served on the Board of Directors. Her most recent on-screen work has been *My Sister's Wedding* and a TV commercial for Mrs. T's pierogies.

**Miguel, Gloria** (Kuna, Rappahannock). A lifetime member at the Lee Strasberg Institute, she studied drama at Oberlin College. In addition to extensive film and television credits Miguel toured a one-woman show, *Grandma*, and the original Tomson Highway's *The Rez Sisters* and performed in *Son of Ayash* and *Jessica*. She has taught at Rough Rock Navajo High School, Brooklyn YMCA, and Brandon University, and was drama consultant for the Minnesota Native American AIDS Task Force. She attended and performed at the Mending the Sacred Hoop Domestic Violence Conference in Flagstaff and the Native American Writer's and Artist Forum in Red Mesa. She performed in Beijing at the 4th World Woman's Conference (1994). She and Lisa Mayo received a Rockefeller Grant and funding from the Jerome Foundation to create *Nis Bundor: Daughters from the Stars*. In 2006 she appeared in the Spanish film *Caotica Ana* and in 2008 created a one-woman show, *Something Old, Something New, Something Borrowed, Something Blue*.

**Miguel, Muriel** (Kuna, Rappahannock). An original member of Joseph Chaikin's Open Theater, she studied modern dance with Alwin Nikolais, co-founded the Thunderbird American Indian Dancers in New York City, and is Artistic Director of Spiderwoman Theater. In addition to extensive stage credits, Miguel's choreography and directing credits include *Throw Away Kids, She Knew She Was She,* and *The Scrubbing Project,* and she has worked with Turtle Gals Performance Ensemble, Raven Spirit Dance Society, and Indigenous Performance Initiatives. Her one-woman shows are *Hot 'n' Soft, Trail of the Otter,* and *Red Mother* (presented at the National Museum of the American Indian, Washington, 2008). Miguel has taught at Bard College, Indigenous Performance at the Centre for Indigenous Theatre, and the Aboriginal Dance Program at The Banff Centre. She has developed four shows for the Minnesota Native American AIDS Task Force working with inner city native youth on HIV/AIDS issues.

**Mojica, Monique** (Kuna, Rappahannock). An actor, playwright, and scholar based in Toronto, Mojica is former Artistic Director of Native Earth Performing Arts, has published in *Canadian Theatre Review* and *Alt.Theatre,* and co-founded Turtle Gals Performance Ensemble with whom she created *The Scrubbing Project* and *The Triple Truth.* She has collaborated on projects investigating Native performance culture and with Ric Knowles edited *Staging Coyote's Dream* and presented on cross-cultural research. She belongs to the second generation spun directly from the web of New York's Spiderwoman Theater.

**Oliva, JudyLee** (Chickasaw). MFA in directing (Oklahoma) and PhD in theater (Northwestern). A published playwright whose work has been seen coast to coast, actress, lyricist, as well as author of two books on theater and numerous scholarly articles, Oliva has worked in professional theater as well as regional and academic theater, conducted writing workshops and served regularly as Artist-in-Residence. *The Fire and the Rose* and *Spirit Line* received readings at Miami University (1997, 2002), and her *Te Ata* premiered August 2006: see http://www.usao.edu/teata/.

**Pearson-Little Thunder, Julie** (Creek). Co-founder with Jana Rhoads of Thunder Road Theater, and with her PhD from the University of Kansas now Assistant Professor Theatre at Northeastern State University in Tahlequah, Oklahoma. Her dissertation is "Native Emergence Theatre and Indian Theatrical Space: Red Earth Performing Arts Company of Seattle, Daystar Dance Company and American Indian Theatre Company of Oklahoma," and her plays are *Buffalo Gallery, Indian Meadowlark,* and *The Woman Who Was Captured by Ghosts* (a Jane Chambers Honorable Mention).

**Rendon, Marcie** (White Earth Anishinabe). Writer, performer, and consultant in the Twin Cities. Rendon has published *Pow Wow Summer* and *Farmer's Market* and poetry in numerous anthologies and has written some ten plays and screenplays; she received St. Paul Company's Leadership In Neighborhoods Grant to "create a viable Native presence in the Twin Cities theater community." Her *Rough Face Girl* is in repertory with the American Indian Repertory Theatre.

**Reyner, Dianne Yeahquo** (Kiowa). In 1974 she became a founding member of Thunderbird Theatre and in the 1990s returned to Haskell and became part of the Thunderbird national touring and community production companies. Her *Weaving the Rain* was awarded the first place Grant K. Goodman Playwriting Award at the University of Kansas, received national recognition as finalist in the Kennedy Center American College Theatre Festival, ACTF Region V production, Lawrence Arts Center Imagination and Place production, and invited performances at UCLA's American Indian Studies Center, Project HOOP. She is business manager of the American Indian Repertory Theatre (http://aireptheatre.org/).

**Rhoads, Jana L.** (Kiowa with Caddo ancestry). Co-Founder of Thunder Road Theater Company (Tulsa 1993) that produces Native plays by Native playwrights, presents pieces about the human experience from a native perspective, provides training in acting, directing, and technical areas, and offers outreach programming to rural communities. A certified speech/language pathologist Rhoads has worked in public schools and Indian Education programs and is presently cultural coordinator for Tulsa Public Schools Indian Education program.

**Scott, Vincent P.** Producer of Native theater and performing arts at the Rasmuson Theater of the National Museum of the American Indian, Washington. With an MFA in Play Direction (Wayne State University) he has worked in many types of theater, including Native theater, and toured to international festivals in Hong Kong and Edinburgh; producer, director, stage manager; has taught at Fort Peck Community (Montana) and other colleges. A recent directing credit is Drew Hayden Taylor's *Someday* for Thunder Road Theater.

**Spiderwoman Theater.** See Lisa Mayo, Gloria Miguel, and Muriel Miguel. The longest-running women's performance troupe in the U.S. (founded in 1975), Spiderwoman has extensive credits in the United States, Canada, and Europe and is the subject of reviews, critical articles, PhD dissertations, and theater reference books. The group was awarded an Honorary Doctor of Fine Arts (Miami University 1997) and has been an inspiration for Native writers and performers.

**Stanlake, Christy.** Assistant Professor, English and Theater, U. S. Naval Academy, with an Ohio State University dissertation on Native American theater. Author of several articles about Native American drama in journals and reference books (*Oxford Encyclopedia of Theatre and Performance* 2003) and dramaturg for the premiere of JudyLee Oliva's *Te Ata*.

**Warner, Vessela S.** Assistant Professor, Theatre, University of Alabama, Birmingham. Warner has published on modern East European and Balkan theater in *Balkanistica, Serbian Survey, Bulgarian Studies Association Newsletter, Macedonian Studies*, and *Theatre and Performance in Eastern Europe* (Scarecrow 2008).

**Wortman, Susan H.** Information Services Librarian, Miami University. In addition to her collection development, reference, and user instruction activities, Wortman provides training in video production.

**Wortman, William A.** Humanities Librarian Emeritus and director of the Native American Women Playwrights Archive, Miami University. He has published on bibliography, librarianship, research methods, Walt Whitman, and Henry James.

# INDEX